CITY OF SALVE

Christopher Mitchell is the author of the epic fantasy series The Magelands. He studied in Edinburgh before living for several years in the Middle East and Greece, where he taught English. He returned to study classics and Greek tragedy and lives in Fife, Scotland with his wife and their four children.

———

For the Advanced Reader Team

ACKNOWLEDGEMENTS

I would like to thank the following for all their support during the writing of the Magelands Eternal Siege - my wife, Lisa Mitchell, who read every chapter as soon as it was drafted and kept me going in the right direction; my parents for their unstinting support; Vicky Williams for reading the books in their early stages; James Aitken for his encouragement; and Grant and Gordon of the Film Club for their support.

Thanks also to my Advance Reader team, for all your help during the last few weeks before publication.

DRAMATIS PERSONAE

The Aurelians
    Emily Aurelian, Queen of the City
    Daniel Aurelian, King of the City
    Lady Aurelian, Daniel's mother
    Lady Omertia, Emily's mother

The Mortals of the City
    Quill, Commander of the Royal Guard
    Nadhew, Roser Lawyer
    Albeck, Official in Refugee Council

The Former Royal Family
    Yendra, Commander of the Bulwark
    Montieth, Prince of Dalrig
    Salvor, Royal Advisor
    Naxor, Demigod; Former Emissary
    Vana, Demigod; cousin of Naxor
    Yvona, Governor of Icehaven
    Amber, Elder Daughter of Prince Montieth
    Jade, Younger Daughter of Prince Montieth
    Ikara, Former Governor of the Circuit
    Lydia, Governor of Port Sanders
    Doria, Courtier in the Royal Palace
    Collo; Former Courtier
    Mona, Chancellor of Royal Academy, Ooste

The Lostwell Exiles
    Kelsey Holdfast, Blocker of Powers
    Van Logos, Former Banner Captain

Silva, God; Descendant of Belinda
Felice, God; Former Governor of Lostwell
Kagan, Shinstran Gang Member
Dizzler, Shinstran Gang Boss
Elena, Dizzler's Younger Sister
Nurian, Banner Officer
Lady Sofia, Lostwell Aristocrat
Gellie, Fordian Housekeeper
Saul, Torduan Chef

The Exiled Dragons
Deathfang, Dragon Chief
Burntskull, Deathfang's Advisor
Darksky, Deathfang's Mate
Frostback, Deathfang's Daughter
Halfclaw, Green & Blue Dragon
Dawnflame, Blue & Purple Dragon
Tarsnow, Dawnflame's Mate
Bittersea, Dawnflame's Mother
Firestone, Dawnflame's Son

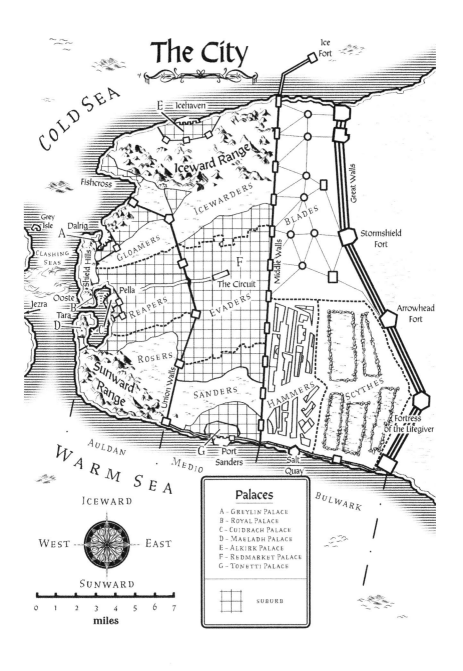

The City

COLD SEA

Ice Fort

E — Icehaven

Iceward Range

ICEWARDERS

Fishcross

Grey Isle

Dalrig

A

CLASHING SEAS

Shield Hills

GLOAMERS

Ooste

Jezra

Pella

B

Tara

D

REAPERS

Sunward Range

ROSERS

Union Walls

SANDERS

AULDAN

MEDIO

WARM SEA

BLADES

Great Walls

Stormshield Fort

Middle Walls

The Circuit

F

EVADERS

HAMMERS

Arrowhead Fort

SCYTHES

Fortress of the Lifegiver

G — Port Sanders

Salt Quay

BULWARK

Palaces

A – Greylin Palace
B – Royal Palace
C – Cuidrach Palace
D – Maeladh Palace
E – Alkirk Palace
F – Redmarket Palace
G – Tonetti Palace

SUBURB

ICEWARD

WEST — EAST

SUNWARD

0 1 2 3 4 5 6 7
miles

CHAPTER 1

THE SAVED

S cythe Territory, The Bulwark, The City – 6th Marcalis 3420
        The red sky shimmered and crackled as if the world was
ending. Kelsey Holdfast narrowed her eyes, trying to adjust to the
strange half-light. The buildings of Old Alea had vanished, along with
the rubble by the western tower of the Governor's residence, replaced
by open fields. The ground glistened pink with frost, and the air had a
cold bite to it.

'Is this the City?' said the silver dragon, her long neck turning.

Next to her, the other two dragons were also gazing around at their
new surroundings.

'We are in Scythe territory,' said Naxor.

Kelsey frowned. 'Was that a yes or a no?'

'It was a yes,' said Naxor. He smiled as he looked around. 'Belinda
sent us to the only part of the City with enough open space to take
every inhabitant of Old Alea.'

Kelsey stared up as the crackling ceased. The sky remained red, as if
in the midst of the most glorious sunset imaginable. The sun was to
their right, hovering over the horizon.

'This is normal,' said Naxor, catching her gaze. 'I'd get used to it, if I were you. Gone are the dazzling blue skies of Lostwell. Welcome to the City.'

Van nudged her elbow.

She glanced down to see him pointing. Small groups of people were milling around, or staggering, their eyes wide in panic and confusion. Servants from the Governor's residence predominated, but Banner soldiers were also in attendance, their weapons ready as they looked around for an officer to lead them. Larger groups could be seen in the distance, mobs of young Shinstrans and Torduan, who, moments before, had been assaulting the mansions of the gods.

'We might be the only ones here,' said Van, 'who understand what has just happened. We need to speak to someone in authority.' He frowned. 'Where are the locals?'

'Dead, mostly,' said Naxor. 'The vast majority of Scythes were massacred by the greenhide invasion, and any survivors will be concentrated in the housing areas sunward of here.'

'Sunward?' said Kelsey.

'Yes. There is no north or south in the City.' The demigod pointed to the right. 'Sunward.' He turned and pointed in the other direction, where the sky was a swirl of darker purples. 'Iceward.'

Deathfang lowered his great head. 'And where are the rulers of the City? It is to them that we should speak.'

Naxor pointed behind them. 'That way, I'd imagine. About fifteen miles from here lies the town of Pella. In the other direction are the Great Walls, and the greenhides.'

A scream tore through the air as a group of Banner soldiers was attacked by a mob of armed Shinstrans. The mercenaries had formed up into a tight mass, their shields and crossbows facing outwards. Other groups of civilians were running in panic, fleeing in all directions across the cold, hard soil of the empty fields. No one was approaching the three dragons, and several groups were trying to hurry away from their location.

'We need to scout,' said Van. He glanced at Naxor. 'What will the City authorities do, when they discover thousands of refugees here?'

Naxor shrugged. 'Who knows? I'd imagine that the Blades will be called out.'

'The Blades?' said Kelsey.

'They are a tribe of the City,' said Naxor; 'responsible for defending the Great Walls and keeping the peace. They will have garrisons close by, within the fortresses that line the walls. They also took a beating in the greenhide invasion, but many more of them survived compared to the unfortunate Scythes.'

'The Ascendant promised me that other dragons had been rescued,' said Deathfang. 'My mate, my children. Where are they?'

'We should hunt for them, father,' said Frostback. 'They will be disorientated and alarmed.'

'I will do so,' said the huge grey dragon. 'Daughter, I want you to circle up and scout while I search for our kin. Halfclaw, you shall remain here, and we will return to this location.'

The green dragon bowed his head. 'Yes, sire.'

Kelsey watched as Deathfang extended his enormous wings and took to the air. Around them, dozens of displaced people from Lostwell turned and stared as the dragon rose into the red sky. More shouts and screams echoed across the fields. Some people were running, as if panic had overwhelmed them, while others crouched by the ground, staring around with wide eyes.

'Kelsey,' said Frostback; 'climb onto my back, and we shall scout as my father has ordered.'

'I should come too,' said Naxor. 'I know the City. I can tell you exactly what you are seeing.'

Kelsey nodded.

'And me?' said Van.

'I cannot carry three humans,' said Frostback; 'not without a harness. You will have to remain here.'

Van frowned, and caught Kelsey's glance.

She shrugged. 'Sorry. We won't be long. Stay close to Halfclaw.'

The former mercenary glanced up at the green dragon, a wary look in his eyes. Kelsey looked at him for a moment. He had come along because... well, she knew why. For her. He had changed since she had last seen him; the way he had looked at her when he had arrived at the Governor's residence had not been the same as the way he had done so before. Despite that, she didn't love him. He caught her looking, turned, and held her gaze for a moment.

'Kelsey?' said Frostback.

She frowned, and glanced up. Naxor was already mounted upon the dragon's shoulders, and a great forelimb was angled out for Kelsey to ascend. She clambered up the silver scales, and positioned herself to Naxor's right, gripping onto the folds of the dragon's shoulders. Frostback beat her slender wings and rose into the sky. Kelsey stared down. The fields of the Scythe territory stretched out for miles beneath them. Nothing was growing, but thousands of Lostwell refugees were milling along the narrow lanes and tracks, or were gathering in the largest fields. Fights were going on, as isolated bands of Banner soldiers defended themselves from the mobs of Alea Tanton youths.

As Frostback gained altitude, Kelsey noticed a high barrier in the distance.

'Is that the Great Wall?' she said.

'No,' said Naxor. 'That's the Scythe Wall. It completely encloses Scythe territory.'

'Why?'

'We are in the Bulwark,' said the demigod. 'The rules are different here, well, they were at any rate. The Hammers and Scythes were both kept within their territories; the Hammers to work in the forges and factories; the Scythes to grow the food for the Bulwark. The Blades policed them, as well as defending the Great Walls from greenhide attack.'

'Were the Scythes slaves?'

Naxor chewed his lip for a moment. 'Some might choose to use that terminology, I suppose. Others would say that the Scythes performed an admirable and necessary role, one passed on from parents to children.'

'Could they leave if they wanted to?'

'No.'

'Then they were slaves.'

Naxor shrugged.

'Which way?' said Frostback, as she circled above Halfclaw.

'Let us observe the Great Wall first,' said Naxor. 'I wish to check that the greenhides are on the opposite side of the defences from us, just to be sure.' He pointed east. 'That way.'

Frostback surged away, crossing the open fields. To the left, Death-fang could be seen in the distance, hovering over another part of Scythe territory, while, ahead of them, the Scythe Wall grew larger. Beyond it was a cleared space, and then Kelsey saw a massive line of defences. They rose to a height that far exceeded that of the Scythe Wall, and were dotted with towers and, directly in front of them, an enormous fortress that stood astride the Great Walls.

'The Fortress of the Lifegiver,' said Naxor; 'where the Commander of the Bulwark, my Aunt Yendra, is based. Let's not go there. No doubt her vision powers will have already spotted the hordes of refugees running amok through Scythe territory, and I have no desire to incur her wrath just yet.'

Kelsey raised an eyebrow. 'Is she someone else that you've pissed off?'

'She might be.'

'That reminds me,' said Kelsey. 'Frostback, don't trust Naxor. He's a scheming little rat.'

'Understood,' said the silver dragon.

Naxor scowled. 'That is unfair; grossly unfair. Here I am, doing my best to help you, and this is what I get in return?'

'Oh, shut up,' said Kelsey. 'You brought this on yourself.' She quietened as the Great Walls approached. Soldiers were on the parapets of the highest of the three lines of defences, and their faces were turned upwards to gaze at the dragon. The soldiers lining the wall were quickly forgotten by Kelsey as her eyes took in what lay beyond the defences. She gasped. The ground seemed alive; a thick green carpet of flesh.

'Pyre's arse,' she muttered.

'Indeed,' said Naxor. 'Still, at least the greenhides are on the correct side of the walls. They penetrated deep into the City during the invasion, after breaching the Great Walls.'

'There must be thousands of them.'

'Millions, probably. The City is an island amid an ocean of greenhides.'

Frostback flew out over the great plain that stood in front of the Great Walls, turning in a gentle arc. Kelsey gripped onto the dragon's shoulders, her fear of falling heightened by the mass of savage beasts below them. The greenhides were attempting to cross a water-filled moat in front of the outer wall of the defences, while projectiles were being loosed upon them in an unceasing stream from the platforms on the inner wall.

'I want to burn some,' said Frostback.

'That's not a bad idea,' said Naxor. 'It will show the Blades on the walls which side we are on.'

The silver dragon swooped down, and opened her jaws. A thick torrent of flame burst from her mouth, tearing a channel through the hordes of greenhides massed before the moat. The beasts shrieked in rage and panic, while a low cheer rose up from the soldiers on the walls. Kelsey glanced down, her eyes stinging from the rising smoke, and saw the bodies of a hundred greenhides, scorched and smouldering. Within moments, the corpses had been trampled over, and the ranks of greenhides closed up, as if the attack had never happened.

'That was enjoyable,' said Frostback, 'but futile. Their numbers are beyond imagining.'

'Take us back,' said Kelsey.

Naxor smirked. 'Scared, are we, Holdfast?'

'Shut up, or I'll push you down there.'

'If you do that, I'll cling on, and take you with me.'

Frostback crossed the lines of the City defences and left the greenhides behind. Kelsey's heart rate began to slow again, and she didn't glance backwards. They passed the Fortress of the Lifegiver and re-crossed Scythe territory.

'To our right,' said Naxor, 'is Blade territory, but keep on in a straight line.'

'There are three tribes in the Bulwark?' said Kelsey.

'Yes. Ahead are the Middle Walls. Can you see them?'

Kelsey squinted into the red light. They soared over the fields of Scythe territory, then passed over a wall separating it from a dense network of brick and concrete buildings.

'Is that it?'

'No. That wall divides the Scythes from the Hammers. The Middle Walls are in the distance ahead of us. Before the construction of the Great Walls, the Middle Walls were the outer defences of the City.'

Kelsey followed the demigod's finger and saw them at last. A high, thick wall rose up beyond the last of the buildings of the Hammers, crowned with turrets and towers. Frostback sped over it, and below them stretched out a huge area of more concrete.

'Those could be the slums of Alea Tanton,' she said.

'They look similar, I suppose. However, it is the Circuit, home of the Evader tribe; another that suffered greatly in the greenhide invasion. The beasts broke through the Middle Walls, and were inside Medio for only a day, but the damage they caused was severe. Do you see that huge building?'

Kelsey looked down and saw an edifice that seemed to be a mile long. It rose up above the grey slums of the Circuit like an enormous rectangular block. She nodded.

'That's the Great Racecourse, where your brother fought the greenhides during that terrible day. And that fire damage? That was Black-rose. Those hills to our right belong to the Iceward Range, part of Icewarder territory, while the Sanders live down to our left. That's my home town – Port Sanders. Technically, my title is Lord Naxor of Port Sanders; did you know that?'

'Didn't know; don't care,' said Kelsey.

'And together,' Naxor went on; 'these three tribes make up Medio, the middle section of the City.'

They flew on, and Kelsey saw another high barrier approach.

'Those are the Union Walls,' said Naxor; 'the earliest defences of the united City. Beyond is Auldan, the only part of the City untouched by the greenhide incursion. It's also the richest part, containing the ancient towns of Tara, Pella, Ooste and Dalrig – the original settlements that combined to create the City.'

They passed over the thick defensive line. To their left were open fields and terraces that rose up the side of gentle hills.

'That's the Sunward Range,' said Naxor.

Kelsey glanced at the great villas that dotted the countryside, then her eyes were drawn to a large bay, where the waters of a sea shone in the red light. Arranged around the bay were three towns, each glistening in the light.

'The town on this side of the bay is Pella,' said Naxor; 'where the King and Queen have their palace. It was from the roof of that palace that we departed the City six months ago. The large suburbs around the town are known as Outer Pella, where the Reapers live, while the Gloamers inhabit Dalrig, and the Rosers live in Tara.'

'It's nothing like Alea Tanton,' said the silver dragon. 'I never knew of any city that had hills and fields within the walls.'

'Half of the City's food supply comes from either the Warm or Cold Seas,' said Naxor, 'but the rest has to be grown somewhere. Mind you, with the drastic reduction in population following the greenhide invasion, feeding the citizenry should now be less of a problem.'

'What are the numbers?' said Kelsey.

Naxor shrugged. 'These details never fail to bore me; you'll have to ask someone else.'

She glanced at him. 'Are you happy to be back?'

'I don't know. It wasn't what I had planned, but if Lostwell has truly been destroyed, then I guess I had little choice.'

'You were in Dragon Eyre, weren't you?'

'For a couple of hours, yes. Frankly, I'd rather have taken my chances on Lostwell than stay there. Blackrose and the others are mad for insisting upon going. No, the City is by far the safest bet, even though I'm not altogether sure of the welcome I shall receive.'

Frostback crossed the glistening bay, then turned in a long, slow curve. Beyond the towns of Tara and Ooste, Kelsey could see more water stretching away into the west, where a thin line of land appeared on the horizon.

'What's over there?' she said.

'The Western Bank; an uninhabited land of forests and more green-hides. The seas enclose the City on three sides, and the Great Wall protects us from the east. There are no other human settlements on this world as far as anyone knows; just the City.'

'And where are we supposed to live?' said Frostback. 'I do not desire to dwell in the City.'

'I have an idea about that,' he said; 'though I'll need to speak to the government first. There will be plenty of time to plan things, once I have been given a job that suits my rank.'

Kelsey laughed. 'What rank is that?'

'I am a demigod with vision powers, my dear Holdfast. My skills will be in great demand, whereas yours will be useless here. Worse than useless, in fact, as there are no enemy Ascendants to foil. All you would achieve is to frustrate the communications of the City.'

'Really? That's excellent news. I'm used to idiots chasing me wher-ever I go; trying to take advantage of my abilities to block powers; it sounds like a dream come true not to be hounded by some maniac or another. I may actually be able to have a normal life here.'

'Speaking of idiots; what do you intend to do with Van?'

'Shut up, Naxor. Van's not an idiot.'

'No? He chased you all over Khatanax, and I heard much of what he had to say about you while we were in Kin Dai waiting for your brother to recover.'

She glanced at the demigod, not sure if she wanted to hear any more.

'Is he in love with you?' said the dragon.

'No!' she cried. 'Well, I hope not. No, he's not. Surely.'

'Then why else did he come here?'

Naxor chuckled. 'Good question, dragon. I think Miss Holdfast is well aware of the answer to that.'

'Take us back to Scythe-land,' she said, ignoring the stupid smirk on his face.

Frostback circled over the bay again, then set out back over the way she had come.

'If Van harasses you, Kelsey,' the dragon said, 'I will incinerate him.'

'Please don't,' she said. 'This situation isn't his fault.'

'So, you led him on?' said Naxor.

'I can't explain it.'

'I'm sure you could try.'

'Alright; I won't explain it; not to you, Naxor. It's absolutely none of your damn business; are we clear?'

'Fine,' he muttered.

Frostback crossed Auldan, and soared over the Union Walls, where dozens of soldiers were staring up at her. For the return journey, the dragon flew a little sunward of her previous route, and Kelsey could see the town of Port Sanders that Naxor had pointed out earlier. Its harbour was filled with vessels of all sizes, and the red tiles covering the rooftops were shining in the strange light of the City. There was something about the nature of the light that seemed familiar to her – then she remembered. The vision of her and Van, when he had been holding a baby, had been lit with the same red light. She closed her eyes, feeling the weight of the future on her shoulders.

Medio passed under them, and they re-crossed the Middle Walls, then the Scythe Wall. The ground beneath them seemed to have erupted in chaos. Large bands of refugees were wandering the empty fields, while several bodies lay dead from the clashes between the Banner soldiers and the youthful mobs who had stormed Old Alea.

'I see my father,' said Frostback. 'He has found the others.'

She soared down, and Kelsey saw nearly a dozen dragons in a large field. The huge form of Deathfang dominated, while the others were assembled round him, including Darksky and her brood of three young dragons.

'I thought there would be more,' said Frostback, as she circled overhead.

She descended, landing close to her father.

'Welcome back, daughter,' said the huge grey dragon. 'I have gathered all of our kin; all those who were transported here from Lostwell.'

'But there are only twelve dragons here,' she said. 'Where are the others?'

Darksky turned to her, her eyes tight. 'The ridge where you left us was unstable,' she said, 'and it collapsed not long after you departed to attack Alea Tanton. We are all that remain of the Catacombs.'

Kelsey and Naxor slid down to the ground.

'Eight adults and four children?' said Naxor, rubbing his chin.

'Six children,' said Darksky; 'for Frostback and Halfclaw are hardly adults.'

'Our priority is to protect the little ones,' said Deathfang. 'Did you see the rulers of the City on your expedition?'

'We saw their palace, father,' said Frostback, 'but we did not approach.'

'That was wise,' said Naxor. 'The sight of unknown dragons flying over the City might cause an unwelcome reaction from its defenders. They have ballistae here, designed for use against the greenhides, but they could easily be turned against you. We need to speak to my aunt, Princess Yendra, to let her know that you aren't a threat.' He frowned. 'Am I correct? You aren't a threat, are you?'

'We will not strike those who leave us in peace,' said Deathfang.

Kelsey glanced around. 'Where's Van?'

'He wandered off,' said Halfclaw. 'I asked him not to, but he ignored me.'

'You were supposed to keep him here,' said Deathfang.

'I'm sorry, sire. Should I have physically restrained him? He was quite determined.'

'Why did he leave?' said Kelsey.

'He said he was looking for someone. A demigod named Vana.'

Naxor's eyes widened and he slapped his forehead. 'Damn it; of course! If she was being held in the Governor's residence, then she would have been transported here as well.'

'Van said that, by his reckoning, she should be a few hundred yards to our right,' said Halfclaw.

Kelsey turned to stare, and saw mobs of civilians roaming over the area. Naxor rolled his shoulders.

'I suppose I should look for them,' he said.

'I'm coming,' said Kelsey.

'Daughter,' said Deathfang; 'cover them from the sky. I owe my life to your rider and I do not wish any harm to come to her.'

Frostback ascended into the air, and Naxor and Kelsey set off. Crowds stared at the two of them as they left the field where the dragons had assembled. Apart from them, no humans had ventured close to the huge creatures. A group of older servants were sitting on the cold earth, shivering in their nightclothes, while a band of blue-sashed youths with weapons eyed the approach of Kelsey and Naxor.

'What are those dragons doing here?' cried one of them.

'They're friends,' said Kelsey. 'They won't touch you if you leave them be.'

The mob glanced up as Frostback soared overhead.

'That one's keeping an eye on us,' said Naxor, smiling.

'In the name of the Ascendants,' said another; 'where are we? What happened? Why is the sky red?'

'You have been taken to another world,' said Naxor; 'as Lostwell was on the verge of destruction.'

'Queen Belinda saved everyone who was in Old Alea,' said Kelsey. 'If it were not for her, you would all be dead.'

'The City authorities will be here soon,' said Naxor. 'Be patient.'

'But there's no food or water, and we're freezing our asses off.'

'And,' said another, 'there are still companies of Banner soldiers around. Why were they saved? They were trying to kill us.'

The voices from the group rose in a mixture of anger and half-panic. Every eye turned to Kelsey and Naxor, as if they held all of the answers.

'Belinda saved everyone she could,' said Kelsey. 'Good, bad, ugly; it didn't matter. You are the sole survivors of Lostwell.'

The people quietened. Some were staring at her with wide eyes, while others looked incredulous. The crowd parted as a man pushed his way through, leading a bedraggled woman by the hand. She saw Naxor and ran towards him.

'Cousin,' he said. 'You look terrible.'

'Ten days in a stinking cell does that to you,' said Vana. She shook her head. 'We're home. How?'

'Belinda,' said Kelsey.

'And the Sextant,' said Van, joining them. 'Listen, we may have some trouble. Lady Felice was also imprisoned in the eastern tower of the Governor's residence, but I saw no sign of her.'

'How do you know that?' said Kelsey.

'I told him,' said Vana. 'I could feel her powers; well, I could until you reappeared. Now, she could be anywhere.'

'Any other gods or demigods come along with us?' said Naxor.

Vana nodded. 'I could also sense Silva.'

'She's here?' said Van.

'Yes, although I've lost her position also.'

One of the crowd stepped forward. 'Are you all demigods?'

'I am Lord Naxor of Port Sanders,' said Naxor; 'and this is Lady Vana of Pella. This is our world; our City – we only happened to be on Lostwell when it was destroyed. We shall speak to the rulers of the City on your behalf, and organise food, blankets and shelter for you.'

Van nudged Kelsey's elbow as Naxor continued to speak to the growing crowds.

'Can we talk?'

Kelsey frowned. 'Do we have to?'

They walked a few yards away, towards the quiet of the dragons' field.

'I came here,' he said, 'because...'

She groaned. He closed his mouth and glared at her.

'Sorry,' she said; 'carry on.'

He shook his head. 'What's the point? It's clear I've made a mistake. I should have stayed with Corthie but, instead, I thought... Look, you know what I thought. You filled my head with your crazy visions, and...'

'Vision,' she said; 'there was only one.'

'Does it matter how many you had?'

'Don't get angry.'

'What was the point of it all? You led me to believe that we were going to fall in love with each other. I couldn't believe it, I admit, not at first, but I...' He lowered his head. 'I don't know what I'm trying to say. I guess you made me feel as if I had no choice – I had to come here, and now... well, it's clear that you still don't like me.'

'You had a choice,' she said; 'I didn't make you come; I didn't even try to persuade you.'

'You don't love me, do you?'

'No. Do you... ah, do you love me?'

Van said nothing, his eyes directed towards the frost-covered ground.

'Oh, bollocks,' she muttered. 'Look, we're both stuck here now; we'll just have to make the best of it.'

'That night in Shawe Myre,' he said; 'I thought... well, it meant a lot to me.'

'You'd just been tortured, and we were in great danger. You shouldn't have kissed me.'

'I know.' He exhaled. 'Alright. I may be many things, but I'm not a complete fool, and I learned long ago how to take no for an answer. If you don't want me, then I'll have to deal with that, but I won't bother you again. I'll find something to do in this City, and I'll leave you alone.'

She glanced at him, wishing for a moment that she liked him more. He was handsome, and brave, and she had seen flashes of a tender side to him, but she had been so occupied with her new relationship with Frostback, that she had no room to explore anything with Van.

'I'd rather be friends,' she said. 'I don't want to cut off all contact with you.'

He nodded, but didn't meet her eyes. 'Maybe in a while; my feelings are a bit raw at the moment. I think I need some time to adjust to our new reality.'

He turned, and began to walk away.

'Hey!' she cried. 'Where are you going?'

'I heard there was a fortress a couple of miles to the east of here,' he said. 'I'm going to hand myself in.'

He continued walking, and Kelsey made as if to follow him.

'Let him go,' said Frostback, landing beside her.

Kelsey said nothing, her eyes on the former mercenary's back.

'I heard you tell him that you didn't love him,' said the silver dragon. 'If that's true, then why are you upset that he's going?'

'I'm not upset.'

'Come now,' said Frostback. 'If you are to be my rider, then I insist upon complete honesty between us.'

Kelsey lowered her eyes. 'I thought he would stay, even though I... Never mind.' She took a breath. 'There are a million things to do. Let's get to work.'

CHAPTER 2
TRIBAL POLITICS

P ella, Auldan, The City – 6ᵗʰ Marcalis 3420

The Gloamer delegate paused for effect. 'And so, therefore, in conclusion,' he said, his sonorous voice filling the small chamber, 'we find these proposals to be without merit, unworkable and, frankly, intolerable.'

Emily kept her expression neutral as the Gloamer delegate sat, while on the throne next to her, Daniel's sigh of exasperation was audible.

Lord Salvor stood. 'Our thanks to the delegate from Dalrig. Last to speak this morning, will be the delegation from Tara.' He nodded to the bench and retook his seat in front of the raised thrones.

'Thank you, Lord Salvor,' said one of the Roser delegates, getting to his feet. He glanced around the chamber. Three lines of benches had been arranged into a rough horseshoe pattern before the King and Queen, representing the tribes of the Bulwark, Medio and Auldan, with three tribes to each bench. The Roser delegate looked down at his notes, then took a sip of water.

'Your Majesties,' he began, 'and my fellow delegates; as you are all aware, this past year has seen unparalleled changes in the governance of the City. The God-King and God-Queen are missing, presumed dead or fled, and of the God-Children, only Prince Montieth and Princess Yendra remain. The monarchy has passed into the hands of ordinary mortals at a perilous time in the history of our home, a time that has seen the unfortunate deaths of over a third of the City's population. Evaders, Sanders, Hammers, Blades – all have seen their numbers devastated; and in the case of the Scythes, the slaughter approached complete annihilation.' He took a moment to sip from his glass as the other tribal delegates shifted in their seats. The five Scythe delegates were directly opposite the Roser who was speaking, but they kept their eyes lowered.

'At such a time,' he went on, 'the temptation to reform the institutions of the City can grow into a powerful force; and I am here, today, to counsel caution. The proposals formulated by the offices of their Royal Majesties advocate nothing less than a revolution in terms of how the City is ruled; a revolution that would not only sweep away centuries, nay millennia, of tradition and custom, but one that would take power from responsible property owners and hand it to the illiterate masses – all in the dubious name of "fairness." Tell me, how can it be fair to confiscate land and property from those whose families have worked hard for centuries, and give it to those who can barely sign their own names? And land reform is merely one aspect of the revolution being proposed. The parliament being suggested would give votes and representation to a section of the City who cannot read, let alone understand the complexities of legislation and the intricacies of politics. Their Majesties talk of individual freedoms, but what use will these freedoms be if the state collapses? And what about tribal freedoms? For generations, the principle that each tribe is autonomous has been paramount, yet the proposals for a single, unifying law code trample on the rights that each tribe holds dear. Our beloved City has thrived for thousands of years without a parliament, and without any of the supposedly necessary and urgent reforms being promulgated this day. Let me be clear; I am not saying that no reform is required, but the current proposals go far beyond what any sensible analysis of the situation would suggest. Therefore, without any hesitation, the Rosers reject the entire package. I beg their Royal Majesties to remove these proposals from consideration, and instead set up a series of Royal Commissions to investigate each individual recommendation. Reform, yes. Revolution, no.'

The Roser delegate took his seat as the chamber sat in silence. Emily could feel the anger simmer from Daniel, but the responses from the various delegates had been in line with her expectations, and she kept her smile steady.

Lord Salvor stood. 'My thanks to the delegation from the Roser tribe,' he said, his hands clasped by his waist. 'This conference shall now adjourn until after lunch, when their Royal Majesties will respond to the points raised, and put the proposals to a full vote of the tribes.'

He nodded to the courtiers by the grand doors of the chamber, which were opened. The delegates got to their feet, bowed towards the raised thrones, and left the chamber, the Dalrigian and Taran representatives whispering to each other as they walked out. The doors were closed once all had departed, leaving Emily, Daniel, Salvor, and a handful of lawyers and court staff present.

'That went well,' said Emily.

Daniel snorted. 'That's not the word I would have used. I was expecting opposition from the Gloamers and Rosers, and the Sanders, as they mimic whatever the Rosers tell them, but from the others too? Only the Reapers and Hammers gave their unconditional support.' He shook his head. 'To say I am disappointed would be an understatement.'

Emily stepped down from her throne to stretch her legs. A courtier presented a tray with a collection of drinks, and she took a glass of fresh fruit juice with a smile. She had warned her husband about the dangers of trying to get all of their reforms through in a single package, but he was impatient for change. She couldn't tell him that she had told him so, at least not in front of the lawyers and officials that remained in the chamber, but she was sure she wouldn't need to – he knew.

'If I may, your Majesties?' said Salvor.

'Of course, Salvor,' said Emily; 'speak your mind.'

He bowed. 'The Rosers and Gloamers will never accept these changes, your Majesties. I have watched them operate in the political sphere for hundreds of years, and have come to the realisation that they will never give up their wealth and privileges without a fight. If we include the Sanders within their grouping, then there are three votes out of nine that we have to accept we will never win over. Unanimity, it seems to me, is an impossibility. When the doubts and caveats of the Blades, Scythes and Icewarders are taken into account, it seems to me that a simple majority among the tribes will also be lacking.'

'I agree,' said Emily. 'Then what is your recommendation?'

'We should accept the suggestion of Royal Commissions, your Majesties, as the Roser delegate proposed.'

'Out of the question,' said Daniel. 'That suggestion was thought up solely to waste time, and to ensure that our proposals are watered down until they become meaningless. We have one opportunity to change the City, and if we don't act now, then that chance will be lost. Land reform, a representative parliament, a single law code, and the freedom of movement for all citizens – these proposals all hang together. Separately, each is not enough; we have to push them through in a single motion.'

Salvor bowed again, saying nothing.

'I think we shall have a bite to eat,' said Emily. She glanced at the assembled lawyers and officials. 'We shall see you after lunch.'

They bowed and left the chamber. Lord Salvor picked up the pile of paperwork he had been using and also bowed.

'Will you be joining us?' said Emily.

'I am due to vision to Princess Yendra, your Majesty. It has been a few days since we had a briefing from the Bulwark.'

'Then do so,' she said, 'and thank you for all your help.'

'It is my pleasure to serve you, your Majesties.'

They left the meeting chamber, and Salvor left to walk to his office, while Emily and Daniel strolled along the wide passageways of Cuidrach Palace towards their private quarters, accompanied by a small number of servants. They reached their rooms, and Emily dismissed the servants, so she could be alone with her husband as they waited for food to arrive.

Daniel tore off his long royal robes and strode to the balcony, his face dark.

'What did you expect, dear?' she said, following him out. She glanced up at the sky, and wrapped the warm robes round her shoulders. Ahead of them, the bay looked glorious, and was reflecting the pink light. A few Reapers on the streets below were gazing up at the balcony, and she gave them a smile and a wave.

'You know what I thought,' he muttered. 'I actually believed that the delegates would look beyond their individual and selfish desires; I thought they would act in the best interests of the City.'

'But it's not one City, is it? There are nine tribes, and each sees themselves as separate. The gods did a good job of dividing us, and these divisions can't be overturned quickly.'

'It's been six months since the greenhide incursion,' he said, 'and we have achieved precisely nothing.'

'Not true. We avoided mass starvation; we managed to clear Medio and the Bulwark of greenhides, and we managed to dispose of the bodies of half a million citizens before disease could take hold among the survivors. The Great Walls are once again guarded by Blades, and the City is at peace. That is most certainly not "nothing."'

He shook his head. 'I don't understand how you can be so sanguine about it. We didn't become King and Queen just to sit on a throne; we did it so we could change the City from top to bottom, and put an end to centuries of injustice. Have you changed your mind?'

'You know me better than that, Danny. Perhaps I am a little more patient than you.'

'We cannot afford patience, not when children in the Circuit are living in squalor because some rich Roser landlords have increased their rent. How dare they complain about illiteracy, when their policies have been responsible for keeping the masses uneducated?'

Emily watched his face as his anger rose.

'At times,' he went on, 'I feel like sending the Blades back into Tara, and Dalrig. If they won't give up their privileges willingly, then perhaps some force should be applied.'

'I doubt history would look kindly upon us if we went down that road.'

'Who cares what history thinks of us? As King, my job is to do the right thing, not worry about how it looks.'

'I'm not sure I agree, Danny; perceptions are important. The people have to feel that we're doing the right thing.'

'Which people? The Evaders or the Rosers?'

'Both, ideally. If we can't take the people with us, then what mandate do we have?'

'We were crowned – that is the only mandate that matters.'

'Not yet. We've been monarchs for six months, as you said – a mere speck in the history of the City. Prince Michael ruled for almost one and a half thousand years. He spent his first decade in power doing nothing, just observing, before he made any changes.'

'Are you saying we should be more like Michael, the worst tyrant the City has ever known?'

'No, of course not. I'm saying that we need to be patient. We want our reign to last, and we want to see it continue beyond our short lives. Without some compromises, that won't happen.'

He glared at her, then the door to the quarters opened. Emily sighed. There was only one person in the palace who didn't knock first before entering. She placed a smile on her lips and turned to greet Daniel's mother.

'Lady Aurelian,' she said; 'do come in.'

'Your Majesties,' she said, giving a brief bow. To her left was Nadhew, the Roser lawyer, who had become a close confidante of the King-Mother. 'How was your meeting with the tribal delegates?'

'Terrible,' muttered Daniel.

'The opening step in a long series of negotiations,' said Emily.

The King-Mother smiled. 'It's lovely to see your minds in such close concert.'

She paused as the door was knocked, and several servants entered, one pushing a laden trolley.

'I see we have arrived in time for food,' said the King-Mother.

'Should we come back another time, your Majesties?' said Nadhew, bowing.

'Nonsense,' said the King-Mother; 'I'm sure the King and Queen wouldn't mind us sitting with them.' She scanned the dishes on the trolley. 'Is this a late breakfast, or an early lunch?'

'Call it whatever you want, mother,' said Daniel, sitting at the table while the servants unloaded the trolley. 'I assume you are here for a reason?'

'Quite,' she said. She glanced from a chair to Emily. 'May I sit?'

'Of course,' said Emily; 'why not?'

'Thank you, your Majesties,' said Nadhew, taking a seat next to the King-Mother.

Emily waited until the servants had finished their work and had departed the room, then she took her seat.

'I'm afraid,' said the King-Mother, 'that someone in the palace has, rather indiscreetly I might add, allowed a copy of your constitutional proposals to leak, and the Rosers are complaining very loudly to me about it.' She glanced at Nadhew. 'Tell them.'

The lawyer nodded. 'The local authorities in Tara have obtained a copy, your Majesties, and are marshalling opposition to the proposals. It's open knowledge that the Gloamers and Sanders are allied to the Rosers, but I have received information that the Blades will also vote against the plan, and the Icewarders, Scythes and Evaders will abstain. That leaves you with only two tribes in favour – the Hammers and the Reapers.'

Daniel frowned. 'The Evaders will abstain?'

'Yes, your Majesty,' said the lawyer. 'My information states that they do not feel that the proposals go far enough. They want the complete abolition of all property rights in the City.'

The King-Mother laughed.

'Do you find this funny, mother?'

'Yes, I do,' she said. 'It's ironic, don't you think, that the very tribe you have been trying to help have turned on you for not pandering to their anarchic notions? You are learning a hard lesson, my dears; one that I learned a long time ago.'

'Yes, mother; and what is that lesson?'

'That nothing you do for the Evaders will ever be enough. They have worn the identity of victims for so long that they know no other way to exist. Everything is a conspiracy against them, according to their point of view. In short, if you decide to put your proposals to a vote, you will lose. Perhaps it's time to re-think some of the more radical parts of your plan.'

'Equality under the law isn't radical, mother.'

'So you say, Danny. Others seem to disagree.' She turned to Emily. 'I suspect that you are one of those, your Majesty? You're being uncharacteristically quiet.'

Emily smiled. 'Daniel and I will come to a decision together.'

'Quite the diplomatic response, dear. What you really mean, I assume, is that you agree with me, and disagree with your husband, but do not wish to say so in front of anyone else. At least you are a loyal wife, which is all a mother-in-law really hopes for. Well, that and grandchildren.'

'Don't generalise, mother,' said Daniel; 'you hardly speak for the entirety of womankind.'

'No, but I do speak for myself, and I would like you to listen, dear. You are making a grave mistake with these plans. You will split the City from top to bottom if you insist on pushing through your changes against such a formidable array of opponents. Is that what you want?'

'We want the City to be secure,' said Emily, 'but we also want everyone that lives within its walls to have the same opportunities. There is no reason why the Hammers, for instance, should be confined to their old tribal territory, or that the inhabitants of Medio are not allowed to own property in Auldan.'

The King-Mother shrugged. 'So, reform, yes; revolution, no?'

Daniel glared at her. 'You heard that, did you?'

'My dear, the Roser delegate's speech was circulating around town yesterday, but I could have predicted their response without having to read the text.'

There was a knock at the door, and Commander Quill entered, dressed in the uniform of the Royal Guard.

She bowed low before the table. 'Apologies for interrupting, your Majesties, but I have a report.'

'Is it confidential?' said Emily.

'No, your Majesty.'

'Then you can say it in front of the King-Mother and Lord Nadhew.'

'Very well, your Majesty. A few moments ago, a dragon was seen flying over Pella. It came from the direction of the Middle Walls, circled over the bay a few times, then flew back towards the east.'

'A dragon?' said Daniel. 'Blackrose?'

'No, your Majesty,' said Quill. 'This one was smaller, and silver in colour. Some of the reports claim that at least one person was seen riding upon its back as it flew. I admit, I did not personally see the beast.'

Emily and Daniel glanced at each other.

'Alert the militia,' said Emily.

'I have already taken the liberty of doing so, your Majesty.'

'Thank you. Summon Lord Salvor, please.'

Quill bowed her head, then left the chamber.

'Salvor?' said the King-Mother, a slight look of disdain on her features.

'Yes,' said Emily. 'I am aware of your feelings towards the demigods of this City, but Lord Salvor has proved nothing but useful to us. His experience of the intricacies of City politics is extensive.'

'It should be, seeing how he has served Prince Michael, Princess Khora and, latterly, Duke Marcus. So much for your grand hopes of excluding the former Royal Family from the government.'

'That's not what we promised,' said Emily. 'We stated that none of them would automatically get positions of authority; those who serve us are there on merit. Princess Yendra, for example; would you recommend that we relieve her of her position as Commander of the Bulwark?'

'Not if you wish to remain in power.'

'Precisely.'

'But Salvor? My dear – he can read your thoughts, your innermost desires and fears. Is it wise to keep him so close to you?'

'I trust him,' said Daniel, 'and so do the Reapers. That's good enough for me.'

'Your naivety astounds me at times, my son. Salvor has been alive for over twelve-hundred years, and has worked for every ruler of the City in that time. To him, you and your dear wife must seem like children, there to be humoured and placated.'

The door was knocked again, and Commander Quill entered, along with Lord Salvor. The demigod glanced round the chamber, giving a small smile to the King-Mother as he did so. She looked away. He bowed before the table.

'Lord Salvor,' said Emily; 'has Commander Quill briefed you on the dragon sighting?'

'She has, your Majesty,' he said; 'however, I bring tidings of far greater import; tidings that I would prefer to relay to you in private.'

Emily frowned. 'Very well.' She turned to the King-Mother. 'If you would please excuse us?'

Daniel's mother bit back a scowl and got to her feet, her lunch untouched. Next to her, Nadhew also rose, and bowed deeply.

'Remember all that I said regarding your plan,' she said, inclining her head a little.

'We shall,' said Emily.

They waited until the King-Mother and Lord Nadhew had left the room, then Salvor bowed again.

'May I begin, your Majesties?'

'Please do,' said Emily. 'This sounds serious.'

'Serious, and... perplexing, if I'm honest, your Majesty. It took me a few moments to contact Princess Yendra, as she was rather occupied with events.'

'What events?' said Daniel.

The demigod took a long breath. 'This morning, your Majesties, several thousand people... appeared in Scythe territory.'

Daniel squinted. 'What? Explain.'

'At the moment, your Majesty, I cannot. One minute, the fields of Scythe territory were empty, and the next, they were full. Estimates are still coming in, but it seems a reasonable guess would be some thirty to forty thousand arrivals, including several dragons. Blades posted on the walls of the Sunward Fort, the Fortress of the Lifegiver, and Arrowhead Fort all claim the same thing. Furthermore, it seems that various factions among the arrivals have been fighting each other, and witnesses have claimed to have seen a few violent deaths.'

'And the Scythes?' said Emily.

'They are safe, according to our reports, your Majesty. The arrivals appeared iceward of the housing district. However, hunger and the cold conditions will no doubt mean that some of the new arrivals will seek food from wherever they can find it, and the Scythes may soon be at risk.'

'Did you use your vision to see them for yourself?'

'Yes, your Majesty. The majority appear like us, but several have green-coloured skin. There is also no luggage among them; no possessions except what they are carrying. Unfortunately, in many cases that appears to be weapons. There are also units of organised soldiers here and there, who have been fighting the groups of civilians.'

Emily and Daniel said nothing, Emily's mind turning over on itself as she tried to grapple with the implications.

'We do not yet know where they have appeared from, your Majesties,' said Salvor, 'but Princess Yendra is currently using her powers to read the thoughts of some of the arrivals in order to gain some understanding of the circumstances regarding their appearance in the City.'

'How many dragons?' said Daniel.

'I counted a dozen, your Majesty; although three or four of these appear to be juveniles. Only one is of a similar size to Blackrose, but several are as large as Buckler was. As far as I know, the dragons have not made any aggressive moves towards the City, or indeed towards those they arrived with.'

'Has anything like this ever happened before?' said Emily.

'No, your Majesty. If I had to speculate, I would say that they were transported here from another world; perhaps the one that Lady Aila and Lord Naxor travelled to at the beginning of summer.'

'Have you ever used a Quadrant?'

The demigod shook his head. 'I never even laid eyes on one until I saw the device Princess Yendra took from Lord Naxor.'

Emily shook her head. 'Forty thousand people appear from nowhere? What in Malik's name are we supposed to do with them all?' She stood, and began to pace up and down. 'Feed them, I suppose. And clothe and house them.'

'Order will have to be restored first, your Majesty,' said Quill. 'From the report, it seems that mobs of these new arrivals are rampaging through Scythe territory. If they locate the winter food stores, they could ruin our plans for feeding the City.'

'Princess Yendra is already assembling troops,' said Salvor. 'Currently, every new arrival is contained within the Scythe Wall.'

'We must not let them break out,' said Daniel. He turned to Emily. 'Belinda; it must be. You asked for dragons, and she sent some.'

'Yes, but I didn't ask for forty thousand civilians.'

'How should we handle the news of this, your Majesties?' said Salvor. 'Rumours of the silver dragon are already spreading through Auldan, and if it flew over Medio, then the same will be true there. I would advise sending a reassuring message to the citizenry, telling them not to panic.'

'I would like you to take care of that,' said Emily, 'while the King and I travel to the Bulwark. I think it's important to see for ourselves what is going on. Please also send a message to Princess Yendra, informing her that we are leaving immediately.'

'Certainly, your Majesty. And the tribal council meeting scheduled for after lunch?'

'Tell them that the meeting is postponed due to these events.'

Daniel scowled. 'They'll think we're postponing because we're afraid to put our proposals to a vote.'

'I am afraid to put it to a vote, Danny,' she said, 'because, as things stand, we would lose. However, the needs of the City outweigh a single meeting, and our presence in the Bulwark is required. Now, leave us, please, as I wish to eat and then get dressed for travel. Have a carriage be prepared for our departure in fifteen minutes. Commander Quill, I want you to come along.'

The commander and the demigod bowed again, then left the room.

Emily glanced at her husband. 'Forty thousand people! Forty! If this was indeed Belinda's doing, then I feel I will need to have some harsh words with her. Food is already tight as it is without so many more mouths to feed – what in Malik's name was she thinking?'

Daniel shrugged. 'Maybe she had no choice.'

Emily took a deep breath. 'On the bright side,' she said, 'there's a lot we could accomplish with a dozen dragons.'

CHAPTER 3

CITY OF WALLS

Scythe Territory, The Bulwark, The City – 6th Marcalis 3420

Kagan shivered as he awoke. His clothes were tangled in the thick undergrowth of a hedgerow, beyond which the sky shone pink and red. The young man tried to lift his hands, but his fingers were sore from the cold, and his teeth were chattering.

Where was he?

The last thing he remembered was the assault on Lord Baldwin's mansion in Old Alea. The enormous house had been surrounded by lush gardens, but he recalled having entered the mansion with dozens of other Shinstran youths, all determined to ransack as much wealth as they could carry from the home of the dead god. They had come up against a squad of well-trained Banner soldiers, and after that his memories became hazy. Perhaps he had been injured, and then dragged back outside?

He groaned, his head throbbing. A shout rang out from somewhere, and he slowly pulled his legs free of the undergrowth, and crawled from the hedgerow. Ahead of him was a field, its surface glistening with frost. He frowned. A field? He couldn't remember seeing any fields up on Old Alea, but it had been his first time on the promontory, and he knew there would be parts of it that he wouldn't recognise. Still, even after squinting into the distance, he could see no buildings, just a few wandering bands of people dressed in what looked to be nightclothes. And the sky – why was it so red? It was like no sunrise or sunset he had even known; was Alea Tanton in flames, despite the floods that had swamped the city?

Freeing himself from the last of the undergrowth, he staggered to his feet, feeling unsteady and dizzy. The back of his head was aching, and he lifted a hand to touch it, feeling a lump that had developed behind his right ear.

That was right, he thought, as more memories came back to him. A Banner soldier had struck him with the butt of his crossbow, and then he had fallen down the wide, marble staircase near the entrance hall of the mansion. He gazed around. There was no sign of any mansion, nor of the gardens that surrounded it. And where were the neat lines of workers' cottages, or the tall towers of the Governor's residence? He noticed a group stare at him, but they looked away when he returned their glance. They were dressed for the hot nights of Alea Tanton, and were shivering in their thin nightclothes.

He approached them, and they began to back away, as if frightened.

'Hey,' he cried; 'wait.'

'We have nothing to steal,' said an older man with a Shinstran accent, raising his empty palms; 'please, leave us alone.'

'Don't be stupid,' he replied. 'Why would I steal from you? Where are we?'

'I don't know, son,' said the older man.

'Maybe we're all dead,' said a woman. 'Maybe this is the afterlife.'

'Don't say that,' said the older man.

'But look at the sky – it's not natural.'

Kagan peered up and around. Vivid splashes of pinks and reds were to his right, while off to the left, the sky darkened into thick purples. He wondered if the old woman was right.

'Do you have any water?' he said.

The group glanced at each other.

'No water, son; no nothing,' said the older man, 'and we've been walking for over a mile. There's nothing but frost and empty fields.'

'And the gangs,' muttered someone else; 'Bloodflies, Blue Thumbs, and we even saw a bunch of Banner soldiers.'

Kagan scowled. 'Have you got something to say about Bloodflies? I don't want to hear any of your cheek, old man.'

The group edged back a little.

'Don't be scared,' said the older man; 'he's on his own. They're only brave in packs. Move along, boy, and leave us be.'

'Gladly,' said Kagan. 'I hope you all freeze to death.'

He turned and walked away from the small group, hearing their low mutters behind him. He crossed the field, seeing another few groups of people in their nightclothes, trying not to think about what the woman had said about them being dead. It was ludicrous, although he was struggling to think of a better explanation. He nearly stumbled over something, then realised it was the body of a dead Banner soldier. His head had been split open, and his skin was shaded with glistening frost. The young man leaned over the corpse, but the soldier's weapons had already been stripped from the body. He was still in possession of his boots, however, which were far superior to the thin footwear the young man was wearing, so he crouched down and began to unlace them from the corpse's feet.

A few people watched him as he pulled his own shoes off and slipped the sturdy boots on in their place. As he was lacing them up, a group of half a dozen men entered the field, all wearing blue sashes over their shoulders. Each was armed, some with stolen Banner cross-bows, and the young man's heart jittered. He knew that the Bloodflies and Blue Thumbs had agreed a temporary truce while they had stormed Old Alea, but he had no idea if it was still in operation. For a moment, he was tempted to remove the red band from his right arm, but the thought shamed him. If he was going to die, it would be as a proud Bloodflies supporter; he would never betray his team, his colours.

The blue-sashed men paid him no attention, and continued on

their way across the field, their Torduan accents grating on the young man's ears.

'Blue Thumb scum,' he muttered, once they had passed.

He got back to his feet, and tried out his new boots. They were close fitting, but much better than his thin shoes had been, and warmer too. He glanced down at the corpse, then strode to the edge of the field, where another long hedgerow seemed to go on for miles. There were gaps in the hedge, some of which looked newly made, and he slipped through onto a rough track. On the far side was another field, while columns of people were trudging up and down the track. Most were older than him, some in their nightclothes, others dressed as courtiers or servants. In the distance, he caught a glimpse of a group with red armbands, and he hurried towards them, pushing past the people on the track.

The group eyed him as he approached, their hands resting on the improvised collection of weapons in their possession. Kagan didn't recognise any of their faces, but their armbands had given him hope.

'Stop there,' said one, his hand clutching an axe.

The young man halted a few yards away from the group, his hands outstretched.

'Who are you?' said the man with the axe.

'He's Bloodflies;' said another; 'look at his armband.'

'He could have stolen that,' said the first man. 'I want to hear his accent first.'

'My name's Kagan,' said the young man. 'I'm part of Dizzler's crew; you know him? We climbed the ramp into Old Alea with the others, but I got separated from them. Have you seen Dizzler?'

The man with the axe nodded. 'Fair enough; you're Shinstran. We haven't seen any of Dizzler's crew, though. We're part of the Baker Street Boys.'

'I know them,' said Kagan; 'well, I know some of them. I used to hang out with Artie.'

'Well, you can hang out with us, if you want,' said the axe-man. 'Safety in numbers, eh? The Blue Thumb bastards have been leaving us alone, but those Banner assholes attacked us an hour ago. I don't suppose you have any idea where we are?'

Kagan shook his head. 'I just woke up in a hedgerow. I think a soldier knocked me out when we were raiding a mansion, and then... and then I'm here. Some old woman I met said she thought we were dead.'

The group glanced at each other.

'Did you not see the sky crackle?'

'Eh? I just told you; I was knocked out.'

'Well, the sky went funny, and then whoosh, we were here. You know how the gods used to appear and disappear at the games? It was like that, except it was us doing the vanishing.'

Kagan nodded. 'What's the plan?'

The axe-man shrugged. 'Stay alive. Find food. And then we can try to work out what's going on.'

The group walked along the road for a hundred yards, then came to a wide entrance to a field. At least a thousand people were in the field, mostly sitting on the hard ground as if in a daze, but others were shouting, or running around in confusion. A large gang of Blue Thumbs was occupying an entire corner of the field, and the Shinstrans gave them a wide berth.

'The Banner forces have cleared off,' said the axe-man; 'there were a hundred of them here the last time we passed. They're better equipped, but out-numbered.'

'Is everyone from Old Alea here, do you think?' said Kagan.

'Looks that way. I reckon half are servants that used to work for the gods, and the rest are gang members like us, apart from the Banner soldiers. I even saw a couple of Fordians earlier.'

'The gods have done this to us,' he said; 'it's the only explanation I can think of. They used their powers and lifted us up from Old Alea and dumped us down here, wherever here is.'

'Kagan!' cried a woman's voice.

He turned, his eyes scanning the inhabitants of the field. Hurrying towards him was a young woman.

'That's Elena,' he said; 'Dizzler's little sister.' He waved.

The woman approached, slowing when she saw the other Shinstrans with Kagan.

'I thought you were dead,' she said. 'I saw you go down at the mansion, clubbed on the head.'

He rubbed behind his ear, where the lump had formed. 'Yeah. I took a sore one. I woke up in a hedge a little while ago, about a quarter of a mile behind us.'

'That's roughly where we appeared,' she said. 'You were in a hedge, eh? That explains why we never saw you.'

'Is your brother here?'

'Yeah. You coming?'

Kagan glanced at the axe-man and the other Shinstrans. 'Thanks, guys.'

'No problem,' said the axe-man; 'take it easy.'

Kagan and Elena left the group, and she led him to the other end of the field, where a few dozen Shinstrans were sitting, all wearing their red armbands.

'Look who I found!' cried Elena.

The eyes of the group lifted, and a few cheered. Kagan looked at the faces; most of the old crew seemed to be there. A man stood, a half-smile on his face.

'Kagan! You've come to join the party, eh? Nice boots.'

'Cheers, Dizzler,' he said. 'I liberated them from some dead Banner guy; he didn't need them any more.'

The man laughed. 'While most folk are running around like headless chickens, or weeping like fools, you stopped to strip a guy of his boots?'

Kagan shrugged. 'My feet were getting cold.'

Dizzler slapped him on the back. 'That's my boy. My sister was nearly in tears, thinking you were dead.'

Elena glared at them. 'I was not.'

'Yes, you were,' said Dizzler. 'You ran off like a hare as soon as you saw him across the field.'

The young woman's face flushed, and Kagan laughed. She stared at him for a second, then turned and strode off.

Dizzler put his arm over Kagan's shoulder.

'You've got her eating out of your hand, mate,' he said; 'but remember, she's my sister, and you'd better not be an asshole to her; right?'

'Of course not, Dizzler.'

'That's my boy. Now, we need to see about getting some food. You got any ideas?'

Kagan frowned. 'Well, if there are fields, then there has to be farms; and if there are farms, there'll be barns and silos and whatnot. We just need to find them.'

Cries rose up from the field, and several people pointed into the sky. Kagan and Dizzler glanced up, and saw a dragon in the distance, silhouetted by the low sun.

'Holy crap,' muttered Dizzler.

'I saw a dragon in Old Alea,' said Kagan. 'If the gods brought us here, they must have brought it as well.'

'Whose side was it on?'

'Ours. I saw it roast a whole company of Banner soldiers.'

Dizzler puffed out his cheeks. 'It's alright,' he called out to the others from his crew. 'The flying lizard isn't an enemy.'

'Unless it's as hungry as we are,' muttered one of the gang.

'Fair point. We need to move, just in case it decides we're lunch.' Dizzler glanced around. 'We'll keep heading away from where we first appeared. If we carry on in a straight line, we're bound to reach something. Come on.'

The crew muttered and grumbled, but did as Dizzler asked. He was a big guy, with broad shoulders, and fists that had seen more than their fair share of fights, and the crew respected him. They set off, with Dizzler in the lead, Kagan striding by his side, while Elena caught up with them, keeping her eyes on the way ahead. Dizzler sent off a couple of the crew to either side to flank them, to warn if any Blue Thumbs or Banner soldiers were approaching, and they crossed the field, avoiding the large groups of shivering civilians.

'They must have been snatched right from their beds,' said Kagan. 'I bet half of them think they're still dreaming.'

'Yeah, sounds about right,' said Dizzler. He glanced at the sky and shook his head. 'Did you know that the sun hasn't moved a bleeding inch since we got here? It's just sat there, hovering over the horizon in a kind of permanent sunrise. I'm not surprised some folk think we might have all died.'

'It has moved,' said Elena; 'not much, but it has moved a bit, and the sky isn't as red as it was when we first got here. It's more pink now, I'd say.'

'I thought the strange light was coming from Alea Tanton,' said Kagan; 'I thought the whole city was in flames.'

'It probably is,' said Dizzler. 'The shock of arriving here has almost made me forget what was happening in the city. I watched the Southern Pits collapse into rubble as we were climbing the ramp, and the water level had drowned every street where we used to gather before the games. Alea Tanton is in ruins.'

They fell into silence as they passed through a line of hedges and entered another huge field. Like the one they had left, it was full of people shivering in the cold. Kagan began to grow hungry as they kept walking. He had eaten nothing since the previous morning, before the first of the giant waves had hit Alea Tanton, and that had been a light and hurried breakfast. A line of tall trees cut across their path, the upper branches rustling in the soft, cold wind. Several small fires had been lit by their bases, and people were gathered round the flames, keeping warm. On the other side was a long irrigation canal, the water level high, and Dizzler's crew stopped for a moment to take a drink.

'It's too wide to jump,' said Dizzler.

'And too cold to swim across,' said Kagan, crouching by the water's edge.

Elena kicked at the frozen mud by the bank of the canal, and a sod of earth came loose, splashing into the water. She frowned and peered down at the hole she had created.

'What's that?' she said.

Kagan stared into the hole, then reached in and pulled out a long, sharp talon.

'It's a greenhide claw,' he said, holding it up.

'Are you sure?' said Dizzler.

Kagan nodded. 'I remember getting a tour of the Southern Pits, and we were shown the greenhides there. Most of them had had their claws removed, and they looked just like this.'

A few of the group shuddered and glanced around.

'Do you think that's why no one's here?' said Elena. 'No one except us, I mean.'

'If any greenhides were here,' said Dizzler, 'we would have heard them shrieking by now. In fact, we'd all be dead by now.'

Kagan tucked the talon into his belt and stood. 'We'll have to find a crossing.'

They turned away from the sun, and walked along the banks of the irrigation canal. Beyond the line of trees, they came to a vast space where the earth was blackened. Kagan knelt, and pushed his fingers through the frost and into a thick layer of ash and dirt. Scattered over the hard ground were small fragments of bone, and more claws.

'This was the site of a huge pyre,' he said. 'Judging by the size, hundreds of greenhides were burnt on this spot.'

'By whom?' said Elena.

He shrugged. 'If I knew that, then I might be able to guess where we are.'

They skirted the blackened earth, and followed the line of the canal until they came to a small bridge. A stream of civilians from Old Alea were crossing it, heading in the same direction as they were, and they hurried over the dark waters, their feet thudding on the thick wooden beams. On the other side was a wide field, and Kagan squinted into the distance.

'A barn,' he said; 'look.'

Dizzler picked up his pace, and the crew strode across the field in the direction of the tall barn. Hundreds of others had already discovered it, and the building had been thoroughly ransacked. Open sacks were spilling their contents of grain by the side of the track, and people were scooping them up on their hands and knees, shoving the grains into their mouths. A man lay dead by the entrance to the barn, a large, gaping wound across his chest. He was dressed in rough overalls, and his boots had been stolen.

Dizzler frowned. 'Do you reckon he was a local?'

'I think he might have been,' said Kagan.

'Poor bastard,' said Elena. 'He was probably only trying to defend his barn.'

'Kagan; go inside and scout for some food,' said Dizzler; 'see if the jackals around here have left any.'

'Righto, boss.'

He strode towards the barn entrance, and noticed that Elena was walking by his side.

'How's your head?' she said.

'Not too bad, but there's a big lump behind my ear.'

'Hold on,' she said, placing a hand on his arm to stop him. She reached up and pushed his shoulder-length hair to the side, and touched where he had been clubbed by the crossbow butt.

Pain leapt through him, but he kept his face straight.

'Looks sore,' she said, 'but it's not bleeding or anything.' She smoothed his hair. 'What my brother was saying; it's not true. I wasn't crying.'

He shrugged. 'This whole thing is messed up, Elena. It would be no cause for shame if you had been.'

'You're only saying that because I'm a girl. Any guy that cried, you'd be mocking them.'

'Not today, I wouldn't.'

They carried on, and paused at the open doors to the barn. Inside was a scene of devastation. It looked to Kagan as if a great store of grain had been stacked inside, but all that remained was ripped sacking and broken wooden shelving. A ton of spilt grain seemed to have been trodden into the mud underfoot, and trails of it led away outside. Kagan walked into the dim interior. Near the back of the barn, he spotted movement and narrowed his eyes. He strode forwards, and saw a child hiding behind a heap of broken wooden pallets. The young boy stared at him as he approached, his face stained with tears.

'Hello,' said Kagan, crouching so his eyes were level with the boy's face. 'Do you live here?'

The boy didn't respond. He pushed backwards against the wall of the barn, as if trying to burrow his way through.

'If you come with us,' Kagan said, 'we'll look after you. Do you know where your parents are?'

Elena reached his side and peered at the child. 'Maybe he doesn't understand our language.'

Kagan nodded. 'Maybe. Can you understand me, little man?'

The boy said nothing.

'Where are we?' said Kagan.

'The City,' whispered the boy.

Kagan smiled. 'Alright. Great. Which city?'

'*The* City.'

'Do you need help? Where's your father?'

The boy pointed at the barn entrance, where the body of the man was lying.

'Shit,' muttered Kagan.

Elena's eyes widened. 'Those bastards killed his dad?'

'Do you want to come with us?' said Kagan. 'We'll protect you.'

The boy shook his head.

Kagan sighed and stood. 'Alright.'

'He'll be safe if he stays in here,' said Elena. 'All the food's already gone.'

Kagan reached for his belt and tossed the greenhide talon to the boy. 'Take that; just in case.'

The boy watched as Kagan and Elena walked back out of the barn, the greenhide claw clutched in his hand. Dizzler was waiting for them, an expectant look on his face.

'The place has been looted,' said Kagan; 'stripped clean.'

'Damn it,' muttered Dizzler; 'we should have come this way earlier.'

He turned to the crew. 'There's nothing for it but to keep going. If we park our asses on the ground, we'll freeze. Come on.'

Kagan counted as the crew moved on through the field. Thirty-nine of Dizzler's crew were there, when he knew for a fact that over fifty had climbed the ramp on their way up to Old Alea, along with thousands of other gang members from the lower city. Still, thirty-nine was a tidy number; enough to dissuade most from approaching them as they made their way out of the field and onto another track. He had seen the faces of the crew every day for years, ever since his mum had moved to an apartment closer to the Southern Pits, near to where Dizzler ruled his little patch of Alea Tanton. Kagan had been nine at the time, and had begun hanging around with the younger members of Dizzler's crew a few days after they had unpacked their meagre possessions. His mum hadn't cared; she had been too busy making sure his dad hadn't followed them to their new address.

They approached a large group of young men and women wearing blue sashes, and the crew quietened. The Blue Thumbs also ceased talking, and stared as the Shinstrans passed them on the track. Despite their proximity, no spiteful words or needless aggression was shown by either group; the weight of their new circumstances prolonging the truce they had forged in Old Alea, but the glances they exchanged were cold and hostile.

Once the Shinstrans had passed the group of Blue Thumbs, Kagan glanced up at the sky. Directly overhead was a small patch of blue, and the sight of it made him feel a touch of despair for the first time since he had awoken in the hedge. Would he ever see the blue skies of his home again? Alea Tanton was a horrible place to live, and had grown considerably worse over the previous day since being inundated by tidal waves and struck with earthquakes; but it was his home. Everyone and everything he knew was contained within the dense housing districts of the Shinstran part of the city; it was familiar.

'I feel like I'm dreaming,' said Elena next to him.

'I know what you mean,' Kagan said. 'None of this seems real.'

She took his hand, in front of her brother; in front of the entire crew. Kagan was mortified for a moment, and had to suppress an automatic urge to pull his hand free. But how would that look to everyone? They would laugh at him, and laugh at Elena; and she would hate him. He glanced down at her, but she was looking the other way. He had known for a while that she liked him; maybe he should give it a try? He had gone out with considerably worse girlfriends over the years, and she was probably feeling frightened and lonely. He decided not to embarrass her, and gripped her hand firmly as they walked along the track.

Dizzler looked over, pretending not to notice that his sister was holding Kagan's hand. He pointed into the distance.

'Do you see that?'

Kagan squinted. Ahead of them, beyond a few more hedgerows, a wall loomed. It seemed to run in a straight line from left to right, with no end at either side that he could see. As they got closer, Kagan could see that it towered over the hedges, and was as high as the tops of the trees that ran to the side of the track.

'There are no parapets, walkways or towers,' said Kagan.

'What does that mean?' said Dizzler.

'It means it's not a defensive wall. There's no way for anyone on this side to see what's happening beyond. In other words, it's designed to keep folk on this side from getting through.'

'Like a prison?'

Kagan shrugged. 'Maybe. We don't know if the wall extends all the way around this area.'

As they came closer to the wall, Kagan glanced at the massive stone blocks that had gone into its construction. They were heavily weathered, but remained solid.

'Do you reckon you could climb it?' said Dizzler.

Kagan thought that sounded like a good excuse to let go of Elena's hand, so he nodded. Elena lowered her eyes as he extricated his fingers from hers, then he turned to the wall. He took a few steps back, then ran at it, springing up at the last second and clambering up. The erosion had formed wide grooves where his hands and feet could gain purchase, and he was soon at the top, the muscles in his legs and arms throbbing from the effort.

He pushed his head up, and rested his arms on the top of the wall. In the distance was another wall, much higher and wider than the one he had climbed, and replete with turrets and towers. In the gap between the two walls was a road, upon which soldiers in strange uniforms were marching. They looked like professionals, reminding Kagan of the Banner forces.

'Hey!' Kagan called out.

Some of the soldiers stopped and glanced around.

'Up here!' Kagan cried.

As the soldiers stared at him, an officer stepped forwards. 'Get down from there!'

'Sure thing,' Kagan said; 'only, where are we?'

'You are in the City. Tell your companions; in fact, tell everyone you see to remain calm. We are coming to you. Where did you appear from?'

'We're from Alea Tanton.'

The soldiers glanced at each other.

The officer pointed to Kagan's left. 'There is a gate a mile in that direction. Do not attempt to break through. We will be coming that way. If there is resistance, then be warned; we will roll right over it. It is in your interests to remain calm and to wait for assistance to reach you; do you understand?'

'Yeah. Make sure you bring lots of food and blankets; folk are freezing to death over here.'

'We've heard reports that many of you are armed,' said the officer. 'No one with weapons will be helped; this is our City, and we're not going to tolerate armed mobs roaming Scythe territory. Now, get down and make your way to the gate – and spread the word of what I've told you.'

'Alright, chief.'

Kagan clambered back down the wall, jumping the last few feet.

'Did you hear all that?' he asked Dizzler.

'Only what you were saying.'

'There's a gate a mile away; soldiers are coming to lend assistance, but not to anyone with weapons.'

Dizzler scratched his chin.

'What do we do?' said Elena.

'We should make for the gate,' said Kagan; 'and make sure we're first in line for any food they bring.'

'Did they say where we are?' said Dizzler.

Kagan shrugged. 'The City. As if we're supposed to know where that is. There's another huge wall beyond this one; seems they like their walls here.'

'Alright,' said Dizzler; 'we'll head to the gates. Kagan, lead the way.'

'Sure, boss.'

Dizzler smiled. 'That's my boy.'

CHAPTER 4

FORTRESS OF THE LIFEGIVER

Fortress of the Lifegiver, The Bulwark, The City – 6th Marcalis 3420

Princess Yendra gazed out from the observation post atop the walls of the Fortress of the Lifegiver. She was used to being up there, but instead of looking out over the hordes of greenhides assaulting the Great Walls, that day she had been directing her gaze in the other direction – towards Scythe territory. Even without using her vision, she could see hundreds, maybe thousands of the new arrivals; wandering across the fields, or sitting on the frozen ground.

She hadn't panicked at the news. She led by example, and wanted her officers to convey the same levels of calm confidence that she did; that way, the soldiers would feel reassured.

'All Blade battalions are in position, Commander,' said a mid-ranking officer to her left, his head bowed. 'They await your orders to advance.'

She nodded. 'And the wall leading to Hammer territory?'

'The local Hammer militia is covering every gate between their territory and that of the Scythes, Commander. Salt Quay has also been reinforced.'

Yendra said nothing for a moment. She had fifty thousand troops at

44

her disposal, of which she needed at least twenty in position on the Great Walls. She had decided to keep ten in reserve and send the other twenty thousand into Scythe territory. Mortals would die, no matter what she decided to do; she had to accept that. If she didn't send the Blades in, then hundreds of the poorly-dressed refugees would freeze to death long before they had a chance to starve, and the remaining Scythes, sheltering in their housing district at the sunward edge of their territory, would be at risk. It didn't matter that she felt sorry for the refugees; her priority was the native population of the City.

'Pacify, disarm, protect,' she said, more to herself than anyone else. She nodded to the assembled officers. 'Send them in.'

'Yes, Commander,' said the highest ranking officer present. He gestured to a signalman, who raised a red flag high into the air.

Whistles blew, and the gates leading into Scythe territory were opened. There were three such gates on the eastern flank of Scythe territory, one by each of the massive fortresses on the sunward end of the Great Walls, and Yendra glanced down at the gate directly in front of the observation post. Squads of heavily-armoured Blades in tight formation were rushing through the open entrance, as entire companies waited their turn on the road that ran alongside the Scythe Wall. From within the territory, screams and cries began to rise up from the refugees, and several groups scattered in panic, trying to flee the Blades. The soldiers ignored the vast majority of refugees, instead concentrating on securing the main routes and seeking out those who were armed. If any refugees refused to lay down their weapons, the Blades were under orders to overwhelm them with physical force; killing them if necessary.

Arranged behind the soldiers queuing to enter Scythe territory were dozens of wagons, each loaded with water, food and clothing, along with hundreds of tents from the stores of the fortress-depots.

Yendra focussed, and sent out her vision to Pella. She found Lord Salvor, her nephew, sitting in his office poring over documents.

Salvor, she said inside his head; *the Blades are moving into Scythe territory as agreed.*

He nodded. *The King and Queen have already departed Pella, your Highness. They boarded a fast carriage some forty minutes ago, accompanied by a company of the Royal Guard. I will locate them and inform them; they are probably at the Union Walls by now. Is there any indication of where these... people have come from?*

A city by the name of Alea Tanton. Curiously, they seem to speak the same language as we do, but none of those whose thoughts I have read have any idea why they are here. From what I can gather, they were involved in a conflict against the ruling gods of that city, when they suddenly appeared in Scythe territory. I will keep you posted with any updates.

She withdrew from Salvor's mind before he could ask anything else; she had more important things to do than pass the time chatting to her nephew. She pushed her vision out, observing the progress of the Blade forces being channelled through the gates. To sunward, the first squads were reaching the housing districts where the remnant of the Scythes lived. The soldiers were rushing through the empty, narrow, cobbled streets, racing to get into their positions. Their objective was to prevent any refugees from entering the district, and to protect the Scythes from any aggression. That tribe had already suffered enough.

She worked her way along the Scythe Wall. By the Sunward Fort, soldiers were fanning iceward, sweeping up along the abandoned farm tracks. They were making good progress, so she moved on. By the Fortress of the Lifegiver, and by Arrowhead, things were different. There, the Blades were confronted with the mass of refugees, including the bands of uniformed soldiers that had appeared alongside the civilians. Progress was slow, as Yendra had insisted that no squad move too far away from support; it would be all too easy for a small detachment of Blades to find itself cut off amid thousands of desperate refugees. She smiled as she watched a large mob of youths with blue sashes over their shoulders throw down their weapons and surrender, then she was distracted by panicked cries of terror. She shifted her vision, and witnessed the first Blade casualty of the day – a young woman of the Fifteenth Infantry Battalion felled by a crossbow bolt through her neck; a bolt loosed by a soldier in a strange uniform. The Blades closed ranks around the group of foreign soldiers, who had taken possession of a derelict barn. The officer on the ground showed no sign of hesitation, and the Blades advanced swiftly, killing any who resisted, until the soldiers dropped their weapons and raised their hands in the air.

Yendra glanced away, feeling powerless. Watching every individual encounter would only increase her anxiety levels; she had to let the Blades do their jobs. She turned to Captain Brunwick, her favourite staff officer.

'Their Royal Majesties are coming to the Fortress of the Lifegiver; we must be ready to greet them. Have a light luncheon prepared for them and the company of Royal Guard accompanying them.'

The captain bowed. 'Yes, ma'am.'

'And summon Lady Jade, please. I will be in the office on the first floor of the Duke's Tower.'

The captain bowed again and hurried off. Yendra took one last look at the scenes playing out below her, then turned and headed for the stairs, a small retinue of messengers and aides following. She descended the outer steps of the curtain wall and walked across the large courtyard of the fortress. Buildings crowded the yard, dominated by two huge barracks blocks and the Duke's Tower, from where Marcus had ruled the Bulwark for three centuries. Blades bowed to her as she passed wagons being loaded with supplies for the refugees. She strode into the entrance of the tower, and made her way to the large office on the first floor. It was still decorated in the fashion that Marcus had liked, and she hated it, but knew how bad it would look if she had prioritised the refurbishment of her new quarters over the other emergencies besetting the City. She had removed the various busts and portraits of Duke Marcus from the tower, leaving bare spaces on the walls where they had been displayed, but otherwise had left everything untouched.

A handful of staff officers were waiting for her. They bowed.

'Word has arrived from Port Sanders, Commander,' said one. 'Boats are being loaded with clothing, blankets and heating oil. Lady Lydia has promised that they should be arriving at Salt Quay by nightfall.'

Yendra nodded. 'And the other tribes?'

'The Reapers have pledged three hundred tons of grain supplies; half to go by ship, the other by wagon, and the Icewarders are sending supplies of fresh water and winter clothing. The Hammers are standing by, ready to enter Scythe territory with food supplies once permission has been granted. The other tribes have yet to respond to our requests for assistance.'

A surge of anger rippled through her, but she kept her features impassive. The Hammers and Reapers were among the poorest inhabitants of the City, and yet they had responded before the Rosers or Gloamers. The Evaders had enough of their own difficulties to deal with, and she wasn't expecting much from that quarter.

'I want a census put into effect as soon as it is logistically possible,' Yendra said. 'We need to know exactly how many refugees we are dealing with. Assign a support battalion from Arrowhead to begin preparations for this.'

'Yes, Commander.'

The doors to the office opened and Captain Brunwick entered. Next to him was Jade, wearing long, dark green robes that shimmered in the light. Her hair was tied up, and she looked angry. The staff officers quietened, and every one of them averted their eyes.

'Ah, there you are, Jade,' said Yendra.

'What is it, Aunt? I was busy.'

Yendra glanced at the officers. 'Please leave us for a moment.'

She kept her smile on her lips as the officers hurried from the room, then turned to her niece.

'What have I told you, Jade? I am the Commander of the Bulwark, and you are my Adjutant. That means you show me respect in front of the officers. When we are alone, you are free to speak your mind, and to have your little tantrums, but I expect you to behave with a certain amount of decorum.'

Jade rolled her eyes. 'Yes, Aunt.'

'So, what were you doing?'

'What do you think? I was killing greenhides. What else do I do here? When we arrived, you said "Kill greenhides," so that is what I do every day. It's getting a little boring, to be honest. No matter how many I kill, there are always more the following day.'

'But there are no more coming,' said Yendra. 'The nest was destroyed. Every greenhide you kill means one fewer to threaten the walls. You must have disposed of thousands over the last six months.'

Jade glared at her. 'Tens of thousands.' She crossed her arms over her chest. 'Something else happened today.'

'Yes?'

'A dragon appeared.'

'I heard about that. It killed several greenhides, or so I was told?'

Jade nodded. 'I might have... panicked a little. I wasn't expecting a dragon.'

'I see. What did you do, Jade?'

'I lashed out. I couldn't help it. I thought the dragon was going to burn me.'

'And what happened?'

'Nothing.'

Yendra frowned. 'Sorry; I'm not following. You used your powers on the dragon?'

'I tried to, but nothing happened. My powers didn't work on it. It flew past, then flew away, as if my powers were completely useless. Once it had gone, I made sure my powers were still working – they are, you'll be glad to know.'

'But the dragon was immune?'

'That's what I just said. Immune. How could that be?'

'Corthie Holdfast was immune to death powers,' said Yendra, pondering for a moment.

'Do you think he's turned into a dragon?'

Yendra laughed, unable to stop herself, as Jade fumed.

'It was a serious question,' said the irate demigod.

'I don't think that sort of thing is possible, Jade. Look, we'll get to the bottom of it, but you'll have to promise me that you won't try to kill any of the dragons that have arrived, not unless they show themselves to be hostile.'

Jade's eyes widened. 'Dragons, plural?'

'Yes. There are a dozen within Scythe territory at the moment. One extremely large male, seven medium-sized dragons, and four young ones, three of which are very little indeed. Their minds are hard to penetrate, but I managed to access the thoughts of the biggest dragon. He is the patriarch of the group, and the one we shall need to negotiate with.'

'We should kill them all.'

'Why, Jade?'

'They are a threat to the City. A dozen dragons could burn it from end to end.'

'Or, if they are friendly, they could assist you in destroying the greenhides beyond the walls. Remember how loved and valuable Buckler was to the Blades, and then imagine that times twelve.'

'Then we could kill the older ones, and chain up the youngsters; raise them as slaves to do our bidding. We could condition them through fear and turn them into useful weapons.'

Yendra said nothing for a moment. Centuries of living in Dalrig's Greylin Palace had warped Jade's sense of morality, but Yendra was confident that, given time, she would be able to change.

'Do you remember we talked about the concept of consent, Jade?' she said.

'Yes. It means that no one can make me do anything unless I agree to it.'

'That's correct, but it also means that we shouldn't do things to others that they don't agree with.'

'Why?'

'These concepts are universal, Jade; they apply to everyone.'

'Why?'

'Because everyone is of equal value.'

'Are they? Says who?'

Yendra paused. They had been round these loops of logic before. For nine hundred years, Jade had believed that her life was worth that of a hundred mortals, and nothing that had occurred since leaving Greylin Palace had changed her mind.

There was a welcome knock on the door, and Captain Brunwick peered into the office.

'Apologies, ma'am, but I have someone here whom I think it would be useful for you to meet.'

'Yes; who?'

'One of the new arrivals, ma'am. He was waiting by the gates, and surrendered to us as soon as they had opened. He claims to be a military officer, and says he knows how and why the refugees got here. He's been questioned by the battalion staff, and they felt that you should speak with him.'

Yendra thought for a moment. 'Send him in.'

'Yes, ma'am.'

The captain closed the door again, and Yendra turned to Jade.

'On your best behaviour, please. Let me do the talking.'

Jade sighed. 'Fine.'

The door opened again, and a man was led into the room, a squad of Blades guarding him. Yendra looked at the man, resisting the temptation to peer into his mind. Better to let him speak, and then she could check the veracity of his statements afterwards.

'This man claims to be Captain Van Logos, ma'am,' said Brunwick; 'of the Banner of the...'

'Formerly of the Banner of the Golden Fist,' said the man, inclining his head a little.

Yendra nodded. 'And what is the Banner of the Golden Fist?'

'A mercenary unit, ma'am,' said Van; 'until it was destroyed by Corthie Holdfast and Belinda.'

'I see. Are Corthie and Belinda your enemies?'

'They were at first, ma'am. However, Corthie ended up being my most recent employer. I last spoke to him and Belinda this morning. It was Belinda who sent us here.'

'Why? Wait; don't answer that yet. Are you hungry? Thirsty? Take a seat.' She glanced at Brunwick. 'Please organise some refreshments for our guest.'

The captain nodded. 'Yes, ma'am.'

Van glanced around, and sat by a long table, its surface covered in maps. He wasn't dressed as a soldier, but he had that look about him, and Yendra had believed his words.

'I am Princess Yendra,' she said, 'Commander of the Bulwark. Corthie Holdfast was my friend.'

'I know that, ma'am,' said Van. 'I heard him mention you on more than one occasion.'

'Then you know where you are?'

'I do, ma'am. Belinda told us where she was going to send us.'

'Is Corthie here too?'

'No, ma'am. I was under the impression that Belinda was going to send him back to his homeworld, with a demigod called Aila.'

'Aila? And how is she?'

'Fine, ma'am. Pregnant.'

Yendra smiled, and sat down opposite Van. 'Tell me everything.'

For two hours, Yendra sat and listened to what the young mercenary officer had to say. Refreshments were brought, and he continued to talk as he ate and drank, telling her about the plight of Lostwell, and the immense power of the Sextant. They were finally interrupted by an announcement that the Royal party had arrived at the gates of the Fortress of the Lifegiver, and Yendra stood at the news.

'May I ask one more thing, ma'am?' said Van.

'Of course.'

'I'm looking for a job, to be frank. I have fifteen years of military experience, ma'am, and have served on multiple worlds. I feel I could offer a range of differing perspectives and expertise.'

'You wish to become a Blade?'

'Is that possible, ma'am? I don't know.'

She glanced at the door, impatient to greet the King and Queen, then turned to face the man. She swallowed her qualms and delved into his mind. He was being honest, she could see that, but his emotions were in turmoil, despite his calm exterior.

'Why didn't you mention your attachment to Kelsey Holdfast?' she asked. 'And, yes; I have just read your mind. It may seem rude, but I knew of no faster way to establish if you were telling the truth.'

'I understand. My mind has been read by gods countless times in the past. Regarding Kelsey, my feelings are personal, and I wanted to provide you with the facts.'

'But you love her?'

'I don't know, ma'am. However, she has made her feelings clear, and I need to work; otherwise I'm liable to sit around moping and giving in to... unsavoury temptations.'

Yendra nodded. 'Stay with me, Captain. For the moment, you can serve as my liaison officer regarding the refugees, and we will reflect upon your position after the immediate crisis has passed. Does that sound fair?'

'More than fair, ma'am.' His eyes almost seemed to well up for a moment. 'Thank you.'

She gestured to Jade and the other officers in the room. 'Come; let us welcome their Royal Majesties to the fortress.'

They filed out of the room, Yendra ensuring Brunwick, Jade and Van were close to her as they walked.

'You didn't explain the dragons properly,' said Jade to Van as they walked.

'Excuse me, ma'am?'

'You said that there were three dragons at the place where Belinda used the Sextant, yet we have been told there are a dozen in Scythe territory. Were you lying, mortal?'

'No, ma'am. There were three with us. The others were gathered by Belinda from various locations across Khatanax. She told us that she was rescuing every dragon that still lived, so I imagine that a dozen were all that remained.'

Jade narrowed her eyes at him. 'I don't trust you, mortal. But you are handsome, and I might select you for my harem. Well, I would if Aunt Yendra allowed me to have one. Shall I slay this Kelsey girl for you?'

'I'd rather you didn't, ma'am.'

'I have death powers.'

'Is that so?'

'Yes. Does that scare you?'

Van suppressed a smile. 'Yes, ma'am. Consider me terrified.'

'Good,' said Jade. 'Later, I'll tell you where my quarters are, and then you can...'

'That's enough, Jade,' said Yendra. 'Focus on the job at hand.'

They walked out of the Duke's Tower and into the large forecourt of the fortress. A line of carriages had arrived, and the King and Queen were stepping down from one. Yendra, Jade and the officers present all bowed deeply.

'Good morning, Commander,' said Emily, striding forwards, Daniel a pace behind.

'Your Majesties,' said Yendra. 'You honour us with your presence. Two hours ago, I authorised the Blades to enter Scythe territory in order to gain control of the situation.'

'How many?' said Daniel.

'Twenty thousand soldiers, your Majesty, with a further ten thousand in reserve. We estimate forty thousand refugees, as well as the twelve dragons.'

Emily's eyes scanned the officers, halting at Van. 'I don't recognise you.'

'This is Captain Van Logos,' said Yendra. 'He arrived with the refugees, and the information he has brought us has proved invaluable.'

Emily kept her gaze on Van. 'Is Belinda responsible?'

Van bowed. 'She is, your Majesty.'

Anger flickered across the Queen's features.

'I fear she had little choice, your Majesty,' said Yendra. 'Lostwell has been destroyed. The forty thousand refugees in Scythe territory are all that remains out of a population of millions. It seems she was trying her best to save as many lives as possible.'

Daniel's mouth opened. 'Lostwell has been destroyed? An entire world?'

'Yes, your Majesty,' said Van. 'The Ascendants did it.'

'The who?'

'The Ascendants, your Majesty; the oldest gods. They are hunting for this world, as they desire to secure the supply of salve.'

'Belinda already told us this,' said Daniel.

'And are we now safe?' said Emily. 'Did Belinda resolve this problem?'

'I cannot answer that question with full certainty, your Majesties,' said Van. 'As far as I know, Belinda prevented the Ascendants from getting their hands on the Sextant, and from that I would guess that this world is safe, but there may be information I am lacking. Lord Naxor may know more.'

Emily groaned. 'Naxor's back?'

'Yes, your Majesty, along with Lady Vana.'

'I thought she was dead.'

'It appears, your Majesty,' said Yendra, 'that she was abducted by Naxor and taken to Lostwell.'

'Are they any other gods or demigods currently among the refugees?'

'Yes, your Majesty,' said Van. 'One Lady Silva, who was a faithful friend of Belinda. She has powers similar to Lady Vana and, in my opinion, she can be trusted. Unfortunately, a certain Lady Felice was also brought here. She has vision powers, and was part of the government ruling Lostwell. I would advise that she be treated as a potential enemy.'

'And the dragons?'

'Fundamentally, your Majesty,' he said, 'they are neutral. They helped us overcome the Ascendants, but more through desperation than noble principles. I do think that they would be open to negotiations. They need somewhere to live, and if they are treated with respect, then they could become allies.'

Emily glanced at Yendra. 'You were perfectly correct, Commander. This man is indeed rather useful.'

Jade scowled at the Queen. 'I saw him first.'

Emily frowned for a moment, while Daniel chuckled to himself.

'Shall we walk up to the observation post, your Majesties?' said Yendra. 'From there, we shall be able to see the progress the Blade forces are making.'

'That sounds like a good idea, Commander,' said Emily, 'although I also wish to enter Scythe territory, so we can see the situation for ourselves.'

'I would advise waiting a few hours, your Majesty,' said Yendra. 'Episodes of violence are still taking place. It will be safer once the district has been pacified, and the food wagons have begun feeding the refugees.'

'Very well.'

They climbed the steps up the side of the curtain wall, then ascended the tallest tower of the flank of the fortress facing the rest of the City. Yendra looked down over the frozen fields of Scythe territory, as the King and Queen did the same next to her. Large groups of refugees had been corralled into certain areas, each surrounded by Blade soldiers, while piles of discarded and surrendered weapons were heaped up by road junctions.

'What is the significance of the red and blue markings?' said Daniel.

Yendra glanced at Van.

'The citizens of Alea Tanton were divided by tribe, your Majesty,' he said. 'The reds are the Shinstrans, the blues, the Torduans. There are also greens, which are the Fordians. The rivalry among the three peoples was quite ferocious, but they allied together against the Banner soldiers.'

'I see we have much to learn,' said Daniel.

Below them, on the road between the fortress and the Scythe Wall, the laden wagons were starting to move through the open gates. A group of a few dozen youths wearing red armbands were waiting on the other side, and they swarmed round the lead wagons as food was thrown to them by soldiers.

'I don't see any elderly people,' said Emily, 'or children, for that matter.'

'No, your Majesty,' said Van. 'The population of Old Alea was made up of soldiers, and servants of working age. Add to that the gangs from the three tribes, then the ages of the vast majority of the refugees would range between late teens and late forties. There won't be many on either side of that.'

Emily nodded. 'Sorry to sound callous, but that means they can all work? That appears to be good news. The City is suffering from critical shortages of labour in certain areas following the greenhide incursion.'

'Then you may be in luck, your Majesty. The best craftspeople in Alea Tanton were concentrated in Old Alea, so they could serve the gods – blacksmiths, jewellers, scribes, brewers, potters, and so on.'

She glanced at him. 'Any farmers?'

'Unfortunately not, your Majesty. No farmers.'

Emily nodded.

'I have a question, mortal,' said Jade.

'Yes, my lady?'

'Why didn't my death powers work on the silver dragon? Are they immune?'

Van said nothing.

'You must know,' said Jade.

'I hesitate to answer,' said Van, 'because I don't think it's my secret to reveal.'

'You can speak freely here,' said Emily. 'Everyone standing on this observation post is privy to the inner counsels of the City.'

'I'm sorry, your Majesty, but I feel obliged to keep certain confidences to myself.'

Emily and Daniel glanced at each other. Yendra frowned, then entered the mercenary's mind. The reason for the dragon's immunity was in the forefront of his thoughts, and she saw that Kelsey Holdfast's strange powers were responsible. Van had told them much about the circumstances of their journey from Lostwell to the City, but Yendra could see that he remained loyal to the Holdfast girl.

'I understand,' she said.

'I don't,' said Jade. 'Why is he keeping secrets from us?'

'Be patient,' said Yendra. 'All will become clear in time.'

CHAPTER 5

COY

F ortress of the Lifegiver, The Bulwark, The City – 7th Marcalis 3420

The following day, Emily awoke in a small chamber near the top floor of the Duke's Tower. Next to her, Daniel was in a deep sleep, and she pulled the thick blankets from her legs and got up from the mattress. Officially, the Fortress of the Lifegiver was one of the eight palaces of the City, and Emily had made of point of trying to sleep in each one since she had been crowned Queen. The only one she hadn't managed to stay in was Greylin Palace in Dalrig, but as Prince Montieth lived there, she was happy to forego that experience.

She washed in the dim light seeping through the shutters, then dressed, picking warm clothes from a large trunk they had brought with them. The servant who usually did her hair each morning had been left in Pella, so Emily sat by a small mirror and pulled a brush through her tangled blonde locks as Daniel snored softly.

The previous day had been frustrating. She had wanted to enter Scythe territory, but Princess Yendra had insisted upon waiting until she was sure the area was safe enough for the Royal party, and when Yendra was determined about something, Emily usually let the god have her way. She sometimes seemed to treat Daniel and Emily like fragile children, who needed to be protected from the world. She found it irritating, but knew it came from a place of kindness. Yendra had always advocated rule by mortals, and now that this had been achieved, she was determined to do her best to nurture it.

She noticed that the snoring had stopped, and glanced at Daniel, who was looking at her.

'Good morning, your Majesty,' she said.

He smiled, then grimaced. 'I think I might have had too much wine last night.'

She raised an eyebrow. 'You did seem to be enjoying yourself. You and that mercenary captain were certainly getting on well.'

'He has a lot of good stories. He's been to half a dozen worlds, at least, and he was able to tell me all about what Corthie and the others got up to on Lostwell. I'm paying for it now, though.'

'Did he say much about Corthie's sister?'

'Which one?'

'Kelsey; the one who is in the City.'

'No, not really. That was the one subject he was coy about.'

'I get the impression that he knows more about her than he's letting on.'

Daniel shrugged. 'Ask Yendra to read his mind.'

Emily turned back to the mirror. 'I already did. While you were talking to Captain Logos, Yendra was telling me a few interesting things. For instance, it was Kelsey who blocked Jade's death powers. It seems that Corthie is not the only Holdfast with unusual abilities.'

'Kelsey did what? I thought Jade had attempted to bring down a dragon.'

'She did. Kelsey happened to be riding on its shoulders at the time, and her blocking ability was enough to shield the dragon as well. And listen to this – Yendra tried to locate Kelsey, using her vision powers, but she was unable to. She said that her powers couldn't penetrate the immediate vicinity of where the dragons were gathered. Consequently, she was unable to contact Naxor or Vana, as they must have been close to Kelsey.'

Daniel sat up and stretched. 'So, she can disrupt communications? Wherever Miss Holdfast ends up living, we'll have to ensure it's not too close to Yendra or Salvor, not if we want to be able to contact the various areas of the City.'

'I have an idea about that.'

He smiled. 'I thought you might.'

'Kelsey is very close to one of the dragons, so perhaps we should leave her with them – she could be our link with the beasts. As for where – well, I was thinking of reviving the Jezra plan.'

'I thought you'd given up on that.'

'I had, but imagine the difference that eight adult dragons could make. Even four would probably suffice. It would keep the dragons busy while we worked out what to do with them, and it would keep Kelsey away from the palaces. I mean, she might very well be a lovely young lady, but we can't have her disrupting our communications network. And on that topic, we still have to decide what to do with Naxor.'

Daniel laughed. 'Maybe we should assign him to Tarstation.'

'It's not a laughing matter, Danny. That corrupt, back-stabbing scoundrel will read our minds the moment he meets us, and then he'll... well, who knows what schemes he'll cook up? Hopefully, Kelsey will be present at our initial meeting, but we can't keep her too close to us.'

There was a soft knock at the door. 'Your Majesties?' said a voice. 'Breakfast is being served.'

'Thank you,' said Emily. 'We'll be down in a moment.'

They had breakfast in the princess's quarters, and then prepared to enter Scythe territory. Yendra had been up for most of the night, scouting the entire region, and issuing orders to the thousands of Blades that had moved in. She still had some reservations about the

Royal party travelling beyond the Scythe wall, but admitted that the chance of violence towards them was low.

That was good enough for Emily, and they boarded a carriage once they had finished eating. A long line of supply wagons was also preparing to enter Scythe territory, along with Blade reinforcements who were being sent in to relieve units of the initial force, and the carriage joined the queue on the road leading to the gates. Daniel had asked the mercenary captain to join them, and he sat in their carriage, along with Commander Quill, who had arrived from Pella that morning. Quill had known Corthie Holdfast well, and she chatted to Van as they waited for the convoy to get moving.

Van changed the subject as they got underway.

'I was wanting to speak about the Banner forces, your Majesties,' he said. 'I realise that they were on the side of the enemy gods in Lostwell, and I know from what Princess Yendra said last night that they have been responsible for casualties among the Blades, but I want to ask that you show them mercy.'

Emily caught his gaze. 'Why?'

'They're just doing their jobs, your Majesty. Every soldier in every Banner signs a contract, and once they've done that, they obey whatever orders they're given. They're disciplined and well-trained, and could be an asset to the City, if treated with a little tolerance and understanding. Any one of them could have been me. If I hadn't been captured by Corthie, then I'd probably still be under contract to the Banner of the Golden Fist.'

'Do you think they would be prepared to work for us?'

'I do, your Majesty,' he said, 'but you should be aware that they will each have a clause in their contracts that determines their actions if captured by a hostile force. There's a fifty-day period where they will still technically be under contract, but after that expires, each one of them will be free to choose a new employer.'

'But being a Blade isn't like having an employer,' said Quill. 'It's in our blood. If these Banner soldiers want to join up, then they should become proper Blades, and that means for life.' She lifted her left sleeve to reveal her Blade tattoos, showing each of the regiments and detachments that she had been a part of during her career. 'We aren't mercenaries,' she went on, 'and our duty outweighs any contract.'

Van nodded. 'I understand, but many of the Banner soldiers will take issue with that concept.'

'Even though they are now on a different world?' said Emily.

'Yes, your Majesty,' said Van. 'Most of the soldiers will have been on other worlds, and half are probably expecting an Ascendant to turn up to tell them what to do. It might take a while for them to realise that they are effectively stranded here.'

The convoy got underway as Van was speaking, and the carriage trundled along the wide track. To either side marched squads from the Royal Guard, their dark blue uniforms marking them out from the Blade soldiers also heading towards Scythe territory.

'Will the Banner soldiers follow Lady Felice?' said Daniel.

'Some might,' said Van, 'but she wasn't in the direct chain of command, so most will probably ignore any orders she gave out.'

'Lady Vana should be able to locate her,' Daniel went on, 'assuming, of course, that Kelsey Holdfast is not close by.'

Van fell silent, his eyes wide.

Emily smiled as she watched him. 'I don't think our guest was aware that we know about Miss Holdfast's special abilities.'

Daniel looked embarrassed for a moment. 'Oh.'

Van glanced out of the window. 'I should have guessed that Princess Yendra would have read it from my mind. I implore you not to spread this information around, your Majesties. Kelsey has a painful history of being hunted by those who wish to hide themselves from the gods, and the fewer who know, the better.'

The carriage was pulled through the gates, and the occupants hushed as they glanced out of the windows. There was a heavy Blade presence by the gates to ensure none of the refugees could leave Scythe territory, and the convoy was waved through. In a field to the left, several rows of tents had been pitched on the frozen ground, and hundreds of refugees were queuing up in front of a wagon distributing food and blankets, all under the watchful eye of armed Blades.

Quill pointed. 'There's one with green skin. What are they called?'

'Fordians,' said Van.

Quill nodded. 'It might be difficult to integrate folk with green skin into the City. I can already predict what some of the less imaginative citizens here will call them.'

'They were hated in Lostwell,' said Van, 'but they were the original inhabitants of that world, there long before others arrived. They're used to being discriminated against.'

'We won't stand for that here,' said Emily.

Van nodded, and Emily thought about her words. How exactly was she going to prevent the Fordians from being insulted and bullied? She knew the low esteem in which Evaders were held by Rosers, and nothing she or Daniel had done had made any difference to that, so why did she think it would be any different for the Fordians?

Quill shifted uncomfortably in her seat. 'Can the Fordians, um... interbreed with humans?'

'Yes,' said Van. 'They *are* humans; they just have differently-coloured skin, which allows them to go longer without food, as long as there's plenty of sunshine.'

'Just like the greenhides, you mean?'

'I suppose so. It's the same principle, I think. Lostwell was the only world where they lived, so those who made it here will be the last survivors of their people.'

'We'll know how many there are when the census is carried out,' said Daniel, 'and then we can work out a plan to ease them into the life of the City. In the meantime, the Blades will keep order, and stop any of them from being assaulted.'

Quill looked sceptical, but said nothing.

The carriage turned left at a junction of farm tracks, and approached the field when the dragons were gathered. Squads of Blades were keeping their distance from the giant beasts, and had sealed off the field to prevent anyone from straying too close. The carriage pulled up by the entrance to the field, and several wagons also stopped. Yendra and Jade climbed down from the wagon directly ahead of the Royal carriage, and a Blade officer opened the carriage door, bowing.

Emily waited for Quill and Van to disembark, then stepped down from the carriage, taking the offered hand of the officer as he helped her down. The wagons and carriage were surrounded by Blades, and Emily could barely see anything beyond their thick ranks. It was nice to feel so protected, but at times she wished she could walk freely through the City without armed guards.

Yendra bowed before her and Daniel. 'Your Majesties; if you remain here, I can go forward and speak to the dragons on your behalf.'

'No,' said Emily. 'We haven't come all this way to hide behind rows of soldiers. I wish to speak to the dragons in person.'

'But, your Majesty; I will be unable to guarantee your safety.' She glanced at Van for a moment. 'Jade's powers will be ineffective against the dragons should any initiate hostilities.'

'If they were going to be hostile, they would have shown signs of it by now. Let's show a little trust, and hope we get some in return.'

Yendra frowned.

'Send in the food wagons first,' Emily went on. 'That will prove our intent towards them.'

'Yes, your Majesty.'

Yendra signalled to an officer, and he waved the wagons onwards. Each was loaded with fresh meat for the dragons, enough to feed a hundred humans. The wagons rolled into the field, and the dragons turned their long necks to watch. By their feet, Emily could see a small group of people, and she recognised Naxor among them. The Blades pushed the wagons to within a dozen yards of the nearest dragon, then they backed away, keeping their hands raised to show they were empty.

The largest dragon, a massive grey male, stretched his neck over to the wagons and sniffed. He glanced at the Blades assembled by the entrance to the field, then picked up the carcass of a pig in his jaws and ate it, his teeth crunching and grinding the bones and flesh in seconds.

He turned to the other dragons, and they approached. A dark blue dragon cajoled three little ones forward, and pulled meat from the back of a wagon for them; then she stood by and watched as they ate. The other dragons swooped down on the remaining wagons, and within minutes, the food was gone, the hungry beasts devouring the lot.

Emily glanced at Yendra and Daniel, and strode forwards. Blades formed up beside her as she walked, then Yendra caught her up, Daniel by her side. Emily side-stepped a pile of pig intestines that lay on the ground and approached the grey dragon.

'Greetings,' she said, as the dragons watched.

The grey dragon lowered his head to within a foot of Emily's face. 'Who are you?'

'This is her Majesty, Queen Emily of the City,' said Yendra, her fingers resting on the handle of the Axe of Rand.

The dragon drew back a few feet. 'The Queen of the City has come to visit?'

Emily smiled. 'It's not every day that a dozen dragons appear from nowhere. We came to speak to you in person. That is why the King and I have both come.'

'The King?'

Emily gestured to Daniel.

'This is his Majesty, King Daniel of the City,' said Yendra.

'Welcome to the City,' Daniel said. 'I'm sure we can come to an arrangement that satisfies everyone. What is your name?'

'I am Deathfang,' said the grey dragon, 'leader of this small band. I see you have Van Logos with you. I assume he has informed you of the events that led to our arrival here?'

'You assume correctly,' said Emily. 'He has led me to believe that you are not a threat to the City, and that if you are treated fairly, and with respect, then you will reciprocate.'

'So far, no one from the City has acted aggressively towards us,' said Deathfang; 'and I wish to thank you for the food. If we are to live here in peace, then we will have to come to an understanding.'

Naxor stepped forward from under the shadow of Deathfang. 'May

I?' He bowed low before Emily and Daniel. 'Your illustrious Majesties,' he said; 'I have returned.' He glanced at the dragons. 'It's been a pleasure, but this is where I leave you.'

'Hello, Naxor,' said Emily.

He smiled. 'Might I say how resplendent you are looking, your Majesty? Your ever-radiant beauty dazzles my eyes. My only wish is that I will be able to serve you, and so I put my skills at your disposal. I am yours to command, your Majesty.'

'Doesn't he make you sick?' said a young woman that Emily didn't recognise. 'Honestly, Naxor, do you think anyone here is buying your act?'

Naxor frowned. 'This,' he said to the Queen, 'is Kelsey Holdfast; a most delightful companion. And, somewhere back there is my cousin, Lady Vana... oh, yes; there she is.'

Vana walked forward, accompanied by another, older-looking woman. They both bowed, something that Kelsey Holdfast had yet to do.

'Your Majesties,' said Vana; 'and your Highness,' she said to Yendra. 'I am very happy indeed to be home. Very, very happy.'

'It's a pleasure to meet you, Lady Vana,' said Daniel. 'There are quarters in Cuidrach Palace waiting for you if you wish to move back into your old home.'

Vana started to cry. 'Thank you; I would be most grateful.'

Emily glanced at the older woman. 'And you must be Lady Silva?'

The woman lifted her chin. 'I am, your Majesty.'

'Welcome to the City. Captain Van Logos has told us about you, and you are welcome to return with us to Cuidrach Palace. I understand the loss you must be feeling, and I can barely begin to imagine what losing Lostwell must feel like, but I hope you will be able to settle here in safety.'

'Thank you, your Majesty. Did Van also tell you that Lady Felice is here?'

'He did. I understand that either you or Lady Vana could assist us in locating this god?'

'I would be happy to help, your Majesty, but...' The demigod stumbled over her words, then glanced at Van.

'They know about Kelsey's blocking ability,' he said.

Kelsey glared at him. 'And I bet you just couldn't wait to tell them, eh? You rat. You ran straight to the rulers of the City and flung yourself before them. Did they pat you on the head like a good boy? Treacherous little weasel.'

The small crowd fell into silence for a moment, then Deathfang started to laugh. It was a strange sound, Emily thought, and a little disconcerting.

'My daughter's rider has a tendency to speak her mind,' said the grey dragon.

'You should know, Kelsey,' said Yendra, 'that I read the information from Van's head. He refused to tell us about your ability to block powers.'

'Oh,' said Kelsey. Her frown deepened. 'The rest was true, though, wasn't it?'

'Captain Logos has behaved honourably, in my opinion,' said Yendra.

'And in mine,' said Daniel.

'Yeah,' said Jade; 'so shut up, Kelsey.'

Kelsey glanced at the faces around her. She crossed her arms over her chest. 'So, this is the way it's going to be, eh? Van's already turned the King, the Commander of the Bulwark, and... whoever you are, against me?'

'Could you possibly be over-reacting?' said Naxor.

'Let's not get off on the wrong foot,' said Emily. 'Any sister of Corthie Holdfast is welcome here, as is any friend of his or Belinda. And we are more than happy to supply the dragons with food until they are settled into their new homes.'

'And where will that be?' said Deathfang.

'I have a few thoughts about that,' said Emily, 'but for the moment, I would tentatively suggest the old quarries up in the Iceward Range. They are about as far away from humans as it is possible to get within the confines of the City, and they are a short flight from the seal grounds, where food can be hunted. The quarries are large enough for a dozen dragons to fit, at least until we find somewhere more permanent.'

'I would be delighted to guide the dragons there,' said Naxor.

'I accept your offer, Queen,' said Deathfang. 'Kelsey will accompany us there, once Naxor has shown the way. How long will this cold weather last?'

'We have four months of winter ahead of us,' said Yendra, 'followed by Freshmist; a time of heavy rains and storms. Are you finding it cold here?'

'Lostwell was a warm world,' said the grey dragon, 'with blue skies every day. However, it was also a dying world. Tell me; are there earthquakes and volcanoes here?'

'None,' said Naxor. 'Endless deserts to sunward, and endless darkness and snow to iceward, but no earthquakes. If you wish to feel the warmth of the sun at this time of year, all you have to do is fly sunward for a few hours.'

'I might do that today,' said a young, silver dragon. 'I miss the warmth.'

'This is Frostback, my daughter,' said Deathfang. 'She is the first of my family to have taken a human rider.'

'And she'll be the only one,' said the dark blue dragon with the three small infants beside her. 'Dragons do not need to carry insects about on their backs; it is shameful.'

'And this is my mate, Darksky. Her views on the subject differ from my daughter's.'

Emily glanced at Darksky. 'I would prefer not to be called an insect.'

Darksky said nothing, and the silence felt as cold as the frost on the ground.

Silva coughed gently. 'Regarding Lady Felice, your Majesties? If I were to move away from Kelsey, then I would be able to begin a search for the rogue god.'

Emily nodded. 'Did you know this Felice?'

'I know her, your Majesty.'

'Is she dangerous?'

'She has upper vision, but no other powers, your Majesty. I do not believe that she represents a significant threat to the City, but left to her own devices she may be able to stir up trouble among the refugees.'

Emily glanced at the demigod. Her eyes were red, as if she had been crying, but she had a determined look upon her face.

She turned to Quill. 'Commander, please escort Lady Vana and Lady Silva back to the Fortress of the Lifegiver. Make sure they are fed and comfortable, and then report back when you have the location of Lady Felice.'

The tall Blade saluted, then she and a handful of soldiers led the two demigods to a wagon.

Emily turned to Kelsey. 'I would like to talk with you alone for a moment.'

'Why?'

'Talk with me, and you'll see.'

Kelsey said nothing, then gave a brief nod. Emily and the Holdfast woman walked away from the centre of the field, out of earshot of the dragons and soldiers.

'From what Van said...' Emily began.

Kelsey sighed.

Emily waited a moment. 'From what Van said, it appears that Corthie Holdfast has returned to his home. I assume that you were also given this opportunity, but for some reason you decided to come here instead. Am I correct?'

'Aye.'

'Why? It seems a little strange to me that you would willingly be separated from your family, in order to travel to a place that you know nothing about.'

Kelsey nodded. 'Did you know Maddie Jackdaw?'

Emily smiled. 'Yes. She was my sergeant in the Blades for a while.'

'Then you probably also know how attached she is to Blackrose?'

'I see. You have formed a bond with the silver dragon, Deathfang's daughter?'

'Aye. I wasn't planning for it to happen, but it did. And when Belinda did her thing with the Sextant... wait; I'm guessing that Van told you about the Sextant?'

'He did, yes.'

She frowned. 'Of course he did. Anyway, Belinda knew that Lostwell was about to be destroyed, and she figured that this was the best place for the surviving dragons to go. Once it was clear that Frostback was coming here, I decided to go with them.'

A realisation dawned on Emily. 'And Van followed you?'

Kelsey glanced away. 'Yup.'

'And when you got here, you told him you weren't interested?'

'Pyre's tits; did he tell you everything?'

'No; I'm deducing the facts for myself. Van was extremely coy about you; he refused to be drawn into a discussion regarding anything to do with you. I thought you were a little harsh with him earlier, and, as he now works for me, I would rather you were less abrasive with him.'

'Piss off. You know what? You can have him; you're welcome to him, but remember this, Queenie, I'm with the dragons, and I don't work for you. You may rule this City, but you don't rule this world, and I don't like being told how to speak to people.'

Emily said nothing for a moment. It had been a long time since anyone had sworn at her, and she wasn't sure how to react.

'Do you have anything else you want to say?' Kelsey went on. 'Any other useful advice for me? Perhaps you want to show me how to curtsy properly, or maybe you want to give me a lesson in elocution?'

'Why are you so angry?'

Kelsey glared at her. 'Because I trusted Van; I thought he was my friend.'

'He is your friend. He has shown you nothing but loyalty.'

'Then why did he walk away? He knew he'd be leaving me alone with a dozen dragons, several of whom would quite like to eat me, and he didn't care. And now he's ingratiated himself with you and Yendra, and... who was the other woman?'

'Lady Jade.'

'Aye, and her too. I saw the way she was looking at him; like a damn vulture waiting to pick his carcass clean. Pyre's arsehole, I don't even know what I'm saying. It's been a stressful couple of days.'

Emily smiled. 'You remind me of Corthie.'

'Aye?'

'Yes.'

'Is that a good thing?'

'Corthie Holdfast is a hero to everyone in the City. If you tell people that you're his sister, you'll never have to pay for a drink. Do you want to come back with us to the fortress? You can have a bath, some warm food and there are clean clothes available.'

Kelsey glanced at the dragons. 'I think I'd better stay. The dragons are putting on a brave face, but I know how disorientated they feel. If I left them, they might think I wasn't coming back.'

'Alright. I'll have Naxor show you the way to the quarries in the Iceward Range. I assume an adult dragon can lift a wagon?'

Kelsey nodded.

'Then I'll have a few wagons prepared that they can carry to the quarries, and I'll make sure the contents will include plenty of home comforts for you. And then, once I've had a chance to think things through, I'll send word about a permanent place to settle. How does that sound?'

'That sounds fine,' said Kelsey. 'Thanks, Queenie.'

CHAPTER 6

THE JEZRA PROPOSAL

The Sunward Desert – 23rd Marcalis 3420

Kelsey closed her eyes and smiled, letting the sunshine warm her face.

'It pleases me to see you happy,' said Frostback.

The young, silver dragon was stretched out onto the golden sands, basking in the strong light. Two hundred miles sunward of the City, and the sunlight felt much as it had on Lostwell – bright and hot.

'It reminds me of home,' said Kelsey. 'The Holdings is just as warm in the summertime.'

'Is the City not now your home?'

Kelsey's eyes glanced at the dragon. 'I suppose so.'

'You don't sound convinced.'

'It's taking me longer than I'd thought to settle in here. On Lostwell, I always knew that my time would be limited; I knew I'd never be staying there forever, and it felt more like an adventure. Here? I don't mean to sound ungrateful, and I appreciate the time we've had to get to know each other better, but...'

'You're lonely?'

'Am I that easy to read?'

'You miss the company of other humans; I understand. You miss your brother and your aunt; and you miss Van.'

Kelsey raised a hand to shield her eyes from the light. The dragon was right, but Kelsey had no desire to admit it openly. Travelling to the City had been her choice, and she had to accept the responsibility for the decision she had made. She had wanted to become Frostback's rider, and her wish had come true; but the price had been high. For sixteen days, she had been living with the Catacombs dragons in a large quarry in the Iceward Range. She saw humans every day, but she was the only one who slept every night in the quarry. Each red dawn, soldiers from the local Icewarder militia would arrive up the steep hill track with wagons filled with food for the dragons, and representatives of the King and Queen had also visited. They had been polite, and had asked Kelsey for a list of things she required to make her stay more comfortable, and then they had climbed into their nice, warm carriages and returned down the slopes.

'I assumed that he would have visited you by now,' said Frostback.

Kelsey frowned, then recalled that they had been discussing Van.

'Perhaps you shouldn't have called him a weasel,' the dragon went on. 'He might have taken it personally.'

'I wanted him to take it personally; that's why I said it. I've called him all manner of things since I've known him. "Weasel" was fairly tame.'

'But, Kelsey, if you like him, then why are you pushing him away?'

'Who said I liked him?'

'If you don't like him, then why do you miss him? And don't deny it, rider; I can sniff out human lies.'

Kelsey frowned. 'It's complicated.'

The dragon moved her head closer to Kelsey. 'Explain.'

'Alright,' she said, lowering her eyes. 'It's time for that conversation, the one I've been avoiding. The one where, by the end of it, you'll stare at me as if I'm insane.'

'I tend to the opinion that all humans are a little insane, each in their own way. Come; let there be no secrets between us. Do you require me to promise that I will keep whatever you tell me to myself?'

'Aye, that would be helpful.'

'Fine. I promise; now, tell me.'

'I'll keep it brief. Here goes – I can see into the future and I've seen Van and me together, so I know that we're going to fall in love with each other. Van knows; that's why he followed me here.'

Frostback kept her gaze on Kelsey, but remained silent.

'It's a power of mine,' Kelsey went on. 'My sister can do it too. A crazy Holdfast trait; a curse, more like. Seeing snatches of the future has defined my life. Knowing little things that are going to happen has almost sent me mad, and sometimes I dread looking into people's eyes in case a vision comes.' She gave a crooked smile to the dragon. 'There. Now you know my deepest secret.'

Frostback continued to stare at her in silence.

'Do you smell any lies?' said Kelsey.

'I do not.'

'Then you believe me?'

'I am still trying to understand the ramifications.'

'Is that a polite way of saying no?'

'Imagine if I had made a wild claim, that I could fly to the sun, or that I could turn stone into water; would you believe me without proof?'

'I don't know,' said Kelsey. 'Dragons don't seem to lie much, if at all; so, probably. If we have a bond, like Sable and Sanguino, or Maddie and Blackrose, then we should trust each other.'

'You are right. In truth, if anyone else had made such claims, I would have dismissed them out of hand. It is only because the words came from your mouth that I am giving them serious consideration. How does your power work?'

'I can't read minds, but I can enter someone's mind, if that makes sense; and sometimes I can see out from their eyes and look at something that has yet to happen. Usually, they're mundane, trivial events that are due to occur a few minutes after I have the vision, but occasionally they are of important matters. I looked into Van's eyes, and I saw him; he was gazing at me, and I could feel the love we shared pass between us.'

'And you told him this?'

'I had to.'

'Did he believe you?'

'No.'

'Then why did he follow you here?'

'He had no choice, I guess.'

'What about free will? Does Van not possess the ability to think for himself?'

'From my point of view, free will is an illusion. I know that, because my visions always come true.'

Frostback glanced away, her red eyes glowing. 'Have you had any vision that involves me?'

'No.'

'Good. If you do, I'd rather not know.'

'I don't think my powers work on dragons. At least, I've never had a vision through a dragon's eyes.'

'All the same, I would like you to promise me.'

'Fine. If I ever have a vision with you in it, I won't tell you.'

'Thank you. I would prefer my free will to be left alone, be it an illusion or not. Who else knows of this power?'

'Aila and Corthie know, but I didn't tell Naxor, and I'd rather everyone didn't find out. They already look at me like I'm crazy; this would only confirm it for them.'

'I agree. The other dragons would scorn you for making such a claim. Some of them do not like you very much.'

Kelsey narrowed her eyes at the silver dragon. 'Do you think I'm unaware of that? Out of every dragon in the quarry, I reckon only you, Halfclaw and your father wouldn't eat me if given the chance. Darksky hates me, and Burntskull would kill me just for fun.'

'It is fortunate that my father is so fond of you; his oath to protect you saves me from having to fight the others.' She stretched her long wings and began to lift herself from the sand. 'Come; let us return to the City.'

Kelsey got up from the side of the dune and brushed the sand from her clothes. It had been their fourth trip down to the vast desert on the sunward side of the City, and she had enjoyed the opportunity to spend time with Frostback, who seemed to be the only friend she had. The dragon offered a forelimb, and Kelsey scrambled up onto her broad shoulders. Frostback lifted into the hot air, turned away from the sun and soared through the sky.

————

They travelled in silence, Kelsey's attention distracted by the views. They crossed the desert and flew over the vast stretch of marshlands that shielded the sunward flank of the City from greenhide invasion. Birds scattered at the sight of the dragon, rising up from the swamps in thick flocks, their cries piercing the air. Compared to the marshlands, the Warm Sea was small, just a thin strip of water, and then the City began. Frostback flew over the harbour town of Port Sanders, its red roofs glowing as the light changed and the temperature lowered. After that, the grey monotony of the Circuit passed under them. Many districts appeared to be abandoned, and workers were out demolishing empty and derelict tenement blocks, clearing more space to plant food. Beyond the Circuit, lay the fields farmed by Icewarders, and then the slopes of the Iceward Range loomed ahead of them. It was clear to Kelsey that the hills had been covered in trees not long before, and the acres of desolate stumps reminded her of Northern Kinell. The trees had been felled in the greenhide emergency, when every effort had been made to shore up the inner defences of the City, and the current shortages of wood and paper had been the result. Several coal and iron mines dotted the miserable-looking landscape, along with deep quarries that had supplied the City with building stone. Frostback aimed towards the largest, and descended, Kelsey feeling the cold air swirl around her.

'It seems we have visitors,' said Frostback, as her claws struck the ground.

Kelsey slipped down from the dragon's shoulders and glanced

around. The dragons were all outside, gathered together by the entrance to the most spacious cavern, while a row of carriages sat at the head of the track leading down to the town of Icehaven. Soldiers were also present, flanking the carriages, and dressed in the blue uniforms of the Royal Guard.

Frostback strode towards the other dragons.

'It is well that you have returned, daughter,' said Deathfang. 'The Queen of the City has arrived, and she wishes to speak to all of us.'

Kelsey hung back a little, nervous when so many dragons were assembled in the same place. Darksky gave her a glance filled with disdain, and nudged her three infants behind a protective wing. Next to her was a purple dragon named Dawnflame, the mother of the fourth child-dragon to have escaped Lostwell. Her young son, Firestone, was playing by her side, chasing a glint of light reflecting off a soldier's breastplate. Dawnflame's mother had also survived, and so had her mate, a striking black and white dragon who, after Deathfang, was the most powerful dragon among the group.

The doors of the carriages opened, and Kelsey turned to watch as a small party climbed down to the ground. Queen Emily was there, along with Princess Yendra. Behind the two women, several others were walking, and one of them was Van. Kelsey frowned. She hadn't seen him in sixteen days, since he had arrived in the company of the Queen when she had visited them in the fields of the Scythe territory. He noticed her gaze upon him, and she looked away. She began to get angry. Van had left her alone in a strange place, at the exact time she had needed a friend. She had felt like crying on her first night in the quarry, with no one around her but a dozen frightening dragons. Even Darksky's infants were larger than ponies – any one of them could have killed her with their razor-sharp claws and teeth.

Yendra strode forwards. 'Good day, dragons. I trust everything here is to your satisfaction?'

'Good morning,' said Deathfang. 'We are more than satisfied with the generosity the City has shown us.'

Yendra nodded. 'Her Majesty, Queen Emily, has come to discuss the future with you.'

'That pleases me.'

A group of workers emerged from a wagon, and arranged two lines of chairs in front of where the dragons had assembled. When they were ready, the Queen sat down in the middle of the front row, and the others she had brought also took their seats.

Emily smiled. She was of a similar age to Kelsey, but had a regal look about her, the Holdfast woman decided, as if she had been born to be a queen. A band of gold sat upon her brow, its simplicity matching the skirts of her pale blue dress. Kelsey felt self conscious for a moment about her own scruffy appearance, then frowned. Emily might be a queen, but she was a damn Holdfast.

'My greetings to you all,' said Emily. 'I don't think that I've been introduced to everyone.'

Deathfang took a pace forward. 'There are a mere dozen of us remaining. When we last met, I was filled with relief that any had survived, but the more days that have passed, the more I feel the loss of those who were killed in Lostwell. Just a short month ago, I ruled over a colony of eighty dragons, and now barely two families have survived. Half of those gathered here are part of my family – my mate Darksky, and my daughter Frostback, and the three little ones. The other family to have survived spans three generations.' He gestured with a forelimb to the oldest dragon in the quarry. 'This is Bittersea, the mother of Dawnflame, who, in turn, is the mother of Firestone.' He gestured to the black and white dragon. 'Tarsnow is Dawnflame's mate. That leaves two dragons without any family – Burntskull and Halfclaw.' His gaze lowered. 'Our losses scorch my heart with the fires of grief.'

'We commiserate with your suffering,' said Emily. 'The City has also suffered. Six months ago, the greenhides broke through the walls and killed over a third of the population. Even now, we face several daunting challenges. Our food supplies were calculated to get the citizens through winter and Freshmist, but with the addition of forty thousand refugees from Lostwell, it will be a struggle to feed everyone. The emergency also stripped much of the City's remaining resources. We are short of wood, stone, fuel, metals, and we have lost most of our skilled farmers and industrial workers. However, every challenge brings opportunities, and I feel that we could help each other.'

'How so, Queen?' said Deathfang.

She nodded to the man sitting on her left, who stood.

'My name is Lord Salvor,' he said to the dragons. 'We have a proposal for you. First, though, let me ask you – what do you want? I don't refer to immediate needs; no, what I mean is, where do you see the future of the dragons upon this world?'

Deathfang glanced down for a moment. 'I desire safety,' he said. 'A secure place to live, with access to food, water and shelter. On Lostwell, we lived in a location far from any human settlements, a place that was almost impossible for anyone else to reach. Our experiences of humans have not been good.'

A few of the dragons muttered their agreement.

'On Lostwell,' Deathfang went on, 'we lived at constant risk of being captured and forced to fight in the pits of Alea Tanton. If we flew too close to any human habitation, we were shot at by ballistae, and soldiers would be sent against us if we ventured too far from the Catacombs.'

'That will not happen here,' said Emily. 'As part of our pledge to you, we promise to treat you and your kin with respect.'

'So you say,' said Deathfang, 'but long years of bitter experience have taught us to be wary of the promises of humans. Don't misunderstand me; we are grateful for the wagons of foods that trundle up the hillside every morning, but it will take time for any trust to develop between us. On the other hand, I do foresee a certain level of cooperation being possible. We can help you, if you help us.'

Salvor bowed his head. 'Thank you. As her Majesty stated, the City is experiencing severe shortages of many resources. To give but one example; wood is in such scare supply, that there is none available to make paper, and that means no written documents, no news sheets informing the citizens of events, and no materials to record the vast amount of information to be garnered from the refugees in the upcoming census. In the long term, it will mean no wood to repair ships, and without ships, the City will starve. The Evaders of the Circuit are currently subsisting entirely upon a diet of seaweed and seafood, and any break in that supply would have catastrophic effects. In short, the City is facing serious difficulties.'

'Get to the point,' muttered Burntskull. 'You want us to do something for you; isn't that correct?'

'Indeed, Lord Burntskull,' said Salvor. 'Here is our proposal. To the west of the City lie the Straits, where the Warm Sea meets the Cold Sea. Beyond is the Western Bank, a mere handful of miles from Pella. The ruins of a town are there – Jezra. It has been occupied twice during the long history of the City, and each time it was over-run and destroyed by greenhides. The terrain there is covered in vast forests, with ample supplies of stone, leather, and the potential to farm enough land to feed the City many times over. Unfortunately, it is also infested with greenhides. We are thinking of sending a powerful force to the Western Bank, to reclaim Jezra for the City. With it, we would stave off the threat of starvation, and we would gain access to enough resources to last a thousand years.' He smiled. 'To do this, we need your assistance. The plan will only succeed if we have the support of multiple dragons operating from the air.'

Deathfang's eyes burned. 'You want us to kill greenhides?'

'Yes,' said Salvor. 'We want you to slaughter them in their thousands. A defensive wall can only be built if the land has been cleared of the beasts, and work can go on only if there is a minimal threat of attack.'

'And I thought,' said Deathfang, laughing, 'that you had come here today to tell us where we were going to be living.'

'We can discuss that too,' said Emily. 'There are a few options open to us. Firstly, there's here. We could send stonemasons and labourers to the quarry, and tunnel out much larger caverns for you. Secondly, there is a range of mountains a few hundred miles to the east of here; Naxor knows its location. And, thirdly, there may be somewhere on the Western Bank that suits you, or, perhaps, upon the Grey Isle.'

'There are mountains to the east of here?' said Darksky. 'We should go there, and as soon as possible. We don't need to negotiate with these insects; we should leave them be, and make our own lives on this world.'

'But the humans have helped us,' said Frostback. 'Do we not owe them something for that help?'

'We shall refrain from killing them,' said Darksky; 'that shall be their reward.'

'I agree,' said Burntskull. 'What would we get out of burning thousands of greenhides? We are dragons; we can take what we wish from humans without waiting for them to grant it to us.'

Emily's eyes tightened. 'We did not feed you so that you would help us; we fed you because it was the right thing to do. We are also feeding the forty thousand human refugees, without any conditions attached. What we are proposing is an alliance between equals. Together, humans and dragons can push the greenhides back, and then we can all live safely in peace.'

Deathfang scratched the ground with his claws. 'We shall need to consider this among ourselves. Thank you for your visit.'

Aside from Frostback, the dragons turned from the queen, and began to stride back to the cavern. Emily glared at their scaly backs for a second, then regained her composure.

Kelsey chuckled, and walked over to the rows of chairs.

'Good morning, Kelsey,' said the Queen.

'Good morning. Don't be disheartened; that went quite well, I thought.'

Emily stood. 'There was no outright refusal, so I suppose you are right. How have you been getting on up here?'

Kelsey noticed Van's eyes on her. 'Fine,' she said. 'Just great. No one's eaten me yet, but only thanks to Frostback. No thanks to anyone else.'

If Emily noticed Kelsey's anger, she pretended not to. 'Do you think the dragons will agree to our proposal?'

Kelsey shrugged. 'I don't know. They'll do whatever Deathfang orders them to do, but he'd only order something that he knew they'd go along with.'

'I will help you,' said Frostback; 'unless my father directly forbids it.'

'Thank you,' said Emily.

'That means Halfclaw will probably help as well,' Kelsey said. She leaned in towards Emily. 'He fancies Frostback.'

'That doesn't mean he will assist,' said the silver dragon.

'Aye, it does,' smirked Kelsey. 'He'd follow you anywhere.'

Frostback sniffed. 'A rider should not embarrass their dragon in public.'

'Tough,' said Kelsey. 'You know how I feel about those kinds of rules.'

'Very well,' said Frostback. She turned to Van. 'Kelsey misses you deeply, and wishes you hadn't left.'

Kelsey's face flushed. 'Hey!'

'What's wrong?' said Frostback. 'I was merely behaving as you were.'

Van walked over.

Emily eyed him. 'Do you need a moment?'

'Thank you, your Majesty,' he said.

The Queen smiled, and returned to where Yendra and Salvor were standing by the carriages as the chairs were being collected. Frostback gave Van a glare, then turned, and strode for the cavern.

'How are you?' he said.

'Fine,' said Kelsey. 'The dragon was lying. I don't miss you.'

'I thought dragons couldn't lie?'

'Aye? Well, I've been teaching this one; she's getting quite good at it. So, what do you want?'

'It's... it's good to see you.'

'It can't be that good; it's taken you sixteen days to visit.'

'I needed some time.'

'I needed a friend. Funny that; you got your wish, but I didn't get mine.'

'I don't understand – you made your feelings clear, and I took the hint. If you don't want me, then how could you miss me?'

'Is that how your mind works? If we're not in a relationship, then we can't be friends? I've been alone up here, surrounded by some fairly enormous and hostile lizards, freezing my arse off in a cavern. I could have done with a friend.'

'Did you assume that I would follow you around once we got here?' he said. 'I searched for you all over Khatanax...'

'Not very hard.'

'Your brother was sick! I couldn't leave him. During that time, I thought about you a lot, and... I worried. A lot. For some reason that right now I'm having trouble understanding, I slowly started to care about you. I wanted to know you were safe. When I saw you in Old Alea, up on the mound of rubble with the others, I felt something...' He shook his head. 'I'm sorry I left you. I couldn't bear to look at you, knowing that you didn't feel the same way about me as I do about you.'

She looked up at him. He sounded sincere, but it was his actions that mattered, not his words. He had walked away from her when she had needed him.

'I'd better go,' he said. 'I think the Queen is waiting for me so she can leave. Listen, would you mind if I came back here in a couple of days? We can have a proper talk, and maybe some food?'

'I don't know. Why?'

'Because I want to be your friend. I've missed you.'

'And will friendship be enough?'

'I'd rather that than lose you.'

'Maybe. Alright.' She frowned. 'Something looks different about you.'

'It's the same thing that looks different about you. Neither of us are smoking.'

'I gave up ages ago, when I was imprisoned by Amalia. When did you give up?'

'As soon as the packet of cigarettes I brought from Lostwell ran out. There's no tobacco in the City.'

She laughed. 'Maybe it's best that you weren't here; I was a nightmare when I gave up.'

He smiled, and she looked into his eyes.

A dark room; night. Faint light coming through shutters. Van, in bed. Under him, a woman. Like him, she is naked. He looks into her eyes, and Kelsey Holdfast looks back at him, her hungry gaze locking with his as her hands grip his back.

Kelsey staggered back a step, nearly falling, then righted herself, her face flushing, and her eyes wide.

Van frowned. 'Are you alright?'

She stared at him, then slapped him across the face. Before he could react, she sprinted off towards the cavern. Frostback, who had been watching, extended her neck out.

'What happened?' the dragon said. 'Did he insult you? Should I incinerate him?'

Kelsey reached the dragon's forelimbs and turned, out of breath. Van was still standing where she had struck him, a hand on his cheek. He shook his head, then walked back towards the carriages, which were ready to go.

'Rider?' Frostback went on. 'Did he harm you in some way?'

'No,' she said, her heart rate starting to slow as the carriages and soldiers left the quarry. She closed her eyes, trying to dispel the vision from her head. The worst part had been seeing her own face, and the look of desire and naked lust that had been in her eyes. She cursed her powers, and she cursed the way they made her react. Van, and everyone in the carriages, had yet more evidence that she was little other than a crazy witch. One minute they had been laughing together, and the next, she had slapped him in front of the Queen. But all of that paled with the knowledge that she would end up in bed with him. Until it happened, she would live with the assurance that it would happen, the inevitability. She began to cry, and Frostback nuzzled her, and drew her in to the protective area behind her giant forelimbs.

'I won't let him hurt you,' the silver dragon said.

Kelsey said nothing, pressing herself against the silver scales of the dragon. Her dragon.

CHAPTER 7

CAMP 24

Scythe Territory, The Bulwark, The City – 6th Monan 3420

Kagan watched as five Fordian men were escorted between the rows of tents. Blade soldiers flanked them, protecting the men from the Shinstrans and Torduans that filled the camp. It was for their own safety, the soldiers had said. A Fordian had been murdered in a nearby field, the body left in the deep toilet ditches at the rear of the last line of tents, and the City authorities had decided to remove the rest.

'Good riddance,' muttered an old Shinstran, as the small group walked towards a row of wagons by the entrance to the camp.

Rumours about where the Fordians were being taken had been circulating throughout the camp all day. Some claimed that they were getting preferential treatment, and were heading to luxurious new accommodation, leaving the Torduans and Shinstrans to freeze in the miserable tented camp; while others insisted that the City was taking them away to execute them – there were too many mouths to feed, and the Fordians had been selected to die. Without solid facts, rumours had become the lifeblood of the camp. Every day, some new nugget of garbled misinformation would spread from tent to tent – the Torduans were being sent to fight the greenhides; the City authorities were deliberately starving the refugees to death because the granaries were empty; the dragons had been taken away and slaughtered for food; the Blades worshipped dark gods that demanded human sacrifice, and every refugee who was taken from the camp was on their way to a temple where their blood would be spilled upon an altar.

Kagan found most of the rumours to be funny, though he generally kept his true feelings to himself. People who had been sane and sensible in Alea Tanton had regressed into gullible fools, their behaviour bordering on hysterical; and violence could erupt at the slightest provocation, real or perceived. In such an environment, Kagan knew it was better to keep his mouth shut, rather than risk being assaulted by an unhinged refugee who thought he was being mocked.

'It's not fair,' said Elena, her eyes narrow as she watched the Fordians board the wagons.

Kagan said nothing.

'Why are they getting to leave?' she went on. 'Green-skinned bastards. A month we've been in this stinking camp, and they get to go? It's favouritism, pure and simple.'

A bitterly cold wind gusted across the camp, and a few flakes of snow swirled through the air. The sky was a deep red, and the snow took on the colour of blood as the flakes fell.

'I hate it here,' Elena said, moving closer to Kagan, using his stature to shelter from the wind. 'Do you think we'll ever go home?'

'The Blades told us that Lostwell had been destroyed,' he said.

'Yes, but they would say that, wouldn't they? They aren't going to tell us the truth; we're their slaves now.'

A group of Bloodflies passed, nodding to Kagan and Elena as they tramped over the frozen mud. Dizzler's face and name was well known in the camp, and his sister and his second-in-command were accorded a wary respect by the other gang members. By the entrance to the camp, the Fordians had been loaded onto the wagons, and they trundled away, heading along a track that led to the Scythe Wall. The inhabitants of the camp returned to their tents, while others began queuing by one of the half dozen food distribution points. Kagan and Elena joined the queue, their bowls clutched in their hands, while Blades with crossbows kept an eye on them. Several of them were female, and Kagan was still getting used to the sight of armed women in uniform. A few of the others Shinstrans had mocked them at first, but they had since learned that every Blade was tough, disciplined and well-trained, regardless of their sex.

'Stay in line!' cried one of the soldiers.

'Bitch,' muttered Elena under her breath.

Kagan suppressed a smile. 'Would you not fancy being a Blade?' he said.

'Are you mad?' she said. 'They're worse than the damn Banner soldiers. And they hate us. They treat us like animals.'

Kagan glanced at the jostling queue. Resentment was simmering among the refugees; an anger at the cold and hunger that had turned into a hatred of anyone in authority. The threat of violence hung in the air, and Kagan stayed alert. Ahead of them, two Torduans, wearing soiled and ragged blue sashes, started shoving an older Shinstran man who had muttered something to them. Within seconds, punches were flying, and the queue began to disintegrate amid panic.

The Blades reacted, piling into the queue, using the butts of their crossbows to clear a path. They dragged the two Torduans from the crowd and beat them, while the rest of the refugees watched in silence. A Blade sergeant glared at the crowd.

'Violence will not be tolerated,' he growled; 'unless it's us doing it.' He pointed at the beaten bodies of the two Torduans lying in the mud. 'You break the rules; that's what happens. Now, get back into line.'

The queue re-formed as Blades carried the two Torduans away.

Kagan glanced at Elena. 'You alright?'

She shook her head, and he noticed that her hands were shaking.

'I don't know how much more of this I can take,' she whispered. 'I wish I could sleep in your tent; I don't feel safe at night.'

Kagan said nothing. Elena was usually waiting outside his tent for him and Dizzler every morning when the sun rose above the horizon, as the Blades had segregated the men from the women in the camp.

Kagan agreed with the policy, but to Elena it was just another example of injustice.

They reached the front of the queue and held out their bowls. The Blades behind the table filled the bowls with hot green soup, and handed them each a small loaf of flatbread flecked with green. Kagan and Elena moved on, and they went to sit by the front of the tent Kagan shared with seven other men.

Kagan stirred his soup with a spoon, eyeing the small pieces of pork floating amid the salty seaweed. He dipped the bread in and took a bite. It was the same food every day; hot, filling, but monotonous. The refugees had been incredulous at first when they had been told what they were eating. In Alea Tanton, consuming the seaweed from the polluted ocean would probably have been poisonous, whereas it appeared to be a mainstay of the diet in the City.

Dizzler emerged from the tent, bleary-eyed and scratching his head. He noticed Kagan and his sister, and grunted.

'Good afternoon,' said Elena.

'Whatever,' muttered Dizzler, sitting on a low stool by the tent opening. 'I would literally kill someone for a cigarette. I was dreaming about smoking last night; smoking and drinking a cold beer in the sunshine; and then I wake up to this nightmare.'

'There are no cigarettes in the camp,' Elena said. 'We've checked.'

Dizzler glared at her. 'Do you think I don't know that? You're an idiot; an utter moron.'

Elena's eyes flickered towards Kagan, as if she was hoping he would intervene, but he said nothing. He would defend her in front of anyone else, but wasn't going to place himself between her and her brother.

'On days like this,' Dizzler went on, 'I'd like to burn the camp to the ground. That would show those Blade bastards. They can't treat us like this.' He glanced at Kagan. 'I'm going to take a dump.'

Elena screwed up her face. 'I'm trying to eat.'

Dizzler belched as he got to his feet. He nodded to one of the younger members of his crew, and together they walked off towards the toilet ditches behind the tents. Dizzler always took someone to the ditch with him to keep a look out, paranoid that a rival crew leader might ambush him at his most vulnerable.

Elena glanced at Kagan. 'Do you think I'm a moron?'

'No,' he said, 'but it's probably unwise to state the obvious to Dizzler when he's just woken up. You know what he's like.'

She frowned. 'Why are you so loyal to him? I've never understood. You could have had your own crew in Alea Tanton, and yet you decided to stick with my brother?'

'Dizzler looked after me when I was young. Ten years I've been in his crew.'

'And you're happy with always being second-in-command? My brother's scared of you, did you know that? You're the only person in the crew that he knows would do a better job.'

'I have no desire to be a crew leader; and what would it mean out here, anyway? Who knows what's going to happen to us? At some point, we'll be resettled, and then we'll have to get jobs. Will the crews even exist by then? I'd be willing to bet that the City has its own gangs, and there's a lot more of them than there are of us.'

He glanced at her, but her eyes had glazed over, and he wondered at what point she had stopped listening. The cold wind blew between the rows of tents and she shuffled closer to him. Dizzler returned, a deep scowl on his face, and Elena edged away from Kagan again.

He sat, and leaned over to Kagan. 'Eyes left. Check that guy walking by the end of the tents; black hair. You see him?'

Kagan nodded.

'Asshole was giving me cheek at the toilet ditch. Tried to push in front of me.'

'Did he know who you were?'

'No. I want you to enlighten him. Now.'

Kagan nodded and got to his feet, ignoring the frown on Elena's face. He slipped into the flow of people threading their way between the tents, and caught up with the young man he was following; a Torduan from his accent. He was walking in the direction of the corner of the field where the Blue Thumb gang members slept, and Kagan quickened his pace. He checked the positions of the nearest Blades, then waited until their backs were turned. As soon as the soldiers were looking the other way, he gripped the young man by the shoulder, and hauled him off to the right, shoving him into the hard mud behind a tent.

The man's eyes widened, and he clenched his fists. He opened his mouth to say something, and Kagan punched him on the nose, twice. He put a hand round the man's throat and pulled his head close.

'That guy in the toilet ditch you disrespected,' he hissed into the man's ear, as blood streamed down his face. 'That was Dizzler. You disrespect him again, you lose a finger. Nod if you understand.'

The young man looked like he was going to cry out, so Kagan gripped him by a thumb, and twisted. The man fell to his knees, his face crumpled with pain. He nodded.

Kagan released him, and he fell onto the frozen mud. Kagan glanced over his shoulder. An old woman had been watching, but she looked away as Kagan rejoined the flow of people. He made his way back to his tent and sat down by Elena and Dizzler. The crew leader glanced at him, and Kagan nodded.

Dizzler grinned. 'That's my boy.'

'He was heading towards the Blue Thumbs in the opposite corner of the camp.'

'So?' said Dizzler.

'That means it was deliberate,' said Kagan. 'They have a toilet ditch by their own tents. Are you sure he didn't recognise you? It sounds like something the Blue Thumbs would get a new recruit to do.'

Dizzler narrowed his eyes.

'Which means,' Kagan went on, 'that the Blue Thumbs will know we got him, and we should prepare for them to retaliate.'

Elena sighed. 'See what you've started?'

'Shut up,' said Dizzler. 'They started it, not me.' He glanced around at his crew, who were sitting by the openings to their tents, then turned back to Kagan. 'Maybe I should send one of our boys round to their toilet ditch. They could wait for a gang leader to take a dump, and then kick him into the pit.'

'That would be a laugh,' said Kagan, 'but whoever you pick will get the shit kicked out of him. Maybe wait a day or two, until their guard is down?'

Dizzler frowned, then nodded.

'Hey,' said Elena, glancing towards the end of the row of tents, 'look who's coming.'

Kagan and Dizzler turned, and saw a large group of Blades. They were talking to each other, and gesturing towards the tents.

'What do those assholes want?' muttered Dizzler.

Elena's eyes darkened. 'Did they see you attack that guy, Kagan?'

'No.'

'Are you sure?'

Dizzler frowned at her. 'He said no; are you deaf?'

'Your attention, please,' shouted a Blade officer. A hundred faces turned to him as he looked down the row of tents. 'The City authorities are going through the refugees, looking for people with certain skills,' he went on. 'Today is the turn of Camp Twenty-Four, and everyone here is going to be asked a few questions.'

None of the refugees responded.

'Form a queue!' cried a sergeant. 'Line up next to your tent.'

Kagan frowned and got to his feet and, within moments, the other refugees in their row had done the same. Their tent was close to the front, and Kagan watched as the first six refugees were led away to be questioned.

'Certain skills?' muttered Dizzler. 'What's that supposed to mean? Do you think they're trying to root out the crew members?'

Kagan shrugged.

'Tell them nothing,' Dizzler said, turning to the rest of his crew. 'You hear me? Nothing.'

They waited until it was their turn, then followed the soldiers towards a series of large tents by the entrance of the camp. They were separated, and Kagan was taken into a tent, flanked by two armed soldiers. Inside, a woman was sitting at a small table, a few documents in front of her.

'Sit,' she said, her eyes scanning him briefly.

Kagan sat opposite her on a low chair.

'Name?'

'Kagan.'

'Second name?'

'Haven't got one.'

'Age?'

'Nineteen.'

'Do you have a trade? A skilled profession?'

Kagan thought for a minute, sensing that a correct answer could lead to an escape from the camp.

'I can read and write,' he said, 'and I'm good with my hands; I can fix anything.'

The woman looked sceptical. 'You can read?'

'Yes.'

She held up a document. 'What does this say?'

He glanced at the sheet of parchment. 'It says, "By order of the Commander of the Bulwark, the following professions among the refugees are to be prioritised…"'

'That's enough,' she said.

'Do you believe me now?'

'It may surprise you to learn that many refugees lie at these interviews. You also say that you can write?'

He nodded.

She handed him a pencil and a scrap of torn paper. 'Write your name.'

He did so.

'Thank you,' she said. 'You are one of the very few younger refugees who happens to be literate. Did you work in Old Alea?'

'No. I lived near the Southern Pits.'

'So, that makes you a Shinstran, yes?'

'Yes.'

'I was led to believe that no one was schooled in the Shinstran districts of Alea Tanton. How are you able to read and write?'

'My mother taught me.'

'And what was her profession?'

'She was a barmaid.'

'And your father?'

'I have no idea. I haven't seen him in ten years. I think he worked on ships for a while.'

She nodded. 'What was your last job?'

Kagan hesitated. He had never had what the Blade would deem to be a proper job. He had worked, yes, but only for Dizzler, enforcing his rules and making sure his orders were carried out. His future could hinge on his response, but if he was going to lie, it would need to be related to something he could actually do.

'A clerk for a building company.'

'A clerk? In an office?'

'Yes.'

'The City has no need for clerks. Unlike Alea Tanton, the majority of the children in the City are given educations. Your ability to read and write might have been a rare skill where you come from, but it's common here.' She pushed the document across the table for him to read. 'Look through this list of occupations and tell me if you have any experience of working in these fields.'

He scanned the list. At the top was farmer, followed by stone smith, blacksmith, shoemaker and a dozen other specialised professions, none of which Kagan had ever done. He felt his hopes sink. He could try lying, but was sure that the woman sitting opposite him would make him prove any claim.

He slid the paper back to her and shook his head.

'A pity,' she said; 'you seem bright.'

'What's going to happen to the Fordians that were taken away?'

'What do you think's going to happen to them?'

'I think that they're getting moved to a new camp, for their own protection.'

'That is correct. If you knew the answer, then why did you ask?'

'Because the rumours in the camp are all anyone listens to. Where are the dragons?'

'There were moved to the Iceward Range.'

'The what?'

'A range of hills in Icewarder territory.'

He laughed. 'I know nothing about the City. I don't know how big it is, or who lives here. I hear rumours about greenhides, and other rumours about powerful gods, but I don't actually know anything. Is there a book I could read? How could I get access to some history books? I'd work to pay for them; I want to work. I'd do just about anything to get out of this camp.'

She pursed her lips. 'Well, I have a note of your tent, and I shall add your name to the list. If anything comes up, we'll be in touch.'

'Is that it?'

'Yes. You may leave.'

Kagan stood, and a soldier walked him out of the tent.

'That was depressing,' said Elena, who was waiting by the track. 'According to them, I'm completely useless. I have no skills, apparently. How did you get on?'

'The same.'

'But you can read.'

He shrugged. 'So can most folk here.'

She turned to go. 'Come on.'

'What about your brother?'

'He's already gone. His interview lasted about twenty seconds, and then the soldiers pretty much threw him out.'

Kagan nodded, and they began to walk back to their tent.

'What did you do to that guy?' Elena said. 'The one Dizzler got you to follow?'

Kagan shrugged. 'Not much. Just a warning, really.'

She narrowed her eyes. 'You hit him?'

'Yes, I hit him. I didn't break anything, though.'

'Is that what you want to be? A thug? A henchman? Beating up folk for my brother? You could be so much more, Kagan.'

'Maybe if we were still in Alea Tanton, but we're not. My priority right now is surviving; making sure that we get through this alive.'

'Am I included in that "we?"'

'Yes.'

She nodded. 'Good, because there's a group of Blue Thumbs over there pointing at us.'

Kagan turned. Twenty yards away, a dozen or so blue-sashed men had gathered, and one of them had a bloody face, his nose a mess. He was pointing at Kagan.

'What do we do?' hissed Elena.

'Stay calm, and get ready to bolt.'

He started to walk towards the group.

'What are you doing?' said Elena, her voice urgent.

Kagan approached the group, and they fell silent.

'I couldn't help but notice,' he said to the Blue Thumbs staring at him, 'that you assholes were pointing at me. You got something to say?'

'Kagan,' said one. 'Our boy here says you beat him up.'

'Yeah. I did. You shouldn't be sending your lads over to our toilet ditch. You stay clear of us; we stay clear of you. He broke the rules. He was lucky I didn't kick his teeth in. If he sets foot in our corner of the camp again, he'll get more than a bloody nose.'

'Bastard,' one of them muttered. 'We should beat him senseless.'

'Quiet,' said another, whom Kagan recognised as their leader. 'He's got a point. Our boy shouldn't have been shitting in their ditch; who knows what he might catch from those dirty Shinstran bastards?'

The other Blue Thumbs laughed.

'Now, run along,' said the leader, 'and take that little whore with you.'

Kagan had been in these situations before. He had learned, the hard way, how much advantage accrued to those who acted first. Words were all very well, but nothing spoke louder than a fist in the face. He also knew that he could not return to Dizzler without responding to the insult given to his sister, regardless of the consequences. He noted where the closest Blades were, and took a guess as to how long it would take them to intervene.

Then he acted. He started to turn, as if he were about to walk away, then raced forward and rammed his fist into the face of the Blue Thumb leader, cracking his jaw, and feeling a tooth scrape down the back of his hand. The leader staggered back, and Kagan got another two punches in before the others in the group had time to react. They lunged at him, their arms swinging, and Kagan took a blow to the side of his face, along with others to his back and shoulders. He raised his hands in front of his face to defend himself, and stopped punching, aware that a dozen Blades were racing towards them.

From experience, Kagan knew that the Blades never bothered to ask questions when they intervened in a fight. They merely took hold of whoever was doing the hitting or kicking, hauled them off and gave them a severe beating. He went down to one knee as the Blue Thumbs continued to attack him, and took the punches without striking back. Within seconds, the Blades were piling in, pulling his assailants off him and battering them with the butts of their crossbows. He remained motionless, his hands raised, and the Blades left him alone. He felt Elena grab his shoulder, and he stood. Around him, seven Blue Thumbs were groaning in the mud, blood covering their faces.

'Go back to your tents,' barked a Blade at him and Elena, and they slipped away.

As soon as they were out of sight of the Blades, Elena stopped and looked up at Kagan's face. She shook her head.

'Did you know that was going to happen? Did you know the Blades would intervene?'

He shrugged.

'Why did you do that?' she said. 'Your eye's going to swell up; and your fist is all cut. I thought you were going to be beaten unconscious.'

'Did you hear what they called you?'

She frowned at him. 'You mean you did that for me? Next time, do me a favour, and don't. I don't care what they call me.'

'I do.'

She glanced at him, her eyes meeting his. 'You can't go back to Dizzler looking like that,' she said. 'His head will explode if he sees the blood on your face. I've got an idea; come back with me to my tent, and I'll clean you up.'

He nodded, and they changed direction. They walked between the long rows of grimy tents. Kagan knew where Elena's tent was, but had never been in it. Sitting outside its entrance were three older women, scrubbing clothes on a small washstand. They glanced up as Elena and Kagan approached.

'Hi, lass,' said one. 'You can't be bringing boys back here.'

'But look at his face,' said Elena. 'He got those cuts defending my honour from a gang of Torduans. The least I can do is patch him up.'

'Fine,' said one of the older woman, a smile on her lips; 'as long as that's all you'll be doing in there.'

Elena took Kagan's hand and they went into the dark and empty tent. She sat him down on a pile of blankets, then left again, returning a few moments later with a basin of water and some cloths. She sat down next to him, dipped a cloth into the basin, then started cleaning the blood from his face. It was sore, but he kept his features steady, watching her movements as she concentrated. It had been a long time since he had been alone with a girl, and there had been no privacy whatsoever within the camp. He glanced at the entrance to the tent. The old women would keep anyone else from entering, and he found himself longing for some physical contact that didn't involve punching someone.

He reached out with a bruised hand and touched her face. She jumped, then looked embarrassed, then stared at him as he brought her face closer to his.

'Kagan,' she murmured, her eyes gazing at him; 'I love you.'

He pretended he hadn't heard, and kissed her, then pushed her down onto the blankets.

An hour passed before anyone else tried to get into the tent. Kagan and Elena were lying on her pile of blankets, their clothes back on, her head resting on his chest as he ran his fingers through her long hair.

There was a low cough. 'I'm coming in,' said a woman's voice. 'I hope you're decent in there.'

'It's fine,' said Elena.

The tent opened, and one of the older woman peered into the darkness. 'It's time for you to leave, son,' she said. 'It'll be curfew soon, and the Blades will be around.'

'Thanks for keeping folk away,' said Elena.

The old woman raised an eyebrow. 'What it is to be young. And anyway, you were only cleaning his cuts, isn't that right?'

Kagan sat up and pulled his boots on as the old woman withdrew from the tent.

'I wish you didn't have to go,' said Elena. 'It's so unfair that the Blades are keeping us apart. Did you know that married couples are allowed their own private tents? Yet we have to skulk about like criminals.' She paused for a moment. 'Are you going to tell Dizzler?'

Kagan finished lacing up his boots. 'I wasn't planning on it.'

'Good. Don't tell him. He'd only try to interfere.'

He moved towards the entrance and she grabbed his hand. 'Once we're out of this camp, we'll be together, won't we?'

He glanced at her. 'I hope so. See you later.'

She released his hand with some reluctance, and he scrambled out of the tent. The old women broke off from their conversation to look at him.

'You're Kagan, yeah?' said one.

He nodded.

'Dizzler's man? Are you sure it's a good idea to get involved with his sister?'

He frowned. 'Involved? She was cleaning my cuts.'

The woman gave him a wry smile. 'Fair enough, lad, if that's your story. Let's hope Dizzler believes it.'

'You aren't going to tell him any different, are you?'

'Not me, son, but remember; this is a small camp, and word gets around quickly.'

'Don't you worry about me,' he said.

Kagan glanced up at the darkening sky, the streaks of purple mingling with the reds and dark pinks. He rolled his shoulders and started walking back to his tent, a smile on his bruised face.

CHAPTER 8

DIVINE ANCESTRY

F ortress of the Lifegiver, The Bulwark, The City – 17th Monan 3420

Yendra closed her eyes. Her elbows were resting on the surface of the large desk in her office, and she supported her chin with her hands. She took a breath, calming herself and suppressing the tears that were threatening to roll down her cheeks.

The mask. She never admitted it to anyone, but sometimes the memories of the mask overwhelmed her. Her body had been healed, and was strong, but the mental scarring persisted. She had calculated the amount of time she had been held within the restrainer mask, and it came to one hundred and eighteen thousand, one hundred and eighty-seven days, each one identical to the last, and each filled with nothing but pain. The King and Queen looked at her as if she were the strongest, most resilient god they had ever known, and it pleased her that they had such confidence in her abilities, but the truth was a little more difficult. Maybe after a century, she thought, once the memories had faded, maybe then she would know peace, and her dreams would quieten down. Sometimes, she would go for several days without sleep, preferring to be tired rather than risk the nightmares of being confined within the cell upon the Grey Isle; the darkness, the chains, the pain; the never-ending pain.

But it had ended; thanks to Corthie Holdfast. The memory of hearing his voice while she had lain in agony never failed to bring her to tears, although she hid that from the others. They needed to see her as enduring and indefatigable, a tower of reliable strength, the anchor that steadied the City while chaos reigned beyond the walls. She couldn't let them see the darker moments that would creep up on her, and, in time, she would heal.

'Are you sleeping?'

Yendra cleared her thoughts and opened her eyes. Jade was standing a few feet away, peering at her.

'Well?' the demigod went on. 'Were you having a nap?'

'No, Jade; I was just resting my eyes for a moment.'

'Why?'

'I have a lot to think about.'

Jade frowned. 'I could have killed you.'

Yendra straightened her shoulders. 'I very much doubt that.'

'I thought I wouldn't be able to sneak up on you, but I managed it fine. I thought you were always using your vision powers, but you weren't. The Axe of Rand is leaning against the desk; I could have picked it up and removed your head.'

'And were you tempted?'

Jade laughed. 'No. Do you think I'm secretly working for my father? Do you think I've been tricking you all this time? That would be funny.'

'Very funny.'

'So, you don't use your vision all the time?'

'Of course not.'

'Good. I get some pretty strange thoughts in my head, and I'd rather you didn't know what they were.'

'I've been in your head, Jade; I've seen those thoughts. They are one of the reasons I tend to stay out of your mind.'

Jade flushed. 'What kinds of thoughts have you seen?'

'All kinds. Mainly a mixture of blood and savagery, combined with kittens and flowers. Dead flowers.'

'I used to kill Amber's flowers all the time. It annoyed her. What about Van? Have you seen any of my... thoughts regarding the mortal?'

'No.'

Jade grinned. 'Good. Anyway, where is he? You told me he was returning from Pella today, at last.'

'He hasn't arrived yet.'

Jade glanced around, then sat in a chair by the window. 'I'll wait.'

Yendra narrowed her eyes. 'Do we need to discuss consent again?'

'No.'

'Then you realise that Van is not your slave to command?'

'If you're referring to the fact that you have forbidden me from ordering him into my bed, then we don't need to talk about that again. I still don't understand it, though. Marcus had a harem, and so did Kano. And Malik. If it was fine for the damn God-King, then why isn't it fine for me? I'm not going to kill or maim him, after all; I'm only interested in having him please me. I have urges that need to be satisfied.'

'And what did you do in Greylin Palace when you had these urges?'

'I would summon one of the servants to my room. None of them were as handsome as Van, though, and many were too terrified to perform adequately.' She paused for a moment. 'I'd let father take those ones for his experiments, so I wouldn't have to look at their faces again.'

Yendra watched Jade. 'Do you understand why that was wrong?'

The demigod shrugged. 'So you say. I can work round these rules. I don't need to order Van into my bed; I can charm him into it instead. That's allowed, isn't it?'

'If Van agrees, then yes, I suppose so. I wouldn't get your hopes up, though; he's clearly still in love with Kelsey Holdfast.'

'That horrible little witch? I'm much better looking than her, and taller. Kelsey looks like a grubby peasant girl, while I am clearly royalty.'

Yendra drummed her fingers on the desk. 'I have a lot of important matters to discuss with Van when he gets here, and I shall require you to listen rather than speak. Are you going to manage that?'

'We'll see.'

Yendra stood and walked over to a table, where she poured herself a glass of water. She glanced out of the window, and watched the soldiers in the fortress forecourt going about their business. A carriage was parked by the entrance to the Duke's Tower, complete with the standard of the Pellan monarchy emblazoned on its side doors – the twin swords of the Fated Blades, with a double crown. She sent her vision out, and found Van, climbing the stairs of the tower to her office.

She glanced at Jade. 'Best behaviour, niece.'

She frowned, then the door was knocked.

'Enter,' said Yendra.

Captain Brunwick opened the door. 'Ma'am,' he said, bowing. 'Major Van Logos is here to see you.'

'Thank you. Send him in.'

Van walked through the door. He smiled, and bowed towards Yendra, then towards Jade, who giggled.

'Welcome back to the Fortress of the Lifegiver, Van,' said Yendra. 'How was your time in Pella?'

'Enlightening, ma'am. I now know a little bit more about the City and its people.'

'Excellent. Congratulations on your new commission, Major. How are you feeling about it?'

'It was a lot more than I was expecting, ma'am. I don't know if any Banner soldiers will listen to what I have to say, but I'm willing to give it a try.'

'The King and Queen seem to think you're up to it.'

Van nodded, a frown creeping across his face.

'Take a seat,' said Yendra. 'Drink?'

'Yes, please.'

'Jade, pour Van a glass of wine.'

The demigod sighed. 'What about my consent?' she said, standing. 'These rules don't make sense.' She walked to the table and poured herself a glass of wine. She took a sip, then poured another glass for Van. She picked it up and went over to where he was sitting.

'Thank you, ma'am,' he said, taking it.

She frowned. 'Do you love that stupid Holdfast girl? I heard she slapped you across the face.'

Van blinked. 'What?'

'Not now, Jade,' said Yendra.

'Then when?' she said. 'When am I allowed to proposition him?'

'Later.' She glanced at Van, who shifted uncomfortably in his seat. 'Right now, I need to brief the major. Much has changed since your last visit, Van. A lack of paper has caused the census of the refugees to be less accurate than I'd hoped, but even so, much progress has been made. The three thousand Banner soldiers have been removed from Scythe territory, and re-housed within empty Blade barracks. Their officers have been gathered here, in this fortress, and I will be taking you down soon to meet them. Aside from the Banner forces, a total of seventeen thousand refugees have been transferred to Hammer territory – everyone with a skilled occupation; and they have been put to work.'

'How are they settling in, ma'am?'

'Quite well, and the Hammers have been welcoming, on the whole. It's the twenty thousand who remain in Scythe territory who are causing us difficulties. Once the skilled workforce was removed, we have been left with a large group of mainly young, but unskilled refugees. Most of them are illiterate, and most were part of gang culture in Alea Tanton. We had to evacuate the Fordians from the camps, as they were being preyed upon by the Shinstrans and Torduans. The camps are bleak places to be, and thousands of Blades are required to maintain order.'

'If the Queen's plan is successful, then all twenty thousand of them could be gone by the end of winter.'

Jade frowned. 'Is she going to have them killed?'

'No,' said Yendra. 'We are not savages, Jade. Her Majesty's plan remains somewhat speculative, as it depends upon the agreement of the dragons, and the success of Van's mission to persuade the Banner forces to work for the City.' She glanced back at Van. 'Has there been word from the dragons?'

'As far as I'm aware,' he said, 'they are still deciding.'

'Let's hope they don't take too long,' Yendra said; 'otherwise winter becomes Freshmist, and the entire operation will have to be postponed until summer.'

'That is also the Queen's worry, ma'am.'

Yendra nodded. 'Is Kelsey still living with the dragons?'

Van looked awkward. 'She is, ma'am. I haven't seen her since we all visited last month.'

'When she slapped you?' said Jade.

'Yes,' said Van, his eyes tightening; 'when she slapped me.'

'If I'd been there,' said the demigod, 'I would have peeled her flesh off with my powers.'

'Kelsey is immune to your powers,' said Yendra; 'I've mentioned this before.'

'Then I would have bashed her over the head with something sharp and heavy.' She glanced at Van. 'Why did she slap you? Were you asking her to leave you alone? Were you telling her that you'd rather be with me?'

Van shook his head. 'I don't want to talk about it.'

'Jade; enough,' said Yendra. 'You're embarrassing the major, and I haven't finished my briefing.'

Jade waved a hand at her aunt. 'Continue, then.'

'This next part,' Yendra said, catching Van's gaze, 'is strictly confidential, and must not leave this room. It concerns the reliability of certain sections of the Blade officer class. As you might have learned in Pella, during the greenhide emergency, the City was governed by the God-Queen and Duke Marcus. Marcus went against centuries of convention, and moved the majority of the Blades into Medio and Auldan, using them to keep order and maintain his rule, rather than employing them in their traditional role of defending the Great Walls. It was a catastrophic decision. Not only did it allow the greenhides to break through into the Bulwark, but it has also tainted the Blades in the eyes of many in the City. Before Marcus, the Blades were apolitical, and were trusted by the citizens of Auldan and Medio. Now? The Blades are reviled and feared by large swathes of the population. There were atrocities. Hundreds of Evaders were slaughtered by ill-disciplined companies of Blades rampaging through the Circuit. Their immediate commander, Lord Kano, encouraged this behaviour, and the ordinary soldiers took his lead.' She sighed. 'I do not blame the common ranks. They were following their orders. But as for the officers, unfortunately, many of them were complicit in the mismanagement of the Blade battalions. Many of them were utterly loyal to Marcus, obeying even the most destructive and cruel commands. Blades killed hundreds of Hammers and Sanders who were trying to flee the greenhides in Medio; shot them from the Union Walls; desperate, frightened civilians; butchered.' Her voice tailed off as she remembered the carnage.

'I was there,' said Jade. 'I was with Emily at the end, when the greenhides were attacking from the east, and the Blades were shooting us from the west. The Hammers would have torn the Blades to shreds with their bare hands if they had been given the chance.'

'The City will heal in time,' said Yendra, 'but I have an immediate problem. The ordinary soldiers have lost their trust and faith in the officer-class, and feel that they were betrayed by bad leadership; and they are correct. I have removed over two hundred officers from their posts in the last seven months, but here is a vital difference between the Banners and the Blades. Banner soldiers are paid professionals, who can be dismissed from their Banner; whereas, one is born a Blade, and remains a Blade until death. I cannot throw the dismissed officers out of the Blades; I can only demote them, or have them imprisoned. Regardless, I am now faced with a dearth of decent, trustworthy officers.'

Van nodded. 'How can I help, ma'am?'

'The Banner officers,' she said. 'I want to know if any would be willing to become Blades. I understand that her Majesty the Queen has appointed you as commander of all Banner forces within the City, but I would ask if you could spare some of the officers? There are a few captains and lieutenants among them, and if there are more than you require for the Jezra operation, then I could use them to plug the gaps in the Blade battalions. They would need to be reliable, of course.'

'They would be reliable, ma'am, once they had signed a contract. Banner officers are renowned for their loyalty, but a contract would be essential.'

'Thank you, Major. Now, let's go and see the officers; I believe they have been summoned from the barrack where they are being held.'

They stood, and Yendra pulled on a cord. A bell tinkled somewhere in the tower and Captain Brunwick appeared at the door.

'Lead us to the Banner officers please, Captain,' said Yendra.

He bowed, and they went down the stairs to the ground floor of the tower. They crossed the forecourt and entered one of the massive barrack blocks that sat inside the fortress, then Brunwick took them to a common room, which had a squad of armed soldiers outside. The soldiers saluted Yendra as soon as they saw her.

'Are the Banner officers inside?' she asked.

'Yes, ma'am,' said one. 'They have been assembled as requested.'

He passed Yendra a wax tablet, upon which had been marked counts.

'Two colonels, one major, fifteen captains and over thirty lieutenants of one variety or another, ma'am,' the soldier said as she glanced at the tablet. 'They are the remnants of three Banners – the Winged Heart, the Undying Flame, and the Black Crown.'

Yendra nodded. 'Are you ready, Major Logos?'

He took a long breath. 'Yes, ma'am.'

The soldiers opened the doors and Yendra entered the large common room, followed by Jade, Van, Captain Brunwick and the squad. Almost fifty faces turned to them as they walked in. Yendra glanced at them, then kept walking, until she reached a small platform at the end of the room, from where briefings were conducted. Van and the others followed her, and they turned to face the expectant Banner officers, all of whom were sitting on chairs. It had confused Yendra a little that the Banners had no women among their numbers, but it didn't matter, so long as they were professionals.

'Good afternoon, gentlemen,' said Yendra. 'My name is Yendra, and I am the Commander of the Bulwark, appointed by their Royal Majesties to protect the Great Walls of the City from greenhide attack. To my left is Lady Jade, the Adjutant of the Bulwark, and to my right is Major Van Logos, formerly of the Banner of the Golden Fist.'

A few gasps came from some in the crowd of officers, and many stared at Van.

'Firstly,' said Yendra, 'I wish to thank you all for your patience. You have been confined to barracks for many days now, while the City authorities have been dealing with the unexpected arrival of so many refugees from Lostwell. As you are aware, you were removed from Scythe territory to prevent the outbreaks of violence that were taking place between the civilians from Alea Tanton and your own forces. None of that will be held against you, as you were following the orders you had been given. However, your situation has changed, perhaps irreversibly. You are no longer in Alea Tanton, and Lostwell has ceased to exist. As far as we know, the Ascendants have no means to travel to this world, and therefore it is likely that you will spend the rest of your lives here, in this City. How you use that time will be up to you. You are currently prisoners of war, but that status will soon elapse. Major Logos will now speak to you about what you can expect once your contracts expire.'

She gestured to Van, who took a step forward. He scanned the crowd in the room, then nodded. 'I can see what you're all thinking,' he said. 'How did a captain from the Golden Fist end up a major in the Bulwark? When the Golden Fist was destroyed by Corthie Holdfast and the Third Ascendant, I was captured. For fifty days, I remained true to my employers, but once my contract had expired, I was employed by the Holdfasts to work for them. My objectives were to prevent the Ascendants from gaining access to two worlds: the salve world, and the world of the Holdfasts.' He paused for a moment. 'This world, is the salve world.'

The officers stirred. Some called out, while others stared in confusion.

Van stared at the crowd. 'That's right. We're on the very world that the Ascendants have been searching for; the world for which so much Banner blood has been spilled. Belinda, the Third Ascendant, sent us here, to save our lives. She saved the life of every Banner soldier who made it here; she didn't discriminate between her friends and her enemies; she saved us all. Some of you might be hoping that the other Ascendants will suddenly appear to take you all home to Implacatus, but if they knew how to get here, they would have arrived by now, and in your hearts you know this. There will be no rescue, and no return home. This world is now your home, and the sooner you accept that, the better.'

He held up a scroll. 'Due to the nature of our circumstances, I have invoked Section Seventeen of the Banner Charter, and have founded a brand new Banner, here, in the City. As of this morning, the Banner of the Lostwell Exiles is now in existence, and I am its commanding officer.'

'Hold on a moment,' said a man in a colonel's uniform. 'This seems a little irregular.'

'I have the right to establish a new Banner,' said Van. 'Section Seventeen is clear. Any mixed units that find themselves cut off from home with no rescue deemed likely, can band together. I served the Banner of the Golden Fist for thirteen years, so I have the authority to take such a step. I am not under contract, and was free to do so.'

'But we are still under contract,' said the colonel.

'Yes, but only for ten more days. When that time comes, you will have passed the mandatory fifty-day period, and you will all become unemployed. I will accept any Banner soldier or officer into the Lostwell Exiles. Pay and conditions will match what you have been previously offered; you have my word on that, and all contracts will be drawn up in the traditional manner.'

A captain raised his hand. 'Would we have an operation, or would we be guarding the walls from the greenhides?'

'Some officers will be transferred to Blade units here in the Bulwark, but the bulk of the new Banner will be sent on an operation.

Unfortunately, I cannot divulge any details about the operation at this stage, as negotiations are on-going with the dragons that were also rescued from Lostwell.'

'And how long would the contract last?' said a lieutenant.

'Annual, rolling.'

'What's the catch?' said the colonel. 'We were captured as hostile forces; what's changed? Are we expected to believe that our enemies are willing to treat us as friends?'

'I have told the City authorities that Banner forces are the most professional and loyal in existence. If you join the new Banner, you will work for the City, and I have no doubt that you will serve it faithfully.'

'And if we refuse?'

Van glanced at Yendra.

'If you refuse,' said Yendra, 'then you will be released in ten days, and moved to a camp in Scythe territory while we process the remainder of the refugees. You will no longer be prisoners of war, and will have the same rights as any other refugee.'

'I remember you from Implacatus, Logos,' said the other colonel. 'You had a good operational record but, if I recall correctly, it was stained by some pretty awful off-duty behaviour. Dullweed, salve, alcohol abuse; you used to drive Major Ahito to despair. Why should I, a colonel, take orders from the likes of you?'

'Because I served five tours on Dragon Eyre and survived,' said Van; 'because I fought the Ascendants in Yoneath and Old Alea and survived; because I know the dragons, I know the City, and I'm Banner through and through. But, if you don't think you could take orders from someone like me, then you're free to decline; no one will be coerced.'

He glanced around to see if anyone else had any questions. 'I'll be staying in the Fortress of the Lifegiver, at least until the Banner's operation has been approved, and you are free to come and ask me anything. You have ten days to consider this offer.'

He stepped back and glanced at Yendra.

'We will leave you now,' she said to the officers. 'Your future is in your own hands. Tell the men in your companies what we have told you, and allow them to make up their own minds; that is all we ask. Good day.'

She descended from the platform, followed by Van, Jade and the others, and they left the common room. She turned to Van.

'Good job,' she said, 'although the intricacies of contracts and paid loyalty confuse me somewhat. I am used to soldiers serving out of duty, not from the terms of a written document.'

'It's early days,' he said. 'Once it's sunk in that they'll be here forever, their attitude will change.'

Jade frowned. 'What about what that man said? Awful behaviour? What was he talking about?'

'I've had my problems in the past,' he said; 'I'd be stupid to deny it. I've never made a good civilian, and I probably never shall.'

'What kinds of things did you do?' said Jade.

Yendra went into Van's head as he pondered the question. She hadn't wanted to, but needed to be sure about him. Behind his confident façade, his thoughts were in turmoil. Confusion about Kelsey was bubbling to the surface, his fondness for her mixed with anger at being slapped, and Yendra could also sense fear – a fear that he would become addicted to salve again. After all, he was on the salve world, after so many years of trying to avoid coming into contact with the substance. He was managing to suppress his inner conflict, but it was a struggle, and he was fighting to remain professional, especially in front of Yendra.

She started walking. 'Another time perhaps, Jade.'

'But I want to know,' said the demigod. 'If I'm going to invite Van into my bed, then I want to know what awful things he's done.'

She glanced at her niece. 'Whatever they were, I doubt they were as awful as some of the things that you've done.'

Jade flushed. 'Auntie! I'm trying to charm him, not scare him away.'

Van raised an eyebrow. He opened his mouth to speak, then closed it again, and they carried on walking.

They came back out onto the forecourt and strode towards the Duke's Tower.

'Could I ask a favour, ma'am?' said Van.

'Of course, Major,' said Yendra.

'I understand that Lady Felice is incarcerated within this fortress?'

'That's correct. We picked her up after Lady Silva isolated her location.'

'May I see her?'

'Why?' said Jade. 'Do you like her?'

'No,' he said. 'She killed me in Old Alea.'

The small party stopped. 'Excuse me?' said Yendra.

'One of the Holdfasts went into my head and persuaded me that Felice was a traitor, so I ended up accusing her of a crime. She didn't take it well, and then she and three other demigods tortured me to death. Then they brought me back.'

'How awful,' said Yendra. 'Why would you want to see her again?'

'To let her know that I survived. It might be petty of me, but I want her to know.'

Yendra considered for a moment. 'Very well. Follow me.'

She led them to the right, and they passed the Duke's Tower and entered a row of chambers cut into the high curtain wall of the fortress.

'She was shackled and hooded upon arrival,' Yendra said, as they descended a flight of steps into the semi-darkness of the dungeons. 'It was a necessary precaution to ensure she cannot use her vision powers. Other than that, she has been well treated.'

They entered a guarded area of the dungeons, and a soldier opened the door to a long passageway, with cells running down one wall. Yendra paused outside a cell door, and gestured to a guard to unlock it. He did so, and the door was swung open. Inside the dark cell, a woman was sitting on a low mattress, her wrists bound, and a thick leather hood over her head, with a series of air holes punched through the material.

'Lady Felice,' said Yendra. 'You have a visitor.'

The woman turned towards the door.

'I'm going to remove your hood,' said Yendra. 'I urge you to remember how powerful I am compared to you. If you attempt to use your powers, even for a second, you will be severely punished.'

She stepped forward, unbuckled two clasps, and pulled the hood from the demigod's head. Felice blinked in the light, scrunching her face up, her eyes bloodshot.

She squinted up. 'Yendra?'

'That's right,' said the god. 'You remember me, don't you? It was I who captured you, while you were skulking in the fields of Scythe territory, pretending to be a civilian.' She smiled. 'Even now, I can sense you bursting to use your powers, to attempt to send a message. Don't waste your time. There is no one to send it to. You are stranded upon this world, and your only hope is to behave yourself and cooperate.'

Felice frowned. 'Are you a full god?'

'I am. My ancestry is divine, as I am the daughter of Malik and Amalia. I sense you recognise the name of my mother.'

'We were hunting for her on Lostwell. We didn't find her.'

'And now Lostwell is destroyed.'

Felice bowed her head.

'Your visitor,' said Yendra, gesturing to Van.

'Hello, Felice,' he said.

She lifted her gaze, her eyes widening at the sight of him.

'Van Logos? You filthy little traitor.'

'I wanted you to see that I was still alive. Baldwin, Maisk, Joaz – they're all dead; you are the only one of my torturers who's left.'

'Did you come to gloat?'

'I did, but now that I'm here, I almost feel sorry for you.'

'Don't. If I had a knife in my hand, I would stick it into your heart, so that I could watch the life in you eyes go out again.'

Jade stepped forward and slapped Felice across the cheek. 'Don't threaten him.'

'Don't hit her, Jade,' said Yendra. 'I am a firm believer that people can change, and I have hopes that Felice can be rehabilitated over time.'

Felice laughed. 'Lord Edmond will come here, and when he does, he will kill every last one of you, from the lowliest mortal to the highest god. You are nothing compared to him, Yendra. You think you have divine ancestry? You haven't the first idea of what's coming. The Ascendants will never give up their search for this world. It will be your grave, and I will dance upon it.'

Yendra nodded, then pulled the hood back over Felice's head in silence. They left the cell, and the guard locked the door.

'I was wrong to want to see her,' said Van, as they returned to the forecourt. 'And, as much as I admire your sentiments, ma'am, I'm not sure that gods like Felice are capable of changing.'

'She seemed sure that the Ascendants will find this world,' she said.

'It's the only hope she has,' Van said; 'she needs to cling onto it, but it's not that simple. The Ascendants cannot find this world without one of three things – a Sextant, a Quadrant that has been here, or someone who has used a Quadrant to get here. They have none of those things, and no prospects of obtaining any.'

They emerged out into the red light of late afternoon.

Yendra breathed in the cold winter air. 'I hope you're right.'

CHAPTER 9

APPRECIATION

Pella, Auldan, The City – 4th Darian 3420

Vana and Silva bowed before the twin thrones.

'Greetings,' said Emily, smiling at the two demigods. 'I hope you are well.'

'Thank you, your Majesty,' said Vana. 'We have come to the Royal Court to inform you that we have completed our survey of the City. You can rest assured; the former God-Queen is not here.'

Daniel puffed out his cheeks. 'That's excellent news. We had suspected that she hadn't returned to the City, but it's good to hear it confirmed.'

'I apologise that it took so long,' said Vana, 'but I wanted to check every inch of the City, especially around Tara, where the former God-Queen used to live. We needed to be sure.' She glanced to her left, where Lady Silva stood. 'My colleague in this endeavour agrees.'

'Quite so,' said Silva. 'I have detected no traces of Lady Amalia's powers anywhere, your Majesties. We even asked Kelsey Holdfast to temporarily vacate the quarry in the Iceward Range, to make sure that the former God-Queen was not hiding close to the Catacombs dragons.'

'We also surveyed Tarstation and the Grey Isle, your Majesties,' said Vana, 'as well as the shipping traffic in the Warm and Cold Seas.'

'You certainly have been thorough,' said Emily; 'and we are very appreciative of your efforts, both of you. Lady Vana, we know you have had a difficult time, and we thank you again for you assistance in this matter. We now wish to grant you a period of rest, to help you settle back into the life of the City. And Lady Silva, your participation in this survey was most welcome. It must have been hard to adjust to a new world, and we are happy that you seem to have found your feet. We would like you to remain in our Court, if you please, so that you can continue to enrich our knowledge of affairs beyond this world.'

'It would be my pleasure, your Majesty,' said Silva.

The two demigods bowed low, then Vana turned and strode from the small reception chamber, while Silva went to stand to the left of the thrones, where the other royal advisors were gathered.

Naxor raised an eyebrow. 'Your Majesties, might I ask – did you just relieve Lady Vana of her position?'

'Lady Vana has no position in the government of the City,' said Emily. 'She helped us, for which I am grateful, but the days of automatic jobs for the members of the former Royal Family are over.'

'That's a courageous stand, your Majesty,' said Naxor. 'However, might I advise caution? Already, here in Cuidrach Palace, a small number of disaffected and unemployed demigods are together under the same roof. Lady Vana might well add herself to that number.'

'You mean Lady Ikara and Lord Collo?' said Daniel. 'I hardly think they amount to much of a threat.'

'Lady Ikara was Governor of the Circuit for centuries,' said Naxor, 'and Lord Collo was a secretary to Princess Khora and then Duke Marcus. They know everything there is to know about the City, including all of its weaknesses. I have learned from palace gossip that they are both aggrieved with having been stripped of any authority; is it wise to antagonise them?'

Daniel rolled his eyes. 'They were both utterly incompetent,' he said. 'Ikara ran the Circuit into the ground, and Collo hasn't made a single useful contribution to the City throughout his long life.'

Naxor and Salvor exchanged a quick glance.

'The City is very grateful for all the hard work carried out by the former Royal Family,' said Emily, before Daniel could say anything else, 'but we believe it might be time for some fresh thinking. We are not prejudiced against immortals. Lady Silva, for example, is a demigod, and we have asked her to assist us as part of the Royal Court.'

Naxor frowned, then glanced back at Salvor, who was standing to the right of the twin thrones. Emily saw their eyes meet, and knew they were communicating with each other. They were brothers, and Daniel had just insulted their family; of course they were communicating with each other, using their damned powers. They would need to be split up. Prior to Naxor's return, Salvor had been impeccably loyal, but Emily had seen signs of a slight disdain in his eyes in recent days. Worse, she was starting to loathe Naxor, but his wide range of vision abilities had made him indispensable.

'Would honorary titles be appropriate for these otherwise unemployed demigods, your Majesties?' said Silva. 'Something that lends dignity without any real power?'

'That might be a good idea,' said Naxor.

'No,' said Daniel. 'That would give the ordinary citizens the impression that we are still favouring the old Royal Family. We are attempting to govern the City in a new way.'

Naxor bowed his head, a slight smile on his lips. 'Of course, your Majesty.'

'What's next on the agenda?' said Emily, anxious to change the subject.

'A delegation from the Evader Council is due to arrive shortly, your Majesty,' said Salvor.

'Oh yes,' said Emily. 'Good. I'm looking forward to hearing what they have to say about the constitutional proposals.' She turned to Silva. 'I would be interested in listening to your views as well. I want to know how these things work on other worlds.'

'I will study the proposals and offer my humble advice, your Majesty,' said Silva.

'Thank you. Now...'

Emily paused as the doors to the chamber were opened and a junior officer in the Royal Guard entered.

She bowed. 'Your Majesties; a dragon has just landed on the roof of the palace.'

'Which dragon?' said Daniel.

'A silver one, your Majesty.'

The King and Queen nodded to each other.

'That sounds like Kelsey Holdfast might soon be here,' said Emily. 'If that is the case, please have her shown into this chamber.'

The guard bowed and left the room.

'I wish she had told us in advance that she was coming,' said Daniel. 'Now we'll have to re-arrange things.'

'The Evader Council can wait,' said Emily. 'If this is about the Jezra operation, then I want to know now.' She didn't mention it, but she was also looking forward to being able to think without the risk that either Naxor or Salvor were reading her thoughts. She glanced at the two demigods, wondering how far she could trust them.

The doors to the chamber opened again, and Kelsey entered, looking as scruffy as she usually did. A squad of soldiers escorted her to the area in front of the thrones.

'Miss Holdfast,' said Emily; 'how good to see you.'

Kelsey half-smirked, her eyes scanning the demigods standing close to the throne. She folded her arms across her chest. 'I see Naxor has managed to ingratiate himself into the Royal Court – why am I not surprised? I'm more surprised to see Silva up there, especially as I know how much she hates Naxor.'

Silva glanced away, her cheeks reddening slightly.

'Anyway,' Kelsey went on. 'I thought I'd better stop by. It might have taken them forty days, but the dragons have finally come to a decision about your proposal.'

'That's wonderful news,' said Emily.

'Wait until you hear it before saying that,' said Kelsey. 'You have to appreciate that the dragons were not unanimous about this. Deathfang could have tried to impose his will upon them, but that might have led to a split in the group, and he doesn't want that. He's in favour of your plan, by the way, and he spent ages trying to persuade the others. Burntskull and Darksky are both bitterly opposed to helping the City in any way – they think that merely allowing us insects to live is generous enough.'

'I see,' said Emily. 'Was a compromise worked out?'

'Aye. Any chance of a formal alliance between the dragons and the City has been ruled out. Deathfang himself will lead a small group to help in this Jezra operation, but there are a few conditions. First, they want to take you up on your offer of enlarging the caverns in the quarry. They want the roofs made higher, and gates at the front to keep out the wind, and a whole manner of other improvements. Second, Darksky and Dawnflame are going to scout out to the east; they want to find those mountains you mentioned.'

'Naxor can help with that,' said Emily. 'He knows their location.'

'If I may, your Majesty?' said Naxor. 'The dragons will not require my help. The mountains lie two hundred miles to the east, and stretch for over a hundred miles from iceward to sunward. They will be able to find it without my intervention.'

'Oh. I thought that you knew exactly where Blackrose had stayed?'

'I do, your Majesty, but there is nothing particularly interesting about that small valley. I'm sure the dragons could locate somewhere better, and they might take offence if I tried to intervene.'

Emily nodded. 'Alright. Kelsey, please disregard my earlier statement. Were there other conditions?'

'No. As I said, Deathfang will lead a small group to Jezra. Frostback, Halfclaw and Tarsnow will assist him, while Burntskull and Bittersea will stay behind in the quarry to watch the little ones. Will four dragons be enough? How long will they be needed for?'

'The offer of four dragons is very helpful, Kelsey,' said Emily. 'Yes, that should be enough. It's difficult to say how long they will be required, but it should be in the region of a month or so. Certainly, the operation will have to end at the start of Freshmist, which is now only two months away. How soon could they be ready to leave?'

'Within the next few days. They want to see the enlargement work begin at the quarry before that, though.'

'That won't be a problem. We can have workers and materials sent up to the Iceward Range by tomorrow. There is one other aspect of the operation that I feel we need to tell you about. We have appointed Van as the commander of the ground forces that will retake and hold Jezra.'

'Van?' said Kelsey, her eyes narrowing. 'Why would you do that? I mean, I guess he's a decent officer, but what does he know about leading Blades?'

'He won't be leading Blades,' said Emily. 'He has founded a new Banner, and the vast majority of the Banner soldiers that were brought here have joined. They shall be the spearhead that assaults the Western Bank. Similarly, the remainder of the Lostwell refugees; the ones without skills, will be shipped over to the Western Bank to provide the labour force. The infrastructure and defences of an entire town will have to be built.'

Kelsey shook her head, her eyes cast down. 'And you're using the refugees to do the work? The dragons, the Banner soldiers, and the Alea Tanton civilians. I should have guessed. Is this how the City gets rid of its refugee problem – by using them as greenhide fodder?'

'I don't know what you mean,' said Emily. 'We need a labour force, and twenty thousand refugees are sitting in cold and dismal camps in Scythe territory, doing nothing but festering. This way, they will be contributing to the future wealth and stability of the City that has fed them for the last two months. It's simple.'

'It stinks.'

Emily kept her composure. 'Of what, Miss Holdfast?'

'Of a cynical disregard for the welfare of the refugees.'

Emily glanced at the demigods standing to the side. 'Leave us.'

Naxor gave a low bow, then he, Salvor and Silva departed the chamber, leaving the King and Queen alone with Kelsey.

'Are you trying to antagonise us?' said Emily.

'Not particularly,' said Kelsey; 'just pointing out some uncomfortable truths. It's political, isn't it? This Jezra operation was your idea, or so I've been told, but I imagine you've had some difficulties finding volunteers. Then, out of the blue, dragons and refugees arrive. How soon did you come to the realisation that you could use them to sail off to Jezra? I can see how it fulfils several political objectives – you don't need to find any local citizens to sacrifice themselves, and you get rid of the undesirable elements among the refugees at the same time. Very clever.'

Daniel frowned. 'You presume too much.'

'Do I?' Kelsey laughed. 'You're forgetting that I've been mentored by an actual Empress, someone who rules a far larger area than this tiny City. She had to make compromises all the time, and I watched her do it. It's amazing how many enemies you can make, even when you're trying to do the right thing. Someone always gets pissed off, no matter what decisions you reach. In this case, you've chosen to piss off the refugees, which is probably sensible, if a little cowardly.'

'You are an abrasive young woman,' said Daniel.

'Boo hoo. I'm going to cry now. Or, maybe not. You know, you two strike me a bit inexperienced at this game. I heard that you gained power because of some bullshit old legend, rather than through actual talent. I also heard that Princess Yendra is the real source of power in the City, and that, without her, your reign wouldn't last a month.'

'You suck the joy from my soul whenever we meet,' said Emily. 'Part of me wants to appoint you as an advisor, while the other part wants to slap you round the face, just as you slapped Van in the quarry.'

Kelsey shrugged. 'I often get that reaction.'

'Why did you slap Van?' said Daniel. 'I asked him, but he refused to say anything about it.'

'He was annoying me.' She glanced around the chamber. 'Where is he? He's not about to appear here, is he?'

'He's in the Bulwark with Princess Yendra,' said Emily; 'organising his new Banner. They will be transferred to Pella a few days before the operation is due to commence. As the only human with a personal relationship with the dragons, we need you to liaise with Major Logos, in order to coordinate your tactics.'

'"Major?" Pyre's arse; you promoted him?'

'If he is to lead a Banner, it was a necessary step. Princess Yendra will remain as overall commander of the operation, but you and Van will be working closely together. One more thing, before I forget; we have had a new harness made for your dragon. Would she be willing to wear it, do you think? It would make flying much safer for you.'

'You made me and Frostback a harness?'

'Yes, with a padded saddle, and straps for baggage – it was modelled on the harness that was made for Blackrose. We actually had two made, in case any of the other dragons find themselves with a rider.'

'Where is it?'

'I can have someone take it up to the roof for you.'

Kelsey nodded. 'Thanks, I guess. I'm not sure what Frostback will have to say about it, though I can guess the response of Darksky and Burntskull. Can I ask another favour?'

'Of course.'

'Can I have a bath and some clean clothes?'

Emily smiled. 'Certainly. Please do.' She raised a hand, and a courtier who had been standing by the doors came forward and bowed. 'Take Miss Holdfast to the guest rooms on the first floor and have servants draw her a hot bath. Allow her to select some clothes from the wardrobes there, and ensure that she is well fed before she leaves.'

The courtier bowed, and gestured to Kelsey.

'Thanks,' she said, then followed the courtier out of the chamber.

Daniel groaned. 'What an awful girl. Rude, discourteous, opinionated. You were extremely patient with her; I wanted to throw her out onto the street.'

'She's very clever.'

'So? What use is that if she can't control her manners?'

'She was an advisor to an Empress.'

'So she told us, but how can we possibly know if it's true or not? I can't imagine any Empress putting up with her for more than a few minutes. Let's hope she likes it in Jezra and decides to stay there.'

Emily stood up from her throne and stretched her arms and legs, stiff after sitting for so long.

'Greenhide fodder, that's what she called them,' she said. 'Is that what people will think?'

'We have no alternative, if we want the plan to go ahead. Look, darling, if you're having doubts, then it's not too late to call the whole thing off.'

She shook her head. 'We can't. The City needs the resources that are lying just five miles from here. Otherwise, living conditions will only worsen. This might be our only chance to act. We both know that we won't get any help from the majority of the tribes – only the Blades are willing to supply volunteers to cross the Straits, and we need them to stay where they are, especially as we promised to keep all Blades in the Bulwark. But, at the same time, I have a feeling Kelsey might be right – are we betraying the refugees?'

'No. Think of it as their initiation into the City. By doing this, they will have proved themselves to the other tribes; they will have earned their place as full citizens.'

'Many will die.'

'Not if the dragons do their jobs.'

'But now we only have four, when I was hoping for six or seven. And once they find a suitable place to live in the Eastern Mountains, we won't be able to stop them all from leaving.'

A courtier entered, and Emily retook her place on the throne.

'Your Majesties,' she said, bowing. 'Kelsey Holdfast has been escorted to the guest suite as requested.'

'Thank you,' said Emily. 'Ensure she is well looked after. Also, have someone take a dragon harness up to the roof, along with water and food for the dragon, if it is still there. And send the demigods back in.'

The courtier bowed again, then departed. A moment later, Naxor and Salvor walked in, talking together, while Silva strode behind. They took their positions on the platform, and bowed.

'Your Majesties,' said Naxor; 'has Miss Holdfast departed?'

'She's refreshing herself in a guest room,' said Emily. 'Leave her be.'

'Of course, your Majesty. As I have mentioned before, Miss Holdfast can have quite an acerbic tongue. I have been on the end of it more than once.'

'She is a foul-mannered young lady at times,' said Silva, 'but she has a good heart, and she is more intelligent than she appears.'

Salvor remained silent. As Emily had long noted, the demigod only gave his opinion if directly asked for it.

She turned to him. 'Salvor, we need to organise workers, building materials and tools to be sent to the dragons' quarry, by tomorrow. Could you please contact Lady Yvona in Icehaven and explain our requirements to her? The Royal Treasury will pay for everything, naturally.'

Salvor bowed. 'At once, your Majesty.'

He took a step back, and his eyes glazed over.

'The Evader delegation is here, your Majesties,' said Naxor. 'I have just used my powers to observe them getting down from their carriages in the palace forecourt.'

Daniel nodded. 'Thank you, Naxor. Could you escort them here?'

'Of course, your Majesty.' Naxor bowed and left the chamber.

Daniel rubbed his hands together. 'I have high hopes for this meeting; we are on the cusp of success with the constitutional proposals – I can feel it. With the Blades and Scythes both deciding to abstain, if the Evaders join us, then we shall only need one more tribe for a majority.'

'It will have to be the Icewarders,' said Emily. 'The Sanders, Rosers and Gloamers will never change their minds on this.'

Daniel nodded. 'Lady Yvona is persuadable. Once the Evaders are with us, we can approach her to see what amendments would satisfy her tribe.'

Salvor blinked. 'I have passed on the message, your Majesties.'

'Thank you,' said Emily. 'Did you speak with Lady Yvona?'

'Her ladyship was busy, your Majesty. I spoke with her chief-of-staff. They have agreed to our requests, and will send the bill to the palace.'

'Excellent. Let's hope the dragons' tastes in interior design are not too expensive.'

The doors of the chamber opened and Naxor strode in, leading a group of Evader councillors.

'Your Majesties,' said Naxor with a flourish; 'may I present the delegation from the Circuit, led by one Councillor Beckhton.'

The five Evaders formed a line before the twin thrones, and Emily raised an eyebrow at the severe frowns that each wore on their lips. At their centre was a man in his forties, with greying hair and sharp eyes. He bowed his head a fraction.

'Councillors,' said Daniel, smiling; 'how good it is to see you. How was your journey from the Circuit?'

Beckhton kept his face expressionless. 'Uneventful, your Majesty.'

Daniel nodded. 'Good. Straight to business, then. I trust you have familiarised yourselves with the text of the proposed bill? If you have a list of amendments that you would like to suggest, we can discuss those, as well as any areas of concern.'

'There would be little point, your Majesty,' said Beckhton.

'And why would that be?' said Emily.

'Because, your Majesty, the Free Evader Council rejects the bill in its entirety.'

The chamber fell into silence. Daniel's mouth was hanging open, his eyes wide in disbelief. Emily's anger started to build.

'We would like to hear your reasons, if you please,' she said.

'Certainly, your Majesty,' said Beckhton. 'The bill does nothing but perpetuate the rule of the rich over the powerless. A tiny handful of Rosers and Gloamers will still control the majority of the land and wealth in the City...'

'But the land reform clauses will change that,' said Daniel.

'Perhaps, your Majesty; but if any changes were to come about due to this bill, they will be too gradual for anyone now alive to notice. The bill is too cautious in every area. Land ownership should be abolished, whereas this bill merely tinkers around the edges. Wealth and land should be in the hands of the common people, not the rich lords and ladies of Princeps Row. The aristocrats that have been living off the blood of the poor for centuries should have their lands and property confiscated, and the rich tried in public courts for their crimes against the poor workers of the City. They should be made to answer for centuries of exploitation and virtual slavery; otherwise there will never be justice. Therefore, we reject your bill, and will vote against it.'

Emily glared at him. 'You will vote alongside the Rosers? They will laugh at you.'

'They will not laugh, your Majesty,' Beckhton said, a glint in his hard eyes; 'the Rosers fear us, as they should. The Evaders will never forget the way the inhabitants of Auldan acted during the greenhide incursion. The Rosers were holding parties to celebrate the destruction of Medio, while Gloamer militia shot at us from the Union Walls. Well, you can tell your Roser and Gloamer friends that if the greenhides couldn't finish us off, then they have no chance.'

Emily shook her head. 'Your demands are too extreme to be countenanced, and your aggressive tone is not helping matters one bit. This meeting is over. Come back when you decide to negotiate like reasonable people.'

The five Evader delegates bowed and strode from the chamber.

'I can't believe it,' said Daniel.

'Your mother did try to warn us,' said Emily. 'Even so, I found it difficult to keep my temper.'

'You did an excellent job, your Majesty,' said Naxor. 'The Evaders were downright hostile. If they had spoken to Princess Khora in that manner, she would have had them locked up in the dungeons. Is there a possibility that they no longer fear or respect the Crown? If that were the case, then perhaps a lesson needs to be applied, to avoid the appearance of your Majesties' rule being weak.'

Emily eyed him. 'What do you suggest?'

'Arrests, your Majesty. It's open knowledge that many Evader activists are calling for the overthrow of the monarchy, and the mass execution of all non-mortals. I'm sure that some of them will have strayed over the line into criminality. Arrest one hundred of the worst offenders and charge them with sedition. That should serve as an example to the others.'

Silva stared at Naxor for a moment, as if seeing him for the first time.

'Salvor,' said Emily; 'what is your opinion?'

The demigod bowed his head. 'Lady Ikara arrested many thousands of Evaders during her tenure as Governor of the Circuit, your Majesty, and she also exiled hundreds every year to serve in the Bulwark as enforced labour. It made no noticeable difference to the attitudes of the Evaders then, and I struggle to see why it would do so now.'

Naxor shot his brother a glare.

'I quite agree,' said Emily. 'Naxor, I would like you to travel to the Circuit, and enter negotiations with the Evader Council as our representative. You will have no authority over the Circuit, but will work towards trying to agree a compromise.'

'But, your Majesty,' said Naxor, 'the delegates seemed in no mood to compromise.'

'Nevertheless, I want you to go to Redmarket Palace in person. We need someone there with experience of the Evaders.'

'Then I suggest Lady Ikara, your Majesty; she has much experience in that area.'

'Absolutely not,' said Daniel. 'There would be a riot if we sent her. Do as the Queen commands.'

Naxor glanced from face to face, then frowned and bowed his head. 'Of course, your Majesties; I am but your servant, and I shall obey your will.'

'Thank you, Naxor,' said Emily; 'sort it out for us, but remember – no arrests, if you please.'

Naxor bowed again, and left the chamber.

'Do you think he'll manage to accomplish anything?' said Daniel, once he had gone.

'Probably not,' said Emily; 'but if he remained here in the Royal Court for another day, it would be him I'd fling into the dungeons.' She glanced at Salvor. 'No offence towards your brother, of course, but he can be a little trying at times.'

Silva chuckled, while Salvor inclined his head, saying nothing.

CHAPTER 10

LIAISON

I ceward Range, Medio, The City – 14th Darian 3420

'So, you live up here all on your own?' said the man, leaning on a long pickaxe, his toned arms glistening with sweat and dirt.

'Aye,' said Kelsey; 'that is, if you don't count twelve dragons.'

She dipped her mug into the large water butt as the workers crowded round for their morning break. Dozens of Icewarders had been labouring in the quarry for nine days, and tons of rubble had been removed.

'If you ever get lonely...' said the man, grinning at her. A few of his mates laughed.

'You'll what?' said Kelsey. 'Come up here and dance for me?'

He winked. 'You could call it a kind of dancing, if you like.'

'I see,' she said. 'Fine. Great, but you should know – any guy who comes up here to see me, I offer to my dragon as a human sacrifice. Those are the rules.'

'For you,' he said, 'it would be worth it.'

Kelsey rolled her eyes then drank from her mug. The labourers could be annoying at times, and some of them tried to proposition her on a daily basis, but she enjoyed their company after so many days of isolation from other humans up in the hills of the Iceward Range. Most of the Icewarders were friendly, and had boundless curiosity about who she was, and what she was doing with so many fierce, enormous dragons. She had kept them guessing, dripping out pieces of information here and there. They loved to hear her talk about Corthie – it seemed that the Icewarders almost worshipped her brother for his part in the greenhide emergency, and she had raided her memories for stories about embarrassing things he had done as a boy.

Corthie's big sister; that was how they referred to her; either that or the Dragon Lady, which she quite liked.

Their supervisor blew a whistle to call them back to work, and the labourers moved away, heading into the cavern as Kelsey stood and drank her water. A couple of them waved as they went, and she nodded back to them.

'Miss Holdfast?' said a voice.

She turned, and saw a young man standing in front of her, wearing what looked like a modified Banner uniform.

'Aye?' she said.

The man stuck his hand out. 'I am Captain Nurian of the Banner of the Lostwell Exiles, your new liaison officer.'

Kelsey glanced at his hand. 'Oh aye? Did Van send you?'

'I was asked to come here by Major Logos, yes,' he said, slowly pulling his hand back.

'Why didn't he come himself?'

'The major is extremely busy, ma'am. He always seems to be travelling between the Bulwark and Pella, organising the new Banner, and preparing for the upcoming operation.'

'So, he's not just avoiding me after I slapped him?'

The captain blinked, looking embarrassed.

'Ignore that question,' said Kelsey. She glanced around, and saw a carriage parked by the entrance to the quarry. A handful of Banner soldiers were standing alongside it, wrapped up warm from the chill wind. 'So,' she went on; 'what do you want, Nurian?'

'Major Logos requested that I brief you on the plan for the operation.'

'I've read the plan.'

'Then I am here to answer any questions you may have about it, or to help you with any requests.'

'If I had questions, I would have asked. Same goes for requests. Has the date changed?'

'No, ma'am; the operation is due to commence at dawn on the fourth day of Yordian; twenty days from now. I work out of a small office in Cuidrach Palace in Pella that has been turned into an Operations Command Post, but the rest of the Banner should be transferring to Pella by the start of Yordian. If you like, you can come down to Pella and see what we've been doing.'

'Why would I want to do that?'

'Major Logos thought it might be a good idea, ma'am. He wants the dragons and the ground forces to be as integrated as possible prior to the start of the operation. Close coordination is his aim, to ensure that the two branches work well together.'

Kelsey frowned and walked a few paces away, so that she could glance down the slopes of the hills. In the distance was the plain of Medio, where the Circuit lay, and the red sun was hovering over the horizon. It had been ten days since she had visited Emily and Daniel in Pella, and had been told that Van was going to be commanding the ground forces, but she still hadn't spoken to him; and now he had sent one of his officers to talk to her instead of coming in person. It was probably for the best. She had been haunted by the vision that had prompted her to slap him, and wasn't sure she would be able to look him in the eye.

'Did Van give you the order to come here?' she said.

'Yes, ma'am. I spoke to the major yesterday about it.'

'And did he say anything about me?'

'He, uh... Yes. He told me a fair bit about you, ma'am. He said you were brave, resourceful and intelligent.'

'Anything else?'

'Well, ma'am, he also said that I wasn't to take it personally if you were rude to me. I told him not to worry on that account; after five years of service in the ranks of the Banner of the Undying Flame, I have a thick skin.'

'Here's how you could help me,' she said.

'Yes?'

'Find me a book on the history of Jezra. I want to know more about where we're going.'

His eyes lit up. 'I can do that for you, ma'am. There is a library within Cuidrach Palace, and there is also the Royal Academy in Ooste, which, I believe, has the largest collection of books in the City.'

At that moment, Deathfang and Tarsnow emerged from a cavern, and the Banner captain turned to stare at the enormous beasts as they approached.

'Kelsey,' said Deathfang. 'Be aware – Dawnflame and Darksky will be returning soon, and once they arrive, I wish to begin our scouting mission.'

Kelsey nodded. 'Sure thing, big guy. Is Frostback ready?'

'She is,' said the huge grey dragon.

'Then where is she?'

Deathfang's head tilted a little. 'She is too embarrassed to come out of the cavern. She thinks the others will laugh at her for wearing a harness.'

Kelsey's eyes widened. 'She's put it on?'

'She has. It was painful for me to see my daughter with a harness on her shoulders, as if she were a beast of burden, but I understand the reasons behind it. We cannot risk you falling to your death, and as I have sworn to protect you, I thought it for the best. She will come out when it is time to go, and not a minute sooner.'

'I have to see this.'

'Please go in,' said Deathfang. 'She needs some assistance with a few of the buckles, and your tiny hands should suffice.'

Kelsey strode off towards the entrance to the cavern, then paused and turned to the Banner officer.

'Come on,' she said; 'you can help.'

Nurian glanced at the dragons for a second, then hurried after her.

They entered the largest cavern, where dozens of Icewarders were hammering and cutting the stone around the walls and ceiling, making a tremendous racket. Scaffolding had been erected, and Kelsey led the officer into the side cavern where Frostback, Halfclaw and Burntskull slept. Halfclaw was out somewhere, stretching his wings, while Frostback was sitting in the dim cavern, a pained expression on her face. Kelsey looked at the harness. It extended across the dragon's shoulders, with the saddle dead centre, and long, trailing straps and hoops of leather were hanging down either flank.

'I am ashamed,' the dragon said. 'Look at me.'

Kelsey's first reaction was to laugh, but she managed to suppress it. 'It looks fine,' she said, moving closer. 'Let me do these straps for you, and tighten it up a bit.'

Frostback noticed Nurian and glared at him. 'What is he doing here?'

'Van sent him.'

'Why? Is Van too much of a coward to visit you himself?'

'I think he's busy.'

'What – too busy to visit? Or too afraid that I will eat him?'

Kelsey glanced at Nurian as she fastened some straps by Frostback's flank. 'She doesn't mean it; she wouldn't really eat him.'

'I might,' said the dragon. 'He deserves it after hurting you.'

'He didn't hurt me, Frostback.'

'Then why have you been crying every night when you go to sleep?'

Kelsey sighed. 'Not in front of the officer, please. And I haven't been crying every night.'

'Oh.' She turned to Nurian. 'If you repeat what I said to Van, I will render you to ash.'

'I... I won't say anything,' Nurian said, his voice high.

Frostback regarded him. 'You are Banner?'

'Yes.'

'Have you ever fought dragons?'

'No, ma'am. I've never been to Dragon Eyre. This is the closest I've ever been to one of your kind.'

'Are you impressed?'

'Impressed, and... terrified, ma'am.'

'Good. That is as it should be. Help Kelsey with these straps; make yourself useful.'

He hurried forward. 'Yes, ma'am.'

Together, the two humans worked their way down both flanks, tightening the straps and fastening the buckles. They adjusted the position of the saddle, then stood back to admire their handiwork.

'That feels more comfortable,' said Frostback, 'but the shame remains. Darksky will mock me, and so will Burntskull and the others.'

'Don't listen to what anyone else thinks,' said Kelsey.

'Yes, that's your way, isn't it, rider? You never seem to care what others think of you, but I am not like that. I have my pride. I know I am a very beautiful dragon, the most beautiful and graceful of the Catacombs, but this harness makes me look ungainly and clumsy.'

'It accentuates your beauty,' said Kelsey.

Frostback shook her head. 'You promised you would stop lying to me. Are your promises worth nothing?'

'It wasn't a lie; it was an opinion. If I say "I like cheese better than apples" and you disagree, that doesn't mean I'm lying.'

'So you truly think the harness makes me look more beautiful?'

'Aye, because it makes you look dangerous. Like you're ready for anything. It also makes you seem less wild and uncivilised, but not tame either. Aye; civilised but dangerous. Nurian, back me up here.'

'Yes,' said the officer. 'I think the harness suits you, dragon. Like wearing a uniform.'

'Insects and their flattery,' Frostback sighed. 'Apologies, I meant humans, of course.'

There was a loud noise from outside the cavern, followed by the sound of raised dragon voices.

'Darksky and Dawnflame have returned,' said Frostback. 'Go, rider, and find out what they discovered in the Eastern Mountains; I remain too ashamed to allow them to see me.'

'Your father said that we were going to leave as soon as Darksky got back.'

'I know, but there will no doubt be a few moments of talking first that I wish to avoid. I will be out in a minute or two.'

Kelsey nodded, and she walked back out of the cavern, Nurian hurrying behind her.

'That was amazing,' he said. 'Aren't you scared of these beasts?'

'Only when they try to eat me, which isn't all the time.'

'Major Logos said that, if it weren't for you, the dragons wouldn't be assisting us on the operation. He said that they're only doing it because of you.'

She shrugged. 'He's exaggerating.'

'He said you'd say that.'

They emerged into the pink light of midday. Most of the dragons had gathered in the open air, and Deathfang was close to Darksky, while Dawnflame was nuzzling her child.

'How long were they away for?' said Nurian.

'A day,' said Kelsey. 'They left yesterday morning, on their second scouting expedition to the mountains.'

They approached the dragons, and Kelsey listened.

'We have found three suitable valleys,' said Darksky; 'all with fresh water supplies. The hunting is also good, with deer and goats, along with a few mountain bears high up above where the greenhides roam.'

'Are there many greenhides?' said Burntskull.

'They are beyond counting,' said Dawnflame. 'Hundreds of thousands between the City and the mountains, and even more on the other side.'

'But,' said Darksky, 'we also found evidence of a great disaster that happened to the greenhides on the far side of the mountains.'

'I know what happened,' said Nurian, his voice lost amid the giant dragons.

'Hey!' shouted Kelsey, waving her arms in the air.

The dragons turned to her.

She pointed at Nurian. 'He says he knows what caused this disaster.'

Burntskull lowered his head down to Nurian's level, sparks flying across his jaws. 'Well, insect?'

Nurian took a step back. 'I, uh, was told in Pella what happened. Back, at the beginning of summer, Blackrose destroyed a greenhide nest on the far side of the mountains. She slew their queen. That means, that in a decade or so, every greenhide between the City and the mountains will be dead, and there will be no others coming to replace them, not until a new queen can establish a fresh colony.'

'Why will they all be dead?' said Burntskull.

'Because greenhides only live that long. Well, what I mean is, that greenhide workers and soldiers only live that long. The queens live much longer.'

Deathfang moved closer. 'Are you an expert on greenhides, boy?'

'I have studied them. I know a little about their lifecycles. I was told that the greenhide population on this world has gone wild; feral. That makes them dangerous, but also vulnerable. Knock out their nests, and the soldiers will wither away.'

'How long will it take before a new nest is established to replace the one that was destroyed?' said the huge grey dragon.

'That depends how close the neighbouring nests are. Twenty years, maybe? And then another twenty for the nest to become fully operational. A young nest is particularly vulnerable, as the soldiers remain small and underdeveloped for quite some time.'

'This is excellent news,' said Burntskull. 'A mere ten years, and the greenhides will be dead?'

'Just the greenhides from the destroyed nest,' said Nurian. 'There could be hundreds of nests on this world altogether. Part of the dragons' role in the coming operation will be to locate and, hopefully, destroy the closest nest to Jezra.'

Deathfang tilted his head. 'And Blackrose was able to destroy one on her own?'

'Yes. Her rider, Maddie Jackdaw, dictated a report which is held in Cuidrach Palace. I have read it.'

'Who are you, boy?'

'My name is Nurian. Major Logos sent me to liaise with Kelsey.'

'Major Logos?'

'He means Van,' said Kelsey.

'Are you accompanying us on this operation?'

'I am,' said Nurian.

'Good,' said Deathfang. 'A greenhide expert would be useful. Come with us today – you can ride on Frostback's harness next to Kelsey.'

Darksky's eyes burned. 'Frostback is wearing a harness? The shame of it. What a humiliation. Where is she? Why did you allow your daughter to degrade herself in this manner?'

'To prevent Kelsey from falling off and dying,' said Deathfang.

Nurian raised a hand. 'Where are we going?'

'Jezra,' said Deathfang. 'It is time to take a look at the Western Bank.'

———

'Don't feel bad,' Kelsey said, as Frostback beat her silver wings and rose into the air. 'Just think, you can fly as quickly and as dangerously as you want, and you won't have to worry about me falling off.'

'That is a small consolation, I suppose,' said the dragon.

Kelsey gripped onto the leather handle that fronted the thick saddle. Her feet were tucked into deep stirrups, and she felt safer than she had at any other time upon the dragon's shoulders. To her left, Nurian was sitting, his eyes wide as he took in the view from above the Iceward Range.

'You can see the entire City from up here,' he said.

'That's because it's so small,' said Kelsey.

'It'll be larger once we've taken Jezra.'

'I guess so. Are you quite happy to be here? No doubts about joining Van's new Banner?'

'Happy isn't the right word,' he said. 'Resigned, maybe. You have to look on the bright side; we're still alive. It could have been a lot worse. I

listened to Major Logos talk to us in the Bulwark, and signed up immediately.'

'How many didn't?'

'A few dozen. Both colonels refused – they said they were unable to
take orders from someone who had been ranked beneath them in
Implacatus. And I got promoted. I was only a lieutenant in the Undying
Flame, and now I'm a captain, even though I'm still only twenty-one.'

Frostback circled in the sky while Deathfang, Tarsnow and Halfclaw
slowly rose up to join her.

Nurian grinned. 'This is great. These dragons are magnificent.'

'I noticed you've stopped calling me "ma'am."'

His face fell. 'Apologies, ma'am; I, uh...'

She laughed. 'Forget it. It's better if you don't; that way, I can pretend
I have a friend.'

The four dragons banked then surged away in a burst of speed,
Deathfang in the lead. They soared down over the slopes of the Iceward
Range, passing the devastated woodlands until they reached the level
ground where the Circuit stretched out before them. They turned
towards the west, and crossed the line of the Union Walls and saw the
great suburb of Outer Pella below them. In the distance was the old
walled town where Cuidrach Palace was located, but the dragons kept it
on their left as they flew. Beyond Ooste rose the small ridge of the
Shield Hills, the cliffs that protected Auldan from the ferocity of the
Clashing Seas beyond. Kelsey saw a bright white building nestled into
the base of the cliffs.

'Do you know what that is?' she said, pointing.

'It's the Royal Palace,' said Nurian, 'where the God-King and God-
Queen used to live. Next to it is the Royal Academy, with the library that
I was talking about. Ooste's a beautiful town, though Tara is even
better.'

The dragons burst out over the Straits, leaving the land of the City
behind them. Directly below was a huge, dense body of thick fog, and
beyond, the shores of the Western Bank were approaching.

'That's the Clashing Seas under us,' yelled Nurian over the sound of the wind. 'No ship can travel through it, which means that nothing can sail between the Cold Sea and the Warm Sea.'

'How do you know all this?'

'I've been studying for days, reading everything I can get my hands on. I reckon that I need to know about this world if I'm going to be here for the rest of my life.'

Kelsey glanced at him. 'Why did Van choose *you* to come and see me?'

'I'm not sure.'

She frowned, and turned back to watch the coastline of the Western Bank draw nearer.

'There is Jezra, ahead of us,' said Frostback.

Kelsey squinted down. The waves were battering against the shore, where a narrow strip of low ground was sheltering under a high ridge of cliffs. At the top of the cliff, the land levelled off, and a great forest began, spreading for miles into the distance. At the base of the cliffs, jutting out into the water, was a twisted mass of stone ruins.

Deathfang began to descend, and the dragons circled over the ruins, the winds calming in the shelter of the little bay.

'It's hard to make out,' said Nurian, 'but the massive stone platform poking out into the sea was built three thousand years ago. It used to be a great harbour, but most of it collapsed long ago. Behind it, that narrow strip of land is where the rest of Lower Jezra was located. And finally, up on the cliff was Upper Jezra, where most of the people lived, farming the land.'

'And look,' said Kelsey, pointing down; 'greenhides.'

'I see them,' said Frostback.

Beneath them, dozens, then hundreds, of greenhides were emerging from tunnels and caverns under the ruins. They scuttled across the eroded stone, their claws clacking in the air, and their harsh cries and shrieks echoing up to the dragons.

'They're horrible,' said Kelsey.

'Your brother killed thousands of them,' said Nurian.

'So I've been led to believe.'

'You doubt it?'

'No. I saw Corthie cut his way through the Banner of the Golden Fist, so I have no reason to doubt that he slaughtered a shitload of greenhides. All the same, I sometimes wonder if I'm really related to him; he's the greatest fighter I've ever seen, whereas I can barely pick up a sword.'

'I'm sure you have other talents.'

Kelsey glared at him. 'What did Van tell you?'

Nurian blinked. 'I was just, uh, being polite. Ma'am.'

'Oh, alright. Good.'

The dragons ascended up to the top of the ridge and wheeled about, banking and circling as each scanned the landscape. The forest started at the edge of the sheer cliffs, but traces of earlier structures were still visible in places among the trees, and the ground undulated, as if more ruined buildings were buried under the soil.

'What do the greenhides eat when they can't get human?' said Kelsey.

'Birds, small mammals, insects, even fish if they can catch them,' said Nurian, 'but they can go without for long stretches, if they have access to water and sunshine. Ultimately, if they're starving, they'll eat vegetation, and then each other. The fact that there's a thick forest here tells me that the greenhides have not been in this location for too long. Their population swells and recedes in waves, depending on the food supply. Once everything's been devoured, the trees will die off, leaving nothing but barren land. The greenhides die off next, and then the forest grows back, in one long cycle that might take a full century.'

Deathfang banked close to Frostback. 'Daughter; let us give the beasts below a small demonstration of our power.'

'Where, father? The forest?'

'No, down by the shore. I wish to land there for a moment.'

The four dragons swept away from the forest and soared over the edge of the ridge, forming a line. The greenhides were still gathering by the base of the cliffs, swarming over the ruined structures amid the spray from the crashing waves.

'Upon my signal,' cried Deathfang, then opened his jaws wide.

Kelsey saw Frostback prepare, the sparks crackling across the sharp rows of her teeth. Just as they reached the bottom of the cliff, Deathfang emitted a great burst of flame, and the other three dragons did the same. The inferno was so bright and hot that Kelsey flinched back on the saddle, her eyes closing as a wave of heat rushed over them. Greenhides shrieked and screamed amid the flames. Some tried to scatter back down into their caverns, while others threw themselves into the sea to drown. The four dragons kept going, each releasing their powerful jets of fire across the ruins of the old port town, then they soared over the start of the Warm Sea. They closed their jaws and banked, then Deathfang landed on a high outcrop of rock, the remnant of what had once been a high tower. The other dragons flew back across Lower Jezra, each picking a high place to land.

They watched the flames over the ruins fall, until they died away completely, leaving nothing but the piled and smoking carcasses of several hundred greenhides.

Nurian's eyes widened as Frostback perched atop a rough wall. He unbuckled his straps before Kelsey could say anything, and within seconds, he had slid down the dragon's flank.

'What are you doing?' Kelsey shouted.

Nurian jumped down from the wall and ran over to a pile of bones and debris, dodging the smouldering greenhide corpses on the way. He leaned down to pick something up, and a greenhide leapt out next to him, its talons flashing in the sunlight. The beast was too close to Nurian for Frostback to use her flames, so she darted forward and slashed her claws across the front of the greenhide. Several more emerged from hiding, and she swept Nurian up in her left forelimb, and ascended into the sky, leaving the greenhides snapping their talons from the ground below. Frostback transferred Nurian to her jaws, then turned her neck, depositing him back onto the saddle.

'If you do that again,' the dragon said; 'I shall leave you to the greenhides; understand?'

'Yes, yes,' he gasped; 'sorry. And thank you, dragon; you saved me.'

Kelsey frowned at him as he re-fastened the straps. 'You numpty. What were you doing down there?'

'Grabbing this,' he said, holding up a sword. It was encased in a tattered leather scabbard, emblazoned with silver insignia.

'This is a Blade officer's weapon,' he said, slowly pulling the sword out of the sheath. 'Ha! Look; it's still in decent condition. A nice little souvenir, and something to show the boys in the Banner – our first trophy from Jezra.'

She stared at it, as Frostback rose higher into the sky. 'I don't understand. Why hasn't it rusted away?'

'Because it's only been here a year.'

'What were the Blades doing in Jezra a year ago?'

'Chasing your brother,' he said, 'after he escaped from Tarstation.'

'Pyre's arse. You know more about what my brother was doing than I do.'

He shrugged. 'Only because I'm based in Cuidrach Palace. They keep all kinds of records inside the library there. You should go and take a look for yourself.'

'Maybe I should.'

'I've got an idea – why don't we go to the big library in Ooste, the one in the Royal Academy? You would definitely be allowed in, and I have permission to visit. We could spend hours in there, browsing and selecting books on politics and history to read. That is, I mean, if you like that sort of thing.'

'That sounds great.'

Deathfang ascended next to Frostback, and the other two dragons also rose into the air.

'We have seen enough,' said the huge grey dragon, 'and now I need some time to ponder our tactics. Let us return to the Iceward Range.'

Frostback turned her head to Kelsey and Nurian. 'Do you wish to go to Ooste?'

Nurian blinked. 'Could you hear what we were talking about?'

'I can hear everything you say when you are upon my shoulders, human.'

'Alright,' said Kelsey. She glanced at Nurian. 'Ooste?'

'Sure,' he said. 'My job is to work with you, so whatever you want to do is fine with me.'

She smirked. 'You should be careful making promises like that.' She turned to the dragon. 'Take us to Ooste. Oh, and we might stop off for booze on the way back home.'

CHAPTER 11

WHITE ARMBANDS

S cythe Territory, The Bulwark, The City – 1st Yordian 3420
Kagan trudged up the long, frozen track, his colleagues from the work team as quiet as he was. It had been another day of back-breaking labour, and the men were exhausted. The cold wind was bringing light flurries of snow from the east, and it was settling onto any patch of ground not regularly tramped over by the soldiers or refugees. Kagan pulled his long coat round his shoulders, the thick fabric keeping out much of the chill. As well as the new coat, he had been supplied with a fresh pair of sturdy boots that fit better than those he had stolen from the dead Banner soldier on his first day in the City.

They reached the field filled with their tents. It still had a sign reading 'Camp Twenty-Four,' but another sign had been nailed up next to it – *Eleventh Auxiliary Brigade (Lostwell)*. The camp had fewer occupants than at any time since it had been established, but no one had departed for twenty days, when a fresh set of rules had arrived along with the new sign. Kagan and his colleagues entered the camp and made their way between the rows of mud-smeared tents towards the food station. Kagan stretched his sore limbs and stamped his feet on the icy ground in an attempt to keep warm, while the queue slowly shuffled forward.

Among those who had left the camp were Dizzler and Elena. Dizzler had disappeared one day, just prior to the new rules being brought into force, and they had later learned that a fellow Shinstran had bribed an official to have Dizzler removed from the filthy, cold environment of the camps. He had been moved to a new apartment somewhere in the Circuit, and had managed to send a message to his sister and his second-in-command, along with some vague promises that he would help secure their release as well. Elena had been removed to another camp on the same day that the new rules had been implemented. One of those rules stated that the camps should no longer contain both men and women, and all females had been relocated, leaving Camp Twenty-Four with only men. The proportion of women in the camps had already been falling, as most had worked in Old Alea, rather than being part of the gangs' invasion of the high promontory, and had skills that the City authorities found useful. The vast majority of those left behind in Scythe territory had belonged to one gang or another – a mass of badly-educated and unemployable youths from the slums of Alea Tanton.

Kagan reached the front of the queue, and was handed a metal tray. Upon it was the usual bowl of seaweed and pork fat, but there was also a plate of oily, fried fish and a large chunk of bread, along with a tall mug of ale and an apple. The improved rations had arrived with the new rules, but the satisfaction of eating well had been balanced out by the introduction of twelve-hour shifts of hard labour. Kagan took the tray to his tent and sat down amid the remnants of Dizzler's crew, who now looked to him as their leader. None of them said much as they ate, tiredness etched into their grimy features. Kagan had just finished when he noticed two Blade soldiers approach. The men by the tents eyed them with suspicion, and continued to stare as the soldiers stopped in front of Kagan's tent.

'We're looking for a Kagan,' said one.

'Why?' said Kagan.

'Never you mind. Are you him?'

'Might be.'

'Then get on your feet; come on.'

'Where are you taking him?' said a refugee, while the others glared at the soldiers.

'None of your business.'

'Don't worry, lads,' Kagan said, standing. 'Sit tight, and I'll be back soon.'

He followed the soldiers to the end of the row of tents, and they turned for the camp entrance. Kagan remained silent, knowing that the Blades would tell him nothing about where they were going, or why. They reached the large administrative tents by the gates of the camp, and escorted Kagan into one, where two dozen other young refugees were already waiting. They were sitting on rows of wooden chairs, and Kagan was shown to an empty one. In front of the refugees, several Blade officers were talking in hushed tones to a small group of civilians, while soldiers stood guard at the entrance.

The rest of the empty seats were filled up as soldiers brought more refugees into the tent, until, when every seat was taken, two men stepped forwards, one a Blade officer, the other dressed in civilian clothes.

'Good afternoon,' said the civilian, as the refugees stared back at him. 'First of all, let me state – I am not a Blade; I am a Hammer volunteer, and I have been asked to speak about the plans that the City has made for you. As you are all aware, twenty days ago, things changed. Every refugee remaining in Scythe territory has been reorganised into fifteen brigades of one thousand men or women, and you have been adhering to a strict training programme, designed to teach you some of the skills that you will soon require. To you, it may have seemed like pointless hard labour, but it had a purpose. It was to prepare you physically for a task that you have been set.'

The refugees shifted in their chairs. Kagan frowned – were they finally going to find out what was happening? As usual, the rumours had been flying around the camps as the refugees had tried to divine the hidden meanings behind the new rules. Better food and hard labour pointed to one thing – that they were being trained for something – and Kagan guessed they were, at last, going to discover what it was.

'You have been selected to pass on the news to your fellows in the camp,' the Hammer civilian went on; 'and you have also been selected because you have all shown leadership qualities during your time here. Each of you has been monitored and assessed, especially since the formation of the new brigades, and you will make up the core of this brigade's officer class, becoming junior lieutenants. Being a brigade officer brings privileges as well as responsibilities. You will have better rations, better clothing and better accommodation, with bathing facilities and a communal indoor mess where alcohol will be allowed. If any here do not wish to be an officer, then please make your way out of this tent.'

The Hammer waited a moment, but not a single refugee budged from their seats.

He nodded. 'Good. That's the reaction I was hoping for. Now, I can go on to tell you what it is that you will be doing.' He nodded to a Blade, who pinned a large map to a board hanging at the front of the tent. Kagan glanced at it. He recognised the vague outline of the City, although he was still hazy on many of the details. The Hammer picked up a long cane and pointed at the map. 'We are, of course, in Scythe territory. In three days' time, at dawn on the fourth day of Yordian, a fleet will leave from here, Pella, and sail across the Straits to here, Jezra. On board those ships will be the three regiments of the Banner of the Lostwell Exiles, supported from the air by a squadron of four dragons. Their mission will be to clear the ruins and cliffsides of greenhides, and then hold a defensive perimeter. Over the following three days, from the fifth to the seventh of the month, more ships will leave from here, Salt Quay, on the sunward flank of the Bulwark.' He glanced at the faces of the refugees. 'That is when all fifteen brigades will be sailing for Jezra.'

A few refugees gasped.

'Your mission,' the Hammer went on, 'or should I say, our mission, as I and several dozen volunteers from the other tribes will be accompanying you, will be to land at Jezra, and commence the building of a defensive wall to encircle the ruined settlement on its landward side. I hope that now, you will start to understand why you have been labouring so hard these past twenty days. Digging ditches, building walls, dismantling and re-assembling mobile cranes – all of that was for a purpose. Our challenge, indeed, our orders, are to complete the first phase of defensive works before the start of Freshmist, which, for those of you who may not know, will arrive at the end of Yordian or thereabouts. You have a difficult month ahead of you, but you will be handsomely rewarded for your efforts. Every volunteer will receive an apartment in the City, along with a cash bonus to help you get settled in.'

Kagan raised his hand.

'There will be time for questions at the end,' said the Blade officer.

'No,' said the Hammer; 'it's fine.' He glanced at Kagan. 'Your question, son?'

Kagan lowered his arm. 'You said "volunteers." Does that mean we have a choice?'

The Hammer smiled. 'Of course you have a choice. However, if you refuse to volunteer, then you will remain here in Scythe territory for the foreseeable future, and your rations and conditions will return to their previous levels. In time, you will be fully integrated into the tribe of the Scythes, as farm labourers. That's your choice. One month of hard work, or a lifetime in the fields. By volunteering for this operation, you will be proving to the citizens of the City that you have earned your place here. The veterans of Jezra will be honoured and respected, and no one will ever be able to say that you don't belong in the City, as equal citizens.' He glanced around the tent. 'Would anyone like to refuse?'

Several of the refugees glanced at each other, but no one spoke or moved.

The Hammer nodded. 'Similarly, when you pass on this news to the others in the camp, make sure you tell them they have a choice, but, if you have any sense, you will strongly encourage them to accept this offer. The City has been through some terrible times recently, and the refugees have, frankly, been a burden we could barely afford to carry. Understandably, there has been some resentment from the tribes. Through no fault of your own, you are being blamed for all manner of shortages currently affecting the citizenry, but, by assisting with the re-conquest of Jezra from the greenhides, you will be helping to alleviate those very shortages. It is not for vanity that the City has decided to re-take Jezra, but to access the vital resources that sit in abundance upon the Western Bank.'

Kagan raised his hand again.

'Yes?'

'If these resources are so vital, why hasn't Jezra been retaken before now?'

A few of the refugees murmured their agreement.

'A simple lack of time,' said the Hammer. 'The greenhide emergency was only eight months ago, and the immediate priorities were to clear the City of greenhides and begin the recovery.' He looked around. 'Any more questions?'

Someone raised their arm. 'Are we lieutenants now?'

'Yes,' said the Hammer, 'as you have all volunteered. You will be given new uniforms before embarkation at Salt Quay, but, for now, Blades will distribute white armbands to you. Do not lose them or let anyone borrow them. Anyone found guilty of doing so will have their rank immediately, and permanently, removed. These armbands will allow you to pick up your extra rations, and you will also be permitted to be out after curfew without needing the usual pass. Tomorrow morning, instead of going with the others in the brigade to the training fields, you will assemble here, in this tent, for instruction in how to conduct yourselves as officers.' He glanced around at the faces, then nodded. 'Dismissed.'

Kagan and the others got to their feet. Two Blades by the entrance were handing out white strips of cloth to each who left the tent, and Kagan took his, and wrapped it round his left arm, copying what the others were doing. Most of the new officers were smiling, though several also had fear in their eyes.

He glanced at the entrance to the camp, and decided to test the limits of his new authority. He strode towards the track that led out of the camp, half expecting the soldiers there to stop him, but they let him pass without a word. Kagan shook his head in disbelief as he walked out of the camp. He knew the location of Elena's camp, and headed there as the sun dipped below the horizon, the sky shimmering in vibrant shades of violet.

With his breath misting in the freezing air, he approached the gates of Elena's camp, passing a sign that read *Fourth Auxiliary Brigade (Lost-well)*. A Blade moved to block his way.

'You can't come in here, mate, even with that armband,' the soldier said.

'Why not?'

'It's a woman's camp, and you ain't a woman.'

'But I'm a lieutenant.'

'It doesn't matter.'

Kagan frowned. 'Can you send someone a message for me?'

'Do I look like your personal messenger?'

'Please?'

The soldier sighed. 'Who?'

'Elena, in tent seventeen.'

'She won't be able to leave the camp.'

'I know, but we can talk through the fence.'

The soldier gestured to a colleague, who took over his position while he strode off into the camp. Five minutes later, Elena appeared, hurrying towards the entrance, a thick coat over her shoulders.

'Kagan!' she cried, breaking into a run.

'How have you been?' he said, as she reached the fence.

She peered between the high slats. 'I'm fine; what are you doing here? How did you get out of your camp?'

He pointed at the armband. 'I got promoted. Extra rations and we get to break curfew. But listen, we're all leaving in a few days, did you hear?'

'Yeah. Some of the girls here have been made into officers, and they told us. Is that what you are, an officer?'

'I guess so.'

'Folk are saying that we only have to work for another month, in this Jezra place, then we'll each get a house and some gold. Only a month, Kagan, and then we can be together again.'

He leaned in closer. 'That's if we survive Jezra. It's crawling with greenhides.'

'But the dragons will kill them.'

'Four dragons against a million greenhides? They'll have to be flying day and night, and there's no way they'll be able to stop them all. It'll be a bloodbath, that's why they've chosen us to go. If there was ever a time for Dizzler to get us out of here, it's now. Have you heard from him?'

Elena's eyes widened a little. 'No. Not for ten days. Do you really think it's going to be that bad? The new officers told us we would be helping to rebuild some old walls. I'll be carrying bricks; well, that's what I've been practising for days. They didn't say anything about fighting greenhides.'

'Have you volunteered?'

'Yeah. We all did.'

He nodded, his eyes lowering to the frozen ground at the base of the fence enclosing the camp. He felt his chest tighten with anger. For all of the City's fine words, they were betraying the refugees, sending them across the sea to be slaughtered, in order to spare their own citizens the horror of facing the greenhides.

'It's good to see you,' she said. 'I've missed you.'

He nodded again, scarcely aware of her words, his thoughts focussed on how he was going to avoid being shipped to Jezra. He would take Elena with him, if he could think of a way; she didn't deserve to be torn to shreds by a greenhide. None of them did.

'Are you alright?' she said.

'Yeah. I'll come back and see you tomorrow – same time?'

'Alright.'

She slipped her hand through the slats of the fence and he took it, pressing it between his palms. He lifted her hand to his lips and kissed it, then let go.

'Take care,' she said.

He nodded, and turned away. He began to walk back to his camp, his spirits lower than at any other time since the refugees had arrived in the City. For three months he had lived from day to day in Camp Twenty-Four, never losing hope that his turn would come, and he would be taken out of Scythe territory and re-housed. Three cold, miserable months; and for what? So he and the others could be sent to face death at the teeth and claws of greenhides? He hated the City. If they would only give him a chance; he was a hard worker, and was prepared to learn any trade that would provide him with money and a roof over his head.

He was so engrossed in his thoughts that he failed to see the group of eight blue-sashed men approach until they were right in front of him, blocking the track.

'Where are you going at this time of night, Kagan?' said one, mockery dancing in his eyes.

Kagan glanced at them. 'None of your business, you Torduan asshole.'

The group laughed.

'I see you've been made an officer,' the man went on.

'Yeah.'

'Us too.'

'So I see. Are you going to get out of my way, or am I going to have to teach you all a lesson?'

'Oh, don't you worry, Kagan,' said the man; 'we're not going to touch you; not yet. If we kicked the shit out of you here and now, we might lose these armbands and that's not something I'm prepared to risk. But we know you, Kagan, and we're coming for you. As soon as we're on the Western Bank, you're finished. It'll be total confusion over there, at least for a while, and you'll just be one more casualty on the list. We'll slash you up good and proper; make it look like the greenhides did it, and then we'll do the same to Dizzler's sister, and nobody will be able to touch us.'

Kagan shoved his way through them, and they laughed again, letting him pass.

'See you on the other side of the Straits, Kagan!' cried one.

Kagan fought his instincts and strode down the track, ignoring the jeers from the Torduans. The guards at the entrance to his camp waved him through, their eyes glancing at the band on his upper arm. He returned to his tent with a knot of tension in the pit of his stomach, as he realised that, for the first time in his life, he feared for his future.

The next morning after breakfast, Kagan split off from the other occupants of his tent and made his way to the administrative area of the camp. Standing outside the large tents was a group of refugee officers, each with a white armband. Among them, Kagan saw the Torduans who had threatened him the previous night, but several Shinstrans were also there, so he gravitated towards them. A few nodded towards him, but everyone knew he was Dizzler's man, and the crew leader's absence from the camp made him feel exposed.

They were escorted into the same large tent where they had been given their armbands, and sat down as a group of Blade officers waited for them to settle.

'Good morning, Lieutenants,' said one of the Blades. 'Now that you've all had a chance to sleep on the news we broke to you yesterday, we are going to assign you to your individual work companies. Each one of you will command forty unranked members of the brigade. You will be responsible for passing on orders to your companies, and ensuring they carry out their allotted work targets. Each company will have its own diggers, runners, builders...'

Kagan lost his patience. 'What about the greenhides?' he cried.

'What's going to stop them from slaughtering us the moment we step foot on the Western Bank?'

The tented room stilled as everyone turned to stare at him.

The Blade officer frowned. 'There will be time for questions later. There will be no more uncontrolled outbursts from anyone sat here. Discipline is at the heart of everything we do, and I will not tolerate dissension. You have all volunteered, and as such, you will obey every order given to you. Is that understood?'

Something snapped within Kagan and he jumped to his feet. 'This is a sick joke. We're nothing but fodder, greenhide fodder. The City doesn't want us here, so they're sending us off to be massacred. They don't care if we all die. Look at the tiny number of so-called volunteers from the other tribes; that tells us everything we need to know about our prospects for success. The Western Bank will be our grave.'

'Sit down, Kagan,' said one of the Torduans; 'you're embarrassing yourself.'

'Eat shit, you Torduan bastard.'

The Blade officer turned to the guards by the entrance of the tent. He pointed towards Kagan. 'Remove this man from the meeting, and strip him of his rank. He shall be going to the Western Bank, but not as an officer. Get him out of here.'

Four soldiers made their way towards Kagan. They grabbed hold of his arms and began to haul him through the interior of the tent, knocking over chairs as the other refugees backed away. Kagan lashed out, punching and kicking, but the soldiers were strong and refused to let go of their grip upon him. They dragged him out of the tent and threw him to the frozen ground. One of the soldiers leaned over him, and ripped the white band from his arm.

'You dumb piece of shit,' a sergeant said, kicking Kagan in the stomach. 'Two minutes ago, you were an officer, and now you're nothing. You won't last a day in Jezra.'

He spat at Kagan, then the soldiers turned from him and went back into the tent. Kagan groaned in pain, the cold from the ground seeping into his bones as he lay doubled up on the mud. He pushed himself up onto his knees, then struggled to his feet, his hands on his stomach. He turned away from the administrative tents, the red glow from the dawn spreading across the horizon as if it were burning. He glanced at the sky, and cursed it. How he longed for the bright sunlit days, and the dark nights of home. He began to make his way back to his tent then stopped. Everyone would be out in the fields, toiling away at the training exercises organised by the Blades; was he supposed to join them?

'Hey, you!' cried a soldier.

Kagan turned to see a small group of Blades approaching.

'What are you doing here?' the lead Blade shouted. 'You should be at work.'

Kagan stared at them. 'I'm not your prisoner. You can't tell me what to do.'

The Blades glanced at each other.

'Don't be stupid, boy,' said one. 'Come with us, and we'll take you to your work company.'

Kagan's rage and frustration boiled over, and he swung his fist, connecting with the side of a Blade's head. Within seconds, they had surrounded him, their crossbows held like clubs as they beat him to the ground. Blows rained down on him as he raised his hands to protect his face.

'That'll do,' said one of the soldiers. 'He needs to be fit enough to get on a boat in a few days. He'll need his strength for Jezra. We'll stick him in the holding pen for a bit; see if he calms down.'

The beating stopped, and Kagan felt his arms get lifted from the ground. Moments later, the soldiers were dragging him along the freezing mud towards the detention area – a group of fenced-in tents in the corner of the camp where trouble-makers were kept. The soldiers went through the gate in the fence and deposited his bruised body on the ground, and he opened his eyes to see them close the gate and lock it behind them.

He rolled onto his back, his chest, legs and arms aching from the blows he had received.

One day, he thought; one day, he would make the City pay for what they had done to him and every other refugee; he would make them pay.

One day, he thought, then he drifted into unconsciousness.

CHAPTER 12

LEADING FROM THE FRONT

Pella, Auldan, The City – 3rd Yordian 3420

Yendra gazed at the assembled crowd of Banner officers and senior sergeants. She hated giving speeches, and was glad it was over. She had delivered countless briefings to mortal soldiers over her long life, and it wasn't the words that she hated, but more the knowledge that she was sending many of the listeners to their deaths.

The audience hall rippled with polite applause as she took a step back. To her right on the platform, Van stepped forward.

'I'd like to thank Commander Yendra for her words of encouragement,' he said, 'and I know that, personally, I take great solace from the fact that her Highness will be accompanying us on the operation tomorrow. With four dragons and a god on our side, I know we'll succeed. Before you go back to your barracks, I want to say how proud I am of all of you.' He paused, and Yendra could see him struggle with his emotions for a moment. 'When we arrived here,' he went on, 'you were alone on a strange world; confused, disorientated, and surrounded by potential enemies. Now, three months later, you have welded yourselves into a new Banner, three thousand strong. Tomorrow, at dawn, you will embark on the Banner of the Lostwell Exiles' first operation, marking a new chapter in your lives. Tomorrow, we will prove our worth to the

City; our new home. I know that none of you will let me down; and I will do my best not to let any of you down.'

He stepped back, and the crowd applauded again. With the briefing at an end, the officers and sergeants began to get to their feet and head towards the main doors, which were opened by soldiers from the Royal Guard.

Yendra glanced at Van. 'Fine words, Major. You have done an excellent job of running the new Banner, and I'm certain that they will perform admirably tomorrow.'

Van nodded, his eyes tight as he watched the hall start to empty.

'Is something wrong?'

'No, ma'am. It's just... I can feel the weight on my shoulders. When I was a captain in the Banner of the Golden Fist, I had two hundred soldiers to worry about – now, I have three thousand. I wonder how many fewer I will have ten days from now.'

'I understand, Major. Unfortunately, I understand all too well.'

'Does it get easier?'

'It does for some,' she said, 'but not for me. I have watched as members of my family have sent mortals to their deaths without a hint of conscience troubling them; but I have never been like that. Given the choice, I would rather remain as I was.'

Van lowered his gaze. 'You are not like any other god we have fought for.'

'Michael, Marcus, and the God-Queen – they thought I was weak because I felt pity for the mortals, but I'd rather experience the pain of empathy than close myself off from my feelings.' She recalled her three daughters. 'I would be lying if I said that the price hasn't been high.'

'Three hundred years in a mask.'

'I wasn't thinking about that, but yes.'

They watched as the last of the Banner officers and sergeants left the hall. On the far left, Kelsey remained, talking to the Banner officer that had been appointed to liaise with the dragons. The Holdfast girl had a smile on her face, which Yendra found unusual. The mood in the hall had been sombre, and she wondered if Kelsey was the type of person who was exhilarated rather than frightened by the thought of the approaching conflict. Corthie had certainly been that way; but the more Yendra looked, the more she realised that Kelsey's smile was directed at the young officer sitting next to her. She glanced at Van, and saw that he was staring at the two of them. Yendra wished she could go into his head to read the man's thoughts, but with Kelsey in the room, her vision powers weren't functioning.

'Miss Holdfast seems to be getting along well with her liaison offi-cer,' she said.

Van frowned.

'Is that a problem, Major?'

'No, ma'am.'

'You chose the young captain, did you not?'

'I did, but...' He stumbled over his words and stopped.

'But what?'

'Nothing, ma'am.'

'Now is not the time for allowing one's feelings to get the better of you. If there is a problem here, I need to know, Major.'

'You don't need to worry, ma'am; I'm a professional. My feelings for Kelsey Holdfast will not get in the way of doing my duty. I admit that it pains me to see her get along so well with him. When I interviewed Captain Nurian for the position, it occurred to me that he was well suited to Kelsey's temperament, and I thought that he would be a good match for her. I hadn't quite appreciated how good.'

'Do you begrudge her a friend?'

'No. I wanted her to have someone she could talk to; I was worried that she might be lonely. But, I'm only human; I look at them together and I feel jealous. I know I shouldn't, but I can't help it.'

'I need to speak to her before she returns to the Iceward Range; shall I do so alone?'

'No, ma'am. As I said, I'm a professional.'

They stepped down from the platform and walked towards Kelsey and the captain. They fell silent as Yendra and Van approached, and the young officer got to his feet and saluted.

'At ease, Captain,' Yendra said.

'Your Highness,' he bowed, seeming a little over-awed by her presence.

'Nice speeches,' said Kelsey, though Yendra couldn't tell if she was being sarcastic or not.

Yendra smiled. 'Is Frostback coming for you?'

'Aye. She'll be up on the roof just now, waiting for us.'

'Excellent. I was wondering if you had any questions about the role of the dragons tomorrow?'

'Nah. It all seems fairly straightforward. Burn every greenhide in sight; don't burn any humans; start off at the harbour and work our way up to the top of the cliffs. I think the dragons are looking forward to it, if I'm honest. Partly because they'll get to incinerate stuff, and partly because they want to get this over with so they can move to the eastern mountains.'

'Have they chosen a location for their new home?'

Kelsey nodded, a smirk not far from her lips. 'They've chosen a few. Be aware that they're probably going to ask the City for more help. There aren't too many cavern systems in the mountains, and none of the dragons have ever dug one out on their own, so Deathfang wants to request help – workers and so on to assist them.'

'And how would the City transport workers two hundred miles through greenhide-infested territory?'

Kelsey raised a finger. 'I have an idea about that. On my world, there are flying gaien, which are kind of like dumb dragons, and we attach a sturdy wooden carriage via chains from four of the beasts, and they carry folk around in them. Each carriage can fit a hundred people – I could draw up a few sketches for you.'

'I think it would work, ma'am, sir,' said Nurian. 'We would only need to construct two of these carriages, and then the dragons could ferry workers and materials to and from the mountains. Lord Death-fang said that he is open to the idea. He'll never wear a harness, but he seemed willing to help transport carriages.'

'We'll look into it once the operation is underway,' said Yendra. 'The

City will do everything in its power to help the dragons. Shall we walk with you to the roof?'

Kelsey stood. 'Sure.' She glanced at Van for a brief second, then her eyes flicked back to Nurian as they began to make their way out of the hall.

'I hear you were in the Royal Academy,' said Yendra, as they walked.

'Aye,' said Kelsey. 'Nurian and I have been ransacking the library there, reading everything we can find about Jezra. I hadn't realised that the second occupation of the Western Bank coincided with the original Aurelian rebellion.'

Yendra narrowed her eyes. 'I don't think I was aware of that, either. It all happened long before I was born.'

'There are documents missing from the records,' Kelsey went on. 'I asked Chancellor Mona about it, and she said much the same as you – that it happened before her time. The second occupation lasted two hundred years, but the records are very patchy. I know it was two millennia ago, but there are still plenty of records from before and after that time.'

'My brother, Prince Michael, was probably responsible. When he ruled the City, he tried to destroy a lot of the older documents from that time, to suppress the existence of the Aurelian rebellion.'

Kelsey frowned. 'Why?'

'He didn't want the people of the City to realise how close the rebellion had come to succeeding. He wanted to portray it as an utter failure.'

'How do you know that if the records were destroyed?'

'Because, Miss Holdfast, Prince Michael wrote a series of letters to his son, Duke Marcus, that Lady Aila discovered. In some of those letters, he detailed his efforts to suppress the past.'

'Can I read them? Where are they?'

'I think they're still in Icehaven. I shall ask Lady Yvona once the operation is over.'

They reached the top of a flight of stairs that opened out onto the roof. Above them, a silver dragon was swooping low over the town of

Pella, silhouetted against the night sky. She turned, and descended towards the roof.

Van gazed up, then glanced at Kelsey. 'Good luck, tomorrow.'

Kelsey nodded, but didn't look at him, her eyes on the dragon.

'And to you, too, sir,' said Nurian. 'We shall see you at dawn.'

The dragon landed onto the roof, her head turning to face Yendra.

'Greetings, god,' she said.

Yendra inclined her head. 'Greetings, Frostback. Please pass on my regards to your father and the other dragons.'

Frostback noticed Van. 'I hope you haven't been upsetting my rider again.'

Van frowned. 'I didn't realise that I had upset her.'

'Then why did she slap you?'

'I still don't know.'

'Frostback, please,' said Kelsey. 'Let's not start an argument with Major Logos. Come on, Nurian, there's a bottle of wine waiting for us back at the quarry.'

She climbed up the side of the dragon's harness. Nurian saluted again, then followed her. When they were both secured on the dragon's shoulders, Frostback lifted into the air, her silver wings glistening in the streetlamps of Pella, then soared away.

Yendra looked at Van. His eyes were dark as he watched the form of the dragon grow smaller in the sky.

'Do you want to talk about it?' she said.

He shook his head. 'What is there to say? You saw the way she acts in front of me; she hates me.'

'May I ask a personal question? You and Miss Holdfast don't seem to have much in common. How did you come to fall in love with her?'

'I didn't mean to, or want to. I've always tried to avoid these kinds of romantic entanglements, but there's something about her, something that draws me in. The more she tries to push me away, the more I want her. I had a choice on Lostwell; I could have gone with Corthie and Aila to his world, but instead I followed Kelsey here.' He shook his head. 'It doesn't matter. I made my choice and, right now, I have tomorrow to think about.' He bowed his head. 'I shall go to bed, I think, and try to get some sleep.'

He turned, and disappeared down the stairs into the palace. Yendra waited a few moments, then left the roof. She walked along the quiet corridors of the palace until she reached the private quarters of the King and Queen. She passed through the guard post and entered a reception room, where King Daniel's mother was sitting with a handful of servants, going over the following day's schedule.

'Good evening, your Highness,' said the King-Mother, rising and bowing.

'Good evening. Are either of their Majesties still awake?'

'The Queen is working late, as usual. I keep telling her that she needs more sleep, but her Majesty rarely listens to anything I say, your Highness.'

Yendra nodded. 'Is her Majesty in her office?'

'Yes. If you intend on interrupting her Majesty's work, then I would be obliged if you reminded her that the Taran Merchants' Guild will be dining with us at breakfast tomorrow.'

Yendra strode towards a door. 'I shall. Thank you.'

She knocked on the door, waited for a reply, then entered. The Queen was working at her desk, surrounded by high piles of books and papers. She smiled as she glanced up.

'Yendra,' she said. 'Nice of you to drop in.'

'I hope it's not too late, your Majesty.'

'It's never too late in the evening to speak to you. How did the briefing go?'

'It went well. Everything is prepared.'

'Are you nervous?'

'No, your Majesty.'

Emily's brow creased. 'I am. Frankly, I'm terrified. So much could go wrong, and so many people might die. It seemed like such a good idea when we were planning it, but now my stomach is all tied up in knots. Are we doing the right thing?'

'I believe so, your Majesty.'

Emily nodded, worry lines under her eyes. 'Do you think you'll get much sleep tonight?'

'I wasn't intending on going to bed, your Majesty.'

'Have a seat, then,' Emily said; 'and we can try to distract each other. Wine?'

Yendra sat down opposite the Queen. 'Yes, thank you.'

Emily filled a couple of glasses and slid one across the desk to Yendra.

She raised her glass. 'A toast?'

'To what, your Majesty?'

'To success tomorrow,' Emily said; 'may the greenhides run in terror; and may all of our soldiers come back alive.'

Yendra raised her glass, but said nothing.

———

Yendra made her way to the harbour an hour before dawn. Jade was walking by her side, her eyes heavy with sleep, and her mood sour. The ships were being loaded with the three regiments of Banner soldiers – eighteen vessels in all, requisitioned by the Crown from the merchant fleet that connected the ports on the Warm Sea. Sitting at dock in Salt Quay was another fleet, waiting to receive its first load of the refugees in the work brigades. At some point that day, it would be Yendra's job to send a signal to the captains of that fleet, letting them know whether or not to set sail, depending upon the success of the dragons and the Banner. If a slaughter ensued, then the operation would be called off, and it would only sail if the Banner's objectives had been taken.

'Do I have to come?' Jade muttered.

'Yes,' said Yendra.

'Why?'

'You have death powers, Jade. You will be very helpful today.'

Jade snorted. 'Waste of time, in my opinion. It's not like you'll be letting me roam free.'

'No. You will stay close to the Banner leadership – you are their last line of defence.'

Jade's eyes lit up. 'You mean I need to stick close to Van?'

Yendra nodded.

'Then why didn't you say so? That changes things. I'll make sure he's safe. I'll keep him very close; you can count on that.'

'I thought you'd given up trying to seduce him?'

Jade raised an eyebrow. 'No. I don't know what gave you that idea. Sometimes, auntie, you are remarkably unobservant.'

They passed a row of Banner soldiers waiting to descend a gangway onto the busy deck of a ship. They were heavily loaded with weapons, armour and equipment, and their sergeants were feeding them a constant stream of advice and admonitions. Several of them turned to stare at Yendra. She was wearing her full battle armour, for the first time in months, and had the Axe of Rand slung over her left shoulder. A few Banner soldiers bowed low, and some even tried to get to their knees as they had been taught to do in the presence of a god, but the sergeants hauled them back to their feet. Gulls were circling over the fleet, their cries punctuating the sound of the ships being loaded. As many of the vessels had come from Port Sanders, the majority of the sailors were from the Sander tribe, and they eyed the Banner soldiers with a mixture of bemusement and suspicion.

Yendra and Jade made their way along the long wharf, until they came to a group of officers. Van was speaking to them, assigning out roles and checking everyone knew what they were doing. He was dressed in steel armour, the Blade symbols replaced by the crest of the Banner of the Lostwell Exiles – a smoking volcano. The officers saw Yendra and Jade, and they bowed before them.

'Gentlemen,' she said, placing a confident smile on her lips. 'I hope you are all in good cheer this morning.'

'Looking forward to it, ma'am,' said a captain.

'That's the spirit,' she said. She glanced at the sunward horizon, seeing the pinks start to spread, replacing the purples. 'Time to embark, I think.'

'Off to your boats,' said Van.

The officers saluted and dispersed across the wharf, leaving Van with a few lieutenants. They walked down the gangway and onto the deck of the command ship. At the stern, the quarterdeck had been fitted with ballista batteries, and more had been positioned along the port side of the vessel, along with large racks of yard-long steel bolts. The deck was crowded with soldiers and their kit, while Sander sailors scrambled over the rigging and prepared the ship for departure.

Yendra glanced towards Cuidrach Palace, which sat by the long waterfront. Using her battle-vision, she could make out a few figures on the high balconies close to the private quarters of the King and Queen, and knew that Emily was watching them.

Van turned to her. 'We are ready to depart, ma'am.'

She nodded. 'Give the signal, Major.'

He gestured to a lieutenant, who raised a flag. The dock workers loosened the ropes connecting the lead ship to the wharf, and threw them onto the deck, and the sails were unfurled. They caught the breeze and snapped full, pulling the vessel out towards the centre of the bay. Pella harbour had no breakwaters, as the sea in the bay was calm, and the ship drove sunward, then tacked to the west, aiming for the gap between Ooste and Tara. Behind them, the other ships of the invasion fleet slipped away from the wharf just as the sun appeared on the horizon. Yendra took a deep breath, filling her lungs with the salt air of the Warm Sea. Van paused from giving orders, and joined her and Jade by the bow.

'There you are,' said Jade. 'I'm your personal bodyguard today, Van. No greenhide will be ripping you to shreds.'

'Thank you, ma'am,' he said.

'Lady Jade will also administer to the wounded,' said Yendra.

The demigod frowned. 'I thought we had brought salve for that?'

'We have,' said Yendra. 'But if the major gets injured, I want you to use your powers to heal him.'

She shrugged. 'Sure. Is it wrong of me to hope he gets injured, so that I can have an excuse to touch him?'

'Yes, Jade; it's wrong.'

Jade gave Van a sly wink. 'I don't care.'

Van half-smiled, then turned to stare at the enormous statue of Prince Michael on the coast next to Tara. It towered into the sky, its gaze turned towards the City.

'So, that's Michael?' he said.

'It is,' said Yendra. 'A similar statue stands in the middle of the Circuit.'

'She killed him,' said Jade. 'Stamped on his head until his brains came out.'

'Had I not done so,' she said, 'then the City would still be under his rule.'

'Oh, I'm not complaining. Father always said that it was the best thing you ever did.'

Van nodded. 'Your father is Prince Montieth?'

'Yes, but I don't want to talk about him. He's not a very nice man.'

The lead ship pulled out of the bay and entered the Warm Sea. The wind picked up, and the swell increased, sending water spraying up the sides of the vessel. Yendra stared into the west as the light grew, her eyesight picking out details of the coastline. Cliffs ran down from a plateau into the crashing waves of the sea, except at one point, where the small bay of Jezra sat.

'Have you been to Jezra before, ma'am?' said Van.

'Never,' she said, 'but I have used my powers to survey every inch of the terrain. Did you read the reports of the Blade expedition that was sent last year?'

'I did, ma'am. I'm sure we'll do better than they did.'

'I have no doubt about that. We shall be hunting greenhides, not Corthie Holdfast.'

'I wish he were with us now. I've never seen anyone who could fight like him.'

Yendra smiled. 'You haven't seen me fight.'

Van returned her smile. 'I've heard the rumours.'

'Look!' cried Jade, pointing upwards.

Yendra and Van turned towards the sky. Four dragons were overhead, spread out over a front two hundred yards wide. On the left was Tarsnow, with his black and white scales, then the huge bulk of the grey Deathfang. On his right was the lithe figure of Frostback, her silver wings shining in the sunlight, and on the far right was the green and blue dragon, Halfclaw. The soldiers on board the lead ship let out a great cheer as the dragons sped over the water towards the west.

Yendra relaxed a little. Upon Frostback's shoulders, she could see two figures strapped onto the harness, and she felt her vision powers return once the dragons had passed a hundred yards from where she was standing on the deck.

'Ma'am?' said Van.

'Yes?'

'About the salve. Was there a reason that you didn't want me taking any?'

She turned to him. 'I won't lie to you. I know you had a problem with addiction in the past.'

'Huh. You know about that? I guess I'm not surprised. You could have heard it from any one of a dozen officers in the Banner. My old behaviour is not exactly a secret, and I'm sure there's been plenty of gossip. The men in the Banner are loyal, but that doesn't stop them from talking.'

'It counts in your favour that you are trying to shed your old habits. I wouldn't have backed you as commander of the Banner if I didn't have faith in you.'

The cliffs of the Western Bank loomed ever larger as they sailed. On their right was a dense bank of impenetrable fog marking the start of the Clashing Seas, and the current grew stronger. The sailors steered the ship in a gentle curve to avoid the worst of the swell, turning slightly to iceward as they crossed the halfway point of the Straits. Van left Yendra's side, and strode down the deck speaking to the sergeants and lieutenants, while she concentrated on the view ahead. The ruins of Jezra came into sight. The lower levels and foundations of an ancient palace comprised the largest structure, and it sat directly beneath the towering cliffs. There were only four paths that led from Lower Jezra up the face of the cliffs to the plateau, and her eyes picked them out. One was to iceward, another to sunward, and the remaining two were on the western flank of the cliffside. A huge burst of flames exploded along the top of the ridge, then, within seconds, fires were raging across lower Jezra. Above the ruins, the dragons were soaring, diving down with their jaws open to flood the ancient town with clouds of thick red flame. Smoke began to billow up into the pink sky, and Yendra heard the cries of burning greenhides reach her across the waters of the Straits. The winds swirled around them as the vessel came to within a few hundred yards of the edge of the Clashing Seas, and the hull rose and dipped on the swell.

Ahead of them, the ruins of the harbour awaited. The ancient docks and wharves had been eroded by centuries of waves battering against them, and the ship edged its way between the ruins into the more shel- tered waters of a narrow basin. Fires were raging on the shores close to them, and greenhides were lying in piles, their charred bodies smoul- dering. The dragons had moved away from the immediate vicinity of the waterfront, and were sweeping back and forth by the ancient palace. Fresh greenhides were starting to emerge from tunnels and under- ground caverns by the ruined harbour, and they were scattering in panic. Some were heading in the direction of the cliffs, while others were trying to escape the flames. A few turned, and saw the approaching ships.

Van nodded to a lieutenant.

'Man the ballistae!' cried the officer, as the ship swung to starboard, its port side now facing the waterfront. Soldiers were already swarming round the eight bolt-throwing machines mounted along the port side of the ship, while the further four on the quarterdeck were also being prepared.

'Select your targets!' the lieutenant shouted. 'Loose.'

A dozen yard-long steel bolts were released from the side of the ship, and the hull rocked back a little from the recoil. The bolts sped through the air, striking the closest greenhides. Nine were skewered through, their shrieks splitting the air.

'Reload, and loose at will!'

Behind them, the rest of the fleet was waiting in the narrow channels that snaked through the ruins of the harbour. Two of the other ships were also in range of the waterfront, and they joined the lead vessel, loosing their ballistae into the fleeing greenhides. Yendra watched as the three ships unleashed two hundred bolts a minute at the greenhides, clearing a large stretch of the waterfront. The lead ship edged closer to the ruins, the sailors using a dozen long poles to push the vessel through the shallows.

Yendra unslung the Axe of Rand from over her shoulder.

'Remember, Jade,' she said; 'protect Van.'

Jade nodded, her eyes transfixed by the spectacle of flames and death upon the shore. Yendra strode down to where Van was directing the attack.

'I intend to jump ashore first, Major,' she said. 'I will take the right flank and get out of the way of the bolts, and keep any greenhides from assaulting from that direction until your men have cleared the ship.'

Van looked at her, and for a moment she thought he was going to object.

He nodded. 'Yes, ma'am.'

'Good luck, Major. See you in Jezra.'

She returned to the bow of the ship, which was closest to the shore, and also on the far right of the hail of bolts that was still being loosed upon the town. She put her right boot up onto the railing, the axe in her left hand, then glanced up. Two of the dragons had moved onto the cliffside paths, and were smothering them in flames from top to bottom, while the other pair was continuing to sweep the lower town.

Yendra took a breath, and jumped.

CHAPTER 13

EXHAUSTED

Pella, Auldan, The City – 4th Yordian 3420

Emily's hands gripped the railing of the balcony as the chill predawn wind gusted about her. Below her in the harbour, the fleet was sailing away, the lead ship passing the enormous statue of Prince Michael that watched over the bay. She had caught a couple of hours of sleep, but it had been fitful, and she felt worse than if she had stayed awake.

A servant coughed, and handed her a cup of the green tea that helped her awaken each morning. Emily nodded her thanks and took it, warming her hands against the delicate ceramic. To her left, the sun split the horizon, bathing the bay in glorious pink light, and Emily couldn't stop herself from smiling, despite the anxiety she felt in the pit of her stomach. Death was on her mind, the inevitable, impending deaths of those who had arrived on her world as lost refugees; and a sense of guilt was weighing heavily upon her shoulders. She had tried to rationalise it, but there was no getting away from the unvarnished truth – people were going to die because of her decision.

The day before, the Tribal Council had taken a break from arguing over the proposed constitutional changes, to debate the status of the refugees. Were they a separate tribe; or should they be subsumed within one or more of the existing tribes? The Rosers believed that they should be forced to join the Scythes and be made to toil in the fields, while the Hammers would be happy to accept the skilled artisans and smiths into their ranks. The Evaders, on the other hand, had insisted that they be treated as a new tribe, just as they had been when they had arrived in the City. They had also been refugees, they had reminded the Council, and the new refugees should be given the same rights as everyone else, as their own tribe.

Emily and Daniel had promised to consider all of the suggestions, and a decision had been deferred to a future meeting, at which Emily hoped to have a few representatives of the refugees present, to allow them to make their case. She wondered how they would react if the fifteen thousand sent to Jezra were slaughtered.

She watched as the last of the fleet disappeared into the distance, sailing round the headland of Tara and out of sight. There had been no choice, she told herself. Without the resources of the Western Bank, the City would continue on its downward spiral, with ever worsening short-ages. Was it a little ruthless? Maybe, she conceded, but the future of the City was at stake, and perhaps a little ruthlessness was what was required.

She walked back into her office and closed the balcony doors. She was already dressed for the day, having bathed before the fleet had sailed, and she glanced at a wall mirror. Her hair had been blown about in the wind, so she spent a moment sorting it, then stepped out into the reception room in the centre of the royal quarters.

'Good morning, your Majesty,' said Daniel's mother.

Emily raised an eyebrow. 'Do you ever sleep?'

'I could ask you the same question, your Majesty. Only, I feel it rather more important that a monarch gets her rest than I. Take the King, for example. He rarely gets out of bed before he absolutely has to, and not all of that has to do with the gin.'

'I couldn't sleep. I wanted to watch the fleet depart.'

'And did staying up half the night contribute to the success of the operation in any way, your Majesty? Mightn't a rested Queen be of more use to her loyal subjects?' She shook her head. 'You need to develop a thicker skin, if I may say so, your Majesty. Rulers sometimes have to send young men and women off to their deaths to deal with some crisis or another. You're not the first to do so, and you certainly won't be the last.'

Emily sat on a couch. 'You being right doesn't make me feel any better.'

'And,' the King-Mother went on, with a slightly pained expression, 'if you're never in bed, I'll never be a grandmother.'

Emily put a hand to her eyes. 'Dear gods.'

'Before the coronation, you had the burden of carrying on the Aurelian name; now, you have the future of the entire monarchy resting on your shoulders. You don't need to work quite so hard every day, your Majesty; you and Daniel can take some time for yourselves.' She glanced at the window clock. 'Speaking of his Majesty, it is time for him to awaken. The Taran Merchants' Guild will be here for breakfast soon.'

'What? No. I'm too tired, and I want to ask Salvor to check the progress of the operation.'

'Did Princess Yendra forget to remind you?'

'No, she mentioned it, but I pushed it to the back of my mind. We'll have to re-arrange.'

'But they have come all the way from Tara, your Majesty; and by road, I might add, seeing as how every ferry has been requisitioned to take soldiers to Jezra. I spent valuable political capital to persuade them that you and Daniel would be open-minded about their demands, which was no easy feat, considering how the majority of Rosers currently view the monarchy. Meeting them would go a long way to winning them over.'

'We'll never win them over. The Taran Merchants' Guild is little more than a protectionist racket. They want us to guarantee that we won't interfere with their system of tariffs, which makes them rich at the expense of every Reaper and Evader in the City. It can't go on, and they know it.'

'They are the most powerful guild in the City, your Majesty. It would be wise...'

'No. I refuse to pander to them.'

The King-Mother frowned. 'Perhaps you're right, your Majesty. In your current mood, which I blame on lack of sleep, you might be inclined to say something you will regret. Very well. If you are not able to put on a brave face, then I will inform them that you are ill. They are unlikely to take it kindly, but that is better than them being offended by a few misplaced words over breakfast.'

The door to the royal bedchamber opened and Daniel walked out, half-dressed and yawning.

'What are you two arguing about?' he said. 'You woke me up.'

He wandered over to Emily and kissed her.

'Good morning, dear,' she said.

He glanced around the room. 'Well? What were you discussing?'

'The imminent arrival of the Taran Merchants' Guild, your Majesty,' said his mother.

'Oh, yes. Is that today? I suppose I'd better wash and get ready.'

'The Queen says that she will not be attending, your Majesty.'

He glanced at Emily. 'Is that right?'

'The Jezra Operation is the priority today,' she said.

The King-Mother smiled. 'Perhaps this is a benefit of having two equal monarchs. What if Daniel goes to the breakfast with me, while you rest?'

'I won't be resting,' she said; 'I'll be working.'

'But if you take my advice...'

Emily stood. 'Your advice is duly noted. The Banner will have landed in Jezra by now, and I'm going to find Salvor. I'll stay out of the public areas of the palace, so you can pretend I'm ill if you like.' She glanced at Daniel. 'Don't give in to any of the Taran demands.'

'You know me,' he said, a half-smile on his face. 'Of the two of us, it's you who is considered the moderate. The Tarans think me a radical. I'll give them nothing.'

The King-Mother grimaced. 'Perhaps this isn't such a good idea, after all.'

Daniel took Emily's hand. 'Go and see Salvor; I'll deal with the Tarans.'

They kissed, and she left the chamber. A courtier was waiting by the door, and began to escort her, along with two soldiers from the Royal Guard. Emily wished she could walk freely around the palace, but had become resigned to being followed about wherever she went. She strode to Salvor's office, smiling at the staff they passed on the way.

The courtier stepped in front of her and knocked on the office door.

A servant opened the door, and bowed before the Queen. She smiled again, a little forced, and went into the large, spacious office, leaving the courtier and guards outside. The office had once been the centre of Princess Khora's government, and had tall bay windows over-looking the town of Pella and a long conference table, with two dozen chairs. In the corner of the chamber, Salvor was sitting at his desk, browsing through the pages of a book, a glass of wine in his hand. His eyes widened when he saw the Queen enter, and he put the book and the wine down.

'Your Majesty,' he said, standing and bowing. 'I wasn't expecting you this morning. I was under the impression that you were meeting with the Taran Merchants' Guild.'

'The King is dealing with that today.'

'Alone, your Majesty?'

'His mother will also be there.'

Salvor nodded. His eyes scanned her face for a second, and she wondered if he were raiding her thoughts.

'What were you reading?' she said.

'Nothing of any great import, your Majesty.'

She glanced at the book. 'Poetry?'

'It relaxes me, your Majesty. I find that the poets of the mid to late Silver Age have a soothing effect on my mind. Have you ever read any of the greats?'

'I studied a few of them at school, but I prefer concrete reality to the surreal whimsy of the Silver Age poets.'

'Quite, your Majesty; but when one has read every single book in the City several times over, one must seek out diversions.'

She approached the desk and sat. 'Have you really read every book in the City?'

Salvor nodded. 'I think so. Chancellor Mona and I used to have a friendly competition to see who would be the first to do so. It's one of the benefits of being immortal, although I don't think many other members of my family were particularly interested.'

'Pour me a glass of that wine, and, when you have a moment, write me a list of the twenty books you think I should read. Hopefully, I will have read most of them, but I'd be interested to see what you recommend.'

'I'd be delighted to, your Majesty,' he said. He poured her a glass of wine. 'Is it advisable for you to be drinking this early? My self-healing can suppress any feelings of intoxication, but, alas, you will not be able to do so.'

She picked up the glass. 'I've been up all night, worrying about Jezra.'

'I see. Is that why you are visiting?' He smiled. 'Was it too much to hope that you'd come to discuss books?'

She smiled back at him. She had rarely seen Salvor so animated, and noted the circumstances, storing them away for the future.

'Shall I take a look at what's happening, your Majesty?'

'Yes, please,' she said.

He set the glass of wine onto the desk and nodded, then his eyes glazed over. Emily picked up the book of poetry and flicked through it while she waited. She shook her head at the verbose and flowery language. It was sheer escapism, the poets of the Silver age being renowned for turning their backs on the mundane reality of day to day life in the City. The change in tone had come with the birth of Prince Michael and his taking up the reins of government, and she wondered if the two events were connected.

Salvor blinked, and took a sip of wine.

She glanced at him, waiting.

'The first regiment of Banner soldiers has landed, your Majesty,' he said. 'I found Princess Yendra, but I decided not to link minds, as she is rather busy at present, slaughtering greenhides. The smoke and flames from the dragons are making it a little difficult to see the overall picture, but the harbour area appears to have been occupied.'

'What about casualties?'

'Lady Jade has remained at the rear with the officers, and she has been healing the wounded. The supplies of salve are also being taken.'

'That's not exactly what I asked. How many are dead?'

Salvor pursed his lips for a moment. 'Several dozen that I could see, your Majesty. The dragons have been clearing the surface area of Lower Jezra, but greenhides are emerging from the many tunnels and caverns that lie beneath the ruins. Right now, the second of the three regiments is about to disembark from the ships.'

Emily nodded. Several dozen could mean anything from thirty to a hundred dead soldiers. In a way, she was relieved – the landing hadn't been a complete disaster, which had been her greatest fear. She thought about the underground caverns.

'Maybe Jade could be employed to clear the tunnels,' she said; 'if the dragons can't reach those parts.'

'Should I communicate this to the leadership of the operation, your Majesty?'

'No. I shouldn't interfere. Yendra is there on the ground; we should leave these decisions to her.'

'Very well, your Majesty. What now?'

Emily sat back in the chair and sipped her wine. 'Keep checking, please; I need to know everything.'

———

An hour passed, while Salvor used his vision every ten minutes or so to provide the Queen with the latest news from Jezra. In between the bursts of his power, they discussed books and the history of the City. Despite the tension over the operation, Emily felt herself relax in Salvor's company. The demigod had always been reserved in front of her, keeping his opinions to himself, and she was pleased that he had opened up a little.

He was on the point of ordering some breakfast for them, when a member of the Royal Guard knocked on the door and entered.

The soldier's eyes flickered over the Queen. 'Your Majesty,' he said, bowing low.

'Did you come to see me?' said Salvor.

'Yes, my lord. Guards on the roof of the palace have seen a fire raging in Ooste this morning, in the vicinity of the Royal Palace.'

'Have the local militia been in touch to request help?'

'No, my lord. We have dispatched a squad to gather information, and have been preparing a detachment to go to their assistance.'

Salvor got to his feet. He gestured to the Queen. 'I want to take a closer look, your Majesty. Do you wish to accompany me?'

'I do,' she said, rising.

They walked out of the office and went to a neighbouring reception room, which had a long balcony overlooking the bay. Salvor strode out onto the balcony, and the Queen joined him, while a small cluster of courtiers and guards followed behind. Emily gazed across the bay towards Ooste. Several tendrils of smoke were rising from the town.

Salvor glanced at the guard. 'I can see more than one fire.'

'There was only one when I last looked, my lord.'

'Are they in the residential areas?' said Emily.

Salvor frowned. 'No, your Majesty. They appear to be coming from the administrative district. If you'll please excuse me for a moment; I intend to use my powers to find out more.'

The demigod's eyes glazed over as Emily waited. One fire in Ooste was unfortunate, but she could clearly make out four separate plumes of smoke over the town. Arsonists? But why would anyone burn Ooste? Since the deaths of the God-King and Duke Marcus, the town had become a sleepy backwater, the government staff and offices transferred to the seat of royal power in Pella. Mona and Doria still lived there, minding the Royal Academy and the Royal Palace but, at times, Emily almost forgot that the town existed.

Salvor let out a gasp, and turned to the Queen, his eyes wide.

'Your Majesty,' he said; 'we must speak in private, at once.'

She turned, dismissing the courtiers and guards, then Salvor closed the balcony door.

'Well?' she said. 'You're worrying me.'

'Your Majesty; I regret to inform you that thousands of Gloamer troops from Dalrig have entered Ooste. They have occupied the key buildings, and are guarding all approaches into the town. The harbour has been closed, and several hundred arrests have been made.' His eyes darkened. 'Also, Prince Montieth is there, in person. I saw him enter the Royal Palace.'

'What? Montieth? He's left Dalrig?'

'It appears so.'

'I thought he never set foot out of Greylin Palace?'

'He hasn't in centuries, your Majesty.'

'Why? Did you go into his head?'

Salvor looked away, and Emily noticed his hands tremble. 'No, your Majesty. I didn't dare. The prince is far more powerful than I, and he would immediately be aware if I tried to read his thoughts. I have never once even attempted to access his mind.'

Emily gestured through the glass of the balcony doors, and a courtier approached.

'Summon Lady Silva, please,' she said.

The courtier bowed and hurried away.

Salvor waited until the balcony door had been closed again, then he turned to Emily. 'What are your orders, your Majesty?'

'I don't know. Has anyone been killed?'

'Not that I could see. Arrests, yes; but no deaths.'

'I don't understand. What could Montieth possibly want from Ooste? What could he gain by so brazenly flouting the laws of the City?'

'I fear that there is only one thing in Ooste that may interest Prince Montieth, your Majesty.'

'Yes?'

Salvor gazed out over the bay, his hands gripping the railing. 'The salve mine.'

———

Within thirty minutes, the Queen and Salvor had assembled every member of the Royal Court to a meeting in Salvor's office. Commander Quill was there, along with her top-ranking officers, as well as the King, who had excused himself halfway through the breakfast with the Taran Merchants' Guild. Silva sat a few places along from Emily, and the King-Mother was also in attendance, wearing a frown as deep as the Cold Sea.

The Queen had sat in silence as Salvor had delivered the news. Instead of everyone beginning to talk at once, as she had expected, when he finished, the office sat in a stunned quiet. Many of those present had assumed that they were going to be given an update on the operation in Jezra, and none had anticipated a move by Montieth.

'Have the Gloamers issued any demands?' said the King after a while.

'None that we can discern, your Majesty,' said Salvor.

'And the prince is definitely somewhere inside the Royal Palace?'

'I watched him go up the steps and enter that building, yes.'

'And I can confirm it, your Majesty,' said Silva. 'I am not familiar with Prince Montieth, but a powerful presence has left Greylin Palace, and is now in Ooste. I can sense his powers; he is very strong.'

'What about our intelligence?' said Daniel. 'Did we have no indication that this was going to occur?'

'We knew that the Gloamers had been gathering soldiers, your Majesty,' said Salvor; 'but, I'm afraid to say that we assumed that this was because of the three regiments of Banner soldiers who were stationed in Pella.'

Daniel's face darkened. 'You knew they were assembling their militia?'

'Yes, your Majesty. However, this has occurred in the past, whenever the Gloamers have felt that they might be under threat. As I said, we made the assumption that they were reacting to the presence of so many Banner soldiers in Pella. We were wrong. Instead, it appears that they planned their attack to coincide with the beginning of the Jezra Operation.'

'So, our intelligence failed us?' said the King-Mother, her eyes narrow.

Salvor bowed his head. 'This is my responsibility; therefore, I offer my resignation. I was caught out, and unprepared, and I apologise for the lapse.'

Emily stirred in her seat. 'We do not accept your resignation, Lord Salvor. Please continue in your post.'

Daniel rubbed his forehead. 'I still don't understand. We have two demigods working for us who can read minds – three if you count Princess Yendra, and four if we include Chancellor Mona. And yet, no one foresaw this?'

There was an uncomfortable silence as Salvor gazed at the floor. 'I can only apologise again, your Majesty,' he said eventually. 'Our policy has always been to leave Prince Montieth and the Gloamers alone. No one, to my knowledge, has ever read the prince's mind. He made it clear some time ago that he would consider any such intrusion by a member of the former Royal Family as a hostile act.'

'Let's move on from trying to apportion blame for this,' said Emily; 'we need to look ahead, not behind. The reason we are now assembled here is to discuss how to react to the occupation of part of the City by Prince Montieth's forces. Commander Quill, how many soldiers from the nearby militias could we spare for this?'

'There are one and a half thousand Reaper militia on standby, your Majesty,' Quill said, 'plus another two thousand in reserve that could be mobilised within a few hours. We could also assign five hundred from the Royal Guard. Longer term, we could draw on the militia lists and recall up to a further six thousand veterans and part-timers, but that would take several days to organise.'

'Then organise it, please,' Emily said. 'Our first priority should be to cut the roads that lead from Ooste to Dalrig, to prevent reinforcements and supplies from being transported between the two towns, and then to initiate a full blockade of both settlements.'

Daniel glanced at her. 'They may interpret that as an act of war.'

'They have already declared war,' said Emily. 'Ooste is occupied by a hostile military force. We cannot show any sign of weakness.'

'I agree, your Majesty,' said Quill. 'However, from a military point of view, any land blockade of Dalrig would be ineffective without also sealing off their harbour, which we could not possibly attempt without the full cooperation of the Icewarders. A blockade of Ooste would be considerably easier. If we cut the roads and close their port facilities, then they would begin to feel the pinch quite quickly. Another option would be to recall the dragons from Jezra, and send them against the Gloamers occupying Ooste.'

'Out of the question,' said Daniel. 'We cannot use the might of dragons against our own people, not to mention the considerable damage to property that would result. We need to strive for a peaceful solution, and to do that, we need to know what it is that Montieth wants.'

'If I may, your Majesty?' said Salvor. 'It has to be the salve mine; I can think of nothing else in Ooste that would interest the prince, and the fact that he has entered the Royal Palace, which leads directly to the Ooste mine, would seem to confirm this theory.'

'But he has his own mine in the hills behind Dalrig,' said the King. 'Why would he want the one in Ooste?'

Their attention shifted as the doors to the office were opened by soldiers and Chancellor Mona walked in. She looked a little travel-worn, but otherwise was keeping her composure.

'I can answer that question,' she said.

'Chancellor Mona,' said Emily, her eyes wide; 'have you just come from Ooste?'

Mona bowed towards Daniel and Emily. 'I have, your Majesties. And apologies, I was listening in to this conversation while I hurried here from the Royal Academy.'

'Please, take a seat.'

'Thank you, your Majesty.'

Mona walked round the long table, and pulled up a chair between Salvor and Silva.

'You were saying?' said Daniel.

Mona glanced round the table. 'I have spoken to Prince Montieth, your Majesty. He offered me a choice – to remain in the Royal Academy under house arrest, or to leave, and so I chose to come here. I asked him why he had moved his forces into Ooste, and he told me it was because the salve mine next to Dalrig has been exhausted. In short, he has run out of salve, and has moved to secure control of the mine in Ooste.'

'And Lady Doria?' said the Queen.

'She elected to stay in the Royal Palace, your Majesty. She has been confined to her quarters.'

'And Lady Amber?' the Queen went on.

'She is still in Dalrig, your Majesty,' said Silva. 'I can sense her presence there.'

'Prince Montieth has no wish to overthrow the government,' Mona said. 'He desires only the salve that remains in the mine at Ooste. He said he would start executing the thousands of trapped civilians if any attempts are made to re-take the town. He didn't go into any detail, but I got the impression that he is planning on excavating the reserves from the Ooste mine, in order to transport it back to Dalrig.'

Salvor glanced at her. 'And how was his state of mind, cousin?'

'He was coherent. Enthusiastic, even. He did mention that it had been Amber's idea to wait for the commencement of the Jezra Operation before striking. If left to his own devices, I think he would have assaulted Ooste the moment the salve ran out, but Amber restrained him.'

'So Lady Amber is complicit in this criminal act?' said Emily.

'It appears so, your Majesty.'

Emily suppressed her instincts to start shouting, but her head was spinning. At that moment, thousands of innocent civilians were at the mercy of Montieth and his soldiers, but if the Crown retaliated, then those same civilians would start to die.

'Ignore Dalrig, Commander Quill,' she said. 'Blockade Ooste, and Ooste alone. Cut the roads and seal off their harbour, but do not initiate hostilities against the Gloamer militia.' She glanced at Daniel. 'Are we in agreement?'

The King nodded, and Quill rose from her chair.

'One moment,' said Mona; 'there is more.'

Quill sat again.

Mona took a breath. 'Prince Montieth doesn't know this yet, but he soon will. It became apparent to me years ago that the reserves of salve in the Ooste mine were running low. Extremely low, in fact. It seems that the late God-King was profligate in his use of the substance, especially in his latter years. Lady Doria has told me of times when she witnessed him literally bathing in salve. That being the case, the prince is likely to react badly when he makes this discovery. If he is desperate, then there is only one further location that holds significant reserves – the mines behind Maeladh Palace in Tara.'

Emily gasped. 'The mine at Ooste is almost exhausted?'

'Yes, your Majesty. I also believe that the reserves in Tara are only a small fraction of what they once were.'

'The City is running out of salve? How could this be? For millennia, the gods and demigods monopolised the supply of salve, keeping it from the mortals so that they could use it all to remain young, and now there is hardly any left?' She felt her temper rise with every word, and a few seated at the table were regarding her with trepidation. 'Have the former Royal Family squandered the lot?'

'Much was excavated, your Majesty,' said Salvor, 'to buy champions from Lostwell. The payments for the two dragons, and for Corthie Holdfast, came directly out of the Ooste and Tara mines. Naxor must have shipped tons of salve to Lostwell over the last three centuries. It wasn't all squandered by my family.'

'We must warn the Taran authorities, your Majesties,' said the King-Mother. 'Prince Montieth might be headed there next.'

Daniel nodded. 'That would seem prudent.'

Emily put her head in her hands. 'Only yesterday, I authorised the removal of the salve reserves kept in Cuidrach Palace, to be used to treat injuries in the Jezra Operation. I assumed, wrongly it seems, that there was plenty more where that came from. In one stroke, I have reduced our reserves considerably.' She glared at Mona. 'It would have been helpful to know that we were, in fact, running out.'

The demigods at the table exchanged nervous glances.

'The King or I need to speak to Prince Montieth in person,' Emily went on. 'We need to have a grown up discussion about how to resolve this.'

'He won't speak to you, your Majesty,' said Mona. 'He told me that he refuses to recognise the mortal leadership of the City. There is only one person he is prepared to negotiate with.'

'Yes?' said Emily. 'Who?'

'His sister, your Majesty. Princess Yendra.'

CHAPTER 14

REDUNDANT

J ezra, The Western Bank – 4th Yordian 3420

Frostback flew low over the ruins of Lower Jezra, emitting another long burst of thick flames at a group of fleeing greenhides emerging from underground. The silver dragon had swept over the same stretch many times, but greenhides kept appearing from the hidden entrances to tunnels and caverns beneath the ancient town. The noise around the dragon was deafening, from the roar of flames to the incessant shrieks of panicking and dying greenhides, and, occasionally, the scream of a fallen soldier. As bad as the noise was, Kelsey considered the smell to be a million times worse. The odour of burning flesh had permeated the air of the narrow bay where Jezra lay. There was little wind behind the shelter of the curving cliffs, and there was no escape from the reek of slaughter. Frostback banked hard to the right, her turn far sharper than had been the case before the harness had been strapped round her; her fear of Kelsey falling gone. Next to the young Holdfast woman, Nurian was clinging on, his eyes streaming from the rush of air.

Halfclaw soared past, the tip of his right wing almost brushing Frostback in the tight space over the lower town. Higher up, both Deathfang and Tarsnow had moved to the ridge at the top of the cliff, and were driving back the greenhides by the edge of the forest. Every now and then, greenhide bodies would fall from one of the paths that connected the lower town to the upper, and the ground at the base of the cliff was stained with green blood.

'How much longer can the dragons keep going?' cried Nurian over the noise.

'Why don't you ask her?' said Kelsey.

'Frostback,' Nurian yelled. 'How much...'

'I heard you the first time,' the silver dragon replied. 'How long have we been attacking this town?'

'Nearly four hours,' said Kelsey.

'My spirits are high, but my wings are beginning to tire,' she said, wheeling back for another run at the ruins of the ancient palace.

She surged down, sending a wide burst of flames over the ragged remnants of the town. Every bush and shrub had been incinerated, and the low walls and ancient ruins were blackened and scorched. A group of greenhides were running towards the harbour, and Frostback swept to the left, cutting them off before they could reach the defensive perimeter set up by the Banner soldiers. She blasted the greenhides with fire, hovering over them for a second to ensure none escaped, then she beat her wings and ascended into the sky.

'Father,' she called, speeding towards Deathfang.

The huge grey dragon turned from the cliffside path he had been burning, a bright gleam in his eyes.

'Daughter! This fine morning has loosened up my old bones. To burn at will; to watch those vile greenhides die! What a joy!'

'Indeed, father,' said Frostback, circling closer. 'However, midday is approaching.'

'Already?'

'Yes, father.'

'I see. Very well. Speak to Halfclaw, and then the two of you should take a break – go and eat something; I believe the humans are supplying us with meals during the assault. Tarsnow and I will take our break when you return in an hour.'

'I shall do as you bid, father. We shall see you again in an hour.'

Frostback swooped back down the side of the cliffs. She spotted a rogue band of greenhides emerge from a tunnel entrance, and unleashed a short burst of flames that enveloped them, then she turned for Halfclaw.

'Frostback!' he cried, as she approached. 'How goes it?'

'My father has told us to take our midday break. We should return to Pella; I will inform the human leadership.'

'I will wait for you to do so, and then we shall fly to Pella together.'

Frostback circled lower round the harbour, then descended, landing on a tall outcrop of eroded rock. Banner forces had set up their command post nearby, and officers were funnelling soldiers towards the slowly-expanding front lines. As Kelsey looked down, she saw Jade kneeling by some wounded soldiers, and, next to them, were rows of bodies that had been covered in blankets. Van was directing the operation from a lookout point by the edge of the old harbour walls, his armour glinting in the sun.

'May I climb down, Frostback?' yelled Nurian. 'I can pass on the message that you and Halfclaw are going to Pella, and I want to report to my commanding officer.'

'You're leaving us?' said Kelsey.

He grinned at her. 'Only until you come back,' he said as he unfastened the buckles securing him to the harness; 'don't forget to pick me up when you return.'

'We shall come for you,' said Frostback.

Nurian clambered down from the side of the dragon, and ran off towards the command post, making his way through the dead and wounded. Frostback beat her wings again, and soared into the sky. She joined Halfclaw, who had been circling overhead, and they surged to the east, crossing the Straits. Kelsey looked back as they flew, watching the carnage and confusion recede into the distance, along with the noise and the smell.

'Have you grown tired of so much death yet, rider?' Frostback said to her.

'In a way,' she said. 'It's horrible to watch, but at the same time, witnessing the power of four dragons working together has been incredible. You must have killed hundreds of greenhides between you – maybe even thousands.'

'And yet they keep appearing from their filthy caverns and tunnels,' the silver dragon said; 'while there are thousands more up on the high ridge, skulking in the forest. This assault would be considerably easier if we were permitted to burn the forest down. Regardless, were it not for us dragons, the humans would have been slaughtered. I hope they are grateful.'

'I'm sure they are very grateful. Their biggest worry will be how many days they can keep you all here. They know that you could choose to leave them at any moment, and fly to the Eastern Mountains.'

'What about you, rider? Do you wish to travel to the Eastern Mountains? I fear that you will be lonely if we go – one human among a dozen dragons, two hundred miles away from any other humans.'

Kelsey didn't respond. She had been struggling with the idea of moving so far from the comforts and company of the City, but hadn't summoned the courage to expound her worries to Frostback.

'Perhaps Nurian could be enticed to come with us?' said Frostback. 'You two are well suited. I think he likes you. Have you considered him as a mate?'

Kelsey groaned. 'I do like him,' she said, 'but you know what my vision showed me. I thought you believed me?'

'I do believe you, rider. However, you cannot live your life on the basis of a single fragment of a vision.'

'It's two visions now; I had another one.'

'Involving Van?'

'Aye. Intimately.'

The two dragons cleared the Straits and soared over the wide bay. To their right was the gorgeous little town of Tara, while the streets of Ooste lay to their left.

'Smoke,' said Frostback. 'Parts of Ooste appear to be burning.'

Kelsey frowned at the thin columns of smoke rising from the town, then they had soared past it, the dragons speeding over the bay towards Pella. They crossed the shoreline and circled over Cuidrach Palace for a moment.

'We shall continue our discussion of Van and this second vision later, rider,' said Frostback as they descended.

A small group of guards were waiting for them in the ornamental gardens to the east of the palace buildings, and Frostback and Halfclaw landed amid the neat lines of flowerbeds and gravel paths. A wagon was pulled out from an out-building, and was guided by soldiers into the gardens.

'Welcome back, dragons,' said an officer in the Royal Guard as she approached. 'We have lunch prepared for you. Will the other two dragons be returning any time soon?'

'My father and Tarsnow will be here in an hour,' said Frostback.

'Perfect; thank you.'

Soldiers pulled the tarpaulin cover from the back of the wagon, revealing a great heap of raw meat. Next to the wagon was a long drinking trough, filled with fresh water, and Frostback drank, while Halfclaw pulled the carcass of a pig from the wagon and began to eat.

Kelsey climbed down from the harness and stretched her limbs on a gravel path. A soldier approached with a basket of food, and she took it, then sat on a bench overlooking the gardens.

'May I sit with you, Kelsey?'

She looked up, and saw the Queen standing close by. She had a thick coat wrapped round her shoulders to keep out the cold, but was still managing to look regal. Behind her, a squad of guards were keeping a close eye on the dragons as the giant beasts tore their way through lunch.

'Sure,' said Kelsey.

The Queen sat next to her on the bench. 'Please keep eating,' she said. 'I only wanted to see how you were.'

'Do you have demigods and suchlike watching what's been happening in Jezra?'

'We have, yes.'

'So far, so good,' said Kelsey; 'although I've seen a few casualties. The damn greenhides keep popping up all over the place.'

'You have been doing a magnificent job.'

Kelsey glanced at the Queen, and frowned. Despite Emily's calm demeanour, there was a tension around her eyes that Kelsey couldn't help but notice.

'You seem a little preoccupied, Queenie.'

'I do? Damn it. I was hoping to present a brave front.'

'What's up? Is it something to do with the fires in Ooste?'

'Yes. There is another little crisis I have to deal with.'

'On the same day as the start of the operation? Is that a coincidence?'

'No. It was planned that way to cause us the maximum amount of discomfort. I would ask, though, that you try not to think about it. I need the dragons to keep their focus on Jezra.'

'Does this "little crisis" affect them in any way?'

'It shouldn't, no. However, I wouldn't plan any more trips to the library within the Royal Academy any time soon, if I were you.'

Kelsey pursed her lips, then she blinked. She glanced around the gardens. Something about them seemed familiar, even though it was her first time there. Then it hit her. It was the location of the vision she had seen of her and Van with the baby, when they had been gazing lovingly into each other's eyes. The backdrop had been of the palace, and the pink sky fitted perfectly. She bit down on a rising sense of help-lessness; it could be months away; years even.

'Have you seen Princess Yendra fight?' the Queen asked.

'What? Oh, aye. I have. It's like watching my wee brother in action. The poor greenhides don't stand a chance. One difference though; I saw her get a wound on her leg from a greenhide talon, and she just shrugged it off. The next time I looked, it had healed completely. My brother recovers quickly, but he can't do that.'

Emily smiled. 'I want to have a few words with Frostback and Half-claw before you return to Jezra; if you'll excuse me?'

'Aye, no bother.'

The Queen stood, and Kelsey watched as she chatted to the two dragons for a couple of minutes. She finished her lunch and strode through the gardens, looking for the exact location of her vision. She found a pair of benches, and crouched, squinting at the view from the one facing the palace, trying to square it with what she had seen through Van's eyes.

'Rider!' called Frostback. 'It is time to return.'

Kelsey stood, brushed down her clothes and hurried back to Frostback. The Queen was standing back, her guards formed up by her side, and she smiled at Kelsey.

Kelsey gave her a wave, then climbed back up onto Frostback's shoulders and strapped herself in. Halfclaw took off first, his blue-streaked wings beating as he rose into the sky, then Frostback followed. Kelsey turned to speak to Nurian, then saw the empty space on the harness next to her and frowned. The young officer had become a constant presence in her life over the previous twenty days. Despite the traits they held in common, in some ways, they were quite dissimilar. He had retained an almost boyish enthusiasm, along with boundless amounts of curiosity and energy, and she sometimes felt a little jaded and cynical next to him. That's what Van was like – jaded and cynical. Yet she had found it much easier to be relaxed in Nurian's company, whereas every time she saw Van, all she could picture was the most recent vision of the two of them in bed together. Part of her wanted to shun Nurian, to turn her back on him before her feelings towards him had a chance to grow into something else. Was she leading him on, when deep within her heart she knew she would, at least for a time, be in love with Van? She had never been in a situation where two men had been interested in her at the same time, and she didn't like the way it made her feel. The cold air gusted round her as the two dragons sped off, and she tried to push all thoughts of Van and Nurian from her mind.

'I like the Queen,' said Frostback. 'I was unsure of her at first, but she appears to take the well-being of her subjects seriously. The King, on the other hand, has barely spoken a word to us dragons.'

Kelsey said nothing, trying to clear her thoughts as they soared back over the Straits. The weight of her visions felt like it was pushing down on her, constricting her chest. How much simpler life would have been if she had possessed battle-vision instead of her weird collection of powers. Then she could be more like Corthie; carefree and happy. At least, that was the impression her brother gave off; who knew what went through his mind?

The sight of Jezra approaching snapped her back to reality. Torrents of thick smoke were smearing the horizon, while ships were making their way in and out of the narrow channels that lay before the ruined harbour. For all the hours of fighting, she was surprised at how little of the town was under the control of the Banner forces. They had advanced to the old harbour wall, and were pushing iceward through the ruins to the cliffside, but the majority of Lower Jezra remained too dangerous.

'Halfclaw,' Frostback called out. 'Go to my father and tell him that we have returned, and I will land to pick up Nurian.'

He tilted his head towards her as they flew, then they separated – Halfclaw soaring up in the direction of the ridge at the top of the cliffs, while she descended. She pulled in her wings and landed on the same spot where Nurian had left them. A crowd of Banner officers were standing waiting for them, and Kelsey saw Yendra in their midst.

The god climbed the rocky outcrop. 'I hope you are feeling refreshed, Frostback,' she said when she had reached the top; 'and ready for another shift?'

'Indeed, I am,' said the silver dragon.

'I have a request to make.'

Frostback lowered her head until it was a foot away from Yendra's face. 'I'm listening.'

'My suggestion may cause offence,' said the god, 'but I deem it necessary under the circumstances.'

'Go on.'

The god glanced up at Kelsey. 'The underground tunnels are making it difficult for us to advance into the main part of Lower Jezra.

Wherever we go, more greenhides emerge from the darkness. The sweeps carried out by the dragons have been invaluable, but I feel that a greater amount of precision is required for the next stage.'

'And how would we achieve such precision?' said Frostback.

Yendra took a breath. 'By allowing Captain Nurian to fly upon your back, without Kelsey.'

'What?' cried Kelsey. 'You want me to stay on the ground while Nurian flies on Frostback?'

Yendra raised her palms. 'I understand that a rider has a bond with a dragon and I mean no disrespect. This is a purely tactical decision. If Nurian is alone on Frostback, I will be able to communicate directly with his mind, and direct the flames onto individual targets that might otherwise escape the notice of dragons in the air. Unfortunately, Kelsey, your ability to block powers is hampering our efforts to clear certain pockets of greenhides. It is only temporary.'

'How is it only temporary? Won't you want to do the same tomorrow?'

'I have another suggestion for that.' She turned back to Frostback. 'How would Halfclaw feel about wearing a harness? If he agrees, then as from tomorrow, Nurian could ride upon Halfclaw, and your rider will be returned to you. I have no wish to come between you and Kelsey, but can you see a better solution?'

'I am not happy about this, god.'

'I understand that, but will you do it for the greater good? One afternoon without your rider, that is all I ask.'

The dragon's eyes burned. 'No, you are also asking that Halfclaw wears a harness. He may refuse.'

'He may. If that happens, then we can have a further discussion. For the rest of today, though, I would request that you allow Nurian to ride alone. It will save the lives of many Banner soldiers.'

Kelsey glanced down from the dragon's shoulders. The group of Banner officers were close enough to have heard the conversation, and they were gazing up, waiting for a decision. Among them, Van and Nurian were standing, and Kelsey felt a creeping sense of humiliation come over her. She had achieved something remarkable – persuading a wild dragon to select her as a rider, and now she was going to have to dismount in front of everyone, and pass her dragon into the hands of someone else. On her homeworld, and on Lostwell, her powers had been fought over, but in the City, they were utterly useless. She was a hindrance to the operation; a liability rather than an asset.

Frostback turned to face her. 'This suggestion displeases me, but I can see the utility of it. However, I will not allow it unless you give your consent, my rider.'

'What do you think Halfclaw will say about tomorrow?'

'I shall do my best to persuade him, rider. I am not completely oblivious to his feelings towards me, and I suspect he will do as I suggest.'

'So, it would just be for the rest of today?'

'I would hope so. At least I am used to Nurian. Do you consent?'

Kelsey scowled. 'Fine,' she muttered, unbuckling the straps holding her to the harness. She tried to ignore the watching faces as she climbed down from the dragon's shoulders, but she could feel their gazes upon her.

Yendra nodded to her as she reached the rocky surface of the outcrop. 'You have my thanks, Kelsey. I realise that this must be hard for you, and ask that you think of the lives your sacrifice will save.'

Kelsey said nothing, shame burning her cheeks.

Nurian clambered up to the top of the outcrop. He looked a little embarrassed when he glanced at Kelsey, but she found it hard to blame him for it. He was Banner; he obeyed orders.

'When you are in the air, Captain,' said Yendra, 'wait for my signal. I will be in a forward position, by the foundations of the old palace, and will contact you from there.' She turned to the dragon. 'I will imprint into Nurian's mind each location I wish you to target. Halfclaw and the others can continue as before, but you shall strike the specific areas that I indicate.' She took a step back. 'Good luck.'

Nurian climbed up the leather straps fastened to Frostback's flank, and sat in the centre saddle. The dragon tilted her head towards Kelsey, then rose into the sky, and Kelsey had to fight back the feeling that she was about to burst into tears. She must not show weakness, she said to herself, trying to channel her some of her mother's iron will. Yendra offered her a hand to help her climb down the outcrop, but she ignored it, and scrambled down to the ground on her own. Yendra followed her, then addressed the officers.

'I shall strike directly ahead, and make for the ruins of the palace. Allow no one to advance to my position until Frostback has secured the area.' She turned to Kelsey. 'Miss Holdfast, I must ask that you stay at the rear, to ensure that there is a hundred yards between us.'

Kelsey nodded, but said nothing.

Yendra set off, the officers clearing a path for her as she hurried towards the centre of the town. The officers watched for a moment, then got back to work.

'Thank you,' said a voice.

Kelsey turned, and saw Van next to her.

'That couldn't have been easy,' he went on, 'but you did the right thing.'

'Shut up, Van. I wouldn't be surprised if this was your idea. Was it?'

'It doesn't matter whose idea it was.'

'You just couldn't bear to see me happy; you had to interfere.'

Van frowned. 'I'm not jealous of you and Nurian.'

Kelsey laughed. 'I wasn't even thinking of that; I was talking about you splitting me and Frostback up. But, if you say so.'

Van paused, looking as though he were trying to choose his words carefully. 'I want you to be happy.'

'No, you don't. If you did, then you wouldn't have abandoned me the moment we arrived in the City.'

'I thought we'd been over this?' he said, getting angry. 'Yes, that's right; we discussed it, and I thought we were starting to get on again, and then you slapped me in the face for no reason.' He took a breath. 'I have to get back to the command post to coordinate the next stage of the landings. Goodbye.'

'Hey!' she cried, and started to follow him. 'I hadn't finished.'

He turned on his heels. 'Don't come after me; you have to stay back here, out of range of Yendra, so she can use her powers. Don't move from this area; understand?'

She glared at him as he strode away, her rage bubbling under the surface.

'That's the first time I've ever seen him angry,' said Jade, who was approaching her. 'He really doesn't like you, you know. I can tell.'

'Shut up, you crazy witch.'

Jade smirked. 'It's not my fault that no one likes you. It's your fault; you're rude and unpleasant. And it's not my fault that you have nothing useful to contribute to the operation. Poor little Kelsey, despised and alone. As for calling me a "crazy witch," I suggest you look in a mirror if you want to see one of those. Oh, and while you're gazing at your reflection, it might be a good idea to tidy your appearance; you're a mess. No wonder Van doesn't like you. Now, if you'll excuse me, I have to heal more wounded soldiers, though I will have to touch each one of them, as your malign powers are polluting the air. Feel free to stand around here uselessly, while I save some lives.'

Kelsey clenched her fist and punched Jade on the chin. The demigod's head flinched back an inch, then she shrieked and fell to the ground, clutching her face.

'She hit me!' the demigod cried, and every soldier in the vicinity turned to watch.

'Get up,' muttered Kelsey, standing over her. 'You're a damned demigod; heal yourself.'

A couple of soldiers ran over and helped Jade to her feet.

'Are you alright, ma'am?' said one.

'Yes, thank you, boys,' said Jade, 'though I'd feel safer a little further away from Miss Holdfast.'

She strode along the ruined harbour front, her long dark green robes trailing over the rough ground of the ruins.

Kelsey stood motionless for a moment, her eyes on the ground. Around her, soldiers were moving back and forth – some heading forwards to the front lines, others moving to the rear for a break in the action. Several looked exhausted, while to the right, a line of walking wounded were being administered to by Jade. Others were taking doses of salve; the substance healing them in seconds, and filling their eyes with a lust for battle. One soldier hobbled by on a makeshift crutch, and Kelsey got out of the way to let him pass. She knew that, somewhere overhead, Frostback was flying with Nurian on her shoulders, but she couldn't bring herself to look up. Instead, she climbed back up onto the top of the rocky outcrop and turned to gaze at the waters of the Straits.

Her rage slowly started to subside as she watched the waves hit the ruins of the harbour. Yendra's suggestion had made sense, and she knew that the princess was only doing what she thought was best for the success of the operation, but it hurt. Feeling more alone than ever, she made sure that no one else could see her, then she allowed herself to cry in silence.

She knew her mother would chide her for her tears, but she didn't care.

She wanted to go home.

CHAPTER 15

CORRUPTIBLE

Salt Quay, The Bulwark, The City – 5th Yordian 3420

Kagan shivered on the low mattress, a cold draft blowing between the gaps in the wooden window frame. He pulled his blanket over him and tried to keep his eyes open. Over two hundred men were sleeping in the dilapidated old barracks, and a dozen of them were keeping a close watch on Kagan, waiting for him to fall asleep so they could... well, he wasn't sure what they had cooked up, but he wasn't going to give them the chance to put their plan into operation.

The entire Eleventh Brigade had been loaded onto wagons the previous evening and transported sunward, arriving at Salt Quay as the sun was setting. The enormous, walled-off port had many old stone warehouses and barrack blocks, and men from his brigade had been shoved into one, and then the doors had been closed and locked.

Kagan had been released from the holding pen in Camp Twenty-Four just prior to the wagons being loaded. He had spent four miserable days there, cut off from any contact with his old crew, and he was hungry, thirsty and exhausted. He peered through the grimy window. Outside, there was nothing to see but the wall of another block, but the sky was growing pinker and brighter by the second. He took a breath. He had survived the night. Men were starting to stir in their beds, and a few were queuing at the door to the toilets, their expressions haggard. Every man knew that they were going to be sailing that day; they had all seen the flotilla of ships docked in the harbour. They would be crossing the twenty miles of sea to land at Jezra, where they would be expected to begin the process of constructing a defensive barrier around the town, and the atmosphere in the barracks was one of grim foreboding.

Sensing the men awakening around them, the dozen Torduans who had been watching Kagan throughout the night slipped away to their own beds, and Kagan let out a breath in relief. He had lain fully-dressed all night, with his boots on, in case he had needed to fight or run. Despite the clothes, he had never been so cold. Frost had formed on the outside of the window, and he could see a plume of breath whenever he exhaled. Even in the worst winter he could remember in Alea Tanton, the cold had never bitten so deep. He swung his legs off the bed and scratched his face. He needed a shave. The holding pen had, for obvious reasons, banned the use of any blade, and his stubble was now five days old.

For some reason, his mother popped into his mind. She had died a couple of years previously, after a short but awful illness. He had been living in Dizzler's tenement at the time, but had visited every day during her final month, and had watched her rapid descent. He had been tormented in the days after her death by one thought – that there were gods living in Old Alea who possessed the power to have healed her, but they hadn't. They never did. Mortals were nothing to them. It had been then that Kagan had developed a strong hatred for the gods of Lostwell, a hatred he could feel transferring to those who ruled the City. He had begun to see the Blades in much the same way that he had regarded the Banner soldiers who protected Old Alea – oppressive bullies who carried out the orders of their tyrant masters. In some ways, the City was worse - the authorities of Alea Tanton had never corralled them in camps, or forced them to join an expedition that was bound to lead to a massacre. He was glad his mother hadn't lived long enough to end up a refugee. Without any skills that the City valued, she would have been heading to Jezra along with her son.

He stood, and joined the queue for the toilets. The men around him edged away, keeping their distance. They all knew that his officer rank had been stripped from him, and they all knew that the Torduan gang had marked him for death, and no one wanted to be close to him if something happened. Kagan found himself not caring what anyone thought, his mind fixated on how he could get away from Salt Quay, and the boats that were due to leave for Jezra. The City was small, but he had heard that there were places to hide in the Circuit.

He sensed movement behind him, but the wooden bat smacked down on his head before he could react. He fell to the floorboards, his arms instinctively moving up to protect his face as the kicks and blows rained down on him. So, this was how it ended, he thought; beaten to death in a cold barracks, alone and friendless.

A whistle blast ripped through the air, and the blows stopped. Kagan heard footsteps run from him, and then the sound of heavy boots approaching. A hand gripped his shoulder, and he flinched, then opened his eyes.

'Kagan from Camp Twenty-Four?'

He squinted at the soldiers, the pain in the back of his head making it hard to see. He nodded.

'On your feet,' said the Blade; 'you're coming with us.'

Kagan heard mutters from the other refugees as soldiers pulled him up.

'Where are you taking him?' said one of the Torduans.

'None of your business,' snapped a Blade.

The four soldiers hauled Kagan down the central aisle of the barracks, passing the rows of bunk beds.

'I hope you hang the Shinstran rat!' cried someone, but the Blades ignored him. They reached the entrance and brought Kagan outside. Without a word, they pulled him across a forecourt that led towards the harbour front. Kagan tried to walk, but his head was splitting, and he kept stumbling. The harbour was quiet, with just a few soldiers on patrol, but no one seemed to pay any attention to the small group leading Kagan. They came to a long, stone wharf, then descended a set of steps to a narrow jetty. A fishing vessel was tied up, and the crew were watching from the deck.

A man stepped out of the wheelhouse and jumped the small gap to the jetty. He frowned, then peered at Kagan.

'Are you sure this is him?'

'As sure as we can be,' said a soldier. 'It was the right barrack block, and he identified himself as the target. He was also in the process of getting the crap kicked out of him.'

The man nodded. He reached out and gripped Kagan by the chin. 'What's your name, son?'

'Kagan,' he said, his voice sounding strange to his own ears.

The man turned back to the boat. 'Bring out the other one.'

There was movement on the deck that Kagan couldn't make out. A hatch opened and a figure emerged.

'Girl,' said the man; 'can you confirm the identity of this person?'

There was a gasp. 'It's Kagan. What have you done to him?'

Somewhere in Kagan's brain, he registered the owner of the voice – Elena.

'We didn't touch him,' said one of the Blades; 'we rescued him; they were going to kill him.'

'Get him on the boat,' said the man.

Kagan was dragged over to the side of the jetty, then he felt himself being lowered onto the deck of the vessel. Elena crouched down next to him, and placed her hand on his face.

'Are you alright?' she said.

He tried to focus on her eyes.

Next to them on the jetty, the man handed something over to the four soldiers, who took it and disappeared back up the steps to the wharf.

The man jumped onto the boat. 'Cast off. Take us to Port Sanders.'

Kagan felt the motion of the boat beneath him increase. He had never been on a boat before, and the movement felt like a slow earthquake. He sensed the man kneel by his other side. He was holding something in his hand, and he brought it close to Kagan's face.

'Lift his head,' he said to Elena.

She pushed her hands under Kagan's hair and raised his face a little, then the man poured a drop of something onto Kagan's tongue. A fierce burning sensation gripped Kagan, starting in his throat, but working its way through his entire body. He began to convulse.

'What's happening?' cried Elena.

'Don't worry; it's salve. He'll be fine in a moment.'

Kagan spluttered, imagining that he was about to die – then all pain ceased. He felt a golden glow of well-being fill every part of his body. He opened his eyes again. Everything seemed brighter, more full of life. He glimpsed Elena's worried face, and smiled at her, a broad and genuine smile of relief.

'See?' said the man. 'He's probably fitter now than he's been in years.'

Kagan turned to him. 'Who are you?'

'The name's Albeck, son.'

'Albeck?' said Kagan, sitting up on the deck. 'Should we know you?'

'Not likely,' the man said. 'Let's just say that a mutual friend asked me to collect you both from Salt Quay, and for now, we'll say no more.'

The three of them stood. Elena made as if to help support Kagan, but he was able to stand unaided. In fact, he felt able to run. He took Elena's hand, feeling the warmth of her skin against his.

'This is amazing,' he said. 'I feel great.' He laughed and looked at the view. The little boat had left the breakwaters of Salt Quay harbour, and had turned to the west. The sun had yet to rise, but the sky to their left was a dazzling pink, with streaks of deep red. The sea stretched out before them, reflecting the resplendent colours of the approaching dawn. Gulls were circling over the boat, calling out, and, to Kagan, it was if he was hearing them for the first time. After so many days of listless torpor, he felt alive, and alert; awake at last.

He blinked. 'We're not going to Jezra?'

Albeck chuckled. 'No, son. The rest of the refugees will be getting loaded onto the ships in the next hour or so, but you and Elena here won't be joining them. We're off to Port Sanders.'

It occurred to Kagan that what they had just done was probably illegal. He glanced at the small crew of the fishing boat.

'Don't worry about them, son,' said Albeck. 'Each one of them's been paid to keep their mouths shut. Times are tough, and there's not many who would refuse a little extra to line their pockets.'

'Your accent; you're not a Blade.'

'Clearly,' Albeck said, smiling. 'No, I'm of the Evader tribe, myself. Funny, this time last year, I would never have been able just to get a boat from Port Sanders – the local militia would have stopped me before I'd gotten to within a hundred yards of the harbour; but now? Thanks to the new King and Queen, us Evaders can travel about Medio unhindered, with no questions asked. Ironic, eh? The freedoms of the new regime have allowed me to break the laws of the new regime. Still, it was an act of mercy, as far as I can see, saving you two from the green-hides at Jezra.'

'We're very grateful,' said Elena. 'Thank you.'

'Don't be thanking me, girl; thank the one who paid me to come and get you.'

'Who was that?'

Albeck tapped his nose. 'Never you mind about that for the moment. Let's get you safely to Port Sanders first.'

The voyage took less than an hour, and the sun was splitting the horizon as the vessel turned into the harbour of Port Sanders. The docks were far larger than those at Salt Quay, and a multitude of small fishing vessels were tied up at the many piers that snaked out into the calm harbour basin. Behind the waterfront rose the most beautiful town Kagan had ever seen. Rows of tall, painted houses with red roofs, and a palace with dozens of narrow spires that reached over the town. A market was bustling by the harbour, its stalls opening with the dawn light. The crew of the vessel lowered the sail, and they slowed as they approached the end of a long pier. The boat bumped against the wooden side of the pier and one of the crew jumped out to secure the ropes.

Albeck nodded to the crew, then led Kagan and Elena onto the pier.

'Keep your heads down,' he said, as they walked towards the busy wharf ahead of them. 'No offence, but the pair of you look like refugees, and your accents will give you away. Just keep quiet and follow my lead.'

Despite the warning, no one on the wharf paid them any attention. Fishing vessels were being made ready to set out, and the market stalls were already doing busy trade. Everywhere Kagan looked, he could see wealth. The clothes worn by the locals were well made, and the women had gold necklaces and earrings, while the market sold a range of food that Kagan had never seen before – bizarre sea creatures with red shells and sharp claws. His stomach began to rumble, despite the unfamiliarity of the goods on display.

Albeck led them through the market and up a street that rose on a steady incline away from the harbour. He took a left, and they entered a dense warren of tightly-packed streets, where flowers of a dozen vibrant colours adorned each window. The tenements on either side of the road were clean and well-maintained, and Kagan had a glimpse of what Alea Tanton could have been like, had only the gods of Lostwell cared about the people under their rule. Albeck selected a narrow, winding back-street, and took a set of keys from a pocket.

'Remember how to get here,' he said to Kagan and Elena, as he unlocked the door.

They entered a tenement close, and ascended the stairs to the top floor. Albeck knocked twice upon a green door, then waited.

A woman opened the door, glanced around the landing, then moved to the side to let them in.

'Good morning, all,' Albeck said. 'I have a delivery.'

Kagan glanced around the large apartment they had entered. It was how he had imagined the houses in Old Alea to have looked. The ceilings were high, and the rooms felt airy and spacious, while the furniture and décor reeked of money. A dozen men and women were sitting around on long couches in a large room, and Kagan frowned as he realised he recognised a couple of them from Alea Tanton.

A man stood, his face breaking into a wide grin.

'Sister!' he yelled, hurrying towards Elena and hugging her close.

Kagan gasped. 'Dizzler?'

The man turned to Kagan. 'That's right, my boy; did you think I had abandoned you? My own sister, and my loyal second-in-command? Not likely.' He grasped Kagan's hand and shook it, as the others in the room watched. 'Come on, take a seat.' He clicked his fingers. 'Food; bring them some breakfast; they must be starving. After that, we'll sort out baths and fresh clothes, and get down to business.'

There was a dining table next to a wide bay window overlooking the town, and Dizzler led Kagan and Elena to it. Albeck followed, and sat next to them.

'All go well?' Dizzler asked him.

'No hitches, boss,' said Albeck. 'Calm and smooth.'

'You're a good man,' Dizzler grinned.

One of the others started bringing plates and bowls of food to the table, while another poured white wine from a large jug.

Dizzler nodded to Kagan and Elena. 'You eat; I'll talk.'

Kagan didn't wait for any other instruction. The food sitting before him was making his mouth water, and his stomach was groaning in anticipation. He picked up a fork and attacked the food.

Dizzler laughed. 'Least you've still got your appetite, eh? That's my boy. Listen, first things first; for the purposes of the local law enforcement officers, you are now both Evaders – got it? I've been in Medio for over a month now, and I've made some friends in that time. As you probably know, the greenhides tore a swathe through this part of the City – hundreds of thousands dead, terrible; shocking. But, that has left certain opportunities open for men and women like us. When I first got here, there were only a tiny handful of Shinstrans living in Medio – hiding out in the slums of the Circuit, or working as skilled tradesfolk, but now I'm looking after a crew of over eighty former Bloodflies; and let me tell you, my crew is in demand. The gangs here suffered massive losses from the greenhides, and we, my friends, are here to fill the vacuum.' He watched them eat for a moment. 'It does pain me how long it took to get you both out. After the Blades reorganised the camps into brigades, they were watching the place like hawks, and I had to wait until you were in Salt Quay before I could act. But, this isn't Alea Tanton, and the Blades are not the same as the Banners. Turns out that Blades are just as corruptible as anyone else in the City.' He laughed. 'Imagine trying to bribe a Banner sergeant? They'd have you in chains before you could blink, but not the Blades; they're amateurs in comparison with what we're used to. And the Sander and Evader militia are so unprofessional that I'm almost embarrassed for them. We've pulled off over a dozen robberies in the last month, with some pretty decent hauls, and no one's come close to catching us.'

Kagan pushed his plate away. The food had been strange, but he had enjoyed every last mouthful of it.

Dizzler grinned at him. 'So, are you up for a job?'

'You know me, boss,' he said; 'I'm up for anything.'

'Did you hear that?' Dizzler asked the room. 'That's my boy. There's a job been brewing for a few days, and as soon as it came up, I immediately thought of you two. It's not going to be your straightforward robbery – some subterfuge and deception will also be required – and a little patience. There will also be perks, but after your stretch in the camps, I think you deserve it.'

'Is it in the Circuit?' said Kagan.

'No. It's right here, in Port Sanders. Two vacancies have recently opened up at the mansion of this rich lady. She had four staff working for her, but two of them seem to have done a runner; there's been no sign of them for a while, and her ladyship is looking for new folk to replace them. And get this – she only wants folk from Khatanax.'

Kagan raised an eyebrow. 'Why?'

'Because that's where she's from. She's a refugee, just like us. And she's loaded.'

'How? I mean, if she arrived the same way as we did; how does she have any money?'

Dizzler frowned, as if this had never occurred to him. 'Eh, I don't know. Does it matter? Either way, she's become one of the richest folk in Port Sanders, but she likes to keep a low profile. Here's what we're going to do. This afternoon, Albeck will take you to her mansion for an interview. I need both of you to be at your most polite and professional; we've got smart clothes already sorted for you. Get the jobs, and then you'll move into the mansion. After that, we'll be in touch. Learn what you can about the workings of the mansion; all the ways in and out, and her ladyship's routine, and make sure you do a good job. Kagan – you're up for the role of bodyguard, and Elena – you'll be the junior house-keeper. The two other staff there are older, and they might be a problem – I want you to work out a way to neutralise them.'

'Are they Shinstrans?'

'Nah,' Dizzler said; 'one's a Torduan, the other's Fordian.'

Kagan grimaced. 'A Fordian?'

'Yeah. I know, I know, but you're both going to have to hold your noses and get on with it. Working alongside those two assholes will be difficult, but if this woman is as rich as she's supposed to be, it'll all be worth it in the end.

'Is she from Alea Tanton?

'Nope. She hails from the Southern Cape. I think she was on some sort of business trip to Old Alea when the whole place went to shit. From what I hear, she doesn't care if you're Shinstran or Torduan or whatever, as long as you're from Khatanax. I guess she doesn't trust the locals, eh?' He smiled. 'Well? What do you say?'

Kagan thought for a moment. His circumstances had utterly changed from where he had been only a few short hours before, but he felt energised, and ready for anything.

He nodded. 'Count me in.'

———

The sun was starting to set as Albeck led them along the streets of Port Sanders. Kagan and Elena had rested throughout the day, washing the stench of the camps from their skin, and dressing in smart new clothes. A hairdresser had called round at the apartment after lunch, and had trimmed and styled Elena's locks into the fashion of the local women in Port Sanders, while Kagan's hair had been cut short, and he had been given a proper shave. Looking at their reflections before leaving, he had been amazed at the transformation. He and Elena looked respectable, like a pair of decent, hard-working youths. Dizzler had given them both new coats, lined with thick wads of cotton to keep out the cold, and it was the most elegantly tailored item of clothing that Kagan had ever worn.

As they strolled along the streets, Kagan seemed to be looking at everything with fresh eyes. Somewhere in his mind, he knew that he had faced death that very morning, but the atmosphere in Port Sanders seemed designed to lift his spirits.

They came to a gap in the road, and Albeck pointed towards the sea, where a line of ships was sailing on the horizon.

'More brigades,' he said, 'heading for Jezra. The first boats left this morning, so that lot are probably the last of them.'

Kagan stopped for a moment to gaze at the ships in the distance.

'That could have been us,' whispered Elena, taking Kagan's hand.

Albeck coughed. 'None of that; no hand-holding. You're not supposed to be a couple. In fact, it's better if you pretend to hardly know each other. Let's say that you knew of each other, if you're asked, but that you're not close. Got it?'

Elena withdrew her hand with a frown.

'If we're supposed to be Evaders,' said Kagan, 'then she won't hire us.'

'You're Shinstrans for the interview. If you don't get the jobs, then you're back to being Evaders.'

'What's she like; this woman?' said Elena.

A smile flickered across Albeck's face. 'Wait and see.'

They came to a street with large mansions running down either side, and Kagan almost gasped. Each house was as large as a tenement, and had high walls surrounding them. A few citizens were out on their balconies despite the cold weather.

'The greenhides never got as far as here,' said Albeck, his eyes tightening a little; 'they were too busy eating the Evaders.'

He led them to the gates of a huge mansion. Two local militia were patrolling the street, and they stopped Albeck, Kagan and Elena as they were about to pass through the gates. Albeck showed them some identification papers, and explained about the job vacancies. The militia waved them past, and went back to their patrol, while Albeck led Kagan and Elena up the path to the front doors of the mansion. He knocked, and they waited.

When the door opened, Kagan saw a green-skinned woman standing in the entranceway, her eyes scanning them with suspicion.

'Good evening,' said Albeck, bowing. 'I am from the Board of Refugees. My two clients here have an appointment with her ladyship regarding the job vacancies.'

The Fordian narrowed her eyes. 'Let me hear them speak.'

'My name is Kagan, and I'm from Alea Tanton.'

'I'm Elena, from the Shinstran district.'

The Fordian nodded, then opened the door wider to let them in. As they entered, Kagan noticed Albeck slip the green-skinned woman a small bag of silver. She tucked it into her robes and led them to a large reception room on the ground floor.

'Wait here,' she said. 'Elena, Kagan, you will be called for one at a time. Make yourselves comfortable.'

The three of them sat on a luxurious couch as the Fordian left the room and closed the door.

'Her name is Gellie,' Albeck said. 'She's the senior housekeeper. Be careful around her. She might take the odd bribe, but she's loyal to her mistress.'

'And the Torduan?' said Kagan.

'He's the cook and gardener. A miserable bastard by the name of Saul. Stay out of his way, if you can.'

'What about the two who ran away?' said Elena.

'Both were Torduans, like Saul. I wouldn't be surprised if the mad old cook chopped them up and put them in a stew for her ladyship.'

'And the lady herself?' said Kagan. 'What's her name?'

'Sofia.'

Kagan nodded. He glanced around the chamber. Rich tapestries hung from two of the walls, and a thick, warm carpet was underfoot. He felt like he was in a palace, the room being bigger than his mother's entire apartment in Alea Tanton.

The door opened and Gellie entered. 'Mister Kagan, if you would please follow me?'

Kagan glanced at Elena, then stood and followed the Fordian woman out into the hall.

'I understand that you have experience of guard duty?' she said, as they ascended a wide flight of stairs.

'That's right, ma'am.'

'And you are literate?'

'Yes, ma'am. Self-taught.'

Gellie nodded, then escorted Kagan to a door. She knocked once, and entered. Inside was a plush little study, with bookshelves lining the walls, and a window that looked out towards the harbour in the distance. Kagan's attention drifted from the view, and he caught sight of a woman sitting next to a low table. He blinked. She was the most beautiful woman he had ever seen. She stood, and he almost stepped back, conscious that he was staring.

She smiled. 'Kagan, I presume?'

'Uh... yes. Yes, ma'am.'

'Leave us, Gellie. I have a few questions for our applicant.'

The senior housekeeper bowed and left the room, closing the door behind her.

Lady Sofia gestured to a chair. 'Let us not stand on ceremony. Take a seat and tell me why I should employ you.'

Kagan sat. His mouth was dry, and he felt almost over-awed by how beautiful she was. He took a breath. Stay calm. Be professional – you need this job.

'I am loyal and hard-working,' he said, 'and I have experience of guarding people.'

'How old are you?'

'Nineteen, ma'am, but I had what you might call a hard upbringing.'

'I see. You are from the Shinstran district of Alea Tanton, is that correct?'

'It is.'

'Were you part of the mob who invaded Old Alea?'

He hesitated. A lie would seem to be in order, but something about the woman told him that she would see through him in an instant.

'I was. When the city began to be destroyed, I ascended the ramp and entered Old Alea. If I hadn't, I would be dead.'

'Quite. Were you involved with the gangs in Alea Tanton?'

'Yes, ma'am. The Bloodflies. They were my family in Alea Tanton, and I don't want to try to mislead you about my past. However, everything has changed, and here we are. I want to make a new life; a better one. I may have done some things in Alea Tanton that I'm not proud of, but even there, I was always loyal to those I worked for.'

'Do you think you deserve a second chance?'

'Does anyone, ma'am? If someone tries to change, can they be redeemed? I hope so, otherwise the future of many refugees will be bleak. If you employ me, I will devote myself to being the best guard you could have. I'm reliable, and I don't drink too much, and I'm good in a fight. I can also read and write.'

'Yes; I know. If you weren't literate, you wouldn't be sitting here.'

'May I ask a question, ma'am?'

A flicker of a smile settled on her lips. 'Of course.'

'I can see that you are rich, ma'am, but what I don't understand is how you managed to bring your wealth to the City. I saw servants and staff in their nightclothes when we first arrived.'

'Did you also arrive in the clothes you were in?'

'Yes, ma'am.'

'And, whatever happened to be in your pockets at the time, did it also come with you?'

He frowned. 'Yes, ma'am.'

'Then it shouldn't be too difficult to understand. I was in Old Alea on a business trip, hoping to organise a deal for the goods in the Southern Cape I was trying to sell. When the waves hit the city, I tried to escape, but the gates were sealed. My servants fled, and the carriage I ordered failed to arrive. I was making my way on foot, alone, through the streets of Old Alea when we were all whisked here. In my right hand, I had been carrying a suitcase; a suitcase full of the valuables I was able to rescue from the apartment in Old Alea where I had been residing. That suitcase was all that stood between me and the refugee camps. I bribed a few officials, and ended up in Port Sanders. Within a day, I had the local militia at my door, demanding to know how it could be that I had so much gold – and I told them the same story I have just told you. I made a considerable donation to the coffers of Port Sanders, and that seemed to do the trick, as they have left me in peace ever since.'

She smiled again. 'Does that satisfy you, Mister Kagan?'

He felt a twinge of embarrassment for having broached the subject, and glanced away. 'Apologies, ma'am.'

'Oh, don't be silly. It was a perfectly reasonable question to ask, and the fact that you had the sense and courage to ask it speaks well in your favour. Stand up for me, and take your coat off.'

He got to his feet, and laid the coat on the back of the chair.

'Turn around,' she said.

He did so, feeling her eyes upon him. He swallowed.

She nodded. 'Good. Sit. Thank you. Now, tell me about the girl. Elena, I believe she is called? Would she make a reliable junior housekeeper?'

'I don't know much about her, to be honest, ma'am; but I believe so, from what I've heard.'

'I noticed that she looks the same age as you, Kagan. If I were to employ both of you, I do have a condition, a condition that applies to all of my staff. You are not to engage in any romantic relationship with her, not if you are living under my roof. Is that clear?'

'Perfectly, ma'am.'

She got up and walked to the window. As she stood gazing out at the view, Kagan kept his eyes on her. She didn't look much older than he was; maybe twenty-one? And yet, she seemed to have a confidence and self-assurance beyond her years. Was that what the privileges of wealth and beauty gave you? His thoughts drifted to Elena. She wouldn't be pleased about the 'no relationship' rule, but Kagan didn't care. The more he looked at Lady Sofia, the more he realised how much he wanted the job. Not for Dizzler, not for the gangs, and not for Elena, but just so he could spend his time in Sofia's company.

She turned to him and smiled. 'Alright. I'll give you a month in the role. If you please me, we can see about making it permanent.'

'Thank you, ma'am,' he grinned. 'I won't let you down.'

CHAPTER 16

PANDERING TO THE ENEMY

J ezra, The Western Bank – 5th Yordian 3420

Yendra watched as the first load of refugees disembarked onto the ruined harbour of Jezra. Three full brigades, numbering three thousand mortals from Lostwell, were spilling out from the ships, to be herded forward by the Banner forces on duty. The first task of the refugee work groups would be to secure the defences of the harbour itself, while the soldiers would push ahead into the areas cleared by the dragons.

The greenhides had taken back much of the town overnight, but Yendra had been relaxed about it; it had been foreseen. The four dragons couldn't patrol night and day, and the Banner forces had pulled back to a defensible perimeter at sunset. Each dragon had been assigned to a different part of the night, and had remained close to the soldiers, keeping the worst of the attacks at bay. Come the dawn, Yendra and Van had three dragons at their disposal again, and the advance had restarted. Kelsey may have glowered and frowned, but the new tactics had worked better than Yendra could have hoped. With Nurian on the shoulders of a dragon, she had been able to direct the previous afternoon's attacks with far more efficiency than before.

Yendra glanced up. As of that morning, Nurian had been riding on

Halfclaw's shoulders, the green and blue dragon proving himself willing to wear a harness. This had allowed Kelsey to return to Frostback, but the mood of the young Holdfast woman had barely improved, especially after Yendra had asked her to ensure that she and Frostback kept at least a hundred yards away from wherever Halfclaw was flying. Consequently, Frostback had been confined to patrolling the paths that ran down from the high ridge into Lower Jezra, and Yendra had hardly seen Kelsey all morning.

Deathfang had taken responsibility for sweeping over the main part of the ruins that day, with Tarsnow resting after his predawn shift. The huge grey dragon was soaring over the remnants of the ancient palace, creating a long buffer of flames, while Halfclaw was striking individual targets closer to the harbour.

Next to the command post, refugees were assembling a row of mobile cranes under the watchful eye of Banner soldiers, while others were unloading bricks from the ships. Thousands of bricks had been ordered for the operation, and they were already being used to seal up the gaps in the frail ruins surrounding the harbour.

Yendra strode along the waterfront with Jade by her side, inspecting the new arrivals as they piled off the ships. Many of the refugees looked terrified, and a few were trembling in the cold wind that gusted across the Straits. Their officers were young, she noted, and several were trying without success to cajole their comrades forwards. Some of the refugees were staring open-mouthed at the sight of Yendra and Jade. Yendra was dressed in her full battle armour, and stood taller than any of the mortals, while Jade had wrapped herself in dark green robes, and had a sinister air to her that she made no effort to allay.

She saw Van approach.

'Good morning, ma'am,' he said; 'good to see you back from the front. How was it?'

'It went very well, Major,' said Yendra. 'Nurian is a fast learner, and so is Halfclaw for that matter. They did a splendid job. We should make good progress today.'

Van nodded. 'I hope so, ma'am; otherwise there won't be enough room to fit the work brigades. I believe there are a further twelve thousand refugees due to land today?'

'That's right, Major. This is just the first three brigades.'

'If we don't push the greenhides back to the base of the cliffs, then we might have to keep some of the brigades aboard their ships tonight, rather than risk them sleeping in undefended areas.'

'We shall reach the cliffs today, Major. The schedule cannot slip.'

'Yes, ma'am.'

A voice appeared in her mind. *Your Highness, apologies for interrupting.*

Yendra frowned. 'One moment, please, Major. My nephew, Lord Salvor, wishes to discuss something with me.'

She turned away, and gazed out towards the Straits.

Yes, Salvor?

As I said, apologies for interrupting. I have been asked by their Majesties to contact you about a rather urgent matter.

Go on.

Yesterday morning, just after the operation had set out for Jezra, Prince Montieth sent his forces into Ooste, and he is currently occupying the town with five thousand soldiers.

Yendra clenched her fists. *Montieth is in Ooste?*

Yes, your Highness.

And this happened yesterday? Why wasn't I informed at once?

Their Majesties felt it would be better to allow you to lead the operation free from distractions. But now that you have had a day in which to oversee the retaking of Jezra, they wished to let you know.

What are his demands? What does my brother want with Ooste?

There have been no demands from Prince Montieth, your Highness; in fact, there has been no direct communication with anyone in Ooste since the troops moved in. However, thanks to the testimony of Chancellor Mona, we strongly suspect that his motive is the mine behind the Royal Palace. It appears that the prince has run out of salve.

Yendra took a moment to control her anger. *What are my orders? What do their Majesties wish me to do?*

Prince Montieth has indicated that he will only speak with you, your Highness. Their Majesties ask if you can spare a few hours today to talk to your brother, but they made it clear that you were not to consider this an order. They wish you to make the decision, based upon the situation in Jezra. If you feel that it is imperative that you stay in person, then their Majesties wish you to do so.

I see.

Do you need a moment, your Highness?

No. Tell their Majesties that I will be on my way shortly. The dragons are due to change shift soon, and I'll hitch a ride to Ooste. Seeing a dragon approach might give my brother something to ponder.

Very well, your Highness. Farewell.

Salvor left her mind, but she remained where she was, gazing out across the Straits. On the horizon she could see the low line that marked the Shield Hills, which protected Dalrig and Ooste from the storms in the Clashing Seas. Montieth must have been planning this for a while, to have organised five thousand soldiers to attack on the very day the operation was launched. Her eyes narrowed. She had known that, eventually, she would have to confront her brother. Before the Civil War, Michael had kept Montieth under control, but the Prince of Dalrig had remained quiet and in his palace for centuries, seemingly happy to ignore the rest of the City. Lady Amber had attended the coronation of Emily and Daniel, but her father had declined the invitation, stoking hopes that he would continue to present no problems.

And now he was in Ooste.

She turned. Van and Jade had been waiting for her, and they gazed at her, waiting.

'I need to return to the City for a short while,' she said.

Van's mouth opened.

'Don't say it, Major,' Yendra went on; 'I am perfectly aware that the timing is terrible, but I have faith in the abilities of you and all of the officer corps. You will remain in command until I complete the short task that I have been set.'

Jade frowned. 'Why are you going back? Do I have to stay?'

'Now is not the time to go into details, Jade, and yes; you will remain here. I want you to take a more active role, closer to the front. Support the advance of the Banner soldiers through the ruins.'

Jade's eyes lit up. 'Killing instead of healing? Sure, I'll stay for that.'

Yendra turned to Van. 'I believe that Halfclaw is about to go for a rest in Pella. It would speed things up considerably if I could persuade the dragon to take me as well. I will contact Nurian now.'

She sent her vision out through the crowded ruins of the harbour, and saw Halfclaw hovering over the entrance to a tunnel, spraying a thick jet of fire all around it.

Nurian. Please instruct Halfclaw to return to the harbour. I need to speak to him.

She broke off contact without waiting for a response from the captain.

'How long will you be, ma'am?' said Van.

'I don't know, Major. Hopefully no longer than a couple of hours. I'm sorry to leave you in the lurch like this. Walk with me to the old tower where Halfclaw likes to land.'

They hurried along the busy wharf, weaving their way through the groups of arriving refugees and the enormous piles of bricks, tools and supplies. Yendra glanced up, and saw the blue and green dragon approach.

'Don't take any rash decisions, Major,' she said, as they walked. 'If in doubt, play it safe; even if that means we miss our target for today. Understood?'

'Yes, ma'am.'

'Jade, you are now under the direct command of Major Logos, pending my return. If he gives you an order, follow it.'

'I suppose so, auntie.'

They reached the base of the heavily-eroded tower. Worn and uneven steps wound up its flanks, and they climbed to the top, just as Halfclaw was descending.

The dragon peered down at Yendra. 'You asked for me, Commander? You should know that I'm due to rest soon.'

'That's why I called for you, Halfclaw. I need to travel, at speed, to Ooste, which is on the way to Pella. I ask you – will you please take me?'

The dragon emitted a groan. 'Yesterday, I was asked if I would carry an insect about and... I meant a human; I was asked to carry a human, and now I'm being asked to carry another? I am not a beast of burden. I agreed to carry Nurian against my better judgement, and I...'

'Yes or no, dragon,' said Yendra. 'I don't have time for a debate. If you refuse, then I will bear no ill will against you, but I need to know.'

The dragon regarded her with cold eyes.

'I would be very grateful,' said Yendra, holding the dragon's gaze.

Halfclaw turned away, as if bored. 'I will take you.'

Yendra nodded to Van and Jade, then began to climb up the dragon's harness before he had a chance to change his mind. She reached the top of his shoulders, where Nurian was already strapped in.

'Ma'am,' he said, his eyes wide.

Yendra settled down on his right, and pulled the buckles round her waist.

Nurian pointed. 'You tuck your feet in there, ma'am.'

She nodded her thanks. 'Dragon, I am ready.'

Halfclaw grunted in reply, then lifted into the air. Yendra had imagined that she wouldn't be impressed by flying – after all, she had been using her vision for many long centuries, but the wash of wind against her face as they ascended brought a smile to her face. She noticed Nurian glancing at her, and regained her composure. People were dying, and smiling was inappropriate, even if one was riding on a dragon for the first time.

They circled once over the harbour, then Halfclaw soared to the east, only yards above the waters of the Straits. Yendra clung on to the harness rail, her senses flooded; she felt exhilarated, her heart swelling. She closed her eyes to better feel the wind against her face, and wished she could remain in the moment forever.

'Ma'am?' said Nurian.

She frowned and turned to him. 'Yes, Captain?'

He pointed ahead of them. Tarsnow, the black and white dragon, was on his return leg from the City, heading back to Jezra to re-join the landing forces. He soared down as he flew, angling towards Halfclaw. When the two dragons came closer, they circled each other.

'Greetings, Halfclaw,' called Tarsnow; 'are you...' His voice tailed away as he noticed Yendra on Halfclaw's back. 'What is this I see? Carrying two insects now, Halfclaw? Did Deathfang's daughter talk you into this new act of craven submission? For shame.'

'What I do is none of your concern, Tarsnow,' Halfclaw called back. 'I suggest you mind your own business.'

'Are you being impertinent to me, your elder? You, a child? You are letting these insects soil your mind, Halfclaw; have some pride. Are you a dragon, or are you a dog; a tail-wagging servant of creatures who should be worshipping us?'

Yendra bit her tongue. She wanted to respond, to tell Tarsnow that he was being a fool, but decided that it would only make the situation worse.

Halfclaw disengaged, and soared away, leaving Tarsnow behind. Nurian and Yendra glanced at each other.

'Never mind him,' said Nurian to the dragon. 'You have to do what you think is best.'

Halfclaw growled. 'Be quiet, insect.'

They sped on, crossing the rest of the Straits in minutes.

'God,' said the dragon; 'where should I deposit you?'

'The town on the left is called Ooste. Do you see the large white building there, the one with the towers? That's the Royal Palace. Please set me down in the courtyard in front of it.'

Halfclaw said nothing in reply, but banked to the left, the tip of his wing skimming through the surface of the blue water. He ascended as they came to Ooste, passing over the roofs of the town. Yendra watched as soldiers from the Gloamer militia stared up at them, their eyes wide at the sight of Yendra on a dragon. The peal of a bell rang out, and within seconds, soldiers were scurrying through the streets.

Yendra frowned. She had hoped that the soldiers would panic, but they seemed to be heading to certain locations within the town. She pulled on her vision and sent it out, scanning the rooftops.

'Damn it,' she muttered. 'Halfclaw! Pull back; bank right. Now!'

The dragon hesitated for a moment, then veered sharply to the right as a yard-long steel bolt whistled through the air. Moments later, another bolt, and then another, tore through the sky towards them. Halfclaw pulled up, then soared down, heading back towards the coast. A further four bolts were released, but Halfclaw's speed bore them away, and they fell harmlessly into the warm waters of the bay.

'Did they know we were coming?' cried Nurian, his knuckles white as he gripped the harness rail.

'Prince Montieth perhaps anticipated an attack by dragons,' Yendra said. 'I should have foreseen it. Halfclaw, I apologise for putting you in danger. Had I known, I would have asked you to set me down elsewhere.'

The dragon said nothing, and turned towards Pella. Five minutes later, he hovered over the gardens of Cuidrach Palace while Yendra and Nurian clambered down from the harness. He hadn't spoken another word since the attack over Ooste, and as soon as their feet touched the ground, he ascended into the sky and set off in the direction of the Iceward Range.

Yendra watched as he disappeared into the distance.

'I should have handled that better,' she said.

'It wasn't your fault, ma'am,' said Nurian. 'Dragons are touchy creatures. A little sensitive at times.'

'They are proud, Captain. And we need them far more than they need us.'

'I don't think Halfclaw likes me, if I'm honest. It took a lot of persuasion last night for him to agree to carry me around, and in the end he only said yes because Frostback and Deathfang badgered him into it. He's in love with Frostback; did you know that, ma'am? I think she likes him too, although she would never admit it.'

Yendra turned for the palace, and Nurian hurried after her. Guards saluted her as she walked along the gravel paths of the ornamental gardens, and when they reached one of the side entrances, Salvor was there, waiting for her.

'Did you see what happened?' she said.

Salvor nodded. 'I was watching, your Highness.'

'Damn my stupidity,' she said. 'I should have realised that Montieth would have been prepared for a dragon trying to land in Ooste. He must have thought I was launching an attack. In my haste, I neglected to scan the town first for ballistae batteries.'

'These things happen, your Highness,' Salvor said. He glanced at Nurian, as if wondering why a Banner captain was accompanying the Commander of the Bulwark.

'I think I shall get some lunch, ma'am, sir,' Nurian said, bowing as he edged away.

Salvor waited until he had gone, then he glanced back at Yendra. 'The situation has altered again, your Highness. Even before your attempted landing in Ooste, we received word from Lady Amber that Prince Montieth is now refusing to speak to anyone.'

'And you didn't think to tell me?'

'The message was received only a few minutes ago, your Highness. I was preparing to inform you when I saw you approach Ooste. I felt it best not to distract you while ballista bolts were being loosed in your direction.'

'Did Amber say anything else?'

'Yes, your Highness. She wants to speak to the King and Queen, but she wants assurances of her safety first.'

'What did their Majesties say to that?'

'They would like you to negotiate this meeting, your Highness. I have taken the liberty of ordering that a carriage be prepared to transport you to the Gloamer frontier, where Lady Amber is waiting.'

Yendra shook her head at him. 'A carriage?'

'Yes, your Highness.'

Yendra walked past Salvor and entered the palace.

'The, uh, carriage is in the other direction, your Highness,' said Salvor, hurrying after her.

'I am a god with vision powers,' she said as she walked. 'I don't need a carriage to speak to Amber.'

'But... Are you serious, your Highness? Are you going to intrude into her mind? You know how much...'

Yendra halted. 'They have intruded onto Ooste with five thousand soldiers. I'm starting to get tired of pandering to my brother and niece. If the only punishment they receive for this transgression is me inside their heads, then they will have got off lightly.'

She turned and strode away, her frustration boiling up within her. She came to a small reception chamber, went in and took a seat facing the window, while Salvor hovered by the door.

'This shouldn't take too long,' she said.

She sent her vision out of the window, then surged it towards Dalrig. She raced over the walls of Pella, then the houses of the outer suburbs passed beneath her, followed by the farmland that straddled the border between Reaper and Gloamer territory. Each road leading from Dalrig had been blocked by a group of Gloamer militia, who were checking traffic trying to access the town. Yendra spotted a line of carriages bearing the standard of the Prince of Dalrig, and entered the lead one. Inside, Amber was sitting with a couple of advisors. She looked relaxed, and Yendra took a moment to watch her. She was one of the only members of her family that Yendra had never read. Amber and Montieth had always promised to retaliate if anyone penetrated their minds, but that arrangement had ended as soon as they had sent soldiers against their fellow citizens.

She took a breath, and pushed her way into the demigod's head.

Amber. Explain yourself.

The demigod jumped in her seat, the words she had been about to say cut off.

You know who this is, Amber. What does your father want? Why has he violated the laws of the City?

You... you shouldn't be in here. My thoughts are my own; this is an outrage. Get out of my head!

Calm yourself niece. I have no interest in soiling myself by raking through any of your twisted little ideas, nor your sordid memories. You have been allowed to live in peace, despite the disrespect you and your father have shown the Crown, but you have gone too far.

I curse you, aunt. Do you hear me? You will pay for this.

Threats, Amber; really? Do you think you scare me? Let's get this over with – what did you wish to say to me, had I travelled by carriage?

Yendra sensed Amber battle with her own thoughts. Part of her wanted Yendra out of her head at any cost, while the demigod's stubborn streak was holding out, trying to insist that Yendra met her face to face.

Decide now, Amber, or I might change my mind about looking through some of your memories. I'm sure I could find some interesting things buried deep within your mind. You have ten seconds.

You are made of nothing but evil, aunt, and I will never forgive this intrusion.

Five seconds.

Fine! I wished to present you with my father's conditions for leaving Ooste. He has appointed me as his interlocutor and he wants me to negotiate directly with either the King or the Queen, alone. You hear me; no gods, no demigods and no soldiers. Face to face. If anyone tries to read minds or interfere, then the talks will be cancelled immediately.

Do you think I am stupid, niece? Do you think I would allow you to sit in a room, alone, with one of their Majesties?

I don't care what you think. There are ten thousand civilians living in Ooste, and you know my father's attitude towards mortals. He'd kill them all in an instant if he thought it would advance his cause.

His cause? I wasn't aware his selfish actions were underpinned by anything as noble as a cause.

I am the only person capable of restraining my father; you know this. The meeting will be held in five days' time, here at the frontier. There is a guard tower half a mile to the west of this road. The King or Queen must go there, and then I will lay down the conditions for a peaceful settlement.

Why five days? What is your father doing that requires five days?

Yendra heard a laugh echo round Amber's mind. *I'm sure you can work that out on your own, aunt. If you can't, well, you're in my head. Read it.*

Yendra plunged into Amber's thoughts. Much was swirling around in her mind – a loathing for Yendra; contempt for the rulers of the City, and, somewhere buried deep, an almost debilitating fear of her father. Prince Montieth was in the Royal Palace, he had sent a message to his daughter that morning. In it, he had expressed his rage at finding the salve mine in Ooste to be on the brink of exhaustion. He needed time, he had written; time to excavate the last of the salve from behind the Royal Palace; and Amber's job was to buy him that time. Otherwise, his words had hinted, the slaughter of the inhabitants of Ooste would begin in earnest. Amber's mind was ridden with conflict. She craved stability above all else, and her father's actions had threatened everything she had been trying to build. She wanted a resolution, but she also wanted to save face, and Yendra almost felt sorry for her niece's dilemma.

I have seen enough.

Curse you, aunt. I hate you.

You can have your meeting. Five days. However, I warn you, if a single civilian in Ooste is murdered by your father, or by your father's soldiers, then my revenge will be swift and overwhelming. Ponder that, niece.

Yendra severed the link and withdrew from Amber's mind.

Salvor coughed gently. 'Your Highness?'

She turned to him.

'How did it go?'

Yendra smiled. 'She only cursed me twice, so somewhat better than expected.'

Salvor attempted a smile, but she could see the worry in his eyes. 'What do they want?'

'Time. Montieth is digging out what remains of the salve behind the Royal Palace, and he needs five days to complete it. Their condition for withdrawing is a personal meeting with either the King or Queen, so that they can negotiate a face-saving deal.'

'A meeting? Amber would risk arrest?'

'No. She stated that there must be no gods, demigods or guards present.'

Salvor snorted. 'Out of the question. What would prevent her from taking the King or Queen hostage? Amber's death powers are second only to her father's – she could kill either monarch in an instant, or force them to sign any agreement she puts in front of them.'

Yendra nodded. 'I need to get back to Jezra.'

'But what about the meeting?'

'I told Amber it would go ahead.'

'How? We cannot allow it, your Highness. I don't trust them.'

'Neither do I, Salvor, but we cannot risk the lives of the civilians trapped in Ooste. If I had refused, then Montieth would have started murdering them.'

'Then what's the answer?'

Yendra gazed out of the window at the wide ornamental gardens, the scene of the coronation nine months before. She remembered the day clearly, the moment the mortals had assumed control of the City forever imprinted into her mind. It had been something she had fought for all her life, and she would not imperil it, not for anything.

'Don't worry,' she said. 'I have an idea.'

CHAPTER 17

RUTHLESS STREAK

Pella, Auldan, The City – 10th Yordian 3420

'Take this, your Majesty,' said Salvor, holding out his hand.

Emily frowned at the knife. 'Really? Do you think I need to be armed?'

'Frankly, yes, your Majesty. Lady Amber is very unpredictable. She may wish to do you physical harm. Please; I insist.'

She sighed. 'Very well, Salvor. I'll take it, but only to make you happy. If I end up having to pull a knife on Amber, then I think we can safely say that the negotiations have not been entirely successful.'

Emily took the sheathed knife, and slid it into the small bag that she was intending to take to the meeting. She glanced up at the sky, but it was empty.

'They will be here soon, your Majesty,' said Commander Quill, standing a few yards away. Behind her was an entire company of the Royal Guard, waiting by a line of carriages outside Cuidrach Palace.

'I wish I was coming along,' said Salvor; 'or, even better, that I was going to the meeting instead of you, your Majesty. This seems like a foolish risk.'

'If it persuades Montieth to leave Ooste peacefully, then it's worth a try. For six days, we've done nothing but sit back and watch as his troops occupy part of the City. This may put an end to it.'

'That would depend upon Lady Amber's conditions, your Majesty.'

'Her expectations will be all wrong,' said Emily. 'She will assume that I am at her mercy. That will quickly change when she realises her mistake.'

A shadow flickered overhead, and Emily glanced up to see Frostback descending. The soldiers of the Royal Guard tensed a little as the dragon landed in the palace courtyard.

'Good morning, Frostback,' Emily said, striding forwards; 'I hope you are well?'

'I'm getting a little tired of incinerating greenhides,' said the dragon, 'but, other than that, I am doing very well, Queen. This new task displeases me, however. Can you provide me with a guarantee that my rider will come to no harm?'

'She will be fine. Commander Quill will be keeping a very close eye on the situation.'

Frostback's eyes glowed red. 'I notice that wasn't a guarantee.'

Kelsey clambered down to the ground, and Emily stepped back as the Holdfast woman and the dragon exchanged a few personal words. Frostback didn't look happy but, after a moment, she extended her wings and rose into the sky, wheeling in the air before soaring away in the direction of the Western Bank.

'Miss Holdfast,' said Emily. 'How lovely to see you.'

'Aye?' said Kelsey. She glanced at the Queen. 'Is that what you're wearing?'

Emily looked down at the dress she had on. 'What's wrong with it?'

Kelsey frowned. 'There's a lot of skin showing.'

'Excuse me?' said Emily, feeling her temper rise. 'What business is that of yours? Just because I'm the Queen, it doesn't mean I have to dress like a Dalrigian housewife. You remind me of my mother-in-law.'

Kelsey laughed. 'That's not quite what I meant. Look, I don't know what Yendra told you about how my powers work, but I can only block stuff that goes through the air. If this Amber woman touches you, you'll be dead in a second.'

'Oh.' She glanced at Salvor. 'Could you fetch me some long gloves? And a scarf. And maybe a coat, too?'

The demigod bowed and made his way into the palace.

'Listen to you,' said Kelsey. 'You sound like you think you were born to rule.'

Emily raised an eyebrow. 'I was born to rule. I'm an Evader who was brought up as a Roser aristocrat – my credentials speak for themselves.'

Kelsey glanced around. 'Where's the King? Why are you going on this trip? A decent man would have volunteered to spare his wife from walking into mortal danger.'

'My husband is busy.'

'Aye? Doing what?'

'He spends his days fighting over the details of the constitutional reforms with the Tribal Council. That's his area. I deal with the unexpected crises.'

'Constitutional reforms, eh? You thinking of setting up a democracy or something?'

'A what?'

'You know, where the citizens get to vote for their rulers and so on.'

'Do you have experience of this?'

'Oh aye. I could write a book on the various attempts, successful and otherwise, of trying to implement democracy on my home world. My mother is the elected ruler of the Holdings, again, so I should know.'

'You should sit down with the King one of these days, Kelsey; I'm sure you'd find much to discuss with him. He is a little... hmm, obsessed might be too strong a word; let's say devoted. Yes, he is devoted to overhauling every last aspect of the government of the City, but it's proving to be a thankless task.'

'That's more my area of expertise, Queenie, to be honest. All this riding about on dragons and stuff is new to me. Back home, you'd usually find me in a library, nose-deep in musty old books. I used to spend a lot of time in the university. You should get yourself one of those.'

Emily nodded, though she had no idea what the word meant. 'And how are things?'

Kelsey frowned. 'With what? You need to be more specific.'

'Let's start with the landings.'

'Fine, I guess. I'm still annoyed about having to stay far away from Yendra, so she can talk to Nurian on Halfclaw, but the Banner forces have reached the base of the cliffs. Lower Jezra is mostly safe, though greenhides still pop out of tunnels every now and again. I think Jade is going to be sent down into the caverns soon. The dragons are fed up, though. Frostback and Tarsnow keep bickering, while Burntskull and Darksky keep asking how much longer the whole thing's going to take. Halfclaw's still carrying Nurian around, but he's not happy about being shot at over Ooste a few days ago. And poor old Deathfang's coming under a lot of pressure to call off the attacks, so they can all move to the mountains before the rains start.'

Salvor emerged from the palace, bowed, and handed the Queen her long white gloves, a blue scarf and her winter coat.

She pulled them on, then glanced at Kelsey. 'Better?'

'Aye, that'll do.'

Emily nodded to Quill. 'Let's be on our way, Commander.'

The soldiers of the Royal Guard climbed into their carriages, while Quill, Kelsey, Salvor and the Queen walked to the lead carriage. Salvor opened the side door, and helped the Queen ascend the steps, then stood back.

'Good luck, your Majesty,' he said, bowing.

Quill and Kelsey joined the Queen inside the carriage, and Salvor closed the door. Within moments, the ponies hitched to the carriages got underway, and they were pulled towards the palace gates.

'What is Amber likely to demand?' said Kelsey.

'A face-saving gesture, or so I have been led to believe,' said Emily.

'Prince Montieth should have excavated whatever was remaining in the Ooste salve mine by now, so hopefully he is ready to pull his troops out.'

Kelsey shook her head. 'Why have you been appeasing this arsehole?'

'This "arsehole" has the power to murder ten thousand civilians, Miss Holdfast. Should I have gambled with their lives?'

Quill chuckled.

'Is something funny, Commander?' said Emily.

'Hearing you swear, your Majesty. Apologies; I couldn't help but laugh.'

'Maybe I should do it more often if it amuses you. Besides, it didn't count; I was quoting Miss Holdfast.'

'Quit the Miss Holdfast nonsense; my name's Kelsey. I hate how folk say "Miss Holdfast" like they're getting me into trouble. Did you call Corthie "Mister Holdfast?"'

'We called him "the Champion,"' said Quill.

Kelsey scowled and shook her head. 'I'm surprised you don't have a statue erected to honour my big-headed wee brother.'

'That's not a bad idea,' said Emily. 'Thank you for the suggestion, Miss Holdfast.'

'Now you're just trying to wind me up. Maybe there's hope for you after all.'

The line of carriages pulled out of the palace grounds and entered the street network of Pella. Kelsey turned to gaze out of the window. Emily took a breath and tried to relax, but her nerves were jangling. Kelsey was right – their policy towards Montieth had been nothing short of appeasement, and the thought made Emily angry. She loathed being forced to do anything against her will, and had been squirming for days knowing that Gloamer troops were roaming the streets of Ooste. Had it been solely up to her, she might have sent her own soldiers into Dalrig, backed up with Yendra and several dragons, and laid waste to the town to force Montieth out of Ooste. Instead, she had listened to the counsels of Daniel and the others, and agreed to negotiate.

'What's the beach like in summer?' said Kelsey.

Emily glanced out of the window. They had left Pella, and were on the road that led to Ooste. The waters of the bay were lapping up onto the coast twenty yards to their left, and the golden sands were glimmering in the soft pink light of morning.

'Is it warm enough to go swimming?' Kelsey went on.

'Yes,' said Emily. 'The summers can get quite hot here, and the waters of the bay lose their chill.'

'But we've two months of rain first?'

'That's right; Freshmist.'

'Can't say I'm looking forward to that.'

'Without it, the cisterns of the City would run dry, and there would be no water to irrigate the crops.'

'Aye, but rain for two months?'

'Find a library,' said Quill. 'Freshmist is the perfect opportunity for staying indoors and catching up on all the things that you've been neglecting.'

'I'd love to,' said Kelsey, 'but what about Frostback? I can't exactly ask her to sit in a library with me.'

'You're not thinking of continuing to live in that quarry over Freshmist, are you?' said Emily. 'How awful.'

'Is there anywhere else that's indoors that could fit a dragon?'

'There are the old dragon lairs in Arrowhead Fortress,' said Quill; 'where Blackrose and Buckler used to live. I'd guess that four or five dragons could fit in there, at a push.'

'Deathfang wants to be in the mountains by Freshmist,' said Kelsey, 'but I'll speak to Frostback. She's not getting along well with the others; that's probably my fault. She doesn't hate all humans any more, and that's driven a wedge between her and the rest of them.'

'I thought Deathfang was fond of you?' said Emily.

'He is, but only because I saved his life from a god. He still doesn't like other humans. I'm the exception.'

The carriage slowed at a junction, and then took the road that led towards Dalrig, leaving the beach behind.

'We're nearly there,' said Quill.

'What do I do?' said Kelsey. 'Am I going to this meeting, or I am supposed to skulk about in the background?'

Emily glanced at Quill.

The commander shrugged. 'The conditions said no gods, demigods or soldiers, your Majesty. They didn't mention anything about mortal Holdfasts with powers.' She peered at Kelsey. 'You any good in a fight?'

'Eh, no. I'm not that kind of Holdfast. Out of my entire family, I'm probably the only one who's never killed anyone.'

'I can fight,' said Emily. 'Without her powers, I'll be more than a match for Amber if it comes to it.'

Quill frowned.

'What?' said Emily. 'You know it's true, Commander. Becoming Queen didn't magically remove my ability to swing a sword. I think I'll take Kelsey in with me. She can protect me from Amber's powers, and I can protect her if the demigod turns violent. It's been a while since I beat anyone up.'

'Do you have a weapon?' said Kelsey.

Emily nodded, and patted her small bag.

'This is a bad idea,' said Quill. 'This whole thing stinks. What if Amber's planned a trap? What if she has dozens of soldiers ready to swoop in and snatch you?'

'It probably is a trap,' said Kelsey, 'except that she'll be expecting to use her powers to get what she wants. She won't have factored in that they'll be useless.'

'I agree,' said Emily. 'It's settled.'

Quill frowned, and looked out of the window.

A few minutes later, the carriages slowed and came to a halt. A soldier from the Royal Guard opened the door of the lead carriage, and helped Emily step down to the ground. She glanced around. Fifty yards away was the guard tower that Amber had specified, while, ahead of them, the road had been blocked by wagons, and Gloamer soldiers were watching them from behind the barricade.

She glanced at Kelsey. 'Are you ready?'

'Sure.'

'Please be careful, your Majesty,' said Quill. 'If I think there's trouble, I'll send the entire Royal Guard in to rescue you.'

'Thanks, Commander. Wait for us here.'

Emily and Kelsey took the path that led to the tower, leaving the soldiers from the Royal Guard standing opposite the Gloamer militia by the barricade.

'You seem calm,' said Kelsey.

'That's because I am calm. What's your range, again?'

'About a hundred yards or so. If Amber's in the tower, she'll already be unable to use her powers, although she probably hasn't realised it yet. Remember – don't let her touch you.'

'I can shake hands, though?'

Kelsey glanced at the gloves. 'I wouldn't risk it, just in case. Also, remember that her self-healing will still work; I don't affect that.'

They approached the tower, and Emily glanced at the windows. The building seemed quiet. She walked up to the door and pushed it open. Inside, was a stone hallway, with stairs ascending to the upper floors. There was also a side door, lying half open. She frowned, and walked to the door. She looked through the gap, and saw Amber standing in the shadows, alone. Emily removed the frown from her lips and took a breath.

'Good morning, Lady Amber,' she said, striding into the small chamber.

Amber regarded her, a faint smile on her lips. 'You came? I had my doubts.' Her eyes narrowed as she saw Kelsey. 'Who's that?'

'No one to concern yourself about,' said Emily. 'Not a god, a demigod, and certainly not a soldier. No offence, Kelsey.'

The Holdfast woman shrugged.

'She's here as my witness,' Emily went on; 'to observe. To be honest, I thought that you'd have brought someone too. In case, you know, I tried to kill you.'

Amber stared at her. 'I don't know if you're deluded or over-confident, but either way, you made a mistake coming here. What I am about to do gives me no pleasure, but my father's orders were clear.' She raised her right hand. 'This will hurt, but it will be over soon, and when you wake up, you will be in my custody, safely locked up within Greylin Palace.'

Emily put her hands on her hips. 'Do your worst.'

Amber narrowed her eyes, then gasped. She glanced at her hand, then at Emily, her mouth open.

'No,' she whispered.

'Yes,' said Emily. She opened her bag and pulled out the knife. 'Is it my turn?'

Amber took a step back. 'How are you doing this? What's happened to me? Where are my powers?'

'You'll get them back,' said Emily; 'if you behave.' She tossed the knife from one hand to the other. 'I've never stabbed anyone before, but my grandmother would be proud to see me now, knowing that all the training she put me through has proved to be worthwhile. Now, Amber, tell me; what will it take for Montieth to leave Ooste?'

Amber cowered against the wall.

'Answer me, Amber. Clearly, your plan was to hold me hostage, presumably as leverage, so that your dear father could get what he wants without interference. What does he want? He has the salve from Ooste. If he withdraws peacefully, we shall let him keep it.'

'He wants more salve,' Amber said, her eyes wide as she stared at the knife. 'Ooste hardly had any, and he needs more.'

'Why? What does he want with so much? It only takes a small dose to rejuvenate a god, and he's gone through the entire deposits that lay behind Greylin Palace. What is he doing with it all?'

'You... you don't want to know.'

'Trust me; I do.'

'No. I would never tell you that. You may have a knife, but you're merely a wretched mortal, and your life means nothing next to mine. The secrets of Greylin Palace will endure for the ages, and my father and I will still be here, long after your children's children are dead.'

'You should know that I have spoken to Naxor and Aila about this.

They've been inside your palace, and they saw things there; horrible things. Why? What is the purpose of the experiments your father is carrying out?'

'I'll die before I betray my father.'

Emily nodded, and lowered the knife a fraction. 'You said he wants more salve? How much more?'

'Ten tons.'

'That's rather a lot.'

'That's what he was going to demand if I brought you back to Dalrig as a hostage. He wants ten tons of salve from the mine in Tara shipped to Ooste, and then transported by land to Greylin Palace. Once it is secure, he will withdraw his forces from Ooste and go home. Do it, I implore you. If you do it, my father will return to his old life, and everything will go back to the way it was.'

Emily said nothing. She knew from Salvor's report that the mine behind Maeladh Palace in Tara had far less than ten tons of salve remaining in it.

'If I refuse?' she said.

'Then my father's rage will be incalculable. Mortals will die and the City will burn.'

'You would plunge the City back into civil war? Not only are you and your father cruel and selfish, but you are also stupid. If it came to war, we would destroy you. Tell your father about how you lost your powers today. Ask him if he can figure out why. What works on you, will work on him, too.'

Amber shook her head. 'You don't understand; how could you? My father won't be interested in the excuses I make for my failure today, and if you refuse his demands for salve, you will face his wrath. At the very least, he will refuse to evacuate Ooste, and if you try to force him out, he'll give the order for the citizens there to be executed.'

'And if he kills even one innocent civilian, we will descend upon him with everything we've got.'

'If I can persuade him not to retaliate, will you pledge not to attack?'

'And then what? How far will your father go to get his hands on the salve in Tara?'

'There are no limits to what my father is capable of. He may decide to cut off all trade to and from Dalrig. The City needs us more than we need the City, and a trade embargo would bring you to your knees without the need for violence. Or, he may decide that violence is necessary. My father is a violent man, and he abides by no rules other than his own.'

Emily nodded. 'I'm refusing him the salve. The mine next to Maeladh Palace in Tara is the property of the Crown, and we intend to distribute the salve to heal mortals. The gods have controlled it long enough, in my opinion. The salve does not belong to your father. Please ensure that you tell him that when you see him.'

'You're letting me go?'

'Of course. I came to talk, not to take anyone hostage. Tell your father that the Crown does not submit to bullies, but, if he takes the salve he has stolen from the Royal Palace, and withdraws his forces from Ooste, we will consider the matter closed. However, if he harms the civilian population, or if he makes any aggressive gestures towards Tara, then he will feel *my* wrath.' She sheathed the knife. 'Go.'

Amber stared at Emily, her eyes sullen and defiant.

Kelsey coughed. 'Your sister says hello.'

Amber turned to her. 'What did you say, mortal?'

'Your sister; I saw her this morning and told her I might be seeing you today. She said hello.'

'You saw Jade this morning? My treacherous little sister? Tell her that she will never be welcome back in Greylin; tell her that my father and I want nothing to do with her ever again, that she is dead to us. Jade is dead to me.'

Amber strode from the chamber, brushing past Kelsey on the way out.

Emily glanced at the young Holdfast woman. 'Did Jade really pass on her greetings?'

'Nah,' said Kelsey; 'she made it clear how much she hated Amber, but, well, they're sisters, and I was just doing my bit to nudge them back together. Just like how I'll tell Jade that Amber sends her regards.'

'I'm not altogether sure that I want the two of them reconciled. Regardless of that, thanks for your help today; you were extremely effective. It was nice to see a god cower for once, instead of trying to lord it over us; it made me feel quite powerful.'

'After several days of being told that I'm a hindrance by Van and Yendra, it's good to know that someone appreciates me.'

'A hindrance?'

'Aye. Yendra wants to communicate with Nurian while he's flying about on Halfclaw, so I have to stay well clear, in case I interfere with her vision.'

'I see. I suppose that makes sense, although it must feel a little awkward.' She took a breath. 'Amber should be back at the Gloamer lines by now; we should go before Quill begins to suspect that we're dead.'

They walked through the hall and left the tower.

'Kelsey,' said Emily; 'you're clearly a clever woman, and you have experience of working for an Empress. Do you have any advice on how we should be handling Montieth?'

Kelsey looked surprised. 'You're asking me? I've only been in the City for a few months, and most of that's been spent in a cold quarry.'

'You're a fresh pair of eyes. You've seen how governments work in different places. I think your perspective could be valuable.'

The young Holdfast woman puffed out her cheeks. 'Montieth is holding Ooste to ransom, threatening to kill thousands of civilians if you resist. So, you're appeasing him, hoping that he'll get what he wants without bloodshed, and then retire to his palace in Dalrig? Seem accurate so far?'

'Yes.'

'Amber mentioned cutting off trade from Dalrig; would that hurt the rest of the City?'

'We would run low on food quite quickly without access to the fish that Dalrig catches in the Cold Sea. They also supply the City's heating and lighting oil, and bring in timber, building stone and other useful goods from raiding the Western Bank. So, yes; any blockade would hurt us.'

'Then, here's my advice. Carry on appeasing them for now, but prepare yourselves. Jezra's the key, isn't it? If you can hold Jezra, then all of the things that Dalrig supplies could be brought in from there, instead. Wait until your supply lines are secure, then hit Dalrig with a surprise attack, before they decide to blackmail the City again. That does leave a gap in your plans, though. If Montieth needs the salve that's in Tara, then he might send troops there to secure it while you hold off. Send reinforcements to Tara to counteract that possibility. Also, destroy the boats that remain in Ooste harbour to prevent him using those. At the same time, prepare an assassination squad to take out Montieth and Amber, in case the opportunity arises. For the long-term future of the City, those two need to go.'

Emily raised an eyebrow. 'My, Kelsey; you do have a ruthless streak.'

'Not at all, Queenie. If I were truly ruthless, I'd advise getting the dragons to raze Ooste to the ground today; and then they could hit Dalrig tomorrow. Dragons love burning humans and buildings; they'd be up for it. Burntskull might even join in. But that would result in hundreds of dead soldiers, and probably a shitload of civilians as well.'

Quill saw them approach as they walked along the path, and sent out a squad to escort them back to the carriages.

'Ideally,' said Emily, 'no one dies.'

Kelsey smirked. 'I saw how you handled that knife in there, Queenie. I'd say that you have a pretty ruthless streak as well, although you try to keep it hidden. If you want to beat Montieth, then deaths are going to be unavoidable. If you want to save your rule, and stop Montieth from trampling all over you, then people are going to die. They're already dying in Jezra.'

Emily said nothing as they walked towards the carriages. She half wished that she hadn't asked for Kelsey's advice, as it pointed to a future that was harsher than the one she pictured in her mind. She wanted to be a good Queen; a kind and benevolent ruler who was concerned for the well-being of everyone in the City. But the words of the young Hold-fast woman had struck a chord; If Emily wanted to remain Queen, she would need to act ruthlessly, and people would die.

It was too late for second thoughts, she realised. She was the Queen, and she was determined to stay the Queen, no matter the price.

CHAPTER 18

THE SILVER PENNY

Jezra, The Western Bank – 20th Yordian 3420

Kelsey watched the snow fall over the ruins of Jezra, each flake tinted pink in the glow of dawn. Brigade refugees in long, thick coats were swarming over the lower town, which seemed to be covered in red bricks. High walls built from them criss-crossed the ancient ruins, while enormous quantities were still being unloaded from supply ships in the harbour. The humble brick, in Kelsey's opinion, had done as much to defeat the greenhides as the dragons and Banner forces.

She sipped the hot drink from her mug, grimacing at the taste. It was the closest the City had in the way of tea, but it was nothing like what she was used to in the Holdings, nor had they heard of such luxuries as coffee, or sugar, or chocolate... the list went on. She felt a little twinge of homesickness at the thought she might never taste chocolate again, but she put it to the back of her mind. She had made her choice, and would have to live with it.

'Good morning,' said Nurian, looking inappropriately cheerful. 'Did you sleep well? How were your new quarters?'

'It's a brick shack, Nurian,' she said; 'and it's not my new quarters. I was only sleeping in there because Frostback was spending time with

Halfclaw. I'll be back in the quarry tonight. Will, uh, you be coming back with us tonight as well?'

He sat down on the low brick wall next to her and sipped from his mug, a scarf covering much of his face. 'Yes. I mean, if that's alright? I wonder if my dragon and your dragon hit it off last night?'

'For Pyre's sake, don't ever refer to Halfclaw as "your" dragon if he's anywhere within earshot. He'd rip your head off. And I doubt that he got anywhere with Frostback last night; she's playing hard to get. She's of the opinion that, since Halfclaw is the only eligible boy dragon on this world that could be suited to her, she doesn't need to make much of an effort, and so she's letting him do all the running. Poor Halfclaw.'

'Poor me. If Halfclaw comes back all grumpy and frustrated, then it'll me who'll have to listen to his complaints and moaning. And, by the Ascendants, that dragon can moan. He spent days going on about the ballista bolts that nearly hit him over Ooste, and he never stops complaining about Princess Yendra, Major Logos, me...' He met Kelsey's glance. 'And you.'

'Me?'

'He blames you for most of his predicament. He says that if you hadn't become Frostback's rider, then he would never have had to carry me. He also thinks you're meddling in his attempts to woo Frostback. If it weren't for his pride, he would have gone back on his word and refused to carry me around any more. But he promised, so he's stuck with me.'

To their left, Jade emerged from one of the many small brick block-houses that had been constructed to house the Brigades and the troops. She was wearing her usual dark green robes, and had a preoccupied smile on her face. The smile dropped as she caught sight of Kelsey and Nurian sitting on the low wall. She walked through the crowds of refugees lining up to get their breakfast, and approached the wall.

'Good morning, my lady,' said Nurian.

'Be quiet, mortal,' Jade snapped. 'You should know by now never to address me unless I speak to you first, which I have absolutely no desire to do.'

Nurian's face fell, and he glanced away.

'Holdfast witch,' said Jade, standing in front of Kelsey; 'did my sister really pass on her best regards to me?'

Kelsey sighed. 'Not this again. I've told you; Amber was polite about you, and asked me how you were doing.'

'Even after you told her what I said about her?'

'Aye.'

Jade peered at Kelsey, her eyes narrow.

'Why would I lie?' said Kelsey. 'I don't like either of you.'

'Next time you see her, tell her that I curse her, and hope all her hair falls out.'

'I might not ever see her again. That meeting was a one-off, I think. But, are you sure? You know, if your sister is trying to mend bridges, then maybe you shouldn't say anything you might later regret.'

'I hate her. She bullied me for centuries in Greylin Palace. She must want something; that's the only explanation for her being nice about me. She's never been nice about me. She wouldn't allow me to have any cats, and she used to order me around as if I was a servant. You're up to something, Holdfast, and I don't like it.'

A corporal in the Banner hurried up to them, and saluted. 'Major Logos would like to see the three of you in the Command Post. Princess Yendra is also there.'

Kelsey jumped down from the wall, and wrapped her coat around her. Nurian took the mugs over to a kitchen station, and then the corporal led them through the snow towards the largest brick building in the harbour. It had been hastily erected, and housed hundreds of Banner soldiers on its upper floors, while the entire ground level was taken up by the administrative headquarters of the operation. Squat rows of brick blockhouses lined the route, where Brigade refugees were crammed in a dozen to a room. The snow was starting to settle on the roofs of the buildings, and a chill wind from the Straits was gusting through the makeshift streets.

They entered the Command Post via a guarded entrance and went into the relative warmth of Van's office, where two oil-burning heaters were sitting. Yendra was there, looking up at a giant map of Jezra pinned to the wall. The map was stained in several places from the leaks and damp within the building, and the ink had become blotchy, making it hard to read.

Van rose from behind his wooden desk.

'Good morning,' he said; 'thank you for coming.'

Nurian saluted, while Kelsey and Jade didn't respond.

'This won't take long,' Van went on. 'Lady Jade, I need you to accompany a few Banner squads today, over in the iceward sector.'

'More tunnels?'

'Yes, please. We had a greenhide incursion there last night – several emerged from underground and dragged off four Brigade refugees. When you get down there, show no mercy; kill them all.'

'I can do that.'

He turned to Kelsey and Nurian. 'As for our dragon riders, I understand that Frostback and Halfclaw should return to duty at noon. When that happens, I want you both up on the ridge. The Brigades are planning on finishing the wall at the top of the sunward path, and we need you to ensure that they can work without being attacked.'

'We can go together?' said Kelsey. 'You mean I don't have to keep my distance?'

Yendra turned. 'That's right. I won't be in Jezra this afternoon; I'm meeting the Queen in Pella. My boat leaves in fifteen minutes.'

'What shall we do until the dragons return, sir?' said Nurian.

'Rest,' said Van. 'The Brigades will keep working on the wall until it's finished; you might be up on the ridge for a while. I'll be watching out for Frostback and Halfclaw's arrival; be ready to go at noon.'

'Yes, sir.'

Kelsey caught Van glance at her, but he quickly averted his eyes. He was courteous and professional around her, and she almost missed their constant squabbling. She wondered if he had started to move on; maybe he had given up on her, or maybe he was just very good at hiding his feelings.

'I will return this evening,' said Yendra. 'When I speak to the Queen,

I will be sure to mention how proud I am of you all. Within a few days, the upper ridges will be securely in our hands, and we can begin to prepare for Freshmist, when the rains will drive the greenhides back into the forest.'

'Does the Queen need me for anything?' said Kelsey. 'You know, if I've not much to do this morning?'

Yendra smiled. 'The Queen is very grateful for the help you gave her on the Dalrigian frontier, Kelsey. If she needs you again, she'll ask.'

Van nodded to them. 'Dismissed.'

Kelsey, Nurian and Jade walked out of the room and back into the cold street.

'He could have just sent us a message,' said Kelsey; 'he didn't need to summon us for that.'

'Shut up, Holdfast,' said Jade. 'Your stupid powers aren't required today, whereas I am needed.'

She strode past Kelsey and disappeared among the crowds of Brigade refugees and Banner soldiers.

'Her ladyship is charming, as always,' said Nurian. 'Hey; I have an idea. I was speaking to an officer in the Brigades about an underground cavern that was cleared a few days ago. He said that there's all kinds of interesting old stuff buried down there. There are even rumours of someone unearthing an ancient library.'

'Sounds ridiculous. Any books would have decayed into dust long ago.'

'Not if they were kept in an airless environment. Are you not even a tiny bit curious? Come on; even if there are no books, there's bound to be other stuff – artefacts from the second occupation, or maybe even the first.'

Kelsey frowned. 'Where's the entrance? I can't stray too close to Jade, not when she'll need her powers to kill greenhides.'

'It's fine, the caverns are on the sunward side of town.'

'Alright. As long as we're back well before noon.'

They started walking along the busy street, passing Brigade

refugees heading to work, wrapped in heavy layers of warm clothing. Their expressions were very different from those worn when they had first arrived, fifteen days before. A grim determination had replaced the wide-eyed fear that had first prevailed. The Banner bore much of the responsibility for the changes. Following instructions laid down by Yendra, the Banner soldiers had been assisting the refugees – training them, mentoring them, and proving to them that they were on the same side. In return, the refugees had started to forget their old hostility to the Banners, and a mutual trust between the two sides was blossoming. The risks they faced every day were the same, and several Banner soldiers had died protecting the workforce from greenhide attacks. Their discipline, too, was rubbing off on the Brigades, and the work companies would compete to see who could finish their tasks first, revelling in the praise heaped upon them by the leadership of the Banner. Day by day, the ragged refugee Brigades were forming themselves into a formidable and coherent group, with a strong shared identity, toughened by hardship and adversity. Kelsey often wondered what use they could be put to, once the operation was at an end – whoever controlled the Banner and the Brigades would have a powerbase to rival the Blades.

Kelsey and Nurian passed the brick mortuary, which was emptied each day at dawn – a ship taking the previous day's casualties back to Pella for burial. Hundreds had died; too many, but far less than the outright massacre that had been feared. Kelsey had calculated that, on average, someone was killed every thirty minutes in Jezra, losses that were painful, but sustainable.

They reached a section of the harbour where Brigade refugees were demolishing one of the first walls that they had built. It had been constructed when the defensive perimeter had barely encompassed the harbour, and now that the whole of Lower Jezra had been pacified, it was no longer needed. The debris was being carried away in wheelbarrows, to be dumped in the sea by the edge of the harbour. Kelsey and Nurian passed the demolition site and carried on. The ground had been flattened, and the mass of new brick structures made it almost impossible to discern the layout of the ancient town under them. Several entrances to the underground cavern system had been sealed up, while those that remained open had little yellow flags next to them to show that they had been cleared of greenhides.

Nurian pointed at a set of ancient steps descending between two ruined old walls.

'This is the one,' he said. 'The Brigades have taken to calling the ruins here "the library," and they might be right. According to the records we saw in Ooste, there was a second-occupation era library somewhere in this vicinity.'

Kelsey remained dubious, but Nurian's enthusiasm was evident on his face. He went to a large crate by the entrance and took out two oil lamps. He lit them, and handed one to Kelsey.

She peered into the distance.

'Jade's nearly a mile away,' said Nurian, 'at the opposite end of the town. It'll be fine.'

He started going down the steps, and Kelsey followed him. The ancient stonework was scorched and blackened by dragon fire, and the air held the scent of incinerated greenhides, a smell that Kelsey had grown accustomed to. At the bottom of the stairs was a narrow passageway, shrouded in darkness, and Nurian shone his lamp down it. Two young Brigade refugees jumped in the light.

They saluted. 'Sir, ma'am.'

'What are you doing down here?' said Nurian.

'Guarding the tunnel, sir,' said one. 'Making sure no one loots whatever's down here. The Brigade commander assigned us to this post.'

Nurian nodded. 'You can relax; we're only going to take a quick look around.'

'Have you been inside?' said Kelsey.

'Yes, ma'am,' said the Brigade refugee, 'but not too far. If you're looking for the statues, go inside and take the second tunnel on the left.'

'Have you seen any books?'

'Not books, ma'am; scrolls.'

'Scrolls?'

'Yes, ma'am. Shelves and shelves of them. You'll want to go past the statues, and turn right. We're under orders to forbid you from removing anything, ma'am. The Brigade commander said that someone from the Royal Academy will be coming over to Jezra, eventually, and we've not to touch anything until then.'

'Thanks,' she said. 'We'll just look.'

Nurian and Kelsey squeezed past the two refugees and carried on along the narrow tunnel. The side walls were scored with greenhide talon marks. They passed a junction, and Nurian aimed his lamp down each of the openings to reveal empty stone chambers. They carried on, and came to a side tunnel on the left.

'This must be the one,' said Nurian, squinting into the thick shadows.

They entered the new tunnel, which broadened out after a few yards. Kelsey and Nurian came to a halt, their mouths open. Ahead of them were two rows of statues leading away into the distance. Each was standing atop a pedestal, and they were larger than life. Warriors, and men and women in sculpted robes gazed down at them with carved expressions of serenity and resolve. Nurian hurried to the first one, his gaze scanning the pedestal for an inscription.

'Why would anyone put statues down here?' said Kelsey.

'This can't be their original home,' said Nurian, kneeling by the pedestal. 'They must have been moved here before the evacuation. Maybe they thought they'd be coming back. There's an inscription on this one, but it's too eroded to read. That means it must have been outside for a considerable period, exposed to the sea and wind.'

They carried on, walking between the two rows. They came to the largest statue that was in the tunnel – of a man wearing a crown on his head, and with a giant sword strapped to his back. Kelsey's eyes went to the inscription, which had been carved in tall letters. They were eroded, but the meaning of the largest word was clear.

'Aurelian,' said Kelsey.

'The last prince,' said Nurian. 'Alright; my theory's changed. If this is Prince Aurelian, then they must have hidden this statue after the God-King and God-Queen deposed him, and sent him in chains to the Grey Isle to die. This is probably the only statue of the last prince in existence; they did a thorough job of excising him from the history books.'

A faint smile touched Kelsey's lips. 'Emily and Daniel will be pleased. This will help the legitimacy of their rule.'

Something crunched under her boots and she looked down. Scattered across the ground were fragments of pottery, along with scraps of metal and a few tiny coins. She bent down and picked one up. It was a small silver penny, similar in size to those in circulation around the City. She studied the face on one side, long with the markings.

'Aurelian's face is on the money, too,' she said.

Nurian smiled. 'You're holding evidence that the history books are lying. The official records state that the last mortal prince didn't mint any coins, yet you have one in your hand. I wonder what else they've been lying about.'

'Do you have a theory?'

'I have plenty,' he said, grinning. 'Firstly, the rebellion by the mortals was far more successful than the authorities have admitted. If you read the stories, it was all over in a flash, but here we have statues and coins.'

Kelsey smiled. Nurian's enthusiasm was infectious, and she found herself filled with curiosity about the City's secret past. She looked into his eyes, and her vision went black, as if she had been swallowed up. A jarring series of images flashed in front of her. Darkness, shadows, a glint of claws in lamplight, and then the face of a greenhide appeared, mere inches away, the teeth glistening as the hideous jaws opened.

Kelsey stumbled backwards, dizzy and terrified. She fell back against one of the pedestals, slipping on the smooth flagstones.

Nurian frowned at her. 'Are you alright? What happened?'

Kelsey said nothing, her eyes staring at him. Her heart was

pounding from the vision, and she strained her ears to listen, but all around was silence.

Nurian extended his hand to help her up.

'We have to get out of here,' she whispered. 'It's not safe.'

'It's fine,' he said. 'Come on; the scrolls aren't far away now; we'll look at them for a minute, and then we'll head back outside.'

'No. Nurian...' She began to weep.

He placed a hand on her shoulder. 'Kelsey; it's alright. Nothing's down here. What's got into you? You were fine a moment ago.'

She gazed at him, trying to etch every detail of his face into her mind, but her tears were making her vision blurry. She felt sick, and weak, her limbs barely able to work, as if the vision had paralysed her.

A soft sound came from the end of the cavern. Nurian turned to see what had caused the noise, and the greenhide was upon him in a second, springing out from its hiding place. It crashed into Nurian, its long fangs engulfing the man's head; its claws ripping through his torso and sending sprays of blood and gore over the sides of the pedestals. Kelsey cowered back against the wall of the cavern, her eyes closed as she hid in the shadows, the sound of the greenhide devouring Nurian reaching her. She squeezed herself into the small space between the pedestal of the last mortal prince and the wall, and crouched into the smallest ball she could make, her hands over her ears and her eyes shut, while, three yards away, the greenhide ate her friend.

She was going to die, but she didn't care. All she could think about was the vision that she had experienced just prior to the attack, the sight of the jaws opening wide to envelop his head; the rows of stained and jagged teeth; the claws lashing out – everything that Nurian had seen in his last moments. She re-played it over and over in her mind, until she felt like she had shared in his death, while she waited for her own.

Kelsey had no notion of how long she had been hiding behind the pedestal in the dark. Sounds filtered through to her ears, but their meaning eluded her.

Something touched her arm, and she cried out in fright, her eyes snapping open.

'She's here!' called a voice. 'Behind the statue.'

Lamplight flickered through the rows of tall stone figures, and Kelsey realised that over a dozen soldiers were in the cavern. One of them approached and crouched next to her.

'Greenhide,' she gasped, not understanding who was next to her.

'We know, Kelsey,' said the man. 'We're going to seal off the tunnel until Jade can get here. Can you stand?'

Kelsey stared at him. It was Van. For some reason, the knowledge angered her and she lashed out, her hands pushing Van away.

He caught hold of her hands and gripped them. 'We need to get you out of here. The greenhide might come back.'

'Nurian!' she cried.

'He's gone, Kelsey. I'm sorry.'

He pulled her towards him, his strong arms holding her as she struggled. Another soldier lent a hand, and they helped Kelsey to her feet. She gave up resisting, and almost collapsed, but Van held her upright, and they started to withdraw from the cavern. Two of the soldiers were carrying a large sack between them, and blood was seeping through the fabric. Kelsey glanced down, and saw the wide bloodstain on the ground. She cried out again, then felt a hand go over her mouth.

'Quickly,' hissed Van. 'Everyone out.'

———

Some part of Kelsey's mind could remember every tortured moment of their withdrawal from the cavern, and she remembered feeling surprised that it was still daylight outside, as if such a thing could only have happened in the depths of the darkest night. A crowd of Banner soldiers and Brigade refugees were standing by the top of the stairs, and a squad of bricklayers got to work the moment the last soldier had emerged back into the streets of the town. Kelsey noticed the sympathetic looks on the faces of those staring at her, but she didn't want any sympathy. She wanted Nurian.

She was half-carried all the way to the Command Post, where she was put into a small room with a bed. Van knelt by her side, but she turned to face the wall, her mind blank, her emotions stretched and numb, and, eventually, he got up and stole from the room, gently closing the door behind him.

Alone, she abandoned herself to tears, her hands gripping the sheets on the bed, twisting them in her fingers.

Van re-entered the room, carrying a tray that he set down on the small bedside table.

'Leave me alone,' she cried.

Van said nothing, sitting down in silence next to her on a wooden chair.

'I said leave me alone.'

'You shouldn't be alone, Kelsey; not right now.'

She turned, her gaze filled with hate for him. She glanced at the tray, and saw a mug of water and a plate of fish and bread, and she lashed out with her hand, sending the tray and its contents flying across the room.

Van nodded, his eyes full of pain, then he knelt and started to clean up the mess.

'Go away, Van. Leave me, like you did before. You don't care about me, so don't start pretending that you do. '

Van didn't look at her. 'Frostback is on the roof. She wants to see you. I can tell her that you're not ready, if you want.'

Kelsey got off the bed and pushed past Van to get to the door. She came out into a passageway, where a guard was standing, and ran for the stairs. She ascended them two at a time, oblivious to the many looks she got as she shoved people out of her way. She burst out onto the flat roof of the building, and ran straight into Frostback.

'My rider,' the dragon said, drawing her forelimbs round Kelsey in a protective gesture.

Kelsey threw herself at the dragon's neck, her arms hugging the silver scales as she wept.

'You have lost someone close,' Frostback said; 'and nothing I can say will fix it, but I want you to know that I feel your loss. You are beloved to me, and my heart breaks to see you in pain.'

Kelsey howled in grief, any semblance of control or restraint lost as she embraced the dragon's neck.

'Van told me that it was very quick,' Frostback said; 'that Nurian didn't suffer; that it would have been over before he even knew what was happening.'

Kelsey recalled her vision, the lunging jaws imprinted into her mind. Nurian *had* known what was coming, even if only for a brief instant. She cursed her powers, and wished that it had been her who had died.

'Today,' said Frostback, 'I will do whatever you deem best. If you wish to return to the quarry, then I will take you. My advice is that you rest; sleep. Nothing but time will heal your wounds, rider. I wish Black-rose were here to teach me more about the bond between dragons and their riders, so that I knew what to do; what was best for you. I fear that my poor understanding of human emotions and customs has not prepared me for this.'

Kelsey tried to process what the dragon was saying, but her thoughts were incoherent and unanchored. If she had possessed dull-weed, she would have smoked it; anything to blot out the pain she was feeling.

'Major Logos,' the dragon said.

'Dragon,' said Van.

'What should we do?' said Frostback. 'I am unfamiliar with human grief.'

'What would dragons do?'

'Incinerate something. Allow the flames to burn off some of our sorrow. Fire can be cathartic.'

'I will take her,' said Van. 'She can rest in my quarters, and then you can bear her back to the quarry later tonight.'

Frostback lowered her head and nuzzled Kelsey. 'I think he might be right. You should sleep, rider.' She glanced at Van. 'Promise me that you will not leave her alone.'

'I promise.'

'Then I shall fly today, and Halfclaw and I will kill the enemy in the name of the fallen Nurian. Each death, we shall dedicate to his honour.'

Kelsey untangled her arms from the dragon's neck, and Van put a hand round her shoulder. She shrugged it off.

'I will go with you,' she said, 'but don't touch me.'

Van nodded.

'Rest, my rider,' said Frostback; 'rest, and tonight, when I collect you, we shall fly far and wide, and remember the good things about your lost friend.'

The silver dragon extended her wings, and rose into the red sky. Halfclaw was already circling overhead, and the two dragons turned for the cliffs and soared away.

'She loves you deeply,' said Van.

'Yet, she left me, just like you did.'

'That's not fair. Frostback would have stayed if you'd asked. She didn't know what to do. I don't know what to do.'

She lowered her eyes. 'I do.'

Fifteen minutes later, Van was filling two glasses with brandy in his rooms on the first floor of the Command Post. Kelsey sat on a bed, her eyes heavy as she watched him. Guilt had crept into her mind; a niggling feeling that Nurian's death had been her fault. Why hadn't she insisted that they not enter the cavern? Everyone knew that greenhides could be skulking down there; why hadn't she stopped him as soon as he had suggested it?

Van passed her the glass and she downed the contents in one

smooth motion, her throat burning. She passed the empty glass to Van, who filled it again.

He took a large swig from his own glass. 'I've made arrangements for the rest of the day. I won't leave you.'

She rolled her eyes. 'Pretending you care again?'

'I do care, Kelsey. I can't bear to see you hurt like this. Nurian was a good man...'

'Don't start with that! You didn't even like him. You were jealous of him.'

Van took another drink, and re-filled his own glass. 'Yes. I was. I saw the way you got on with him, and I was envious. You used to smile when you saw him. You never smiled at me. But, it doesn't matter; my feelings are not important right now.'

Kelsey drank half of the brandy in her glass, feeling the alcohol work its way through her. Tears sprang from her eyes, but she wiped them away.

Van gazed down at the floor. 'I still love you, Kelsey.'

'No, you don't.'

'I do. I've tried hard to ignore it; I've submerged myself in work, but it doesn't make any difference. You are what I think of when I close my eyes each night; and yours is the face I see in my dreams. I know that you don't like me, but don't doubt my feelings for you. Anything you want or need, I will try to give you. Anything I can do to make you feel better, name it.'

'Go away.'

'I can't; I promised Frostback.'

She glanced at him, and something else stirred within her, as she remembered the other vision. She almost choked, feeling shame that such thoughts could enter her mind at such a time, but she longed for human contact, longed to feel something to take away the pain and guilt that was consuming her, even if only for a short while. She downed the rest of the brandy and filled the glass for a third time. The vision of them together came back to her in waves. She had seen it, so it was going to happen. Once it had happened, then maybe she would cease to be haunted by it. Without meaning to, she reached out with her hand and touched Van's face. He started, then gazed up at her.

'Kiss me,' she said. 'Kiss me like we're the only two people left in the world.'

He swallowed, his eyes darkening with desire for her. 'Are you sure?'

'Don't ask me that,' she said, pulling him closer; 'just do it.'

He touched her cheek, and drew her face towards him. Their lips touched, and then, within seconds, they were tearing each other's clothes off, their bodies pressed together in the dim lamplight.

Kelsey stared at her reflection in the wall mirror. A few feet away, Van was sleeping on the low bed, his bare chest rising and falling, but she paid him no attention, her focus upon her own face. Her eyes were red from crying, and she felt guilty that she had fallen into Van's arms so soon after Nurian's death. Had it helped? She didn't know, though the burden of the vision had been lifted from her shoulders. They had slept together; it was done, and she no longer had to worry about when it would happen. For a brief few moments in his arms, she had almost forgotten her grief and pain, and that made her feel even more guilty. What kind of person was she, that she could do that? A wicked, selfish person, unworthy of Nurian's friendship.

A headache was forming from the alcohol, so she refilled her glass and drank the contents, feeling sick and dizzy. She turned and glanced at Van. He loved her, or so he said. She started to cry again, and swigged from the bottle of brandy, as if drinking would somehow help. She retched, and almost dropped the bottle, her tears spilling down her face. She threw it against the wall, the glass shattering into sharp fragments, the brandy dripping onto the bare floorboards.

Van shot up in bed, his eyes wide. He glanced at the smashed bottle, then pulled Kelsey towards him, his arms reaching round her shoulders.

'I hate you,' she gasped, but didn't resist, her head burrowing into his shoulder as he held her close. It seemed wrong; everything seemed wrong.

Van said nothing, rocking her gently back and forth in his arms as if he were cradling an infant.

'I hate you,' she repeated, as she wept in his arms. 'I want Nurian; I want my mother.'

'I can't bring either of them here,' he whispered, 'but you have me.'

CHAPTER 19

UNCOVERED

P ort Sanders, Medio, The City – 3rd Malikon 3421
    Kagan stared out of the open shutters, his eyes wide. Outside, the rain was torrential. The noise it made was tremendous, a rumbling that covered Port Sanders and the rest of the City. Thunder echoed, and lightning flashed across the sky above the Warm Sea, while the raindrops drummed down on the red rooftops. The sun had vanished, replaced by a thick, dark impenetrable blanket of cloud. The streets were empty of people, and the rainwater was flowing down the middle of the road like a river. Every door and shutter was closed, except for the one he had opened in Lady Sofia's mansion, and all of the flower boxes had been taken inside.

He heard someone approach.

'What are you doing, Kagan?' said Sofia, her voice slightly teasing.

'Just... just watching the rain, ma'am.'

She came to stand beside him, and he swallowed, her proximity unsettling. He sensed her perfume, but kept his eyes on the open window.

'Freshmist,' she said. 'It has begun.'

'It's hard to believe that yesterday was clear and sunny,' he said, 'and now this, ma'am. For two months?'

'I believe so, Kagan. But after that, comes summer.'

'I was thinking, ma'am, about the New Year. It might be the year thirty-four twenty-one here, but back in Lostwell it'll be fifty-two fifty-three.'

'That's right,' she said, 'except, there is no Lostwell, not any more.'

'Do you really believe that, ma'am?'

'I do. The Ascendants destroyed our world, and it's gone, forever.'

'It seems too big, too awful, to imagine.'

'Yes, well, before you think too deeply about that, I need you to assist Saul in the kitchen.'

'Yes. Sorry, ma'am; I was distracted by the rain.'

He bowed and turned away, embarrassed. He had been babbling on about Lostwell to her ladyship as if she were a friend, rather than his employer, when he was supposed to have been working. He couldn't help it; she disarmed him at times, speaking informally to him, and even making jokes with him, and he occasionally forgot she was his boss.

What he couldn't forget, was how beautiful she was. It wasn't just her looks, it was the way she moved; her entire poise conveyed confidence and self-assurance. In some ways, she seemed older than her years, wiser than the average twenty-one year old, and he often found himself day-dreaming about her.

He hurried down the stairs to the ground floor, then took a breath and entered the kitchens.

'There you are, boy,' said Saul, a fierce look in his eyes.

The cook flung Kagan an apron.

'Put that on, boy, then get down to the cellar and bring up today's food crates – they're clearly marked.' He lifted a sharp butcher's knife and stared at Kagan. 'Don't drop anything, or I'll slice your fingers off, one at a time.'

Kagan frowned, and pulled the apron over his head.

'Filthy little Shinstran dog,' Saul muttered. 'Go on; off with you.'

Kagan said nothing in reply, and strode from the kitchen, heading towards the stairwell that led down into the basement of the mansion.

He had learned that there was no point antagonising Saul. For some reason, Lady Sofia over-looked the cook's foul temper and the threats he made to the other members of staff; one time, she had laughed when Elena had complained about some of the things that Saul had called her. Apart from the mistress of the house, only Gellie, the senior house-keeper, seemed immune from Saul's anger. Typical Torduans and Fordians, picking on the two young Shinstrans, he thought, as he descended the stairs.

He didn't mind. Being close to Lady Sofia more than made up for Gellie's contempt and Saul's threats. The food was good, the pay was good; in many ways, Kagan thought it was the best job he had ever done. And he got to see Sofia every day. He lifted the first crate, widened his stance to bear the weight, and carried it up the stairs. Gellie was in the kitchen when he entered, and she and Saul broke off a conversation as he walked in.

Kagan put the crate down onto a long table.

'Have you seen the rain?' he said. 'It's quite something, isn't it?'

Gellie narrowed her eyes as if she had seen something that had disgusted her, while Saul laughed.

'Save your breath, boy; you have another three crates to go.'

'I know, but...'

Saul brandished the knife, and Kagan frowned, then walked back out of the kitchen. No wonder the previous two staff had run away, he thought; that is, if Saul hadn't killed them and cut them up into small pieces. Gellie had forbidden him from asking questions about the fate of the two runaways, and he had been made to promise that he would never bring the subject up with her ladyship, which had only served to make him more suspicious. He descended back into the cellar, and glanced at the thick stone walls, imagining that the bones of murdered members of staff were hidden there.

Three more crates, and then Saul banished him from the kitchen, the cook refusing to allow Kagan to watch him work. Kagan's official position within the mansion was guard, but as there seemed to be very little guarding required, he often served as a general worker, helping out the others with whatever tasks Gellie and Saul dreamed up for him. Before Freshmist had commenced, that had meant daily trips to the market to pick up supplies, and he had got to know the streets of Port Sanders quite well before the skies had opened.

Gellie was waiting for him outside the kitchen.

Kagan bowed his head a little. 'Housekeeper.'

She stared at him for a moment. 'How are you at fixing roofs?'

'Em, I suppose it depends what's wrong with the roof. Is something wrong with our roof?'

'It has begun leaking into the attic.'

'I can certainly take a look. If it's just a couple of loose tiles, then I should be able to sort that. Back in Alea Tanton, I...'

'I'm not interested in hearing stories about your time in the gangs, Kagan. Your old, and no doubt criminal, life in the slums is of no concern to me. Get up into the attic, see what you can do, then report back to me.'

'Yes, ma'am.'

She strode off, and Kagan headed upstairs, stopping off in his quarters to pick up a bag of tools. He slung it over his shoulder and ascended one more flight. At the top of the stairs, Elena was mopping the floorboards. She stopped when she saw him.

'Hi, Kagan; what are you doing up here?'

He pointed up. 'Attic.'

She leaned the mop against the bucket and approached him, pushing him until his back was touching the balustrade.

'It's funny how we live in the same house but never see each other,' she said. She glanced at a side door, and put her hands on his chest. 'We have a few minutes, if her ladyship and the others are all downstairs.' She leaned up to kiss him.

He pushed her away. 'We can't; we'd lose our jobs if they caught us.'

'So? Don't you like me any more? You couldn't keep your hands off me in the camp, and now you're rejecting me?'

'You're being unreasonable, Elena.'

She narrowed her eyes. 'Are you forgetting why we got these jobs in the first place? I think you're getting too attached to that woman.'

'What woman?'

'Don't act innocent with me; I've seen the way you stare at her.'

Kagan frowned. 'Can we talk about this later?'

'No. It's always the same with you; you never want to take responsibility for your actions. You lead me on, and then abandon me as soon as you see someone like Lady Sofia.'

'Keep your voice down, Elena. Do you want the whole house to hear you?'

'When this job's done, I'm going to tell my brother how you treated me.'

'I don't know what you're talking about; I haven't done anything to you.'

'That's what I mean. You're supposed to love me, and you've practically ignored me from the moment we moved in here. I lie awake at night, hoping you'll knock on my door, but you never do. You were happy to break the rules in the camp when you wanted something from me; but now that you're working for some fancy woman, I'm not good enough for you any more. You're a pig, Kagan, a selfish pig. I wish I'd gone to Jezra.'

She turned round and hurried away, leaving the mop and bucket lying in the middle of the floor. Kagan chewed his lip. Everything Elena had said was true. He had used her in the camp, and his feelings for her had evaporated as soon as he had set eyes on Sofia. They had evaporated long before that, if he was being honest with himself. Things had been different in the camp; the atmosphere of desperation and hopelessness had made him long for physical contact, and Elena had been available. She had made him feel alive when he might otherwise have despaired, but he had never loved her.

Did that make him a pig? Probably. Did he care? No.

He glanced over the balustrade to check that no one had overheard, then turned and made his way towards the attic.

Two hours later, he arrived at the door to Gellie's little office, from where she ran the household. He knocked.

'Enter.'

He opened the door and walked in.

Gellie glanced up at him. 'Yes?'

Kagan tried not to stare at her green skin. 'I've fixed the roof, ma'am. The leak has stopped.'

'Who would have thought? So, you do have your uses? And here I was, thinking you were just another mindless brute, employed solely because her ladyship liked the look of you. It's a pity that you're about to lose your position.'

Kagan frowned. 'What?'

'Is that any way to address your superior? "What?" You sound like an oaf.' She shook her head. 'I told her ladyship to employ people with experience of serving the gods in the palaces of Old Alea, but did she listen? She did not. Instead, she hires gang thugs from the slums – semi-literate savages who haven't the first idea of how to work in a civilised environment. I've been looking for an excuse to get rid of you, and today, you handed one to me. As soon as her ladyship learns that you have been conducting a secret relationship with Elena, you will both be put out onto the street.'

'You're wrong,' he said. 'I'm not having a relationship with Elena.'

'Really? Then explain to me what you and she were arguing about at the top of the stairs this morning? I have exceptionally good hearing, and it sounded exactly like a lovers' quarrel. I couldn't make out many of the words, but I did hear her call you a pig. So, either you've let her down, or you've been harassing her. Either way, if I breathe a word of this to her ladyship, your position here will be terminated.'

'If?' Kagan said. 'A moment ago, you told me you were going to tell her, and now you're saying "if" you tell her?' He gave the Fordian woman a wry smile. 'What do you want?'

'You catch on quickly; I'll give you that.' She leaned across her desk. 'Take a seat, boy.'

Kagan hesitated for a moment, then sat.

'Good boy. Do you want to keep your job?'

'Yes.'

'Then you'll listen, and do what I ask. If you refuse, then I will go straight to her ladyship, and tell her everything. I own you now, Kagan.' She articulated his name with venom in her voice. 'I have friends, powerful friends, living here in the City, and I want you to help them carry out a little job. It's simple. A few nights from now, I will make my excuses and stay away for the evening. My friends will arrive after midnight, and you will let them in; and then you will assist them.'

'Assist them with what?'

Gellie smiled. 'What do you think, boy? Lady Sofia is one of the richest women in Port Sanders. Don't worry; no one will be hurt. Elena and her ladyship will be unharmed as long as they don't resist, and Saul will be too drunk to notice; I'll make sure of that. Once my friends have emptied the mansion of its valuables, you will have to run away; but if you do this for me, I will ensure that you get a fair split of the proceeds. That's your choice, Kagan – help me and get rich, or lose your job.'

'You'd betray her ladyship?'

Gellie snorted. 'Is she even a real lady? I've never heard of a Lady Sofia from the Southern Cape. Who's to say that she didn't steal that suitcase full of gold? She might have found it while wandering the streets of Old Alea during all the chaos, and now she's pretending to be someone important. We have only her word that she is who she says she is.' She peered at him. 'Well, what do you say?'

'I'll think about it.'

'Don't take too long. If I have to go back to my friends and tell them that you're being uncooperative, then all manner of nasty things may occur when they arrive. Your friend, Elena, might not be so safe after all. And as for you, well, you'll be unemployed by then. You have until midnight tonight to let me know. Now, leave me.'

Kagan sat in his room, the shutters lying wide open so that he could watch the rain. Lightning streaked across the sky, and the roar of noise was drowning out the argument going on in his head. His natural inclination was to say nothing and go along with the housekeeper's conspiracy. He didn't trust her pledge that he would receive his fair share, but in the confusion of a robbery, he would make sure he wasn't left out. If he helped Gellie's friends, then he might risk the anger of Dizzler, but if other robbers got there first, then that was life. Dizzler would understand. What troubled him more were the vague threats towards Elena and Sofia. If he refused to help, and lost his job, then he wouldn't be able to intervene to make sure that they were safe. Sofia didn't look like she could fight, and he knew that Elena couldn't – they would be easy prey for a robber with a sadistic streak. If it was going to happen, it would be far better if he were there in person, so that he would be able to exert some control over the situation. He had taken part in several house robberies in Alea Tanton, and he knew well how things never went according to plan. There was always an element of confusion and chaos, and he was good at thinking on his feet.

The end result would be the same, however – he would have to leave Port Sanders and head off into the unknown environment of the Circuit, about which he had heard nothing but bad news. He loved living in Port Sanders; it was like paradise compared to the slums of Alea Tanton, and he would miss seeing Sofia. His heart fell at the thought. Everything about her drew him in, and like a moth to candlelight he felt almost blinded by her. What if the robbers hurt her? The idea made him angry, and he imagined fighting off her attackers and beating them half to death with his bare fists. Her safety would be at risk, even if he were there.

Kagan frowned. There was only one thing he could do to keep her safe.

He cursed himself. He barely knew Sofia, and yet he was going to ruin his life to warn her. He stood. No one was going to be happy with what he was about to do. Not Dizzler, who would be angry that he had lost his job; not Elena, who would hate him for putting Sofia first; and not her ladyship, who probably wouldn't even believe him.

The mansion was quiet when he stole from his room. He glanced around the second floor landing, but no one was there. On the floor above, he thought he could hear the swish of a mop. The mansion was organised around a central atrium, the glass covering of which let in the light from outside. At that moment, the sky was a brooding, leaden grey, but there was enough light for Kagan to glance down onto the floors below.

He made his way downstairs to the first floor, and padded along the thick carpet to her ladyship's private rooms. There was a chance that Gellie was visiting her at that moment, but Kagan had made up his mind. He knocked on the main door leading to her suite of rooms, and entered the little reception hall. He listened, but heard no voices coming from any of the side doors. He knocked on the door to the study, where he had been interviewed on his first day, and looked inside, but it was empty.

The door to the sitting room opened and Sofia walked out.

'Oh, Kagan; it's you? With all the creeping about, I thought for a minute there that I was being robbed.'

Kagan blinked.

'What's the matter?' she said. 'Tongue-tied?'

'No, ma'am. I... I mean, I wanted to speak to you about something important.'

She raised an eyebrow. 'So, this is not about the roof? Good. I would have patiently listened to your tale of repairing the tiles, but it would have bored me stiff. Come into the sitting room.'

She turned and re-entered the chamber, and Kagan followed her in.

She pointed at a chair. 'Sit. No, actually; I'll sit. You can fetch me a drink.'

He walked to the cabinet by the wall. 'What would you like, ma'am?'

'Taran brandy,' she said, as if it were obvious.

He opened a bottle and poured her a generous measure, then walked to a low table and set it down in front of her.

'Now, you can sit,' she said.

'I might stand for this, ma'am.'

'Oh.' She sipped her brandy. 'Right, let's hear it.'

Kagan took a breath. 'Your senior housekeeper, Gellie, is planning to betray you. She has friends who are going to rob this house in a few days' time, and she wanted me to help them. She told me a couple of hours ago, but it's taken me a while to muster the courage to come and tell you.'

Sofia stared blankly at him. 'Gellie is planning on robbing me? Is that what you're alleging?'

'Yes; that's what she told me.'

'And she asked you to help her?'

'Yes.'

'But, Kagan, she can't abide you. Why would she trust you? Surely, she'd know that you'd come and tell me?'

Kagan said nothing.

Sofia narrowed her eyes. 'What has she got on you? She must be blackmailing you; it's the only explanation. What does she know about you that I don't?'

Kagan exhaled, wondering if he had made a terrible mistake.

'I lied to you, ma'am, during the interview,' he said. 'I told you something that wasn't true.'

'I see,' she said, a frown descending onto her face.

'When I told you that I didn't know Elena, I was lying. I did know her; in fact, I'd been having a relationship with her back in the camp in Scythe territory. We were advised that it would be easier to get the jobs if we pretended not to know each other, and so that's what we did. But, my relationship with Elena was over before you interviewed us. We were split up in the camps, and I had barely seen her for a month before we came here that day.'

Sofia raised a hand to silence him. 'I think I've heard enough.'

'Can I say one more thing?'

She nodded.

'I'm sorry, ma'am; sorry that I lied to you. But, I'm not lying about Gellie; she means you harm, and I couldn't stand by and let that happen.'

'What is an appropriate punishment for lying to me?'

'I will take whatever punishment you think necessary. If you want to throw me out onto the street, then I'll accept it, but if you let me stay, I'll do anything to prove my loyalty to you. I made a mistake.'

Sofia's frown evaporated, and a strange smile appeared on her lips. She turned her head. 'What do you think, Gellie? Should we let the boy stay?'

The housekeeper emerged from a side door, her eyes narrow as she regarded Kagan.

He gasped. 'What? But...'

Gellie bowed her head. 'He appears to have passed your test, ma'am.'

Sofia laughed. 'I notice that you didn't actually answer the question.'

The housekeeper pursed her lips, as if pondering. 'He is the first to have passed the test, ma'am, so, yes. He has proved his loyalty.'

'A test?' said Kagan. 'All that... was a test?'

Sofia shrugged. 'Call me paranoid, but I like to know if I can trust those who work for me.' She nodded to the housekeeper. 'That will be all, Gellie. Thank you for your assistance in this.'

The Fordian woman bowed, then walked from the sitting room.

'I don't understand,' said Kagan; 'you mean that Gellie isn't going to rob the mansion?'

'Of course not,' said Sofia. 'Every word she spoke to you, I had already scripted. I told her what to say. I know that you were mixed up with the gangs in Alea Tanton, and I needed to place a mixture of fear and greed into your way, to see how you'd react.'

'What about Elena?'

'Did you really believe that neither Gellie nor I would notice that something existed between you and Elena? Did you think we were too naïve to guess that you knew each other? That girl has tried to kiss you several times.' Her smile faded. 'If you *had* kissed her, even once, you would no longer have a job. But, you resisted.'

'What will happen to Elena now?'

'Don't concern yourself with that. Instead, let's discuss how you can make up for your wicked lies.' She regarded him for a moment. 'Get me another brandy, and get one for yourself.'

Kagan got up and walked to the cabinet, aware that Sofia was watching him the entire time. What did she want from him? His nerves had been pulled taut by her 'test' and his head was spinning. She had tried to entrap him, and it looked as though her forgiveness would involve conditions. He poured two measures of brandy and brought them back to the table.

'Have you ever tried Taran brandy before?' she said.

'No, ma'am.'

'Taste it. I think you'll find it acceptable.'

He drank some of the golden liquid, and felt the warm burn on his throat.

'There was nothing on Lostwell that could compete with this,' she said. 'Don't you agree?'

'It is a very fine drink, ma'am.'

She smiled. 'Relax. I'm not going to bite you; well, not too hard. Right, let's get the rules out of the way. If you please me, you will stay; if you don't, then you'll have to leave. I am not looking for love, or a relationship, but I do need a man for... other reasons. Your body belongs to me. In return for your silence and loyalty, your pay will be trebled, and you will become quite a wealthy young man. You can have the freedom of Port Sanders once the rains have stopped, but you must never, ever, find yourself entangled with another woman. If I discover any disloyalty in this regard, I will have you killed. I can be jealous, possessive even, and I will not tolerate sharing you with anyone.' She drained her brandy. 'Hmm, quite lovely. Is there anything about these rules that you don't understand?'

He stared at her, his face flushing. 'You want me to... Uh, I...'

She shook her head at him. 'Don't do that. Don't get all flustered; it's not very attractive. If you have something to say, then say it; if you don't, then remain quiet. Now, did you wish to ask me something?'

Kagan felt dizzy, and he had to suppress an urge to run from the room. He calmed his breathing. Wasn't this exactly what he had wanted? He had been dreaming about Sofia ever since he had arrived in the mansion, and, if he understood her correctly, she was offering herself to him. She didn't want love or a relationship; but didn't that suit him perfectly? She had selected him for a reason, it just hadn't been the reason that he had previously thought was true. His self-confidence started to bubble back to the surface.

'I am at your service, ma'am; and I think we should get started right away.'

'That's better,' she said. 'Yes, that's the attitude I want to see.'

She put down her glass and locked eyes with him, and he felt a rush of desire surge through his body. She stood, and extended her hand towards him. He took it, and she began to lead him to the bedroom.

'Try not to think of this as another test,' she said, a smile playing on her lips, 'but, be warned; I will be judging you.'

The following morning, Kagan awoke in his own bed, the sound of the rain battering off the shutters stirring him from sleep. He opened his eyes and stared at the ceiling. He had spent the entire afternoon, evening, and most of the night in Sofia's quarters, and it had been the greatest experience of his young life. He had considered himself experienced with women, but she had shown him how little he had truly understood. She had known exactly what she had wanted, and he had learned quickly.

He wondered when he would next be invited to her rooms. She had told him that their arrangement was not something to be spoken about openly within the mansion, and that he was to carry on with his duties, waiting for her to take the lead. He was never to boast about it, nor ever speak to anyone else about what went on behind the closed doors of her quarters. Gellie would pretend to be ignorant of the situation, and he was to act as if nothing was going on.

He would still have to deal with Elena, he realised, the thought filling the pit of his stomach with anxiety. Elena would take one look at him and know that something had changed. How long would it take for her to work out what was happening?

He got up, showered, and got dressed in his work uniform.

A noise was coming from downstairs, and he walked out onto the landing and glanced over the balustrade. In the hall below, Gellie was speaking to a man, while a couple of packed bags were lying close to the front doors of the mansion. Kagan squinted at the man, then realised it was Albeck, from Dizzler's crew – the man who had arranged the interviews.

He walked downstairs, and Albeck greeted him, shaking his hand.

'Good morning, son,' he said. 'How have you settled in?'

'Very well, thank you.'

'Good. It's a pity about Elena, but I'm glad that your performance here has been satisfactory.'

'Better than satisfactory,' said Gellie, her perpetual frown imprinted onto her face. 'Her ladyship is very pleased with Kagan.'

Kagan glanced from one to the other. 'What did you mean about Elena?'

'Her ladyship has decided to terminate her contract with immediate effect,' said Albeck. 'I shall file it with the Refugee Council, and see if I can find her somewhere more suitable. You, of course, will be staying.'

Elena emerged from a side room, her eyes red. She caught sight of Kagan, and a look of pure contempt came over her features.

'Are you ready to leave, girl?' said Albeck.

Elena nodded, then looked away.

'Excellent.' Albeck turned to Gellie. 'Always a pleasure doing business with you. Apologies that the girl didn't work out. Does her ladyship require other candidates for the position? I could see what's available at the Refugee Council?'

'Not at the moment, Albeck,' said Gellie. 'We shall make do with three members of staff for now. If anything changes, we shall be in touch.'

'Right you are,' he said, then he picked up the two bags from the floor. He glanced at Elena. 'Time to say your goodbyes.'

She scowled at Kagan, but said nothing.

Albeck shrugged, then nodded to Gellie. 'Pass on my deepest regards to her ladyship.'

Kagan stood back and watched as Albeck escorted Elena out of the mansion.

Gellie gave him a curt glance. 'Back to work, boy. Saul needs today's supplies brought up from the cellar.'

He bowed. 'Yes, ma'am.'

She strode away, leaving Kagan alone in the middle of the hallway. He glanced down at his clenched right fist, and uncurled his fingers to reveal the slip of paper that Albeck had secreted into his palm during the handshake.

Due to Elena's departure, it read, *our mutual friend has decided to delay his plans until after Freshmist. Use the time to look into the sources of her ladyship's wealth, as she appears to have more than we had realised; and wait for summer.*

Kagan walked to the fireplace in the hall, tossed the note into the flames, and watched it burn. Summer. That meant he had two months; two whole months of Sofia.

He smiled. Maybe Freshmist wasn't so bad after all.

CHAPTER 20

THE MOTHER OF THE CITY

Iceward Range, Medio, The City – 23rd Malikon 3421

The rain battered down onto the carriage roof as the small convoy wound its way down from the slopes of the Iceward Range. In good weather, the journey from Pella to Icehaven would take no more than two or three hours, but the storms of Freshmist had reduced the roads to muddy ruins, and their pace across the last stretch of the hills had been slow.

Yendra glanced at Kelsey, who was sitting opposite her in the warm, comfortable carriage. Over a month had passed since the death of Captain Nurian, and the young Holdfast woman remained dispirited and contrary, as if her grief was manifesting itself as raw anger. Under normal circumstances, Yendra would not have asked her to come along, but the invitation from Lady Yvona had specifically named Kelsey. Perhaps the trip would do her good. After all, there was little for Kelsey to do in Jezra during Freshmist. The bad weather had grounded the dragons, but that was fine, as the greenhides had scuttled away into the darkest reaches of the forest as soon as the storms had begun. Lower Jezra was secure, and significant inroads had been made into fortifying the ridge running along the top of the cliff, ready for the next push in summer. But none of that concerned Kelsey, and Yendra had seen her –

listless and restless, drinking too much, and getting into arguments with anyone she came across, especially Van, who had been at the receiving end of several angry tirades.

The carriage came to an abrupt halt as a wheel caught in the thick mud. Soldiers jumped down, and began digging the wheel out, while the incessant rain soaked them through in seconds.

'Stuck again,' Yendra said. 'This truly is the worst time of year to be travelling. On days like this, I wish I had a Quadrant.'

Kelsey said nothing, her gaze directed out of the window.

'Have you ever used a Quadrant, Kelsey?'

She shook her head.

'You must have seen a few, though?'

'Obviously.'

'Please don't take that tone, especially when we get to Icehaven. Lady Yvona has gone to a lot of trouble to make this day a memorable one; you are being honoured.'

'No, I'm not; my brother is being honoured. My big, dopey brother. I just happen to share the same family name.' She glanced at Yendra. 'You all wish he was here, instead of me, don't you?'

'No, Kelsey. Believe it or not, I am very fond of you, and I hate to see you in pain. You are so young...'

'I'm the same age as the Queen.'

'Indeed. Her Majesty is also young. I sometimes feel like the mother of the City, trying to guide and help the younger generation.'

'Don't patronise me, Yendra. You're ancient; I get it. You've seen mortals come and go for centuries. Does it not make you sick, seeing mortals continually make the same mistakes over and over?'

Yendra raised an eyebrow. 'They are never exactly the same mistakes. And I apologise if you thought I was patronising you. The truth is, I find it difficult to talk to you, Kelsey. You are fiercely intelligent, just as Queen Emily is, but you are confrontational, while her Majesty is more... diplomatic, let's say. I'm not saying you need to change, but your stubbornness can be hard to deal with at times.'

'So, it's all my fault?'

'No. I recognise that I am not always easy to get along with. Remember that I can read minds. I know well how I am viewed by some – a self-righteous, arrogant god, who looks down upon mere mortals. Some fear me, some hate me; almost no one understands me.'

'Aye? Tell me one thing about you that's been misunderstood.'

'That I am devoid of human feelings. That's the most common accusation I see in people's minds. They think me emotionless, because I appear calm. That is not true. I suffer from self-doubt and anxiety like anyone else, and I am haunted by the deaths of my three daughters. My last glimpse of Kahlia was when my brother Michael killed her, an image that has been burned into my mind. People say that time helps. It does, but the wound never fully heals; how could it, when the love I bear for them hasn't gone away? Next to the deaths of my three girls, the centuries spent in the restrainer mask pale into insignificance. I would endure a millennium in the mask if it would bring one of my daughters back to me, and I would consider it a cheap price to pay.'

Kelsey looked away, her gaze lowered, and Yendra watched her.

'What happened to Captain Nurian wasn't your fault,' she said; 'you know that?'

Kelsey nodded.

'There was nothing you could have done. Try not to be so hard on yourself.'

'I'm not being hard on myself. I've been through it a million times and I know now that it wasn't my fault, but it doesn't matter – he's still dead. What I'm feeling is not guilt; it's loneliness. I feel so alone here, Yendra; cut off, adrift. Isolated.'

'What about Frostback?'

'Oh, Frostback tries to help, but she doesn't really understand, and she has Halfclaw to keep her company, as well as her father and the rest of them. I have a bond with her, but it isn't as strong or as deep as the bond Blackrose and Maddie share. That's why I sleep in Jezra now, and not in the quarry. I'm failing at being a dragon rider; I can't even get that right. With Nurian, I finally found someone who got me, and then... Then, you know what happened. I keep thinking back to my sister, about when she lost her husband; and I know it's not the same, but all I can think about is what she went through.' She stared at Yendra. 'I don't ever want to go through that. If that's what losing someone close to you is like, then maybe I shouldn't get close to anyone.'

Yendra hesitated. What could she say to Kelsey, when that was how she had lived her life? After the death of her own husband, the mortal father of her three daughters, she had sworn never to allow herself to love anyone in that way again. And she had kept to her word. The other gods and demigods of the City had taken many, temporary, mortal partners and lovers, some to have children with, others because they couldn't bear to be alone. But Yendra had remained apart from that. How could she criticise Kelsey for wanting to do the same?

'I understand, Kelsey,' she said at last.

'Is that it? No advice?'

'No advice.'

'Good. Thank you.'

The carriage got moving again, and the young Holdfast woman turned back to the window.

———

It was evening by the time the carriage rolled through the gates of Icehaven, though, in the depths of Freshmist, it could be hard to tell when the day ended and evening began. The rainy seasons were the only times of the year when Icehaven seemed the same as the rest of the City – with no sunlight visible through the thick cloud cover, the perpetual shadows covering the town made no difference. The carriage went through the empty, rain-washed streets, before pulling into a courtyard at the rear of Alkirk Palace.

Yendra smiled at the sight of it, memories of her recovery from the mask stirring within her. A line of Icewarder courtiers emerged from the building, each holding a wide umbrella.

'Ready to get wet?' said Yendra.

Kelsey frowned.

One of the courtiers opened the side door of the carriage and a gust of freezing cold wind and rain slammed into Yendra as she descended to the flagstones. She and Kelsey hurried through the rainstorm, the umbrellas offering almost no protection from the elements, and entered the palace.

Yendra shook her head, and water flew from her hair. She glanced at Kelsey, who looked bedraggled and windswept, her clothes dripping onto the polished floor.

'Greetings,' said a woman in uniform, as she bowed. 'Welcome back to Alkirk, your Highness.'

'Thank you, Major Hannia,' Yendra said. 'This is Kelsey Holdfast.'

'Good evening, Lady Holdfast; it is an honour to meet you.'

'Don't let my mother hear you call me that,' said Kelsey. 'She's Lady Holdfast, not me.'

'Apologies. Shall I call you "Miss?"'

'Just Kelsey will do, thanks.'

'Certainly, Kelsey. Shall I show you to your rooms, so that you can change into something drier?'

'That would be most welcome,' said Yendra.

Hannia led them up a flight of stairs into the depths of the palace, and they stopped at a door.

'These are the same quarters that Corthie Holdfast stayed in when he lived here,' said the major.

Yendra smiled. 'I remember.'

Hannia opened the door. 'There is plenty of hot water, and I'll have food and your bags brought up in a moment. The ceremony isn't due to start for another two hours, so you should have enough time.'

Yendra and Kelsey entered the spacious compartment, and the god glanced around, seeing the large dining table where she had shared so many meals with Corthie. Hannia bowed and left the apartment, and Yendra sat by the table.

'Have your bath first,' said Yendra; 'I can wait.'

Kelsey eyed her. 'Are you saying that I stink?'

'I never know how to react to your jokes, Kelsey.'

'I know; that's why they're so funny, well, they are to me. They make *you* feel all uncomfortable and awkward, and that sort of brings you down to my level.' She glanced around. 'So, you lived here with my wee brother? Sounds cosy.'

'It wasn't just the two of us, you'll be happy to know. Be aware that your brother is idolised in Icehaven; he made a large impression on the townsfolk here, and they dearly loved him.'

'That's just great. I know a few stories about him pooping his pants when he was a little boy – do you think that'd go down well with this audience? What about the time I cut the head off his toy bear with a pair of scissors, and he cried for days?'

'It might be better to stick to banalities. Corthie was always good at giving a speech, even when he didn't feel like it.'

'Oh, I can give a good speech too; our mother used to drill it into us as children – only, the content of this one might upset a few people.'

'Please tell me you're joking.'

She turned for the bathroom. 'I guess you'll just have to wait and see.'

Kelsey had been correct, Yendra reflected as she watched the young woman speak to the packed hall. She *was* good at giving a speech. Up on the podium, it seemed almost as if a different person was addressing the attentive crowd. Kelsey was confident, relaxed, even charming, as she related a few stories about her brother to the Icewarders. The crowd laughed at the right moments, and stood to give her an ovation as her speech came to an end.

Yendra felt proud of her. It was irrational, but she couldn't help it. She knew how much pain Kelsey was in, and yet she had been able to put her feelings to one side in order to do something that must have seemed like the most awful chore. No one in the crowd would have been able to guess the torment she was feeling about Nurian, or Van, or her increasingly difficult relationship with the dragons.

Kelsey sat and exhaled, and Lady Yvona stepped up to the podium.

'Thank you, Kelsey Holdfast, for that most wonderful, and inspiring speech. The people of Icehaven owe your family a great debt, and I feel honoured to call your brother a friend. It pleases me that he has managed to find his way home, and I sincerely hope you feel at home, here, in our City. You will always be welcome in Icehaven.'

The crowd applauded again.

Major Hannia took the podium as Lady Yvona sat.

'That concludes this evening's ceremony,' she said to the crowd. 'Many thanks to our honoured guests – Princess Yendra and Kelsey Holdfast, and thank you to everyone who has attended; have a safe trip home.'

Yendra glanced at Kelsey as the crowds began to leave the hall.

'Well done,' she said. 'You made it look easy.'

Kelsey shrugged. 'Had plenty of practice.'

'You said your mother taught you?'

'Aye. She spent our childhoods trying to turn us into leaders, or aristocrats, at the very least. She made us speak at the Estate festivals.'

Yvona leaned over. 'May I intrude for a moment?'

Yendra smiled.

'I know you are tired, your Highness, but I would value some of your time.'

'I'm glad,' said Yendra, 'as I have much to discuss with you. Kelsey will join us.'

Yvona glanced at the young Holdfast woman, but Yendra knew that she was too polite to make any objections.

'Of course,' said the Governor of Icehaven. She stood, the long skirts of her honey-yellow dress reaching the smooth floor. 'Let's go upstairs to my rooms, and make ourselves comfortable.'

Major Hannia remained behind to talk with some of the Icewarders who had been in the audience, while Yvona led Yendra and Kelsey up to her apartment. Most of the palace was given over to administrative offices and a hospital, and the Governor occupied only a small section of one floor. There was also a distinct lack of guards, and Yendra worried about Gloamer spies infiltrating the palace. Yvona was kind and acted with integrity, but Yendra wished she paid more attention to the harsh realities of the City.

They went into a small room, where a fire was roaring in a hearth. The shutters were sealed against the rain and wind, and the chamber was warm, and softly lit by a pair of oil lamps. On one wall hung a huge portrait of Yvona's family – her sister, her two brothers, and her mother, Yendra's sister. Yendra glanced at the painting as she sat. Every one of them depicted in it, except for Yvona, had died in the Civil War. Rand was there, in his battle armour, holding the Axe that bore his name, the axe that Yendra now wielded. Yendra's eyes settled on Princess Niomi, her sister. She was wearing a beatific expression close to how she had looked in real life, until her death at the hands of Princess Khora, in one of the most horrific moments of the Civil War. Niomi's death had severed the Royal Family in two, and had hardened Yendra's determination to overthrow the government of the City.

She had failed, but she had then survived to see her vision come true in a way that she had never expected.

'Let's have a bottle of wine,' said Yvona.

Yendra pulled her gaze from the painting.

'Kelsey; do you like wine?' said Yvona.

'If it's got alcohol in it, I'll drink it.'

Yvona smiled, as she uncorked a bottle. 'Now, who does that remind me of? I'm so glad you could come today, Kelsey. How are the dragons?'

'They're grumpy about the rain. It hardly rained at all in Khatanax, especially where they lived. But, they're fine. They should be leaving once summer comes. Deathfang wanted me to remember to say thank you, for all of the hospitality you've shown them; letting them stay in the quarry and all that.'

'Tell Deathfang that he's very welcome, although Icehaven can't take all the credit. After all, the bill is being settled by the Crown.' She turned to Yendra as she filled three glasses with wine. 'Your Highness, aunt; what was it you wished to discuss?'

'You go first, please.'

'Very well. I wanted to go over the constitutional proposals with you. The King wrote to me, and suggested some compromises, and I think a middle ground could be found.'

'Let me stop you, niece,' said Yendra. 'I am not empowered to negotiate in this area. I think it best if I don't get involved.'

'I don't mind talking about politics,' said Kelsey. 'I hear that the Icewarders voted for you, Yvona.'

'That's right,' she said. 'As of now, I remain the only elected tribal leader in the City. The other tribes have discussed it, but we are the only ones who have gone ahead and done it.'

'I have strived to maintain a strict neutrality in these matters,' said Yendra. 'It is not for one of the God-Children to try to dictate the constitutional arrangements of the City. Military affairs – yes; politics – no.'

Yvona's expression darkened a little. 'You wish to discuss military affairs with me?'

Yendra caught her gaze and held it. 'Yes.'

The warmth seemed to drain from the room. Yvona sipped her wine, and glanced away.

'Prince Montieth has not left Ooste,' Yendra went on, 'and the citizens trapped there are suffering great hardship. We cannot strike, as the prince has threatened to kill them all, but we cannot allow the situation to continue. A land blockade against Dalrig would hurt the City, and be wholly ineffective, as Dalrig can get everything it needs from the Cold Sea. The Crown needs the Icewarders' fleet to get involved. Only a combined blockade, from land and sea, will exert enough pressure to force Montieth to back down.'

'Or he'll go to war,' said Yvona. 'The Dalrigians have a larger fleet than us, and they have several heavily-armed merchant vessels. If I ordered our ships to blockade the harbour at Dalrig, then we could be attacked from the other direction, from their base on the Grey Isle.'

'This has been anticipated. What if, niece, I told you that you could have a dragon on hand, to protect your ships from attack? As for the Grey Isle, we intend to occupy it, and use it to force the Dalrigians into submission.'

Yvona stared at her. 'You're going to invade the Grey Isle? With what? I will not permit the Icewarder militia to take part in this; they would be slaughtered. The Dalrigian soldiers are better trained, and better equipped than ours.'

'We wouldn't be using your soldiers, Yvona. All I am asking for is the fleet. You can blockade Dalrig harbour, and still have enough ships left over to sail to the Western Bank and pick up the Banner regiments. It is they who will be doing the fighting; all you need to do is transport them to the Grey Isle.'

Yvona raised an eyebrow. 'The Banner forces? Those mercenaries from Lostwell? Can you trust them?'

'I have complete faith in them,' she said. 'They are the best soldiers I have ever worked with. They make the Blades look like amateurs in comparison.'

'You can't be serious, aunt?'

'I am perfectly serious. I watched them train and organise themselves in the Bulwark, and I've seen them in action every day in Jezra. No other tribe or militia could have achieved what they have achieved. They are disciplined, loyal, and extremely well-trained. More than that, they have transformed the Lostwell Brigades, from a ragged band of bewildered refugees, into a coherent and efficient team of experts in support and logistics. The Banner have trained them, mentored them, and instilled them with their own values. I wouldn't have believed it possible if I hadn't seen it with my own eyes.'

Yvona looked sceptical. She swirled the wine in her glass. 'Let's say that this is all true. The Banner and the Brigades are in Jezra, yes? For my fleet to pick them up, they would need to be on the Cold Sea side of the Western Bank, iceward of the Clashing Seas.'

'There is an ancient harbour on that side,' said Yendra. 'It is heavily used by Gloamers from the Grey Isle, as a base from which to raid the surrounding countryside. Westrig, I believe the harbour is named.'

'I am aware of Westrig,' said Yvona; 'my own ships have used it occasionally. It is where Corthie Holdfast was picked up, when he was rescued from the Western Bank. But, aunt, it is several miles iceward of

Jezra, and the intervening ground will be crawling with greenhides when summer comes. How will the soldiers and their equipment be taken to Westrig? They would be massacred on the way.'

Yendra smiled. 'Do you think we have been idle during Freshmist? The greenhides are skulking within the depths of the forest, leaving us a free hand.'

'To do what?'

'The Lostwell Brigades have been out every day since the rains began, reconstructing the old wall that used to run between Jezra and Westrig. By the time summer comes, Westrig will be safely in our hands.'

Yvona stared at Yendra, her mouth falling open. 'Impossible.'

'Why, Yvona?'

'It's Freshmist. No one can work outside in Freshmist.'

Yendra smiled. 'Did I mention the discipline of the Brigades? A hundred yards of wall a day – that's their target. Ten thousand Brigade refugees, toiling every day in the rain and mud, each competing to build their stretch of wall the fastest. For them, this is the first time they have been able to work without the threat of greenhide attack. Compared to the jaws and talons of the Eternal Enemy, a bit of rain is nothing.'

'You're calling Freshmist "a bit of rain?" Torrential hailstorms? Winds so strong that nothing can sail? And you're forcing refugees to work in those conditions?'

'I'm not forcing them. For this operation, I took the plans to the Combined Council, a group of Banner and Brigade officers elected by the ranks, and sought their agreement first. Had I ordered them, they would have done it, but I find that this approach is far better. Once they had agreed in principle, they set about organising the details them-selves, and I took a step back. Rest assured, niece, that the Banner forces will be ready and waiting in Westrig if you decide to help us.'

'I don't know. Icehaven could lose everything if this goes wrong. We depend utterly on our fleet for food and fuel, and don't forget that we also feed half of the Circuit; the Evaders would also starve if our ships were sunk. And we have no wood to repair damaged ships, let alone to build any new ones.'

'Wood will be in plentiful supply if we succeed,' said Yendra, 'and I promise that the Icewarders will get their fair share.'

Yvona shook her head. 'I'm sorry, but too much could go wrong.'

Kelsey raised a hand. 'I have a question.'

They glanced at her.

'You're elected, right? The Icewarders chose you to lead them. What do they want? How would they react if you did as Yendra suggests?'

Yvona frowned. 'To my shame, most Icewarders would be delighted if we went to war with Dalrig.' She sighed. 'There are many in Icehaven who are still extremely angry about Dalrig's behaviour during the greenhide invasion. The Gloamers sided with Duke Marcus, and locked the gates of the Union Walls against us. Not only that, but their ships hunted ours in the Cold Sea, and sank several. Their worst offence was over Fishcross. They occupied the town, then gave it to the Blades to use against us. When the greenhides came, the Blades panicked and fled, leaving thousands of Icewarders behind to be slaughtered. Fishcross will take years to recover. I have tried to counsel reconciliation and forgiveness, but I can feel the anger that exists here.'

'Then, you'd have no problem finding volunteers?' said Kelsey.

'None, whatsoever.'

'And, if they learned that you'd turned down this opportunity?'

'They would be greatly angered.'

'Could they vote you out?'

Yvona's eyes narrowed. 'It wouldn't be straightforward, but there is a process to remove me. It wouldn't come to that. I have ruled Icehaven for well over two centuries, Kelsey, and my mother ruled for a thousand years before that. If I refused, then the people would be angry, but I would be able to ride it out.'

'Even if the sister of Corthie Holdfast spoke out in favour of the plan?'

'You would do that?'

'Come on, Yvona,' said Kelsey; 'don't you think it's time you picked a side and stuck to it? You did the right thing during the reign of Marcus, or so I've heard. Right now, Montieth is laughing at the City, and the King and Queen can do nothing about it without your help. But, if you swung your weight behind the Crown, then we could take Montieth down a notch or two. Your tribe would love you for it, and I'm sure Emily would be very grateful.'

'And, on a practical level,' said Yendra, 'we would offer you full access to the Grey Isle and Westrig harbours, while keeping the Gloamers out. Your fleet would have a golden opportunity to increase the wealth of Icehaven.'

'And Tarstation?' said Yvona.

'Without support from Dalrig, Tarstation will fall into line,' said Yendra. 'The entire Cold Sea would open to you.'

Yvona got to her feet. She stared at the giant portrait of her family for a moment, then bowed her head.

'I'll need to consult with Major Hannia,' she said. 'Wait here.'

She strode from the room, her yellow dress swishing past where Kelsey sat.

Yendra glanced at the young Holdfast woman sitting next to her. 'Why did you intervene, Kelsey?'

Kelsey shrugged. 'Didn't you want me to? I thought you needed some help.'

'My niece was on the verge of refusing, until you spoke up. You said things to her that, perhaps, I could not. Once again, the Queen will owe you her thanks, if Yvona agrees to help us.'

'Oh, she's going to help us. Her and that Hannia woman are joined at the hip. She wouldn't be asking her if she hadn't already made up her mind.'

Yendra smiled at her, feeling a pride that felt almost maternal.

Kelsey frowned. 'Why are you peering at me like that?'

'I'm just glad, Kelsey,' she said; 'that you're on our side.'

CHAPTER 21

SEEKING PERMISSION

Pella, Auldan, The City – 7th Amalan 3421

Emily frowned at the pieces on the gaming board. She had been distracted by the conversation she had been having with her mother, and realised that it was now impossible to let her win, as she usually did.

'Hurry up, dear,' her mother said; 'even I can see your winning move. What are you waiting for?'

Emily sighed, and moved the piece, ending the game.

'Well done, dear,' said her mother, a slight twinkle in her eye. 'I knew you'd beat me eventually.' She glanced at the closed shutters of her small sitting room. 'I'll be happy when the summer comes. The first month of Freshmist is bearable, but by the time we get into Amalan, I'm desperate for it to end.'

Emily continued to stare at the board, trying to figure out where she had gone wrong.

Her mother laughed. 'You look disappointed to have won, dear.'

'No, mother, I...'

'Come on, dear; do you think I haven't noticed you letting me win? Today, I decided to allow you to take the victory.'

'What? You've been letting me let you win?'

'It seemed important to you, dear. I suspect that you are feeling a little guilty that I have no relevant role to play in the Royal Court, and you think that by allowing me to beat you, I'll feel better. You don't need to worry; the fact that you visit me every day is enough, Emily.'

Emily said nothing.

'I know you too well, daughter. You have achieved more than anyone could have dreamed, and yet you are ridden with guilt that I have been pushed to the side by Lady Aurelian. The Royal Court has room for only one mother of a monarch, and, as Lady Aurelian has often reminded me, I am not your birth mother.'

'She's said that to you?'

'Several times, dear. However, let it go. I can sense your temper flaring, but nothing Lady Aurelian says has the power to offend me. If she dislikes me, that remains her problem, not mine.'

Emily sat back, and took a sip of wine. 'It's the big vote today.'

'Then why aren't you sitting in with the Tribal Council?'

'Win or lose, it's Daniel's baby. He's done all the work to get the proposals to this stage, while I've been dealing with Jezra and Ooste.'

'But, he's going to lose, dear. Will he not need your support?'

'He seemed very confident before the meeting. I asked him if he wanted me there, but he said he would be able to handle it on his own. He said that if I could face Lady Amber alone, then he could deal with some disgruntled Rosers.'

'I imagine that it's not just the Rosers who will be disgruntled if these reforms are passed. However, it matters not, because they will fail. The King's search for a majority has been in vain.'

'Maybe.'

'Looking at the bright side, if the King's reforms do fail, then at least he will have more time to spend with you. At times, the two of you seem more like business partners than husband and wife. Has the flush of romance worn off so soon?'

'Perhaps a little. There's just so much to do. I could work every hour of the day and night, and it still wouldn't be enough. I keep thinking that, some day, it'll all calm down, and then we'll be able to relax and enjoy ourselves. Am I deluded?'

'Having a child might bring you closer together.'

'It might, but it would be me who'd have to take time off work for months, while Daniel tries to cover both of our jobs.'

'You are the Queen, Emily. It is not a "job."'

'Alright, but the fact remains that I'll be the one who has to step away, in order to have a baby. I can't afford the time.'

'Then delegate, dear. You have Yendra, and Salvor, and Quill, and a whole host of other people working for you. Do you believe that only you are capable of carrying out a task to your satisfaction?'

'Frankly, yes. Sorry, but that's the way it is. I trust myself to get things done, and I can't bear the thought of others doing the work for me. Also, I work hard to keep my figure, and...'

'Oh, please. Knowing the way your mind works, you'll have your figure back in no time. And I will be here, to help you. After all, Lady Aurelian won't want to get her hands dirty changing nappies. Let me do this for you, dear.'

Emily glanced down. She did want children, but didn't relish the prospect of being pregnant, or of giving birth. Never mind the pain; it all just seemed so... messy. Anyone present at the birth would see her at her most vulnerable and undignified; would it be worth it to hold a baby in her arms? She pushed it to the back of her mind for later. Much later. She was twenty-one, and there was plenty of time for all that.

'I'd best be going back to work,' she said.

'Of course, dear. Same time tomorrow? I'll allow you to let me win again.'

Emily smiled as she stood. She kissed her mother on the cheek, then left the small apartment. Cuidrach Palace was like a warren, with jumbled wings and floors from different eras of construction, and her mother's rooms were tucked away in a quiet corner of the complex. Courtiers and a pair of guards were waiting for her as she emerged, and they escorted her to the largest wing, where the Tribal Council was meeting.

She heard the sound of raised voices as she approached. Someone was shouting, angrily, about betrayal. A door to the chamber opened, and a group of delegates streamed out. From their dress and accents, they seemed to Emily to be a mixture of Rosers, Sanders and Evaders. All looked furious, and stormed down the hallway.

One halted when they saw Emily.

'This will not stand, your Majesty,' the Roser cried, with venom in his eyes. 'That was nothing short of a disgrace; it will not stand.'

The guards next to the Queen tensed, their hands hovering over the hilts of their swords

More guards piled out of the chamber, and began to move the protesting delegates on. A few resisted, and the soldiers roughly shoved them down the hallway, using their shields to herd the delegates from the area close to the Queen.

Emily waited until the hallway had quietened, then entered the large council chamber. Groups of delegates from the other tribes were standing around, talking, while Salvor and Daniel were up on the platform next to the twin thrones. Daniel was beaming from ear to ear.

Emily narrowed her eyes.

Daniel bounded down from the platform when he saw her.

'We won!' he cried. 'We've done it; the proposals passed.'

'They did?'

He laughed. 'Yes. You should see your face; you don't believe me, do you? Salvor, tell the Queen.'

Salvor bowed before her. 'His Majesty is correct. The Constitutional Proposals passed the vote of the Tribal Council and have become the law of the City.'

'How?' Emily said. 'The Rosers, Gloamers, Sanders and Evaders were adamant in their opposition, and the Scythes had already pledged to abstain.'

'I told you yesterday that the Icewarders had changed to a "yes." I've been writing back and forth with Lady Yvona, and we reached a compromise. And then, just as the meeting started, the Blades announced that they had changed from "abstain" to "yes" as well.'

'But that works out at four votes apiece; not a majority.'

Daniel smiled. 'I used the current crisis to throw out the delegation from the Gloamers. We won four votes to three.'

'You expelled the Gloamers?'

'They're holding the entire City to hostage, darling. I was working from the rules; the rules we all agreed upon. The Gloamers broke those rules when they invaded Ooste. Legally, it would have been fraudulent to have allowed their vote to stand.'

Emily put a hand to her forehead.

'Just think,' Daniel went on; 'two years from now, there will be a fully elected parliament sitting in Pella, with representatives from every tribe. The enormous estates owned by a handful of rich Rosers will be broken up, and Hammers and Evaders will be able to go into Tara without having their papers checked. The children of Scythes will not be forced to follow in their parents' footsteps – the servitude of the Bulwark is over, after a thousand years. We did it, Emily.'

She nodded, words failing her.

A group of Reapers approached, smiles plastered onto their faces, and bowed before the King and Queen.

'A wonderful day, your Majesties; a day that will go down in history,' said one.

Emily tried to smile. 'I'll leave you to speak to the delegates, husband. Well done.'

She turned and strode away before anyone else could speak. Her pair of guards hurried after her, and they eased through the groups milling through the large hall. Emily's face grew tired from the forced smile, but she kept it steady until she reached the Royal apartment. She went inside, leaving the guards at the door, and let out a long breath.

The King-Mother stormed across the reception room. 'He's done it this time; that stupid boy. How could you let him do this?'

Emily gave her a cold stare.

The King-Mother halted. 'My apologies, your Majesty; it was wrong of me to speak out of turn. However, this is a grim day for the City. The

King, my son, your husband, has made a dreadful mistake. Can you overturn it?'

Emily walked to a side cabinet and poured herself a glass of wine. She had already had one that her mother had given her, and didn't usually drink when she was working, but succumbed. She raised the glass to her lips and drank.

'Well, your Majesty? Is there anything you can do? Are the courts able to block it? Can the Gloamers appeal? The Rosers will certainly try. The Evaders will riot, while the Rosers go to court; such was always the way of it.' The King-Mother sat heavily onto a couch. 'The Blades; why?'

Emily glanced at her. 'Perhaps they don't want to force their children to become soldiers.'

'You forget how fragile this City is, your Majesty. In reality, it is a tiny, walled outpost in the midst of a greenhide world. The City might not have been perfect, but its structures have allowed people to live here in peace for thousands of years. Who are we to meddle with that?'

'We're Aurelians.'

'Yes, we are. Let's hope that the legend of our name doesn't turn out to be a curse.'

A cheering sound came from outside, and Emily walked to a window. Down on the streets, a large crowd of Reapers had gathered next to the palace in the torrential rain. They were celebrating the passage of the new laws, and chanting the names of Emily and Daniel, filling the space between Cuidrach Palace and the harbour front.

'They think this is the end of it,' said the King-Mother, who had appeared by her side. 'It's not. Those fools are dancing in the rain as if they've won, but the fight is just beginning. The Rosers will resist this to the end. Don't be surprised, your Majesty, if they look for friends in unusual places.'

'They would never ally themselves to Prince Montieth.'

'Do you think the bankers and merchants in Tara care what Montieth does? Do you think they'll weep if he kills a few civilians in Ooste? They'd hand Ooste over to him in perpetuity if that was his price for tearing down the new laws.'

Emily said nothing, preferring to listen to the King-Mother rant, rather than argue with her. She had a point though, and much of what she had said reflected her own thinking, only she hadn't wanted to say so in front of her husband.

The main doors of the apartment opened, and Daniel strode in, followed by Salvor. Daniel's smile faded as he glanced at the two women by the window.

He shook his head. 'Aren't you even going to pretend to be happy for me?'

The King-Mother rolled her eyes, and folded her arms across her chest.

'I'm too shocked to be happy,' said Emily.

'Did I miss something, Emily? I thought you were in favour of the proposals? Remember we used to talk about tearing down the house, so that we could build a new one on top of it? That is precisely what we have done.'

'It was the manner of it that irks me, Daniel.'

'I followed the rules.'

'It doesn't matter. Appearances are more important. The perception gleaned from today's vote is that you rigged the system; that, at any rate, is what the Gloamers, Rosers, Sanders and Evaders will believe. Half the City, in other words. Half the City will feel that you cheated them.'

Daniel glared at her. 'I didn't cheat.'

'That's irrelevant.'

'No, it's not. Do you seriously believe that I should have allowed the Gloamer delegation to vote, when their soldiers are trampling all over Ooste?'

Emily felt her anger start to simmer. 'Throw them out, by all means; but then you should have postponed the vote. You won a majority with four votes, which, as anyone who can count will tell you, is not a majority of nine tribes. You took advantage of the situation to ram the proposals through, and have thereby tarnished them forever. The biggest changes to how the City is run in over a thousand years; passed on a technicality.'

Daniel's face burned with rage, while Salvor and the King-Mother shared a glance.

'Why are you ruining this?' said the King. 'This is our biggest triumph; my biggest triumph. Is that it? You're angry because the victory is mine? You're jealous that I'll get the credit, as it was I who undertook all of the work; it was I who attended all the meetings and had to sit through endless lectures from lawyers; I who lobbied the tribal delegates every day for months. Forty-two letters to Yvona is what it took to get her vote, and I know, because I had to write each one out by hand. This has been the greatest achievement of my life, and you're standing there, telling me it's tarnished? I knew my mother would be upset, but you? I thought we were a team; I thought you were on my side.'

He turned and strode away, entering his study and slamming the door behind him.

The reception room fell into silence.

'Perhaps we should leave,' the King-Mother said to Salvor. 'Let's give their Majesties some privacy.'

'Unfortunately, I cannot,' said Salvor. 'I have received a message from Princess Yendra that requires a royal decision.'

Emily walked slowly over to the cabinet and re-filled her glass with wine. She felt as if she had been winded, and avoided looking at the mirror in case her face was red.

The King-Mother bowed. 'I shall return to my office, your Majesty.'

Emily gave a curt nod, and the King-Mother stole from the room.

Salvor coughed.

'Do I need to sit down for this?' said Emily.

'I haven't come here to bear bad news, your Majesty,' he said, 'but Princess Yendra is seeking authorisation to proceed with the plan to invade and occupy the Grey Isle. Lady Yvona in Icehaven has pledged to support the operation with the Icewarder fleet, but a certain amount of gold will now have to be spent for the preparations.'

Emily walked to the couch and sat.

'Do you need a moment, your Majesty?'

'When is the operation planned for?'

'As soon as summer begins, your Majesty. They're targeting the first day of Mikalis, but it will be weather-dependent.'

'How big a force is she planning?'

'Two thousand Banner soldiers and two thousand from the Lostwell Brigades, your Majesty. Lady Yvona estimates that she will require between thirty and forty ships to transport them from the Western Bank to the Grey Isle. At least two dragons will also be involved. Apparently, it will be Deathfang's last operation before they set off to their new home in the Eastern Mountains.'

'And the blockade?'

'That has also been agreed. Once the Icewarder fleet is assailing the Grey Isle, Lady Yvona will send the rest of her ships to seal off the harbour of Dalrig. Dragons from the quarry in the Iceward Range will assist, if necessary. At that point, the land blockade of Gloamer territory will begin, with Reaper militia occupying every road leading to Dalrig.'

Emily stared at the floor. She knew what she was going to say, but felt that such a decision required a moment. Once again, she would be responsible for people dying, as they surely would; worse, if it all went wrong, she would be driving the City back into civil war.

She glanced up at Salvor. 'Tell Princess Yendra to proceed; the authorisation she requires is granted.'

Salvor bowed low. 'At once, your Majesty.'

Over two hundred petitioners begged to be allowed to speak to the King and Queen that afternoon – people who wanted to congratulate them on the constitutional changes becoming law; and people who wished to complain about the same changes. The Taran Merchants' Guild sent a dozen men and women to protest vehemently, and Hammers who were loyal to the Crown jostled them in the corridors of the palace.

The King and Queen admitted no one to their private chambers, nor did they leave, and the soldiers outside their doors kept the public at bay. Emily spent the afternoon in her office, and Daniel stayed in his, each ostensibly working, but as the day drifted into evening, Emily, for one, knew that she had done nothing constructive.

Soldiers cleared the passageways and halls of the petitioners once the evening bell sounded, which marked the time the sun set during the two rainy seasons. Emily listened as she heard the last of the petitioners being removed from the palace. They were spilling out onto the wet streets by the harbour, and she walked to the balcony to watch from behind the window. Down on the ground, small groups of Rosers and Evaders were brawling in the rain with soldiers and the remnants of the Reapers who had gathered earlier. More soldiers piled out of the palace, and shoved the protesters down the street with their shields.

Emily closed the shutters. The torrential rain was bad enough, but she couldn't bear to watch her people fighting in the streets. She rubbed her temples. She had a slight headache from the wine she had drunk before, and her argument with Daniel had left her feeling deflated. She opened the door of her study and peered into the reception room. It was empty. The hallway outside had quietened, but she could see the shadows of several soldiers under the main doors. She loved Cuidrach Palace – it was welcoming, and much of it was open to the public, which was one of the things that had attracted her to living there. As she gazed at the slender, very-breakable doors that were the only barrier between her and a potential mob, she wondered if she had made the right decision. The private quarters in Maeladh Palace were hidden far from anywhere the public had access to, and the same was true with the Royal Palace in Ooste. She frowned; she would not be intimidated inside her own home.

Daniel appeared at the door to his study.

'Hi,' he said.

Emily glanced at him.

'Sorry about before,' he said. 'I guess I was disappointed at your reaction, and now, well, now that I've thought it through, I can see why you were angry.'

'You shouted at me in front of Salvor and your mother.'

'I know. I shouldn't have. These proposals have meant so much to me, because I truly want to improve the lives of the people living in the City; and hearing you say that I'd tarnished them forever, well, it hurt, and I lost my temper. They're not tarnished, Emily. The controversy about how they were passed will fade in time, especially once people start to feel the benefits that the new laws will bring.'

'I hope so, Danny.'

'I'm taking the rest of the day off. Tomorrow, I'll have to start preparing to resist the appeal the Rosers will inevitably lodge. They can't win, but it will suck up more of my time over the next few months.'

'Danny, I authorised the invasion of the Grey Isle.'

He blinked. 'When?'

'Before Salvor left. Princess Yendra needed a decision, so I took it. The operation will take place at the start of summer. Two regiments of Banner forces will...'

'Do I need to know the details?'

'No, but I can tell you them if you like.'

He shook his head. 'I don't think I want to know. This is your area of expertise; let me concentrate on the constitution.'

'Are you trying to keep your hands clean?'

'Maybe.'

'Your decision today might end up costing as many lives.'

His eyes narrowed.

'But,' she went on, 'perhaps you're right. Perhaps we should stick to our own areas.'

A tap-tap came from the door, and it opened a crack.

'Come in, Salvor,' said Emily; 'don't lurk by the door.'

Lord Salvor strode in, a sombre expression on his face. He closed the door behind him and approached the King and Queen.

He glanced at Emily. 'You may want to sit for *this*, your Majesty.'

She frowned. 'Spit it out.'

'Word has reached us from the Circuit, your Majesties,' he said, addressing them both. 'The Evader delegation arrived back from Pella in the latter part of the afternoon. As they were emerging from their carriages by the Great Racecourse, they were attacked by a group of hooded men. All five of the delegates were murdered, along with six of their aides. The assailants then fled into the Circuit.'

Daniel stared at Salvor. 'Who would want to kill the Evader delegates? I thought that they were well-liked in the Circuit.'

'Neither the identity, nor the motives, of the assailants has yet been established, your Majesty. Evader militia are searching the region of the Great Racecourse, and we must wait to see if they unearth any evidence. No group has claimed responsibility, but rumours are circulating that the orders to assassinate the delegates came from this palace.'

'The palace?' said Emily.

'Yes, your Majesty. The rumours state that the Crown are the only beneficiaries of the deaths of the delegates; and that their murders were ordered as retribution for voting against the constitutional proposals.'

'That's ridiculous,' snapped Daniel.

'Indeed, your Majesty; however, as you stated, the delegates were popular among the Evaders, and were seen as the leaders of the Circuit. You must remember that, only a year ago, the Evaders were occupied and suppressed by Blade forces, and before that, by militia from Auldan.'

'Of course I remember,' said Daniel; 'I was in the militia posted to the Circuit.'

Salvor bowed. 'Apologies, your Majesty; but then you can see how rumours like this can take root in the Circuit. The Evaders have a tendency to view matters through their own perspective, which is one of constant fear of persecution. The murder of the delegates, to them, would fit that pattern.'

'Is someone trying to frame us?' said Emily. 'Someone who hopes that everyone blames us for the murders?' She rubbed her temples again, feeling her headache build.

'Perhaps, your Majesty,' said Salvor. He raised his chin. 'Could I have your permission to start searching for answers? It would involve the reading of minds without necessarily seeking consent. I could sweep the other delegates, the guards, the carriage drivers, and the staff of the Evader Council in the Great Racecourse, along with any other persons of interest.'

Emily hesitated. Salvor was offering her the power of the gods. Those with vision skills were forbidden from reading minds without the owner's consent, although, of course, there was no way to stop them from breaking the rules. But for Salvor to explicitly offer to raid the minds of hundreds of citizens, was something new to her. She had promised herself that, as a mortal Queen, she would never abuse the powers of the gods, but hadn't she already done that, by taking Kelsey Holdfast along with her to the meeting with Amber? Kelsey was mortal, but Emily had still used her powers for her own ends. Was this any different?

Daniel nodded. 'Do it, Salvor. If someone's trying to set us up, we need to know who it is.'

Salvor nodded, then glanced at Emily. 'I would also like your permission, your Majesty. This sort of request requires the full backing of the Crown.'

'And you will report only to us?' said Emily. 'You will tell no one else?'

'You have my word, your Majesty.'

She suppressed the throbbing in her head. 'Permission granted.'

CHAPTER 22

WESTRIG

Jezra, The Western Bank – 3rd Mikalis 3421

Kelsey shook the rain from her hair as she stepped into the tunnel. Behind her, up the set of stairs, the rains were pouring down, and the ruins of Jezra seemed to be criss-crossed with little streams of water, all tumbling towards the sea. The two Brigade guards in the tunnel nodded to her as she passed, saying nothing. Kelsey's face was well known in the town and, as a dragon rider, she had earned a certain amount of respect from the soldiers and former refugees.

She picked up a lantern and entered the system of caverns. Some had been flooded by the rains, but 'Statue Street', as the Brigade workers had named it, had remained dry. She took the left branch, and entered the long chamber lined with the huge statues. The floor had been swept clean of the dust and detritus, but the bloodstain from Nurian's death still marked the bare stone. Her eyes went to it, and she paused for a moment. Two and a half months had passed, but she still felt her chest constrict at the memory. She carried on, her boots avoiding the stain on the floor, and took the next right, shining the lantern to check that the way was clear. Jade had been down into that network of caverns several times, and had killed the greenhide responsible for Nurian's death, but Kelsey always liked to check.

Access to the cavern of scrolls was through a half-blocked doorway, and she had to lift the lantern and squeeze past the mound of rubble. Once inside, she opened the shutters on the lantern and set it down. The walls of the cavern showed no sign of any damp, and the ground was bone dry. She walked to the long rows of shelving that adorned an entire wall of the cavern. Upon each shelf were tied bundles of scrolls, the paper made from the reeds of the Warm Sea. On the far right was a pile of broken scrolls – ones that workers had attempted to open, and which had half-crumbled to dust in their fingers. They had been left on the shelf as a warning to others – do not touch.

Even breathing on them was probably causing them damage, Kelsey thought, as she gazed at the hundreds of scrolls. What secrets did they contain? Some of the Banner soldiers joked that they were probably filled with boring supply inventories, or shopping lists, itemising how many bricks the town had purchased, but Kelsey hoped that it wasn't true. The scrolls had been stored there for a reason, to preserve them; therefore, to her mind, they must have been important. She walked along the side of the shelves, her eyes looking for anything she might have missed on previous trips to the cavern.

She jumped as she heard a noise echo through the tunnels. She froze for a moment, her heart pounding. If it was a greenhide, she thought, then please, please, let it be over quickly.

'Miss?' said a voice from the gloom.

She turned, and saw one of the Brigade guards from the entrance.

'Pyre's arse, you nearly gave me a heart attack.'

'Sorry, miss.'

'What is it?'

'The rain's stopped. It's summer, apparently.'

'Just like that?'

'Just like that, miss. The sky's already clearing up, and the sun's come out. The major has ordered a muster, and the dragons are on their way here.'

'Are we leaving?'

'As soon as we're organised, miss.'

She glanced at the piles of scrolls, frowned, then picked up the lantern from the floor. She walked with the guard back to the stairs that led to the caverns, and blinked as she saw the red sky overhead. As she ascended the stairs, she could feel the warmth of the sun of her face, and she smiled. The clouds had almost completely gone, a wind blowing them to iceward, and the air was sharp and clear.

'What a difference, eh, miss?' said the guard.

She nodded. 'Like a different world.'

She gazed at the ruined town as she reached the top of the stairs. The streets were still half-flooded, and tendrils of steam were rising as the sunlight grew brighter. She splashed through the deep puddles, passing a new complex of buildings that had been built during Freshmist. Several of the first, makeshift barrack blocks had been demolished to make way for the new structure, which could house two entire Brigades – two thousand workers. Unlike the earlier buildings, it had been constructed without fear of attack, and was solid and comfortable.

Kelsey's own housing block was due to be demolished soon, and its massive replacement was growing every day as hundreds of Brigade workers laboured on it. Huge construction works were also going on down at the harbour, the Brigades acting as if the storms and rain of Freshmist had barely inconvenienced them, and more ships could now safely dock than before.

She reached the Command Post. It was the original, ramshackle, damp and leaky building that had been flung up in the opening days of the occupation, and excess water was spilling from its roof and gutters, forming a series of little falls that sparkled in the warm sunlight. Outside the building, a crowd had formed, of Brigade and Banner officers, awaiting their orders. Kelsey nodded to a few that she recognised. She had gone out drinking with some of them, but had kept her distance, refusing to make any close friends after what had happened to Nurian.

She scanned the skies, feeling a knot of anxiety build. She was looking forward to seeing Frostback, but was worried that their separation would have altered the dragon's attitude towards her. Kelsey had spent very few nights in the cold and miserable quarry during Fresh-mist, preferring to seek human company in Jezra instead. She tried to prepare herself for bad news. She wouldn't be surprised if Frostback had decided to forsake their bond, and if that happened, she had sworn that she wouldn't let herself cry in public, nor would she allow her anger to flare. She would take the news calmly, and walk away.

'Kelsey, do you have a moment?'

She glanced down, and saw Van standing in front of her. He was dressed in his armour as if ready for battle, and the newly-polished steel plates were shining in the sun.

'Sure,' she said.

'Deathfang is leading the other three dragons to the Western Bank for the assault on Westrig.'

She nodded.

'You will be the only rider,' he said. 'Princess Yendra has decided not to request that anyone else fly on Halfclaw for the operation, as she will be coming by ship, while we go overland. I thought you should know.'

'Halfclaw would probably say no, anyway.'

He half-smiled. 'There's something I've been wanting to ask you.'

'Oh aye? What?'

'Deathfang has stated that this will be the last operation that he takes part in. He's promised us a few days, and then they will be off, flying to the Eastern Mountains.'

'I know all that.'

'Alright. But, will you be going with them?'

She shrugged.

'Is that a "maybe?"'

'It's an "I don't know." I've hardly seen the dragons since the start of Freshmist. I don't know if they'll want me to come along. Darksky might decide to refuse to allow it, and I'm not even sure if Frostback and I have a bond any more. But, even if they do allow it, I'm not certain that I want to live with twelve dragons, two hundred miles from the City. I'm not Maddie. I'd do a lot for Frostback, but I don't think I could live in a cave for the rest of my life.'

He nodded.

'Why are you smiling? Did something I say amuse you?'

'No,' he said; 'but that's the most you've said to me in two months. There have been so many times, Kelsey, when I wanted to speak to you, but you've been keeping me at arm's length ever since... well, you know.'

'Since we slept together?'

'I meant since Nurian's death, but, yes. Since then. I know that you regret what we did, but...'

'Who said I regret it? It was what I needed at the time, and I'm not ashamed of what happened. I was, maybe, for a while, but not any more.'

'I don't regret it, either. I had hoped it might be the start of something.'

'Come on, Van; you can't possibly still feel the same way about me. We've barely spoken in months, despite living in the same, small town.'

'But what about your vision? I thought we were supposed to fall in love?'

She sighed. 'That could be years away. There's no baby around, for a start, and, until there is, I'm trying not to think about it.'

He leaned in closer to her. 'I can think of little else.'

'Perhaps you should try to remain focussed on your job.'

He took a step back from her, and nodded. Close by, a Banner officer pointed at the sky. Kelsey glanced up, and saw four large specks approaching. In the lead was Deathfang, his bulk far greater than the three dragons who were following. They circled over Jezra for a moment, then began to descend over the foundations of the ancient palace, the only open space in the town big enough to accommodate four dragons.

'Good luck today, Kelsey,' said Van, then he turned to his officers and began issuing commands.

Kelsey glanced at him, then strode down the wet streets towards the palace. Ahead of her, the four dragons were landing, and she saw Frostback, her silver scales gleaming in the light. Kelsey began to sweat as she walked. Having dressed for the rains of Freshmist, she was now feeling the heat from the sun. She climbed the repaired steps up to the top of the platform of foundations, and waited for the dragons to notice her.

Deathfang saw her first.

'Greetings, Kelsey,' he said, arching his long neck to look at her. 'How wonderful it is to feel the sun on one's wings again. I hope you weathered the rains in good spirits?'

'I'm just glad it's over,' she said. 'The grey skies were doing my nut in.'

Deathfang lowered his head further. 'My daughter is concerned.'

'About what?'

'Father!' Frostback cried. 'Are you meddling?'

'Sorry, daughter,' said the huge grey dragon, lifting his head. He regarded the scenes around him. Hundreds of heavily-equipped Brigade workers were setting off up the path towards Westrig, while Banner soldiers were gathering in their companies.

He stretched his long wings. 'That feels good,' he said to the others. 'Let me say a few words, as I think the occasion demands it. Tarsnow, Halfclaw and Frostback, we four have returned here, to Jezra, in order to give our assistance to the humans, for one final time. I have spoken to Princess Yendra, and we came to a deal – we will spend ten days helping the humans, no more, no less. We four here will assist with Westrig, and then the island, while Dawnflame has volunteered to assist the Icewarder ships in their blockade of Dalrig.' He glanced at Tarsnow. 'I am well aware that some among the dragons have been opposed to helping the humans, and I am grateful that you overcame your concerns to follow my orders, but, it will soon be over. In ten days, we will be leaving the City, and starting our new life in the Eastern Mountains. We have all made sacrifices, but ours has been a noble cause – helping those who helped us. In this way, we have built friendships and alliances for the future, and brought the world of dragons a little closer to the world of humans. I hope that, in time, every dragon who escaped from Lostwell will come to agree with me on this point. That is all I have to say.'

Deathfang and Tarsnow glanced at each other, then they both ascended into the air, rising up to higher than the level of the cliff.

Halfclaw looked towards Frostback, nodded, then joined the others in the air.

Kelsey waited, watching Frostback. The silver dragon kept her glance down, as if embarrassed.

'How are you?' said Kelsey.

'Fine.'

'Good.'

'Well, are you climbing up or not?'

'Do you want me to?'

'Would I have asked if I didn't?'

Kelsey stepped forward, and reached up to grab the leather straps hanging from the harness. Frostback kept her gaze averted, instead studying the sky.

'Strange weather here, isn't it?' Kelsey said, as she climbed up onto the dragon's shoulders.

'Indeed.'

Kelsey strapped herself into the saddle. 'How is everyone in the quarry doing?'

'They are all well.'

Kelsey cringed. She hated trying to make conversation with the dragon, when it had been so easy in the past to talk to her. Frostback took off without another word, and joined the others in the air. Kelsey looked down. The pools and puddles littering the ruins of Jezra were shining in the sunlight, while vast sheets of steam were rising from the forestlands that stretched away on the plateau. Deathfang took the lead, and they soared iceward in the direction of the small harbour at Westrig.

Kelsey kept her eyes on the ground as they flew. The new wall that the Brigades had built during Freshmist stood strong and tall, heading in a straight line from the corner of the defences of Jezra at the top of the ridge. The trees had been cleared for several yards on either side of the new wall, and hundreds of soldiers and Brigade workers were marching along the track that led to Westrig, the ground churned to thick mud under their boots. The wall went on and on, stretching for two and a half miles, maintaining a distance from the coast of around a hundred yards. It had been built with a mixture of large, cream-coloured bricks, and the remnants of the ancient wall that had stood in the same place nearly two thousand years before. On the forest side of the wall, small packs of greenhides were already emerging from the damp gloom of the forest. Some of them were sniffing the wall, but the presence of a solid barrier was enough for most of them to turn away.

The ground rushed beneath them, and the dragons approached the end of the wall. An entire regiment of Banner soldiers had assembled there, waiting for the signal to push down into the little bay where the ancient harbour lay. Behind the Banner soldiers were two full Brigades – two thousand men and women, ready to finish the defensive works that would encircle Westrig. Wagons filled with tools, wooden beams and bricks had been dragged along the track from Jezra, and stood next to the waiting Brigades. A simple series of coloured flags had been pre-arranged with the dragons, and, at the head of the columns, a single, large, black flag had been raised – the signal to the dragons that they were to begin driving the greenhides from the harbour.

Deathfang swooped low over the lead Banner units, then led the other dragons down the slope. Kelsey clung on to the harness rail as Frostback dived. There weren't too many greenhides within the harbour area, and they started to flee in panic as soon as they saw the dragons. Frostback opened her jaws and sprayed a group of greenhides on the steep slopes in front of her, and the four dragons separated, each wheeling off to attack their targets. The old, familiar stench of burning greenhide flesh reached Kelsey's nostrils, and the sound of their shrieks rattled through her head. Deathfang and Tarsnow banked to the west, and began to push the remaining greenhides up the slope on the iceward side, while Halfclaw and Frostback finished off those still down by the water's edge. There was a long stone jetty jutting out into the bay, and several greenhides ran along it to escape the flames, then jumped into the Cold Sea, preferring to drown rather than be incinerated.

Kelsey looked over her shoulder. The black flag had been taken down, and a red flag was in its place, signalling to the dragons that the Banner forces were advancing. A temporary wall at the top of the slope was broken down with sledgehammers, and the soldiers piled through, fanning out as they hurried down the slopes toward the harbour. Frostback and Halfclaw saw the new flag, and joined Deathfang and Tarsnow at the top of the ridge. Their job now was to prevent any greenhides from breaching their defensive cordon, so that the Brigades could get a makeshift wall built in the shortest time possible. Already, the wagons were rumbling forwards, and Brigade workers with saws and axes were starting to fell the trees where the new wall would go.

It was going to be a long, hard day, but up on Frostback's shoulders, where the sun and wind were warming her skin, Kelsey didn't mind. She closed her eyes, feeling better than she had done in a long while.

***

After a massive effort, the first defensive perimeter was complete by sunset. Three hundred yards of brick wall had been put up in that time, sealing off Westrig from the forest. No gates, towers or parapets had been constructed, but they would come in time, along with a taller, thicker wall that could be constructed without fear of attack. Deathfang, Tarsnow and Halfclaw soared away, heading back towards the quarry in the Iceward Range, but Kelsey asked Frostback to take her down, so she could take a look at the small harbour.

The silver dragon landed on a rocky outcrop halfway down the steep slopes overlooking the bay, and Kelsey unbuckled the straps that held her to the harness. She scrambled down onto the outcrop and stretched her limbs. A few passing soldiers waved at them, grins on their faces.

'No casualties,' said Kelsey. 'That went very well.'

'Yes,' said Frostback.

Kelsey frowned. She had been dreading it, but knew she needed to talk to the dragon. It was clear that Frostback was unhappy, but so was she, and it seemed wrong to let it fester.

'Frostback,' she said.

'Yes?'

Kelsey forced the words out. 'Do you want me to stop being your rider?'

The dragon said nothing for a moment, her head angled away, so that Kelsey couldn't see the expression on her face.

'It's just,' Kelsey went on, 'I'm not sure if you want to carry me about any more. I'm sorry if I've done something to upset you. Whatever it was, I didn't intend to drive you away. I know that I can be difficult at times, and I find it hard to hold onto friends; and I'd be sad, but I'd understand if...'

'Stop talking, Kelsey,' the dragon said.

'Oh. Alright.'

'It pains me to hear you apologise to me. You have done nothing wrong; it is I who is at fault.'

'You?'

'Yes, Kelsey, and I don't blame you for wanting to live in Jezra, instead of in the quarry.' She turned her head to gaze at the young Holdfast woman. 'I let you down, several times over. First, when Princess Yendra asked that Nurian ride on my shoulders, instead of you. I should have refused. But worse than that, when Nurian died, I left you alone, when I should have remained by your side. I didn't understand what I was supposed to do to comfort you, so I did nothing. Shame has consumed me ever since, and I could barely bring myself to face you today. It is little wonder that you hate me and want to stop being my rider. If only Blackrose were here, then she could teach me more about the bond between a dragon and a rider. In my ignorance, I have failed you.'

Kelsey felt her eyes well, and she closed them until the feeling passed. She had cried more since Nurian's death than in the rest of her life put together.

'Is this goodbye, Kelsey?' Frostback said.

'Please don't think that I hate you, Frostback. I still love you. I want to be your rider, I do.'

The dragon said nothing, waiting.

'But,' Kelsey went on, 'I can't move to the Eastern Mountains. I need other humans around me. They don't need to be right next to me, but two hundred miles is too far. The quarry's only a couple of miles from Icehaven, but even there I felt isolated.'

Frostback gazed at her. 'If Nurian were alive, would you have gone to the mountains if he was also prepared to go?'

'Aye; I would have. That's what I thought we'd do, back at the beginning of the Jezra operation. If Nurian was there, then I'd be able to handle the isolation, but, Frostback, I can't do it alone.'

'Then what shall we do, my rider?'

'I don't know. I can't ask you to stay here – you'd be giving up something that I'm not prepared to give up for you. It wouldn't be fair to ask you to live among humans, just as I can't live among dragons.' She bit her lip. 'Could Halfclaw be your Nurian?'

'What are you suggesting?'

'Could you imagine living here, on the Western Bank with me, if Halfclaw also stayed?'

'I don't know. I have yet to decide if I want to take Halfclaw as a mate. He and I were friends in the Catacombs, and we have known each other since we were both very young, but I never anticipated us becoming mated for life. Unfortunately, the knowledge that he and I are the only compatible dragons on this world, has increased the pressure upon us. My father is eager for us to be betrothed, and if I asked Halfclaw to stay here in the Western Bank with me, then the others would believe that I had made up my mind. Halfclaw would believe that I had made up my mind.'

'Do you like him?'

'Yes. He is honourable, and loyal, but do I see him as my lifelong mate? I know that if I don't choose him, then I shall be destined never to find a true mate.' She looked away. 'My father would be extremely disappointed. He has pinned the future of our colony here not only upon the prospect of one of his little ones mating with Firestone when they are much older, but also upon me and Halfclaw. Otherwise, he says, the dragons on this world will die out in a mere generation. He wants to see grandchildren before he dies, so that he knows his legacy will endure.'

'That's a lot of weight upon your shoulders.'

Frostback turned back to look at her, their faces inches apart. 'We are both young, you and I, and both trapped by our futures. I have Halfclaw, and my father's expectations – and you have Van, and your vision of what will come to pass. Destiny has forced us down these paths. Perhaps if we share these burdens together, they won't bear down so heavily upon us.'

'But how do we stay together?'

'We will think of a solution. I will leave you now, and fly back to the quarry. We shall return at dawn for the attack on the island, my rider, and I will bear you into battle once again.'

Kelsey leaned her head against Frostback for a moment. 'See you tomorrow.'

The silver dragon extended her wings, and Kelsey stepped back as Frostback ascended into the clear, red sky. She circled once, then sped off to the east.

Kelsey walked down the slope. At the bottom of the hill, the ground levelled off, and a few ruined buildings were dotted around. An entire Brigade was already working on repairing and upgrading the harbour, and a constant stream of loaded wagons was making its way down from the top of the ridge. The noise of sawing, hammering, and yelled instructions filled the evening air as the sun lowered below the horizon, and the sky turned purple.

She made her way to a kitchen operating out of the back of a wagon, and Van saw her as she joined the queue.

'Good job today,' he said to her. 'The dragons did exactly what we asked them to do. Not a single life lost.'

She glanced at him. 'If you don't count the greenhides. And tomorrow might be different.'

He nodded, his expression darkening a little. 'Fighting Gloamers instead of monsters? It'll definitely be different. Anyway, how did it go with Frostback? I saw you talking to her on the hillside.'

'You were spying on me?'

He gave her a wry smile. 'Frostback is an enormous, silver dragon. She can be quite hard to miss.'

'Fair point. Me and Frostback are alright; I'm still her rider.'

'Good. And the Eastern Mountains?'

She caught his gaze. 'I'm working on it.'

CHAPTER 23

BRIGHTER PROSPECTS

Port Sanders, Medio, The City – 3rd Mikalis 3421

Within hours of the rain stopping, the streets of Port Sanders had been transformed. The last of the rainwater had drained into the sea, or had evaporated under the warmth of the summer sun. The populace had opened their shutters, after two months of keeping them closed against the storms, and the flower boxes were being placed back under the windows of the tenements. The fruit trees that lined many of the town's roads had broken out in new life, with leaves and blossom beginning to bud. Down by the harbour, the crab and lobster fleets were preparing to sail, and the markets along the quayside were re-opening.

Kagan walked the streets with his eyes wide, like a visitor, hardly able to believe that the beautiful town was his home. Lady Sofia had sent him out on errands the moment the sun had appeared in the sky, and he had leapt at the chance to get outside after so long spent inside the mansion. Not that he hadn't enjoyed being stuck indoors with Sofia for two months; she had been spoiling him, buying him expensive new clothes, and bringing in a woman to attend to his hair and new, neatly-trimmed beard; moulding him into someone he wouldn't have recognised in the slums of Alea Tanton. Stylish young ladies smiled at him as he passed them on the street and, were it not for the black cloud at the back of his mind, he would have felt that life couldn't get any better.

He glanced at the market stalls by the waterfront, holding Saul's list in his left hand. None of the produce on sale was fresh, all of it having been stored over from the previous harvest, but the selection was wide, and he was able to purchase everything that the mansion's cook required. He took his time, savouring the sensation of the sun's heat on his skin, which reminded him of Lostwell. Six months in the City, and he had almost forgotten what hot weather was like, and he hoped that the summer would be as warm as that on Khatanax.

With a basket full of food held in one hand, he paused by the entrance to a shoemaker's workshop. There was a small window, and in it were pairs of black leather boots on display. With the money Sofia had given him, he could afford to buy a pair, and the thought amazed him. He had spent his entire life in poverty, wearing clothes that had usually been stolen from washing lines or from those he had beaten up.

'Nice looking boots, son; right enough,' said a voice next to him.

Kagan froze, his heart almost stopping.

'And that coat you're wearing; it looks like it cost a tidy sum.'

Kagan turned his head to glance at Albeck. There was no way that the man had bumped into him by accident.

'Have you been following me?' he said.

'I have indeed, son,' Albeck said. 'I figured there was a good chance that her ladyship would let you out of her sight once the sun came out. So, how's life been treating you?'

'Why didn't you just knock on the front door if you wanted to see me?'

'You're not thinking it through, son. I can only risk knocking if I'm on official Refugee Council business. I'm not. Today, I'm on Dizzler business. Come on; there are some wonderful little cafes close by, and I'm thirsty.'

The Evader strode away. Kagan watched him for a second, debating whether or not he should bolt. He could probably outrun the man, but what would be the point? They knew where he lived. He took a breath, and followed.

Albeck led him back to the quayside, and picked a table with a wide view of the harbour and Tonetti Palace, its narrow spires glowing in the red sunlight. They sat, and Albeck ordered a bottle of wine from a waitress.

'Beautiful day, isn't it?' he said, as the waitress walked back into the café. 'I love the way the water glints on the sea. It makes a nice change from rain, and from looking at grey concrete in the Circuit all day.' He paused as the waitress returned to their table with a bottle. She half-filled two glasses.

'Thank you, my dear,' said Albeck. He waited until she had gone, then turned to Kagan. 'You didn't answer my question. How have you been getting on in the mansion?'

'Fine.'

'Her ladyship must have taken quite a shine to you, if those clothes you're wearing are anything to go by. That's a good sign; it means she most likely trusts you, which will certainly help when the time comes. On that topic, stay ready. Dizzler has been trying to untangle the extent of her ladyship's wealth, so you might have to hold tight for a tiny bit longer. You alright with that?'

Kagan nodded. The longer the better, in his opinion. Never, would be preferable.

'Good. The plan is a simple one, as the best always are – I know the layout of the mansion, and the back door to the kitchen is the one that you'll need to unbolt. Neutralising the cook will be your responsibility; Dizzler doesn't care how you do it, just make sure he can't interfere. When the boys enter the mansion, you will present them with a map.'

'What map?'

Albeck eyed him. 'The map you're going to draw, son. It will indicate where her ladyship keeps her gold. Dizzler has some concerns about this, as she appears to have gone on a spending spree recently, and he's worried that she might be running low. Does she still have plenty in the mansion?'

'Yes.'

'Just as well. You give the boys the map, and any other details they request, and then leave the rest to them. Guard the kitchen door until the boys have cleared the house, then you'll escape with them. Follow their instructions, and we'll get you to a location where you can lie low for a while.'

'What will happen to Lady Sofia?'

Albeck shrugged. 'That's none of your concern, son.'

Kagan shuddered, as a host of possibilities flashed through his mind. They might be planning on holding her hostage for a ransom, or maybe they would kill her to stop her reporting the crime. Kagan had taken part in similar jobs with Dizzler in Alea Tanton, and they had nearly always ended messily if the owner of the residence had happened to be in when the robbery was taking place. And Lady Sofia never left the mansion.

Kagan's nerves went taut, then snapped. 'I can't do it. I won't do it. I'm out.' He got to his feet.

'Sit down, son,' said Albeck, 'and think very carefully about what you're going to say next. If you walk away from me, I'll have the Sander militia arrest you this afternoon, for fraudulently avoiding the draft for the Jezra Brigades. You'll be in a prison cell by sunset.'

Kagan swallowed, then sat.

'I'm going to pretend that never happened,' said Albeck. 'It would embarrass me to have to relate that little outburst to Dizzler, especially as he's always going on about how you're his trusted second-in-command. Have some wine, son, and take a moment to think about the concept of gratitude. Who was it that saved you from being put on a ship to the Western Bank? Who was it that set you up with the job in the mansion? A hundred young thugs wanted that job, but Dizzler gave it to you, and you've been living like a little prince off the back of it for months. Still, everything sweet turns to piss in the end, as they say, and your time in the mansion is nearly up. Now, are you going to be a good boy and behave yourself? Don't speak; just nod.'

Kagan nodded.

'Alright. I'm not going to give you a date, but stay ready; it could be any time in the next month. You'll get a few hours notice, on the evening of the job. Remember to draw the map, and remember to keep it hidden, for Malik's sake. Dizzler told me you were a professional – act like one.' He opened his wallet and threw some coins on to the table. 'You can finish the wine.'

Albeck stood, smoothed his coat, and walked away, disappearing into the crowds by the market stalls. Kagan turned his gaze towards the waters of the harbour, anxiety gripping his chest like a vice. Part of him had irrationally hoped that, somehow, Dizzler would have forgotten all about him, and that he would be allowed to continue in the life that he had come to love. He pushed Sofia from his mind, unable to face the possible fates that lay in store for her, if he went along with Albeck's plan. But what choice did he have? He had broken the law when he had avoided the ships heading to Jezra, but he feared the wrath of Dizzler more than being arrested by the local militia. Dizzler never forgave those he perceived to have betrayed him, and, as his enforcer, Kagan had killed for Dizzler in the past, eliminating traitors and informants in the back alleys of Alea Tanton. Dizzler would never let him live if he refused to help with the robbery; better to go along with it, and try to forget all about Sofia.

He drained both glasses, picked up the basket, and started to walk back to the mansion.

———

The ground floor was quiet when he slipped through the main entrance. He locked the door behind him, and placed the key onto a hook. On the floor above, Gellie peered over the balustrade at him.

'It's just me,' he said, 'back from the market.'

He took the basket through to the kitchen, but Saul wasn't around. As he placed the basket onto a work surface, he glanced at the kitchen door. It led out onto an alleyway that ran alongside the mansion, and was locked from the inside by two iron bolts. He remembered that they squeaked when opened; he would have to oil them before the night of the robbery. His nerves churned. He tried to imagine himself letting Dizzler and his crew in, then standing by as they ransacked the house, while Lady Sofia slept upstairs, defenceless.

'Get out of my kitchen, boy.'

Kagan started, then turned to see Saul enter from the kitchen pantry, an open bottle of brandy in his left hand.

'Go on, out,' he snapped.

Kagan strode from the kitchen, and ascended the stairs to the first floor, so he could tell her ladyship that he was back. Gellie passed him, heading in the other direction, but the Fordian housekeeper ignored him. He walked into the small reception hall leading to Lady Sofia's rooms, then paused, hearing voices coming from the sitting room. He listened, and heard a woman speak. She had the soft tones of a Sander accent, and seemed to be talking about the rulers of the City.

Kagan knocked, and entered.

Sofia was sitting on a low couch, sipping from a glass, while a woman of around the same age was on a chair opposite her, her hands folded across her lap.

Sofia smiled. 'How was the town?'

'Gorgeous, ma'am,' he said. 'The sun has really brightened every-thing up. Anyway, ma'am, I just wanted to let you know that I was back, and wanted to ask if you needed me for anything?'

She beckoned him with a finger. 'Come in and sit down.' She turned to the other woman. 'This is Kagan, also from Lostwell. He's my personal assistant. I hired him as a guard, but he's proved to be much more useful than that.'

The woman smiled at him as he sat, and he bowed his head to her.

'This young lady,' Sofia said to him, 'has come on behalf of a group of Sander citizens, to tell me all about the new laws that were passed by the Tribal Council a short time ago.'

'The constitutional laws?' said Kagan.

'That's right.' Sofia turned back to the woman. 'Poor Kagan has had to listen to me complain about these new laws for some time now.'

The other woman's eyes widened. 'You are aware of the content of the new laws, my lady?'

'I am, yes,' said Sofia. 'I might have arrived from Lostwell, but I like to take a keen interest in the political atmosphere of wherever I happen to live. Several clauses of the new constitution have concerned me, particularly those reforming land ownership. I have invested a considerable sum, you see; buying up some parcels of land in the Circuit, as well as this townhouse in Port Sanders, and under the new arrangements, I would be liable for a steep increase in taxation, and may even be forced to sell some of my recently-acquired portfolio.' She smiled at the woman. 'Now, I assume that you came here today in order to request something from me?'

The woman's face flushed a little. 'Several of the local merchants and townspeople have decided to band together to help fund the legal action that the Rosers have lodged against the new laws. Due to certain irregularities in the way they were passed in the Tribal Council, we feel that we have a good chance of success.'

'A legal fund. I see. Unfortunately, due to the nature of my investments here in the City, I am still waiting for a return, and so my present access to cash is a little limited, and I would only be able to spare a modest sum. Does twenty thousand in gold sovereigns seem adequate?'

'My lady,' the woman said, her eyes lighting up; 'that would be an extremely generous donation.'

'Nonsense,' said Sofia. 'It's the least I can do to assist. However, I do like my privacy, and would prefer my donation to be anonymous.'

'I will have to report the source to the correct authorities, my lady; but we shall prevent it from becoming public knowledge.'

'Thank you. Perhaps you could tell me something? I understand that a certain Lady Lydia is the Governor of Port Sanders? I have yet to hear her position on the new constitution; does she have one?'

'Oh yes. Lady Lydia is deeply opposed to the plans, my lady. However, she feels it best to remain officially neutral.'

'Really? Why?'

'After Lady Ikara lost her role as Governor of the Circuit, my lady, I feel that Lady Lydia is worried that she will also lose her position, if she objects to the new laws. The King and Queen are putting pressure on every tribe to call elections...'

Sofia chuckled. 'They would allow the masses to pick the rulers of the City?'

'That is what they intend, my lady. The Governor of Port Sanders would like to delay this, if possible. Lady Lydia has always allowed the local Merchants' Guild a strong role in the governance of Sander territory.'

'So, she is an ally; albeit a silent one?'

'Indeed, my lady.'

'It's a pity that she doesn't have more courage, but I'm sure she must know what she's doing. The gods of Lostwell certainly never bothered about such niceties; if they wanted something, they took it.'

'The noble Royal Family of the City is not as it once was, my lady, and the days of the God-King and God-Queen are over, more's the pity. The new King and Queen are keen on letting mortals take over the organs of government. It hasn't just been Lady Ikara who has lost her job. Lord Collo and Lady Vana, two highly experienced demigods, are also unemployed. And, of course, Prince Montieth's recent actions have done little to restore faith in the gods of the City.'

'He has shown up the mortal rulers as weak and indecisive,' said Sofia. 'If they can't deal with a single rogue element occupying Ooste, I fear they will struggle if a worse crisis emerges.'

The other woman smiled. 'It is gratifying to know that you sympathise with our aims, my lady. The City needs more strong, independently-minded citizens like yourself, and I feel that you will prosper well here in Port Sanders.'

'Thank you. As regards the gold, I'll send a note to the Tonetti Bank, authorising the release of the sovereigns I have pledged towards the legal fund. Will you keep me up to date with any developments?'

'Of course, my lady. The first hearings are due to take place in Tara within the next month or so; a date is still to be set. We shall keep you posted with any news.'

Sofia smiled, signalling that the meeting was at an end. The woman rose to her feet, and Kagan also stood.

'My assistant will show you to the front door,' said Sofia; 'and then he will return here, won't you, Kagan?'

He bowed. 'As you wish, ma'am.'

He escorted the visitor out of Sofia's rooms and down the stairs.

'Your mistress is a remarkable woman,' she said, as they reached the main entrance of the mansion; 'and so generous. Her donation will be very helpful. Back in Lostwell, was her wealth mostly in land investments?'

Kagan smiled. 'I wouldn't like to say, ma'am.'

'Of course, yes. Discretion among the staff is very important. Well, thank you very much for showing me out, and I'm sure we'll be seeing more of you and Lady Sofia, now that you have made Port Sanders your home.'

Kagan opened the doors, and the woman walked away, heading towards a carriage that was parked outside on the street. Kagan closed the door and re-locked it, then made his way back up the stairs. He had managed to keep his expression muted while Sofia and the woman had been talking, but Albeck had never been far from his mind. He entered her ladyship's rooms, and walked into the sitting room to see her opening a new bottle of brandy.

'I am free for the next hour or so, Kagan,' she said, her back to him as she filled two glasses. 'And after all that political talk, I am in need of something to distract me.'

'Can I ask a question, ma'am?'

She glanced over her shoulder at him. 'If it's related to the discussion about the new laws, then make it a quick one.'

'It's not that.' He hesitated, wondering how to put it in a way that she wouldn't find offensive. 'I was just thinking, ma'am. You arrived in the City with a single suitcase, and yet you've been able to buy a townhouse, land in the Circuit, and you're able to afford twenty thousand sovereigns as a donation.'

She frowned. 'Are you worried that I'll run out of money?'

'No, ma'am. It's just; how much could one suitcase fit?'

She turned, carrying the two glasses of brandy. 'A lot. Here; try this. It's the Eighteen vintage, from a little place in the Sunward Range. Tell me if you like it.'

He took the glass, and sipped. 'It's very nice, ma'am. Very sweet.'

'I'm glad you like it, as I now own the distillery. I purchased it yesterday. Intriguingly, it comes with a small villa attached to some vineyards. I foresee a trip there in the near future, Kagan; it'll be pleasant to have a home in the countryside as well as in town, don't you think?'

'Yes, ma'am.'

'So, you can see that you don't need to worry about me running out of money any time soon. Now, drink up, and come with me to the bedroom; we're on the clock.'

Forty minutes later, Kagan and Sofia lay in her enormous bed, their legs entwined. Sofia had brought the bottle of brandy, and was pouring some of it into her glass, as Kagan watched her. She had no inhibitions when they were alone, and his eyes were drawn to the sight of her bare skin. She was perfect; a vision of beauty, and she had chosen him.

She caught him staring, and smiled. 'Do you like what you see, Kagan?'

'You know I do,' he said. 'You are the most beautiful woman I've ever seen.'

'So you say. Still, I like to hear it. Are you happy with our little arrangement?'

'This is the happiest I've ever been. These last few months have been like a dream come true.' An image of Dizzler's crew rampaging through the mansion flashed through his mind. He pictured Sofia's terrified face as they broke down the door of her rooms, and he nearly choked.

She raised an eyebrow. 'You don't look that happy. What's wrong?'

He gazed at her. He couldn't let it happen. He thought back to his talk with Albeck by the waterfront, and how he had persuaded himself to go along with the plan. He had been deluding himself; there was no way he would be able to look the other way if Sofia was in danger; the thought of Dizzler's crew touching her made him want to kill someone. At that moment, looking into her eyes, he realised that he would rather die than betray her to Dizzler. He swallowed.

'Oh dear,' said Sofia. 'I insist that you tell me everything, at once, Kagan.'

'If I do,' he said, 'then you'll kick me out of the house.'

Her eyes narrowed. 'Have you been seeing another woman?'

'No,' he cried. 'Never. Only you, I swear it.'

She shrugged. 'Well, it can't be that bad.'

'It is. It's very bad.'

She sighed. 'Get on with it, Kagan.'

'Do you remember how you and Gellie tested me?'

'Of course.'

'She blackmailed me. She had something on me, and wanted me to help her friends rob the mansion.'

'Yes. I told her what to say, so I'm hardly likely to forget.'

He lowered his glance. 'Someone else is blackmailing me, for the same reason.'

She sipped her brandy, her expression calm.

'They sent someone to follow me today,' he went on, 'and told me their plan.'

'What do they have on you?' she said.

'Someone bribed the Blades to get me and Elena excused from going to Jezra along with the other refugees. Apparently, it's a serious crime, and they're threatening to go to the authorities if I don't help them. They want me to open the kitchen door, at night, and let a gang in to rob the house.'

'When?'

'I don't know. I think they could sense that I wasn't very willing, and I don't think they trust me. They told me that they'd give me a few hours notice, and that it will probably take place some time in the next month.'

'Have you known all along that they might come for you?'

'I was hoping that they had forgotten all about me.'

'A little naïve of you, don't you think? So, I have a lying criminal in my bed? You're lucky that I'm fond of you; very lucky indeed.' She took another sip of brandy. 'I'm going to need names, Kagan.'

He felt shame well in his guts, spreading through his body. He had never informed on anyone before, especially not members of his former gang. The penalty for such transgressions was death, and he had always felt it justified. Informers were the lowest of the low, yet what choice did he have, if he wanted to keep her safe?

'Albeck,' he muttered, his eyes closing.

'What? The man from the Refugee Council? He's allied himself to a gang from Alea Tanton?'

'He has, ma'am. A Shinstran gang. They moved into the Circuit during winter.'

'Alright. Who else?'

Kagan kept his eyes shut. 'Dizzler.'

'Who?'

'Dizzler. He's my old gang boss. I worked for him for years in Alea Tanton. He paid the bribes to get me and Elena out of Salt Quay, and he's Albeck's boss now as well.'

'Dizzler, eh?' She nodded. 'Leave it to me.'

He raised his head again. 'What will you do?'

She pierced him with her gaze. 'I said, "leave it to me." We won't speak of this again, do you understand?'

He nodded.

'Good.'

She got out of bed and walked to a large wardrobe, Kagan's eyes following her. Now that it was done, he didn't feel any relief. He had saved Sofia, but he felt soiled and dirty. He was an informer. He had broken the one rule that Dizzler prized above all others, and sold out his old friend.

Sofia held up some clothes. 'Are there any more secrets that I should know about, Kagan?'

'No, ma'am, but you should know that I've killed people for doing what I've just done.'

She examined a dress. 'You've killed people?'

'Yes. Back in Alea Tanton. For Dizzler.'

'What if I asked you to kill for me; would you do it?'

'I'd kill anyone who tried to hurt you, but I'm not an assassin.'

'That's a reasonable answer, I suppose,' she said, pulling on a blue dress. 'Help me with the clasps.'

He stood, and walked to where she had turned her back to him. He moved her hair over one shoulder, and fastened the long row of little clasps that ran up the back of the dress, feeling her skin beneath his fingertips.

Sofia turned, and placed her hands on his bare chest. 'How many people have you killed, Kagan?'

He gazed down at her. 'Three.'

She smiled. 'Still a beginner.' She kissed him. 'Don't be frightened of Dizzler; he won't be able to touch you here; you're under my protection now.'

'I'm more concerned that he'll hurt you, ma'am.'

'Don't be silly, Kagan. You have no idea how powerful I am, do you? But, don't worry; you'll soon find out.'

CHAPTER 24

MIST AND SMOKE

The Cold Sea – 4th Mikalis 3421

The Cold Sea – 4th Mikalis 3421
    Thick sheets of mist were rising from the calm waters of the Cold Sea. Yendra squinted into the gloom, knowing that the Western Bank was right in front of her, but unable to see any of it due to the dawn fog. The only indication that they were in the right place was from the string of powerful lanterns that had been hoisted up by the entrance to the small harbour of Westrig. Behind her on the deck of the empty merchant's galley, the Icewarder crew were lowering the sails.

'Ahoy!' cried a voice from the mist, and an Icewarder rang the ship's bell in reply.

The vessel glided slowly into the still waters of the small bay, and bumped against the side of the jetty. Sailors threw ropes up to the waiting Brigade workers, who pulled them in and secured the vessel. Yendra climbed up to the jetty, and the members of the Brigade who were there bowed low.

'Good morning,' she said. 'Are the Banner forces ready?'

'Yes, ma'am,' said one of the young Brigade officers. 'Two regiments are lined up for embarkation.'

'And the Brigades?'

'The Second and Ninth are also ready, ma'am.'

'Excellent. There are seventeen more ships, anchored a mile to the north-east. Due to the mist, I have ordered them to approach one at a time rather than risk any collision. Therefore, speed is essential. I want the first four companies on board within the next five minutes.'

'Yes, ma'am.'

The officer took a whistle from a pocket and gave three short blasts. Immediately, the sound of boots echoed through the gloom, and Yendra watched the ranks of heavily armed Banner soldiers march up the jetty towards her. Brigade officers began directing them onto the ship, and they formed queues, each jumping down onto the deck of the vessel, then finding a space to sit for the short voyage.

Van emerged from the mist, dressed in his battle armour. He saluted Yendra.

'Your Highness,' he said. 'Do you think this mist will burn off?'

She nodded. 'Mist is common at dawn during the first days of summer, but it'll be gone in an hour or so, once the sun's had a chance to rise. Did you sleep well?'

'I got an hour or two. The Brigades and Banner have been working through the night, securing the defences and repairing the jetty, and moving the supplies we'll need up from Jezra. Pass on my thanks to the Queen – she's fulfilled every promise about keeping the supplies flowing in from Pella.'

'You'll be seeing her in person after this operation. You're her golden officer, Van; you've proved over the last few months that her Majesty was correct to place her faith in you. I hope you're good at receiving acclaim, because there will no doubt be parties and receptions to celebrate your achievements on the Western Bank.'

He frowned. 'We still have the Grey Isle to take, your Highness.'

'Indeed.'

'Regarding casualties, your Highness; I know that the Queen wants as few dead as possible, and I have ordered the Banner to show quarter wherever practical. However, anything can happen, and I can't guarantee it'll be bloodless.'

'I understand, Major.'

The last soldiers of the first four companies boarded the crowded deck, and Yendra stepped back down onto the vessel, Van following her. She gestured to the Icewarder ship's captain, and the ropes connecting the vessel to the jetty were loosened and thrown back onto the deck. Sailors scrambled over the rigging, and the ship began to move, easing away from the jetty, before turning in a slow arc until the bow was pointing towards the north-east. The sails were unfurled, and the vessel picked up speed, gliding through the calm waters of the bay until the jetty was lost in the mist behind them.

'Is there any new intelligence on the Grey Isle garrison, your Highness?' said Van.

Yendra nodded. 'Reinforcements and supplies were sent out from Dalrig yesterday, as soon as the rains had lifted. Even so, the Gloamers will be heavily out-numbered by the Banner forces.'

'They're expecting us?'

'Yes. I have no doubt that there are Gloamer spies operating in Icehaven, and word will have reached Lady Amber in Dalrig that we were planning an assault upon the island.'

Van nodded. 'I'd better let the company commanders know.'

'Were it not for the dragons, Major, I would be tempted to abandon this operation. Thankfully, we have them for a few more days.'

Van saluted, then walked off along the crowded deck towards his officers. Yendra kept her eyes directly ahead, peering into the blanket of mist.

It took an hour for the six Icewarder ships to load the two Banner regiments. The other dozen vessels would follow behind, carrying the Brigades and their equipment, and the half dozen ships sailed onward to the Grey Isle. A strong wind picked up from sunward, and the swell increased as the sails snapped full.

Yendra was staring ahead of the bow when the mist lifted, burned off by the hot summer sun. In front of them, the high cliffs of the Grey

Isle were jutting up from the waves. Yendra made her way to the quarter
deck, where the Icewarder captain was speaking to the helmsman on
the wheel.

'Captain,' she said, as she climbed the steps.

He bowed. 'Your Highness?'

'Take the ship into the entrance of the inner bay, and weigh anchor
there.'

'We're not going straight into the harbour, your Highness?'

'Not yet. Signal to the other five troop carriers to do the same.'

'Understood, your Highness.'

Yendra watched as the ship tacked a little to the east, so that the
steep cliffs of the island were on their left. She saw the opening in the
cliff wall ahead of them, and beyond, the houses and harbour of the
isle's only settlement. The helmsman brought the vessel close to the gap
in the cliffs, and then Yendra heard a great grinding noise as both
anchors were dropped. The ship carried on for a few more minutes as
the sails were brought in, then it slowed to a halt, the anchor chains
stretched taut. Next to them, the other five ships positioned themselves
in a rough line, so that they were blocking the entrance to the harbour.
Yendra powered her line vision and sent it out towards the small town.
The six vessels had been spotted, and Gloamer militia were running
along the waterfront, while civilians were being ushered off the streets.
To the left of the settlement was the town's castle, where the garrison
was based. Yendra's eyes fell on it, and she grimaced from the memories
it brought back.

She glanced at the captain. 'Get ready to move into the harbour
upon my signal.'

The captain bowed.

She looked up into the skies, in the direction of the Iceward Range,
and smiled. Four dark specks were soaring towards them. Among them,
Frostback's position was clear – her silver scales were glittering in the
light of the morning sun. A few of the Banner soldiers called out,
pointing at the approaching dragons, and soon every eye was watching
the creatures as they drew nearer. Deathfang was in the lead, his

massive bulk unmistakable, and Halfclaw and Tarsnow were alongside Frostback.

The dragons sped over the cliff, then circled over the settlement.

Yendra turned to the captain. 'Now, if you please.'

'Yes, your Highness.'

The crew began to strain at the anchor winches, and the sails were unfurled into the strong wind. The ship rocked, then began to move into the bay.

'This is the part that worries me,' said Van, who had moved to stand next to her.

'There are only five hundred Gloamer militia in the garrison,' she said. 'They must know they don't stand a chance. The rational choice would be to surrender.'

Van frowned. 'Who ever said that people were rational?'

Yendra nodded to the captain. 'Take us alongside one of the central jetties.' She turned back to stare at the town. The Gloamer militia could clearly see the dragons circling overhead, and with six ships also advancing, they must realise that resistance would be pointless. Inside, she had agreed with Van; this was a risk, but she had tried her best to think of a plan that would result in no casualties, and awing the enemy with a display of overwhelming force had appeared the only option.

There was a shout from the direction of the castle, and several yard-long steel bolts shot through the air from the battlements, aimed up at the dragons. All fell short, flying under the height the dragons were circling at, but Tarsnow broke off from the others, and soared down.

'What's he doing?' muttered Van.

Tarsnow pulled up in front of the castle, and sent a blast of fire surging towards the battlements, where several ballistae were positioned. The flames engulfed the machines and the Gloamer militia operating them, their screams echoing across the bay. Tarsnow rose up a few feet, his eyes scanning for more targets. As he turned towards the keep, another ballista battery on the top of a lower tower loosed at him. Two bolts shot upwards, piercing Tarsnow's flank. The black and white dragon let out a great cry of agony, and he seemed to hover for a moment, his head arched back, as blood flowed from the twin wounds in his side. Another two bolts were loosed. One ripped through the dragon's left wing, but the other struck his chest, and Tarsnow began to fall.

The other dragons hurtled down in a blur, and the castle erupted in an inferno of flames. Deathfang sent fire spraying over every parapet, and down into the keep and the courtyards of the castle's interior, while Halfclaw incinerated a mass of running soldiers as they tried to flee along the road to the harbour.

Tarsnow's body crashed into the side of the castle, bringing down a tower and a huge stretch of curtain wall. His head dropped to the ground and lay still, his eyes open but lifeless.

Yendra stared, her gaze fixed on the fallen dragon. Then her attention shifted, as the three surviving dragons turned their wrath onto the settlement. Halfclaw swooped along the shore from the castle, sending blasts of flames at anything on the road, while Deathfang and Frostback were soaring towards the houses of the town.

Yendra tried to enter Deathfang's mind, but Kelsey was riding on Frostback's shoulders, and she was too close to the huge grey dragon, shielding him from the god's vision powers. She turned to Halfclaw, who was dipping in and out of Kelsey's range.

She pushed into the young dragon's thoughts.

Halfclaw; not the civilians, please. Let them not suffer for the soldiers' mistakes; I beg you.

The green and blue dragon hesitated.

Halfclaw, please.

He pulled up from the road, leaving a trail of flames behind him leading all the way to the burning castle. Over the town, Frostback had noticed Halfclaw, and was also pulling out of the attack, but Deathfang was oblivious. He dived over the settlement, his jaws wide open, and emitted a great blast of fire that swept across the rows of stone houses, from the harbour to the foot of the cliffs at the back of the town. Roofs exploded and buildings cracked and shattered under the weight of the inferno. Groups of soldiers and civilians were fleeing, but the fires moved faster than they could run, and they were consumed in the conflagration.

The Banner soldiers on board the lead ship fell into silence as they stared at the burning town. Deathfang ascended, to gaze down on the work his rage had wrought, and he glowed in the reflected light of the flames. Yendra realised that he was far enough from Kelsey to contact, and rushed into his mind.

Let that be enough; please, Deathfang. Let no more die today.

The grey dragon made no response, but she could feel the anger flowing through him. At that moment, the ship bumped against the side of a long jetty, and soldiers began disembarking, climbing up in their squads. The Gloamers who were still alive threw down their weapons, their hands in the air, as they gathered by the waterfront, the fires ripping through the town behind them.

Van ordered the squads down the jetty, and they raced forwards, securing the harbour, and taking the survivors into custody. The other five troop carriers were also docking and within minutes, the harbour was full of Banner soldiers. Deathfang remained over the town like an apparition of death, his great wings extended above the smoke and flames.

Yendra climbed up onto the jetty, the Axe of Rand over her shoulder. The Banner soldiers had grouped the survivors together in a square by the main wharf, and Yendra gazed at the terrified faces of the children among them. A great crack echoed over the bay from the castle, and another tower collapsed, falling into the freezing waters of the Cold Sea. The fires over the town were dying down, but the ruins of the castle were still burning, sending thick plumes of black smoke up into the clear, pink sky.

Van approached Yendra as she stepped off the jetty onto the long wharf.

'The Grey Isle is ours, ma'am,' he said, his face grim.

She stared at the smoking town. 'I take full responsibility for this,' she said. 'I wanted the dragons to scare them, not annihilate them. The Banner is blameless.'

'I approved the plan, ma'am. The blame is not yours alone. We knew what they could do; we've seen them in action countless times against the greenhides...' He paused, his voice nearly cracking.

'We knew,' said Yendra, 'and yet we still brought them here, to face our fellow citizens.'

Deathfang shifted from his position above the town, swooping low over the harbour. The gathered Gloamers wailed in fear as the dragon's shadow swept over them, and some of the children screamed.

'I will speak to the dragons,' said Yendra. 'Alone.'

She strode off along the road, in the direction of the burning castle. Frostback and Halfclaw were circling over the coast between the town and the castle, and Deathfang joined them, then all three descended as Yendra approached. They gathered next to Tarsnow's sprawling body, and Halfclaw sniffed the long steel bolt protruding from the dead dragon's chest.

Deathfang landed between Tarsnow and Yendra.

'You are to blame for this disaster, god!' he spat at her. 'One of my kin has fallen; the strongest and mightiest of my colony, the father of Firestone, the mate of Dawnflame. How am I to tell his mate of this? That the brave Tarsnow fell due to the politics and infighting of insects? Destroying greenhides for you was what we initially agreed, but you couldn't stop there, could you, god? You pushed me into helping one last time; now witness the fruits of your folly. It is enough, for now, for all time. Our agreement is over, and I shall pay for it with bitter tears.' He lowered his head. 'I would curse you, god, as Dawnflame will surely curse me.'

'Then, why don't you?' said Yendra; 'for you are right. This day was my fault. I should never have asked you and your kin to help us take the isle. I was wrong.'

'I acquiesced, god. To curse you for it, would be to curse myself.' He turned to Halfclaw. 'Help me, young one; help me carry the body of our fallen kin home to the Iceward Range, so Dawnflame can consign her mate to ashes. Once that is done, we shall delay no longer. By this evening, every one of us shall be in the Eastern Mountains, far from the corruption of the world of insects.' He faced Yendra again. 'This is goodbye, god. My last favour to you will be to prevent my other kin from seeking revenge for Tarsnow's death. I will not do this from kindness, but because I do not wish my kin to be sullied by any more contact with you.'

He rose up, and Halfclaw joined him in the air. Together, they descended over Tarsnow, and each took hold of the fallen dragon. Their wings beating, they lifted the black and white dragon's body upwards, then they soared over the bay, carrying Tarsnow away.

Frostback landed by the road, and Yendra watched as Kelsey scrambled down the silver dragon's flank.

'Have you come to blame me too, Miss Holdfast?'

Kelsey kept her gaze down, her eyes welling. 'What did you think was going to happen?'

'I thought that the Gloamers would surrender.'

'Aye?' She shook her head. 'The moment those bolts were loosed at us, I knew; I just knew. I tried to stop them, but they wouldn't listen to me.'

'I listened to you, rider,' said Frostback, 'despite my grief at Tarsnow's death. The soldiers in the castle deserved to burn, but we should have left the town alone. Princess Yendra, I am sorry.'

'Thank you, Frostback,' said Yendra, 'but we all have a part in this catastrophe, and I must claim the largest share. It was I who asked you here this day, and now you have lost one of your kin.'

Kelsey glanced up at her. 'Not to mention hundreds of dead Gloamers.'

'The City will be in uproar when they learn of this,' said Yendra. 'I will tell the Queen that the dragons were not to blame, that they were reacting according to their nature, and I will offer her my resignation.'

'She won't accept it,' said Kelsey. 'You're all that's keeping Emily and Daniel upon their thrones. If they lose you, they lose everything.'

'I hope that isn't true, Kelsey. What will you do now?'

'We should return to the quarry in the Iceward Range,' said Frostback. 'Words will be spoken, and tears will be shed over the death of

Tarsnow, and I must be there for that.' She lowered her head to Kelsey. 'I ask you, my rider; come with me. Show my father where your sympathies lie; he will be in a rage with the humans of the City, and he needs to see that you are with him. And then, we shall all go to the Eastern Mountains, and turn our backs on this place.'

Kelsey looked conflicted, her eyes glancing from Frostback to Yendra, then she nodded.

'I will go with you, Frostback.'

'Thank you, my rider. Climb up, and we will leave.'

'I'll see you again, Yendra,' Kelsey said. 'Tell Van... tell him I'm sorry for dragging him to this world, and tell him to wait for the baby – he'll know what I mean. Bye.'

She climbed up the harness onto Frostback's shoulders, and the silver dragon lifted into the air. She circled once over the burning castle, then soared away to the east, until she was lost in the distance.

The harbour of the Grey Isle grew busier as the day passed, as the ships carrying the Brigades arrived. Their first job was to extinguish the fires in the town, and the last of the flames were put out as the sun was beginning to set. The castle had been left to burn, and no one approached the blackened, smouldering ruins all day. The buildings along the waterfront were the least damaged of the town, and Van set up his Command Post in the largest of them – the old Merchants' Hall, which sat in front of the longest jetties. The Gloamer ships in the harbour had also been left untouched by the dragons' fury, and Banner soldiers had removed the crews and were guarding the stores on board.

In a room on the second floor of the Merchants' Hall, Van and Yendra were going through the lists of the dead, compiled by the Brigades, who had been given the task of counting the bodies.

'I can delay no longer,' Yendra said. 'The Queen will be anxious for information.'

Van glanced at the others in the room. 'Everyone out. The Commander of the Bulwark and I need to speak.'

The Banner officers saluted and filed out of the chamber, and Van turned to the princess.

'You shouldn't take the blame for this,' he said.

'I must. I refuse to scapegoat either you or the dragons. Close the door and get me a drink, Major; I will return shortly.'

She focussed, and sent her vision out. She pushed it at speed over the waters of the Cold Sea, pausing for a moment to see the Icewarder ships blockading the harbour of Dalrig, then sped her sight to Pella. She entered Cuidrach Palace and located Salvor.

Nephew.

Salvor blinked. He was sitting with the Queen in one of her private chambers, a map of the Grey Isle spread out on a table in front of them.

He glanced at the Queen. 'Princess Yendra has entered my mind, your Majesty.'

'About time,' said Emily. 'What's the news?'

The Grey Isle is under our full control, Yendra said, *but the news is not all good. Tarsnow is dead, shot down by ballista bolts. In revenge, Deathfang razed the town, killing three hundred and fifty-three civilians. Out of the five hundred Gloamer militia, only forty-one remain alive, the others were incinerated within the town's castle.*

The dragons killed over eight hundred?

In a matter of minutes, Salvor. I take full responsibility. I misjudged how the dragons would react if brought under attack. Tell her Majesty that I apologise, and that I offer my resignation for this disaster. Major Van and the Banner behaved impeccably, and they neither caused nor sustained a single casualty; they and the Brigades are re-housing the survivors of the town, and securing its defences. The castle has been destroyed, along with over half of the houses within the town.

I see, your Highness. Do you wish to stay in my mind while I inform her Majesty of this?

No. I will contact you later.

She severed the connection, and her vision snapped back to her own mind. She focussed her sight, and saw Van holding out a glass of brandy for her. She took it, and drank.

'How did they react?' he said, sitting at the table.

'I left Salvor's head before discovering that,' she said. 'I didn't want to witness the Queen's immediate reaction. I will give them some time to digest the news first.' She drained the glass and got to her feet. 'I'm going for a walk; there's something I need to see.'

She left the chamber, and descended the stairs to the ground floor, passing Banner and Brigade officers as they worked. A squad attempted to attach themselves to her as she left the building, but she waved them away and set off along the coastal road in the direction of the castle. Smoke was still rising from the ruins, and she took a circuitous route, avoiding the area where Tarsnow had collided with the walls. She came round to the side of the castle, and climbed over the collapsed rubble by the main gatehouse. Her hands were scorched from touching the hot stones, but her self-healing repaired the damage as soon as it had been inflicted. She scrambled down into the interior of the castle, and entered the ruins of the keep. The upper levels had been destroyed, but the basements and cellars were intact, and she descended into the gloom, ignoring the stench of death and burnt flesh from the scattered bodies. The walls were cracked and blackened from the flames, and heat was radiating from the stonework as she walked down a narrow staircase into the bowels of the castle. She reached a dark hallway at the bottom of the stairs, and pushed open a door. She stared down the passageway beyond, seeing the lines of old prison cells running down each wall. Her heart pounded as memories flooded her, and she suppressed a feeling of nausea. She walked along the empty corridor, then stopped outside a cell.

Her cell. Her home for hundreds of years. She peered into the filthy dungeon, and saw that her old chains were still lying amid the dirty straw on the floor. She knelt down, and touched a shackle, her hand reaching between the iron bars. Dried blood was mixed with the straw, and she remembered lying in the filth, and the never-ending pain in her head. Her own father had placed her there, chained, bound and masked, in that cell, instead of executing her as he had promised the God-Queen. She stilled, closing her eyes, allowing the recollections to fill her; the hopelessness, the despair. The pain. Then she heard Corthie's voice, the voice that had brought her back, the voice promising that he would never leave her alone in that dungeon, and she started to weep. Silent tears fell down her face.

She had done good things since being rescued and revived, she told herself. She had helped save the City from the greenhides, and she had helped place mortals on the twin thrones. The God-King was dead, and the God-Queen gone forever; and yet eight hundred Gloamers were now dead, because of her.

She opened her eyes and wiped the tears from her face. No one ever saw her cry, and no one ever would. No, she would bury her guilt, and the shame that went with it, because she had no alternative. Kelsey had been right; without her, would the mortal monarchy have any chance of surviving? Emily and Daniel needed her; they needed her to be strong and determined, and they must never know the doubts that tore her conscience to pieces. Her strength was the rock upon which they depended, and she would not let them down again.

She stood, and let her feet guide her from the building. It was time to get back to work.

CHAPTER 25

PULLING THE STRINGS

Pella, Auldan, The City – 14th Mikalis 3421

Emily pinched the side of her leg to keep herself alert. The speech by the Reaper councillor had been going on for so long that she was concerned her attention might drift away, or worse, that she might yawn in front of the half-filled benches of the Tribal Council. She glanced at the faces of those present, and could see more than a few struggling to hide their boredom; and she wished that Daniel was there in her place.

One of the Roser delegates caught her gaze, then frowned and looked away. At least the Rosers were still attending, she thought. The Gloamers had been boycotting the Tribal Council since their votes had been discarded at the session where the constitutional laws had been forced through, and the Evaders had only sent two new delegates to replace those murdered in the Circuit on the same day. The Sanders had also cut the numbers of their delegates, as a protest against the slaughter of the eight hundred Gloamers on the Grey Isle ten days before. The Rosers had been about to do the same, but had relented when the court case to adjudicate the controversial session had begun in Tara that morning. Five Roser judges were examining the rules of the Tribal Council, to discern if any had been broken by the King. Daniel had decided to go there in person to defend his actions, which had necessitated Emily's attendance at the Council meeting.

It was the first time since the conquest of the Grey Isle that Emily had appeared in public, and she could sense a faint tremor of hostility towards her, even from those tribes she judged to be friendly. No one had said anything to her face about the deaths of so many Gloamers, but she knew that she was being held responsible. It may have been the dragons who had killed them, but she had approved the orders that had led to the carnage.

The Reaper councillor ended his speech and sat, and Emily stifled a sigh of relief.

'Our thanks to the Councilman,' said Salvor, rising to his feet. 'He can be assured that the Crown takes his points regarding the standardisation of weights and measures across Auldan and Medio very seriously. Next to speak are the Roser delegates.'

Salvor sat down again, and one of the Roser councillors got to her feet.

'Your Majesty, Lord Salvor, and honourable members of this council,' she said; 'I hereby move that this council session be ended immediately, and the doors of this chamber be closed until the current case being held in Tara reaches a decision. For, if the honourable judges find that his Majesty King Daniel broke the law when he forced the passage of the constitutional reforms, then anything we decide here will be moot.'

A Hammer delegate raised his arm. 'Objection! The chances of that happening are remote. The Rosers are just trying to waste time.'

Salvor glanced up. 'Over-ruled. This council does not intend to pre-judge the outcome of the case being held in Tara.' He nodded to the Roser delegate. 'Please continue.'

'Thank you, Lord Salvor,' she said. 'As I was saying...'

She broke off as the doors to the chamber opened, and the five Gloamer delegates entered. The large hall fell into utter silence as they made their way to their empty seats.

Salvor stood. 'This council welcomes back the delegates from Dalrig. Are we to assume that the boycott is at an end?'

The head Gloamer remained standing, while his colleagues took their seats. 'No, my lord.'

'Then,' said Salvor, 'is there a reason for your attendance this day?'

'Yes, my lord. We bear a statement from Prince Montieth that he has asked be read out to the Tribal Council. Once that is done, we shall vacate the chamber again.'

Salvor nodded, then glanced at the Roser delegate. 'Apologies, but I would ask that you please be seated, in order for us to hear what Prince Montieth has to say.'

The Roser delegate frowned, then sat back down. To the right of the Rosers, the chief Gloamer extracted a folded sheet of paper from his outer jacket. Salvor gestured for him to proceed, and then sat down next to the Queen, who shot him a glance.

'Thank you, Lord Salvor,' the Gloamer said, as he unfolded the document. 'The note from the prince is addressed to the Crown, and to the Tribal Council. It begins, "Ten days ago, in a callous and unprovoked attack upon the sovereign Gloamer territory of the Grey Isle, over eight hundred innocent Gloamers were slaughtered by wild dragons under the direct command of Princess Yendra, Commander of the Bulwark. Her Highness, in turn, received her orders from none other than her Majesty, Queen Emily of Pella. This unprecedented and cowardly assault, and the subsequent sea and land blockade of Dalrigian trade, have caused immense suffering to the Gloamer tribe, out of all proportion to the bloodless occupation of Ooste, for which these actions were ostensibly a response. Prince Montieth wishes it to be noted that not a single life has been lost in Ooste over the course of the occupation, in stark contrast to the cruel and senseless attack upon the Grey Isle. Queen Emily sanctioned the use of wild dragons against the innocent populace of the City; something that not even the former God-Queen had contemplated. In so doing, her Majesty has lost the trust and respect of the citizens of the City, and it is clear that she intends to rule as a tyrant, without any regard for the…"'

The delegate halted, as shouts from the other tribes threatened to drown him out. The Hammers and Reapers, in particular, were taking exception to his words, while the Rosers sat smirking in their seats.

'Silence,' said Salvor. 'The statement comes from the pen of Prince Montieth, who is not here to listen to your objections. Let the man speak.'

'Thank you, my lord,' said the Gloamer. 'Where was I? Oh yes. "... without any regard for the rights of the people she purports to lead. As such, Dalrig has the following announcement to make – as of this morning, the Gloamer occupation of Ooste is at an end. The militia troops are being withdrawn, and will be posted back to their barracks within Gloamer territory by sunset on this day. By this gesture, the honourable and noble Prince of Dalrig hopes to show the other tribes of the City that his intentions have always been peaceful. The population of Ooste has been unharmed, and their property left untouched. In return, the noble Prince of Dalrig demands the immediate lifting of the blockade, on both land and sea, and the evacuation of all foreign and hostile forces from the Grey Isle. Let the peoples of the City unite in peace, and let the Crown swear never to deploy dragons or foreign so-called Banner soldiers against the citizenry again."' The delegate folded the document in two and placed it back into a jacket pocket. 'That concludes the missive from the Prince of Dalrig. We await the response of the Crown.'

He sat, amid a stony silence within the chamber.

Salvor glanced at Emily, and she made a cutting motion across her throat with a thumb.

He stood. 'This session is hereby at an end. The Crown will respond to the Prince of Dalrig in due course. Good day, ladies and gentlemen.'

The Gloamer delegates jumped to their feet.

'This is an outrage!' cried one. 'We demand a response; now!'

'Settle down, if you please,' said Salvor, his voice curt. 'The Tribal Council shall reconvene tomorrow, at noon. Good day.'

Salvor gestured to the Royal Guards by the doors, and they opened them wide. Emily got to her feet, then strode to the rear exit, a squad of soldiers accompanying her, as the chamber filled with angry shouts. She walked from the hall, leaving the raucous complaints behind her, and carried on until she reached Salvor's office. She left the guards at the door and entered alone. The room was empty, so she walked to a cabinet and poured herself a small brandy, which she drained in a single motion. Despite it, her nerves were jangling, and she felt like screaming.

How dare they?

Montieth was the aggressor, not she. He had trampled all over the laws of the City, and then had the audacity to turn it around and place the blame on her shoulders. A tyrant – that's what he had called her. A tyrant, after she had freed the City from the rule of the God-Queen. She tried to think about her next move, but her mind filled with every choice she had already taken. She should have taken Lady Amber into custody that day by the border; or, she should have listened to Kelsey and sent assassination squads into Ooste to eliminate Montieth. She had been too restrained; that was her problem. The City pictured her as ruthless, but she hadn't been nearly ruthless enough.

She sat heavily into a chair. No. She couldn't allow her anger to rule her decisions. She needed to calm herself; she needed to breathe.

The door opened and Salvor strode in.

'The Royal Guards have cleared the council chamber, your Majesty,' he said. He frowned as he glanced at her. 'Do you require some time alone?'

'No. I need you to find out if it's true, Salvor. Are they really evacuating Ooste?'

He walked over to where she sat and took a seat close by. 'I will look for you, your Majesty.'

She glanced up at him as his eyes glazed over. She hated that he could see into her mind; he must sense her confusion and inexperience every time he looked at her thoughts, and she felt like an imposter. She clenched her fists. No. She was the damned Queen, and deserved her title; had earned it through her own blood and sweat.

She turned to the door, half-expecting Daniel to walk through, then she remembered that he was in Tara. She recalled that the letter from Montieth had neglected to mention the King; instead placing the entire responsibility onto her shoulders. The wily old bastard had out-flanked her, and he was trying to drive a wedge between her and her husband in the eye of the public, singling her out as the villain of the affair. And what would Daniel think? He had warned about the potential for casualties in the Grey Isle, and she had dismissed his concerns, thinking that her orders to Yendra would be sufficient to prevent bloodshed. Stupid dragons!

'Your Majesty?'

She glanced at Salvor, and tried to compose her features. 'Yes?'

'The gist of the missive appears to be accurate. Gloamer forces are currently pulling out of Ooste, and the first regiments have already entered the gates of Dalrig. At their present speed, I estimate that the last of them will have left Ooste within three to four hours.'

'And Montieth? Where is that devious little rat?'

Salvor's eye twitched a little. 'I did not see his Highness. Should I call for Lady Silva? Or Lady Vana, perhaps? Their powers would be able to pinpoint his location.'

She nodded, and his eyes glazed over again.

Emily's fingers drummed the surface of the nearby table as she waited. Her anger began to fade, and she tried to think about how she could turn things back to her advantage. If Montieth had truly left Ooste, then hadn't she won? For all his self-righteousness, hadn't he actually admitted failure and gone home? She would be able to lift the blockade, and Dalrigian goods would appear in the markets of Pella again after a ten-day absence. The Icewarder fleet could sail home, slashing the costs the treasury were bearing for its deployment outside the harbour of Dalrig. She wondered about the Grey Isle; it might be wrong, but she wanted to keep it – its possession would keep Dalrig on the back foot, and neutralise the threat of another blockade.

'Lady Vana and Lady Silva are on their way, your Majesty,' said Salvor.

'You summoned them both?'

'Yes, your Majesty. Lady Vana has recently been expressing frustration about her lack of a role within the palace, and I thought it would be wise to include her.'

Emily frowned. 'I was under the impression that she wanted a quiet life.'

'She has been back in the City for almost six months, your Majesty. I fear that boredom may drive her into the arms of Lady Ikara and Lord Collo, if we're not careful.'

'Does she think that, because she's a demigod, she's entitled to a position of power?'

'She has useful skills; they could be quite dangerous in the wrong hands.'

Emily rolled her eyes, then got up and walked to the window, feeling restless.

'I wonder how Daniel's case is going,' she said.

'Should I check, your Majesty?'

'No. I can wait. Were it not for Montieth, I'd be tempted to go to Tara today, so I could stay over with Danny in the old house in Princeps Row. I haven't seen the King-Father in months. Still, on the bright side, I'm glad that the King-Mother decided to accompany the King; at least she won't be looking over my shoulder for a few days.' She glanced at Salvor. 'Obviously, that remains between us.'

'Of course, your Majesty.'

A courtier appeared at the door. 'Lady Vana is here, your Majesty.'

Emily smiled. 'Show her in.'

The courtier bowed, and then Vana strode into the office. She approached Salvor and the Queen, and bowed.

'Thank you for coming,' said Emily.

Vana nodded. 'How may I be of service, your Majesty?'

'I would like you to provide the location of Prince Montieth for me.'

'He is in Dalrig, your Majesty.'

Emily raised an eyebrow. 'Are you sure?'

'Yes, your Majesty. I looked for him as soon as I heard the news of the statement made in the Tribal Council. He had already returned to Greylin Palace by the time the Gloamers rose to speak.'

'I see. Well, thank you, Lady Vana; that was most helpful.'

Vana bowed. 'Is there anything else I can do for you?'

'Yes. Where is Naxor? He has been remiss in keeping us informed as to his whereabouts.'

'My cousin is in Port Sanders, your Majesty, residing in his old mansion.'

'Is he, indeed? Thank you, again. That will be all.'

Vana frowned. 'Your Majesty, might I speak?'

'Of course.'

'I am capable of more than merely locating the members of my family, your Majesty; I have centuries of experience of working for the rulers of the City, and... and, it's been six months since I was informed that I would be taking a rest from active service. I am grateful for such an extended leave of absence, but I am now well-rested, and am looking forward to returning to duty.'

Emily suppressed her impatience. 'Let's examine your record for a moment, Lady Vana. Under Duke Marcus, you were employed to keep a register of the locations of every god and demigod in the City; is that correct? You hunted for Lady Aila, did you not?'

Vana's cheeks flushed. 'I did, your Majesty; however, it was under duress. The duke made it clear that I had no choice; I had to help him, or I would have been punished.'

'I see. And under Princess Khora's rule; what did you do?'

'I was one of her Highness's closest advisors, your Majesty. I accompanied her when she travelled, and, like Lord Collo, I was on hand to perform any task that was required of me.'

Emily nodded. 'Give me an example of something that you advised Princess Khora to do.'

'Your Majesty?'

'You said that you advised her; on what? What areas of expertise did you provide? Were you responsible for policy decisions? If so, please list them.'

'It was in the aftermath of the Civil War, your Majesty, and the governance of the City was in turmoil following the death of Prince Michael. I gave my unconditional loyalty to Princess Khora, when she needed it.'

'Even though the loyalists, of whom Princess Khora was one, were responsible for the deaths of your father and many of your siblings? You switched sides in the Civil War, didn't you, once the rebels looked like they might lose?'

Vana's face reddened, and her eyes shone with anger.

'In fact,' Emily went on, 'before the execution of your father, Prince Isra, you were a rebel. Is that not so? If one were to examine your record closely, it would appear that you pledge loyalty to whoever happens to be in charge. You change with the wind, don't you? If, for instance, Prince Montieth were to stage a bloody coup, you would be the first to offer your services to him, wouldn't you?'

Vana said nothing, her fists clenched.

'Is it not the case,' Emily said, 'that you feel you deserve a place in government based solely upon the fact that you cannot die of old age? Is that a suitable qualification? I think not. I would rather employ those whose hearts are with our cause, instead of those who feel entitled because they happen to be immortal. Therefore, although I am grateful for your kind offer, I feel obliged to politely decline it. Thank you again for your assistance in locating the errant prince. Dismissed.'

Vana remained where she was, shaking with anger, then turned and hurried from the chamber.

Salvor emitted an audible groan.

'Do you have something to add?' Emily snapped.

'May I speak freely, your Majesty?'

'No. I know what you're going to say. You think I was too hard on her. Maybe I was, but I'm tired, Salvor, tired of certain members of your family thinking that they own this City. Vana, Ikara, Collo, Lydia, Amber, Montieth – need I go on?'

'If you feel that way, your Majesty, then perhaps you should dismiss me also.'

'Did I include you in that list, Salvor? You have never once acted as if you feel entitled to your position. Instead, you prove your worth by the quality and diligence of your work. If the others did the same, then I wouldn't be standing here complaining about them.' She took a breath. 'Are you angry with me?'

'Frustrated, perhaps; but not angry. I want your monarchy to succeed, your Majesty; I want the mortals of the City to rule, but the entire project is so fragile; and antagonising the immortals who live here might turn out to be counter-productive. What if something were to happen to Princess Yendra, or even myself? I fear that Yendra and I are the only members of the former Royal Family who are truly with you, and were it not for their fear of Yendra, the others might conspire against you and the King. I know that this goes against your principles, your Majesty, but I counsel a policy of appeasement – appease the demigods who live in the City; give them something to do, lest they turn their idle thoughts to rebellion.'

Emily sat down by the table, feeling her anger drain away.

'Your orders, your Majesty?' Salvor said, his face expressionless.

Emily blinked. 'What?'

'As regards Ooste, your Majesty. Should we send the Reaper militia in to check the status of the civilians living there? Supplies of food and fuel may need to be transported to the town. Should I inform Lady Mona that she is safe to return home to the Royal Academy? And Lady Doria, should she be summoned from the Royal Palace and debriefed? Is the Crown planning on releasing a public statement regarding the evacuation from Ooste, and if so, what are its contents?'

Emily sighed. 'Pour me a brandy, and we'll get started.'

Emily and Salvor worked in seclusion for the afternoon, the demigod issuing the Queen's orders via his vision powers. Two thousand Reaper militia were sent to Ooste, and they reported that the last of the Gloamers had evacuated. Many of the civilians were hungry and exhausted after the occupation, but Montieth had been accurate – none had been killed.

Soldiers from the Royal Guard were brought into Cuidrach to keep away the dozens of petitioners who were demanding access to the Queen, including relatives of those who had been killed by the dragons on the Grey Isle. Emily could hear the low rumble from their voices echoing through the corridors of the palace, but none made it into Salvor's office.

Emily was working on her third draft of a public statement, when Commander Quill entered the room.

'What's wrong?' said Emily, putting down her pen. 'I can tell from your face that something has happened – what is it?'

'Bad news, your Majesty.'

'Well?'

'The King has been abducted, your Majesty.'

Emily's eyes widened. She stood. 'What?'

'In Tara, your Majesty,' said Quill. 'The King was returning to Princeps Row after the court closed for the day, and hooded men attacked his convoy as it climbed the cliffside. Seven members of the Royal Guard were slain, and the King was taken. A boat arrived in Pella harbour ten minutes ago with the news.'

'Who was responsible?' said Salvor.

'We don't know, my lord. There have been no statements or demands from anyone so far. Some of the surviving soldiers from the Royal Guard claim that the King was being taken in the direction of Maeladh Palace, but that hasn't been confirmed.'

Salvor turned to the Queen. 'I will look now, your Majesty; I will be as quick as I can.'

His eyes glazed over as Emily stared at him.

'I'm sorry, your Majesty,' said Quill.

'How many soldiers did Danny have with him?'

'I assigned a full company for his protection, your Majesty, but it appears that his Majesty had requested that only a single squad accompany him today. Tara was deemed to be safe, and the officer in command acquiesced to the King's request.'

'One squad? Twelve soldiers? Dear gods.' She put a hand to her face. 'They took him alive? He's still alive?'

'As far as we know, your Majesty. The men that attacked could have killed the King, if that had been their objective. Instead, he was bundled into the back of a wagon and taken away.'

Salvor blinked, and turned to the Queen. 'His Majesty is being held within Maeladh Palace,' he said. 'I counted perhaps forty armed men, all hooded, who are also in the palace. Roser militia are currently surrounding Maeladh. I instructed their commanding officer not to take action until ordered.'

'Get a ship prepared,' said Emily. 'I'm going to Tara.'

'But, your Majesty,' said Salvor; 'it could be a trap. Perhaps you are the target? There have been some threats made to your life since the incident on the Grey Isle.'

'And there have been threats to Danny's life over his damned constitutional laws. I'm not going to sit here trembling while my husband is being held hostage by a gang of thugs.'

The door opened, and Silva entered the office, her face red.

'My humble apologies, your Majesty,' she said, as she hurried forwards. 'I was out walking when Lord Salvor summoned me, exploring parts of Medio that I'd yet to visit. I came as fast as I could.' She glanced at the faces of those present. 'Is everything alright?'

'No,' said Emily. 'Everything is not alright.' She turned to Salvor. 'Get me a ship; now, if you please, and pack it full of the biggest soldiers we've got. We can be in Tara in an hour if we hurry.'

'At once, your Majesty,' he said, and his eyes glazed over again.

'Can I assist in any way?' said Silva.

'No,' said Emily. 'I asked you here so you could look for Montieth, but that crisis seems to have been supplanted already. Quill, get me a few squads and walk with me; we're going to the harbour as soon as Salvor comes out of his vision trance.'

Quill bowed, and rushed to the door, where she began shouting orders at the soldiers outside.

'May I ask what's wrong, your Majesty?' said Silva.

'The King has been captured. He's in Maeladh Palace.'

Silva gasped. 'The King? Is a coup being attempted? Should I ascertain the locations of every god and demigod in the City?'

Emily glanced at her. 'You mention a coup, and your first thoughts are of the demigods?'

'I don't trust some of them, your Majesty. Apologies if that offends you in any way, but if anyone was going to mount a coup, my suspicions would be on the members of the former Royal Family.'

Emily nodded. 'Proceed.'

Silva bowed, then went into her own trance. Emily glanced around, her impatience growing. Salvor, Quill and Silva were all doing her bidding, but she felt helpless. Danny was at the mercy of someone who clearly hated them, and he was in more danger with every minute that passed.

Salvor nodded to her. 'Your ship is being readied, your Majesty. Should I stay here, or do you wish me to come with you?'

'I'll take Quill, but you'd better stay here to keep an eye on things. Contact me at once if you have any news.'

Salvor bowed.

Quill rejoined them. 'Are we ready, your Majesty? Four squads are outside, waiting for us.'

'One moment,' said Emily, glancing at Silva.

The demigod's eyes cleared. 'No gods or demigods are anywhere near Tara, your Majesty. Shall I walk with you? I can list the locations of all immortals while we go to the harbour.'

Emily nodded. 'Alright.' She turned to Salvor. 'Have my armour and sword sent down to the ship; I'll get changed while we sail. I can't be leading an attack on Maeladh wearing a dress.'

Salvor frowned, but bowed again.

Emily led Quill and Silva to the door, where a large group of soldiers were waiting to escort them to the harbour.

'Start with Montieth,' Emily said. 'I know he's in Dalrig, but I just want to check.'

Silva frowned. 'Prince Montieth is not in Dalrig, your Majesty.'

'What? Then, where is he?'

'He must have left the City, your Majesty – I cannot see his location anywhere within my range.'

'How far does your range reach?'

'The Bulwark in one direction, and as far as Jezra and the Grey Isle in the other, your Majesty.'

'Could he have taken a ship?' said Quill, as they walked. 'He could be going to Tarstation.'

'Why would he go there?' said Emily.

'I don't know, your Majesty; but if he's not in the City, then where else could he be?'

'Damn it,' Emily muttered. 'It's just something else to worry about. First things first – let's get Danny out of trouble, and then we can think about dealing with Montieth.'

Quill nodded. 'Are we really going to assault Maeladh Palace, your Majesty?'

They reached the gates of the palace that led to the harbour, and soldiers pulled them open, letting in the bright, pink sunshine.

'The mood I'm in,' she said, 'anything might happen.'

CHAPTER 26

MOURNING PERIOD

The Eastern Mountains – 14th Mikalis 3421

Kelsey shone the lamp down into the recesses of the dark cave, illuminating the wall carvings, and Frostback leaned forward to sniff the engraved stone.

'Hunters,' said Kelsey, pointing with her free hand, 'animals – that's a goat, I think. Wow, this cave is covered in markings.'

'Why would humans do this?' said Frostback. 'Why would they carve the walls of a cave?'

Kelsey shrugged. 'Art? Religion? Who knows?' She lifted the lamp, and gazed up. The engravings that covered the walls extended onto the ceiling of the large cave. 'There's lots of abstract stuff, too – swirls and patterns that must have meant something, I guess. And more animals, but no greenhides – none. That being the case, I'd say that these markings must be at least two and a half thousand years old, because that's roughly when the greenhides appeared next to the City, and any humans living in the Eastern Mountains would have been wiped out around then.' She glanced at Frostback, and at Halfclaw, who was standing a little further back. 'Ironic, eh? Back on Khatanax, the dragons lived in old human tombs, and here, you've picked somewhere else that used to be inhabited by people.'

Halfclaw snorted. 'A coincidence.'

'I doubt that,' said Kelsey. 'These caves show signs of having been extended and enlarged, with tunnels connecting them, and channels dug out to bring fresh water. This location is perfect for dragons, because humans have already worked on it.'

Frostback's eyes burned. 'Do not repeat that to Deathfang, or to any of the others here; you know how angry they all are with humans at the moment.'

'Well, I don't know, to be honest. You've kept me away from the others since we arrived here, which, you know, I'm grateful for, if it meant that none of them could kill me.'

'Dawnflame's rage would consume you in a heartbeat,' said Halfclaw. 'Deathfang told Frostback and me to make sure that you were kept away from her, and from Darksky, for at least ten days.'

Kelsey frowned. 'Ten days is today. Do you think I might be allowed out of this cave soon?'

The two dragons glanced at each other.

'I will ask,' said Frostback. 'It is not fair that you have to bear any of the blame for what the other humans did, just as we were not to blame for the depredations of Grimsleep.'

'The others don't see it like that,' said Halfclaw. 'Their anger has gone beyond such reasoning. Yesterday, Darksky accused me of being an insect-lover, and said that I was unworthy to be a dragon.'

'Don't listen to her,' said Kelsey. 'You are a very fine dragon.'

'I am torn, I admit it. I do not like insects, and yet, in these last ten days, I have become accustomed to your ways, Kelsey, and do not believe you to be completely evil.'

'Eh, thanks, I guess. But only in the last ten days? What about all that time I spent with you in the quarry on the Iceward Range?'

The green and blue dragon tilted his head. 'I hated you then, and would have eaten you, were it not for the fact that you were under the protection of Frostback and Deathfang. And before you mention what you did in Old Alea to save us, I must tell you that I saw you only as a dangerous and evil witch, who had somehow managed to ensnare

Frostback within a web of lies and deceit. It has only been because I have been forced to spend so much time with you in these caves, that I realise my opinion might not have been entirely accurate.'

'You would have eaten me?'

'Without hesitation. I would still happily devour Yendra, or Van, or any of the other insects from the City. You, however, I would now spare.'

Kelsey frowned. 'And I thought I was just being paranoid in the quarry.'

'You came to no harm because my father and I protected you,' said Frostback. 'We made vows that cannot be broken. Even so, I believe that Darksky would have killed you, were it not for the fact that humans were wheeling dozens of carts full of food up to the quarry for us every day. But here, we are two hundred miles from the City. That, allied to the death of Tarsnow, is why we have had to keep you confined to this little network of caves.'

'I would like to see the sun again,' said Kelsey. 'I'm tired of cowering in the dark.'

The two dragons said nothing, then Halfclaw turned his head to examine the rest of the large cave.

'I might select this cavern as my permanent sleeping place. It is bigger than the one I have been sleeping in, and further from Burntskull. His snoring keeps me awake.'

'I wish we didn't have to share these caves with Burntskull,' said Kelsey. 'He scares me.'

Halfclaw eyed Frostback. 'There is an easy solution to that problem.'

'I know there is,' the silver dragon said, 'but I cannot become betrothed to you just to eject Burntskull from our cave. If we do get betrothed to each other, I want it to be for the right reasons.'

'Could I not act as the chaperone?' said Kelsey. 'I could keep any eye on you both; make sure you don't get up to anything that Deathfang disapproves of.'

Frostback lowered her head. 'You could hardly stop us, my rider.'

'It's not funny,' said Halfclaw. 'Frostback, you know my feelings – I wish us to be betrothed, and not just because that would mean

Burntskull having to leave our cave; I wish it because you are dear to my heart.'

'Not because I am the only young female dragon on this world?'

'I desired you before we left Lostwell; you know that. I understand the pressure we are both under. Your father, in particular, has been pushing us together. It upsets me. Back in the Catacombs, we were best friends for many years, and we used to laugh together; we did everything together. Here, we seem to be carrying the weight of everyone's expectations for the future. They all wish us to hurry up and start producing new dragons for the colony; this is not what I wanted for us.'

'I know,' said Frostback. 'And yet, I cannot give you the answer that you desire. I need more time, Halfclaw.'

'I am patient,' he said. 'In the meantime, we shall all just have to endure Burntskull's snoring.'

The small yellow dragon thrust his head into the cavern. 'I do not snore, and it is impertinent for youths to mock their elders. Do you think for a moment that I like being stuck in these caves with you two, not to mention that foul little insect? Each morning when I awake, I pray that you become betrothed, so that I no longer have to share my living space with you. But, Deathfang's orders were clear – you are not allowed to live together until you are formally betrothed.' He paused for a moment as he noticed the wall carvings. 'What insect nonsense is this?'

'Art,' said Kelsey. 'You wouldn't understand.'

The yellow dragon peered closer at the markings. 'Pah. These ridiculous scratchings are meaningless. They prove nothing but the superiority of dragons over insects, for what dragon would waste their time on such frivolities?' He turned to face Frostback and Halfclaw. 'Regardless, I came into this cavern to tell you that Deathfang wishes us all to gather by the central pool. The ten days of mourning for Tarsnow have passed, and he wants to discuss the future.'

'Does that include me?' said Kelsey. 'Can I come?'

'Your attendance is compulsory, insect,' said Burntskull, not looking at her.

'When does it begin?' said Halfclaw.

Burntskull stared at him. 'Now.'

He strode from the cavern, and the others began to follow him.

'I didn't know that dragons had a ten-day mourning period,' said Kelsey, as they left the cave with the engravings.

'My father has invented a new rule,' said Frostback. 'He says he wants to create new traditions for us.'

They passed through a series of caverns, Kelsey keeping the light from her lamp aimed at the rough ground as they went. They entered the largest cavern, where she and the three dragons slept each night, and Kelsey felt her nerves come alive. For ten days, she had been confined within the interior of the caverns, and she longed to feel the sunlight on her skin again. A thought occurred to her.

'Is it daytime?' she said. 'I've lost track.'

Halfclaw laughed. 'Yes. The sunrise was a few hours ago.'

Kelsey crossed the edge of the cavern, stepping over the imaginary line that she had been kept behind for so long. The cave twisted to the right, and she ran the last twenty yards. She turned the corner and felt the sun on her. She smiled, and took a lungful of fresh air. Ahead of her was a ravine that stretched from left to right, and the cavern entrance was at the foot of a sheer wall of cliffs. Much of the ravine was narrow, but there was an open space in front of the cave where the sunlight could reach. The bottom of the ravine was covered in flowers and grass, except for the rough paths that the dragons had made, and Kelsey ran down the short slope and closed her eyes, savouring the smells, and the feeling of warmth on her face.

The pool that Burntskull had mentioned was a hundred yards along the ravine to the right of the cave shared by the three dragons. Kelsey hadn't seen any of the other dragons since they had arrived in the Eastern Mountains, and was almost looking forward to it.

'Get out of my way, insect,' said Burntskull.

Kelsey laughed. 'Or what, you miserable bastard?'

'Or I'll trample you into the dirt.'

Frostback stepped forwards and scooped Kelsey up in a giant forelimb.

'Do not tease Burntskull,' she said, as the three dragons strode along the ravine in single file.

'Why not?' said Kelsey. 'It's fun to see his face.'

'When we get to the pool,' the silver dragon said, 'I want you to be quiet and respectful, especially to Dawnflame. Her grief hasn't ended just because my father ordained ten days of mourning. One stray word from you might be all it takes to drive her into a rage.'

'Alright; I get it.'

After a hundred yards, the ravine widened into a large open space. A waterfall was streaming over the edge of the cliffs on the iceward side, its waters feeding a circular pool in the centre of the open area. Two other ravines snaked away from the centre. On the left, a narrow valley led to the caverns where Dawnflame, her mother Bittersea, and her son Firestone lived, while the ravine on the right housed the caves where Deathfang, Darksky and their brood of three infants stayed. There were many other caves riddling the cliffs, but most were too small for any dragons to fit, and the colony were occupying the three largest cavern networks. The other dragons were waiting for them, sitting around the pool. Frostback tilted her head to them, then went to the right, taking her place to the left of her father, and ignoring the glare from Darksky.

Frostback released Kelsey from her grasp and set her down on the banks of the pool. On the opposite side from her, Dawnflame was sitting, her head lowered, while her mother was watching the young Firestone as he played in the shallows of the pool. Burntskull and Half-claw joined them, taking up position on Frostback's left.

Deathfang raised his long neck, and gazed at the dragons sitting round the pool, the high cliffs surrounding them.

'My kin,' he said, his voice filling the open space; 'here we are, in our new home. One year ago, I ruled a colony of eighty dragons, and now – we are eleven. We are the only dragons on this world, but our numbers are few, and our future uncertain. I had plans, great plans, but the tragic death of Tarsnow has thrown them into turmoil. I had looked to the union of Tarsnow and Dawnflame to produce a new brood of infants that, one day, might be suitable mates for my own infants, but those hopes have been dashed.'

'Is that all you care about?' growled Dawnflame. 'I have lost my beloved, and there you stand, bemoaning the lack of mates for your children?'

'Hush, daughter,' said Bittersea. 'The leader of our colony is thinking of the future, our future. For our colony to survive, there must be children.'

Deathfang tilted his head towards Dawnflame's elderly mother. 'Tradition dictates that a widow and an orphan should be brought under their lord's protection, unless another claims them first.' He glanced at Halfclaw, who turned away, looking embarrassed. Deathfang nodded, then looked at Burntskull.

'I cannot replace Tarsnow,' said the yellow dragon.

'Not even to save the future of the colony?' said Deathfang. 'With Halfclaw's wooing of my daughter, you are the only other adult male dragon here.'

'Stop this,' said Dawnflame. 'My son and I are not to be haggled over. I am not here just to breed children for you, Deathfang. I need no protection. I can protect myself, and Firestone.'

'We must preserve tradition,' said the huge grey dragon.

'You hypocrite,' snapped Dawnflame. 'You pick and choose your traditions, I see. My mourning has been cut short by your new ten-day rule, and yet you want to enforce some old law regarding widows? Know this – with Tarsnow's death, I shall never mate again. For children, I suggest you look to your daughter.'

'But her offspring will be too closely related to my own,' said Deathfang. 'If you do not see sense, our colony will wither away within two generations. I know this is painful for us all, but...'

'How is it painful for you?' said Dawnflame. 'You aren't the one who will have to mate with Burntskull. I absolutely refuse, and if you insist, then I will fight you, Deathfang. You will defeat me, of that I am sure, but I will never willingly cooperate with this plan.' She turned to Darksky. 'You are my friend, are you not? Will you say nothing?'

'I worry about my children's future,' said the blue dragon, 'but perhaps this is not the time for such a discussion.' She glanced to her left, where Deathfang was sitting. 'Let us say no more about this for now. It can wait.'

'Very well,' said Deathfang; 'I bow to your wisdom. We will say nothing more of this at present, and Dawnflame may remain without a protector, for now. Instead, I want to talk about the City.' He waited, gauging the reactions of the others. 'We helped the rulers of the City, and that is a fact. Whether you agreed with my decision or not, no one can dispute that our assistance was vital, both in clearing Jezra of green-hides, and in conquering the island. Without our aid, they would have failed in their enterprises. Therefore, I say that they owe us, not only for the death of Tarsnow, but for all of the help we rendered unto them. How shall they pay? I suggest that they send labourers, with tools, to enlarge our new home. They could widen the tunnels and raise the ceilings, and connect the caverns where we live, so that we are not isolated in three separate locations. This would go some way to repaying a portion of what they owe us. Does any one object?'

Burntskull, Darksky and Dawnflame all tried to speak at the same time. Deathfang glanced at them, raising a forelimb.

'Eldest first,' he said. 'Bittersea?'

The dark purple dragon looked up. 'I do not object. Despite what happened, if the insects will toil for us, then I see no reason why we shouldn't demand it of them.'

Deathfang turned to Burntskull.

'I object. Let us have nothing more to do with the insects. It's bad enough that we have to put up with your daughter's pet.'

'Hey!' said Kelsey. 'If it weren't for me, every one of you would have died on Lostwell. I know that most of you will never acknowledge it, but deep down, you all know it's true.'

'And that is why you are allowed to stay here,' spat Burntskull; 'but I do not have to like it! As for the City, let us cut off all connection to them – they killed Tarsnow; that was our reward for helping them. Let them give us no other reward, lest another misfortune strikes us.'

Darksky lifted her head. 'Well said, Burntskull; I am in complete agreement, but I would add something else – if we were ever to go back to the City, it would be to raze it to the ground, as a punishment for their murder of Tarsnow. We could burn the City and live in its palaces, leaving a few insects alive to serve us. Yendra is the only powerful god among them; Jade has powers, but the strongest among us could withstand them long enough to have time to burn her to ashes.' She glanced over the dark pool at the other dragons. 'I see some of you looking at me aghast. Know that I do not counsel this course. Like Burntskull, I would prefer to turn my back on them, forever. I just want you all to realise the power we have over the mere insects. We could crush them, if we chose to.'

'No one is debating that,' said Deathfang, 'but why spurn their help in making the caverns here more comfortable? It is a simple thing, and would be over in a short time. Another rainy season is coming, after the four months of summer have passed; do you wish to spend it wet and miserable?'

'How did you sink so low?' said Dawnflame. 'My ears can scarcely believe the words you are saying. The insects butchered my mate, for nothing. They attacked him with their infernal machines, and cut him down, leaving Firestone fatherless. I am doomed to mourn Tarsnow forever, and the blame for that is wholly on the shoulders of the insects in the City. I curse them; may their womenfolk fall barren, and their menfolk die of open sores. May crows pluck out the eyes of their children, and may greenhides gnaw upon the flesh of their fallen. If any insects were to come here, then I warn you, Deathfang, I will show no mercy.' She lifted her claws. 'I will rip them to shreds; I swear it.'

Deathfang lowered his head, and the dragons fell silent, the only sound coming from the waterfall.

'Can I speak?' said Halfclaw.

'You are the next oldest,' said Burntskull.

'I would like the tunnels to be enlarged. They are cramped and uncomfortable, and there isn't enough space to live as we would like. When the rains come, they will leak, and the caves will be damp and cold. Humans could seal up the gaps and widen the caverns. I agree with the chief.'

Deathfang glanced at him, but his eyes looked resigned.

'Did you not hear my vow, boy?' said Dawnflame. 'I will slay any insect that comes here.'

'I heard you,' Halfclaw said, 'and I respect your grief. Tarsnow was a mighty dragon, and his loss has caused great sorrow. But, we will be hurting only ourselves if we hold to our hatred.'

Darksky's eyes burned as they stared at the young green and blue dragon. 'Has that little witch infected your mind, also? I notice that you have started to call them humans, just as Frostback does; and you mention hatred of them as if it isn't justified. They murdered Tarsnow. Every dragon here should join Dawnflame in cursing the insects for this crime. Halfclaw, I want to hear you curse them.'

Halfclaw turned to Frostback.

'Do not look at her for permission,' said Darksky. 'Are you a child? Speak your mind, and curse the insects.'

'I daren't speak my mind,' Halfclaw said, his gaze falling.

'Why not?' said Deathfang. 'All are free to speak, when their turn comes.'

Halfclaw kept his eyes on the pool. 'I have nothing more to say.'

'Then, I'll say it,' said Frostback. 'I'll say the simple truth that everyone knows, but no one wants to hear. Tarsnow's death was his own fault. He disobeyed my father's orders, and attacked a castle. The humans who shot him were defending themselves, against his aggression. To blame them for it is folly.'

Kelsey dived to the ground as Dawnflame unleashed a blaze of fire at Frostback. She rolled to the side of the pool, her arms over her head as Frostback leaned into the flames. The silver dragon launched herself into the air, letting the fires envelop her, then dived onto Dawnflame. Kelsey tried to scamper away as the two dragons collided, but Darksky reached out with a forelimb and brought it down, pinning the Holdfast woman to the ground, a claw embedding into the soil just inches from her face. Deathfang rose in a flurry of wings and descended into the midst of the fight, using his great talons to separate the fighting dragons. Darksky's three infants began screeching and wailing, while Bittersea pulled Firestone out of the way of the clashing teeth and claws.

'Enough!' cried Deathfang. 'Daughter, desist!'

He pushed Frostback to the left, as Dawnflame swung a raking blow with a forelimb. Her claws caught Deathfang instead, ripping three parallel lines of blood down his right flank. The huge grey dragon grunted in pain, then used his weight to shove Dawnflame back, until he was standing between the two dragons.

'Frostback,' cried Darksky. 'You haven't changed. You are still a selfish, disrespectful child. Deathfang, discipline your daughter at once.'

'I was defending myself,' said Frostback, blood dripping from a wound under her right eye.

'Let me slay her,' said Dawnflame; 'she deserves to die for her words. Tarsnow's honour demands her death.'

Kelsey struggled and squirmed under the heavy forelimb of Darksky, but the dragon's grip was too strong.

'I know how she should be punished,' cried the blue dragon. 'I have her pet. Let Dawnflame rip the insect to pieces.'

Frostback turned, her eyes burning in alarm as she saw Kelsey pinned to the ground. Halfclaw was by her side, his claws out in case Dawnflame resumed her attack, while Deathfang was raising both of his forelimbs, his eyes darting from Kelsey to his daughter.

'Dawnflame,' cried Darksky; 'let the price of Frostback's insult be the life of her insect.'

'No,' said Frostback. 'Darksky – if you kill Kelsey, I will break your neck with my jaws.'

'Everyone; stop,' bellowed Deathfang. 'Bittersea, take Firestone and your daughter back to your cavern; now.'

The elderly purple dragon tilted her head. She pushed the young Firestone behind her, and then gripped Dawnflame's shoulder, pulling her back. Her daughter stared at Frostback for a moment, then allowed herself to be led away.

'If Frostback or that insect are here when I return,' she said; 'I will kill them both.'

Kelsey watched as Bittersea escorted Dawnflame and Firestone away. She was starting to find it hard to breathe under the weight of Darksky's forelimb, but no amount of struggling could free her from the dragon's grip.

Deathfang turned from Dawnflame, and rested his fiery gaze upon his daughter.

'Why did you say that?' he cried. 'Why, Frostback? It's only been ten days since Dawnflame lost her mate; have you no honour?'

'I was speaking the truth, father,' said the silver dragon. 'Someone needed to say it.'

'No, daughter; no one needed to say what you said.'

'She'll never change,' said Darksky; 'she needs to be taught a lesson.'

Deathfang turned to her. 'Yes? And I suppose you think we should kill Kelsey? No, Darksky; I made a vow to protect the girl. You didn't see what she did in Old Alea, therefore I can understand why you hate her so, but she saved us all that day.'

'Then, my lord,' said Burntskull, 'what is the solution? You heard what Dawnflame said.'

'I heard her,' said Deathfang. He glanced at the bleeding cuts down his flank. 'It is clear to me that Dawnflame needs time to heal, but that will not happen if my daughter remains here.'

'Are you exiling me again, father?' said the silver dragon. 'Are you siding with Dawnflame over your own flesh and blood?'

'I am saving you, child, from your own stupidity.' He turned to Half-claw. 'I release Frostback into your protection, my boy. In my eyes, you are now betrothed to my daughter.'

'Wait,' cried Frostback; 'this is not your decision to take.'

'I am removing this decision from your control, my daughter,' said

Deathfang. 'You will leave our new home, with Kelsey and Halfclaw, and live elsewhere.'

'But, where?'

'I don't care!' Deathfang thundered. 'Darksky, release the Holdfast girl.'

Darksky stared at Deathfang for a long time, then, slowly, she raised her forelimb. Kelsey scrambled out from under her claws, panting and aching, and ran to Frostback's side.

'Go, now,' said Deathfang, 'before I change my mind and let Dawn-flame have her vengeance.'

Frostback and Halfclaw glanced at each other, then the silver dragon reached out and grasped Kelsey round the waist.

'Go!' bellowed Deathfang.

Halfclaw tilted his head, then extended his wings and rose into the air. Frostback stared at her father, her eyes filled with pain, then she too lifted into the sky. Kelsey looked down as they ascended, and saw the perfectly circular pool recede into the distance. Around them, the high peaks of the Eastern Mountains closed in on all sides, and she felt the warm summer sun on her skin. The two young dragons circled over the ravines, then turned towards the west, and surged away.

Kelsey stamped her feet and rubbed her hands together, her breath misting in the freezing air. Next to her, amid the sparkling frost and snow, Halfclaw was examining the cut under Frostback's right eye, while, above them, the sky was streaked in purple. The sun was low against the horizon, despite the hour, and icefields stretched into the distance at the foot of the high ridge where they had landed.

'We are not betrothed,' said Frostback.

Halfclaw said nothing.

'I don't care what my father said,' Frostback went on. 'I don't need you to protect me, Halfclaw.'

'It's not his fault,' said Kelsey.

Frostback glared at her. 'Are you implying that it's my fault?'

'You and I share some traits,' Kelsey said; 'and not knowing when to shut up is one of them. I have also said things in front of my family that have caused… problems, so I'm not going to criticise you for it, but you have to admit; that was a stupid thing to have said to Dawnflame.'

'The truth is more important than pandering to falsehoods. They wanted us to curse all humans; would you have been happy if I had done so?'

'No, but having a big mouth comes with consequences. Halfclaw, what are your thoughts? You've said nothing since we left.'

The green and blue dragon glanced at her. 'Thank you for asking, Kelsey. My emotions are in turmoil. Part of me agrees with what Frostback said, but I also think it would have been better left unsaid.'

'Are you a coward?' snapped Frostback. 'You would hide from the truth?'

'There are only eleven dragons left here,' he said; 'if living together in peace meant having to compromise, then that is the path I would have chosen. And now, I am exiled, after having done nothing wrong.'

Kelsey shivered. 'I'm freezing my arse off here; can we go somewhere warmer?'

'The chill air is cooling my temper,' said Frostback.

'Where shall we go?' said Halfclaw.

'Jezra,' said Frostback.

'What?' said Halfclaw. 'You want to live next to the humans again? That will only serve to confirm every accusation that Darksky and the others threw at us.'

'I don't care what they think.'

'But the humans may attempt to drive us away,' said Halfclaw. 'They will hate us for killing so many upon the island.'

'We shall go straight to Yendra, and explain what happened. They still need us to assist with clearing the greenhides.'

Halfclaw's eyes tightened, then he looked at Kelsey. 'Can you predict what the humans will do if we return? Will they welcome us, or shun us?'

'I think that those living in the City might try to shun us,' Kelsey said, 'but not the Banner or the Brigades in Jezra – the Lostwell Exiles would be glad to have us back, I think. They know us best; we worked with them for months. But, we'll have to be clever about it; they'll be jumpy and nervous if we come swooping in.'

'Then, we don't fly over the City,' said Frostback; 'we could go west from here, over the icefields and the Cold Sea, then turn sunward once we have passed the City. Halfclaw, are you in agreement?'

The green and blue dragon lowered his head. 'I do not wish to go back to the humans, but neither do I wish to try to find a new home on our own. If you go to Jezra, then I will follow. You may mock me for it, but I take your father's words seriously; and I am your protector, whether you wish me to be or not. I would die for you, Frostback.'

The silver dragon stared at him for a second, then looked away.

'Kelsey,' she said; 'climb up onto the harness. We shall go to Jezra, and let fortune decide our fate.'

CHAPTER 27

THE ROBBERY

Port Sanders, Medio, The City – 14th Mikalis 3421

'You filthy Shinstran dog,' muttered Saul, a cleaver gripped in his right hand.

'Good morning, Saul,' said Kagan. 'Have you started on the gin today already?'

'I will chop you into small pieces and roast you in the oven.'

Kagan nodded. 'I just need a bottle of wine to take upstairs. It has to be white, and cold.'

The cook groaned and pulled himself to his feet. He wiped his free hand on an apron, then dug into a pocket.

'It's a beautiful day,' said Kagan. 'Do you ever venture outside?'

'Piss off,' growled Saul, handing him a set of keys.

'Thanks,' said Kagan, taking the keys; 'well, that was a lovely chat, as always.'

The cook ignored him and sat back down onto his chair in the corner of the kitchen. Kagan went to the locked alcohol cupboard and opened the door, revealing shelves lined with bottles of brandy and gin, and racks of wine. At the bottom of the large cupboard was a brick-lined ice box. Most of the ice had melted, but the water was still cold, and Kagan plucked out a bottle of white wine. He locked the cupboard back up, and threw the keys to Saul, who grunted, then swigged from a bottle of gin. Kagan arranged the wine onto a tray along with a clean, tall-stemmed glass and a bottle opener, then picked up the tray and left the kitchen.

Gellie leaned over the balustrade as he ascended the stairs.

'Kagan,' she said, her tone clipped. 'A delivery of goods is scheduled to arrive in ten minutes, and I will need you to assist with carrying in the boxes.'

'I'll be there, ma'am,' he said.

She nodded, and then disappeared into a room. Kagan continued up the flights of stairs, until he came to the upper floor. There, he walked along the landing to a final set of stairs that led up onto the roof. The steps were narrow, and he took his time, making sure he didn't drop anything as he climbed. At the top, the door was lying open, and he stepped outside into the warm sunshine. The red-tiled roofs of Port Sanders were shining in the sunlight, and Kagan smiled as he felt the warmth on his face. About a third of the roof was flat, while the rest was sloped, covering the mansion's attic and skylight, and Lady Sofia had positioned her chair on the sunward side. She was reclining on it with her eyes closed, and Kagan paused for a moment to look at her. She was dressed inappropriately, compared to the other aristocrats in Port Sanders, with her arms, legs and much else uncovered as she lay in the sunlight, and his eyes wandered over every part of her.

'Stop gawking and get over here,' she said, keeping her eyes closed.

'Of course, ma'am,' he said, hurrying forwards with the tray.

'Pour me a glass, then sit down,' she said. 'The wine is chilled, I hope?'

'The ice has gone, but the water was still cold,' he said, setting the tray down and opening the bottle. He poured her a glass, and she opened her eyes.

'How I love lying in the sun,' she said, catching his gaze. She smiled, and took the offered glass. 'Sit.'

He sat down on a wooden bench next to her reclining chair.

She took a sip of wine, and sighed. 'Perfect.'

'Are you not worried that the neighbours will see you up here?'

'And why would I be worried about that?'

'Well,' he said, his face flushing a little, 'you seem to be dressed in your underwear.'

She laughed. 'So? It's summer, and we're not in Dalrig.'

'Dalrig, ma'am?'

'Yes. The people there are a little uptight, or so I've heard. But this is Port Sanders, so relax. I thought you liked looking at me?'

'I do,' he said, a little too quickly.

'I had no opportunity to just lie out in the sun in my old job, but no one knows me here, and so I shall act as I please.' She smiled again. 'And you're worried about what the neighbours will think? How cute.'

Kagan pulled his gaze away from her bare skin, and tried to think of something else.

'How did you meet Gellie?' he said.

She raised an eyebrow. 'Why would you want to know about that?'

He shrugged. 'Sometimes, I see you talking together, and it seems to me as if you might have known her for a while. Did you meet her before we were taken from Alea Tanton?'

'My, Kagan, you are perceptive at times. However, my relationship with Gellie is really none of your business. And, before you ask, the same goes for Saul. You might find it unusual that I employ a Fordian, a Torduan and a Shinstran, but we're really all just Lost-wellers.'

He smiled. 'Is that a real word?'

'If it isn't, then it should be. The Tenth Tribe; that's us. We should forget all of the old distinctions, just as the Brigades in Jezra appear to have done. They've achieved great things over on the Western Bank; do you ever wish you had gone with them?'

'No. It's true that their trip over there wasn't as disastrous as everyone feared, and I'm glad they've earned the respect of the City; but if I had gone there, then I wouldn't have met you.'

'You're a sweet boy, at times. Don't get too sweet, though; I like you a little rough around the edges.'

She turned over onto her front. 'Rub my back.'

'I can't, ma'am; I have to help Gellie with a delivery.'

Sofia frowned. 'Off you trot, then. Don't be too long, though; I don't like to be kept waiting.'

With some reluctance, Kagan got back to his feet. He gazed down at her, his desire pounding through his body, then walked back to the stairs. They had already slept together that morning, but he could never get enough of her, and felt almost bereft as soon as she was out of his sight. He hurried down the stairs, determined to deal with the delivery as soon as possible, so that he could go back up onto the roof. Gellie was standing in the front hall, directly under the skylight.

'You're late,' she said.

'Lady Sofia wanted to talk.'

She rolled her eyes. 'Come with me.'

He followed her as she led the way through to a side door of the mansion, which backed onto a lane. She unlocked the door, and opened it. Outside, a wagon was sitting, its back piled high with boxes and crates. Two young men jumped down from the driver's bench.

'Good morning,' said one, with an Evader accent. 'We have seven crates for you, ma'am.'

Gellie kept her expression severe, and peered at the crates. 'Kagan; assist them.'

'Yes, ma'am,' he said.

The Evader walked him to the back of the wagon, and lowered the bar at the back.

'Watch; the first one's heavy,' said the Evader. 'Might be best if the two of us carry it inside.'

Kagan nodded, and the young man slid the crate to the edge of the wagon, then they both took hold of it. Kagan braced himself, but the crate was light. He said nothing, joining in the pretence that they were carrying something heavy. They took it inside the mansion, and set it down. As they did so, the Evader glanced around, then leaned forward.

'Albeck says it's tonight; two hours past midnight. Be ready.'

Kagan blinked, but before he had a chance to respond, the Evader was already back outside, getting the next crate prepared. Kagan carried the next six inside on his own, and the wagon pulled away, the shoes of the ponies clattering off the cobbles of the alleyway.

'Thank you, Kagan,' Gellie said, as she closed and locked the side door. 'Take the crates to Saul, and then you can return to your "chat" with her ladyship.'

'Yes, ma'am,' he said, but his thoughts had moved on to other things.

He raced back up the flights of stairs as soon as he had delivered the last crate to the kitchen, and burst out into the sunlight.

Sofia opened her eyes from the reclining chair, frowned, then laughed. 'My, you are keen.'

He ran over to the bench and sat. 'It's happened. I just got word; it's tonight, after midnight. I thought…'

She raised her palms. 'Slowly, please. What's happened?'

'There was an Evader boy with the delivery wagon.'

'That makes sense, since the goods I ordered are made in the Circuit.'

'He passed me a message, from Albeck. They're coming, tonight, two hours after midnight.'

She nodded. 'Alright.'

'What do mean "alright?" I thought you had dealt with Albeck and Dizzler?'

'Calm down, Kagan. And have a little faith in me.'

'But… but… what shall we do? Should we call the militia? I won't be able to keep back a dozen thugs from Dizzler's crew if they get inside the mansion. Tell me what to do, ma'am.'

'You worry too much,' she said. 'And, I've already told you what to do, and yet my back remains unrubbed.'

He stared at her.

'I don't want to have to ask again, Kagan. The day is long, and there's plenty of time before I have to start thinking about Dizzler.'

She closed her eyes. Kagan continued to stare at her for a moment, then he reached out with his hands to touch her.

———

'What do you think of this one?' Sofia said, holding up a pale blue dress.

Kagan glanced at her from the bed. 'It's fine, I guess, ma'am.'

She raised an eyebrow. 'Something tells me that you're a little distracted, Kagan.'

He glanced out of the bedroom window. It was dark, the sun having set a few hours previously, and the shutters were almost fully closed.

'I'm over here, Kagan,' she said.

'I don't understand how you can be so calm,' he said. 'We don't seem to have made any preparations for tonight.'

'I disagree. We have spent a highly enjoyable day together, instead of sitting around worrying about what might happen.' She picked a dark red dress from the wardrobe. 'This one, I think. It will hide any splashes of blood.'

'I'm not sure you understand just what we're up against,' he said. 'These guys are vicious; they'll have no qualms about hurting you if you resist. If you have a plan, then please tell me what it is.'

She slipped the red dress on, then sat at her dresser to put on her make up. 'You should probably get washed and dressed,' she said, as she began to apply some eyeliner.

He got out of bed, and made his way to her bathroom. He showered in the plentiful hot water, then stared at his misted-up reflection in the mirror. He had made his mind up; he would go down fighting when Dizzler arrived, and if they killed him, well, at least he had experienced the best day of his life first. He was aware that Sofia didn't love him, but he didn't care. He loved her, and would do anything for her – he would kill, he would die, and he would betray his old friends; it didn't matter; all that mattered was her. He dried himself and got dressed, then went back into the bedroom.

Sofia was still sitting by her dresser, while Gellie was standing next to her, brushing her hair. They stopped talking as he walked into the room, and he raised an eyebrow, feeling awkward. Gellie never came into her ladyship's bedroom while Kagan was there.

'I was just telling Gellie about tonight,' Sofia said. 'As you know, Kagan, I tell her everything. Well, far more than I tell you, anyway.' She glanced at the housekeeper. 'Kagan guessed that we knew each other before the events in Old Alea. And to think that you thought he was stupid.'

'I didn't think you would choose someone stupid, ma'am,' said Gellie. 'I did think that you might have selected a man who was slightly more refined than Kagan, but if he pleases you, then who I am to object?'

'Precisely, Gellie; and he does please me. I deem him suitable.'

'Suitable for what?' said Kagan.

'Let's get this night over with,' said Sofia, 'and I might tell you. Is Saul ready?'

'He is, ma'am,' said Gellie. 'I have extinguished every lamp in the house; are we expecting company at midnight?'

'Most likely,' said Sofia.

'But the message said two hours after midnight,' said Kagan.

'Indeed, it did,' said Sofia. 'However, as Albeck presumably does not trust you any more, I imagine that they will come a little earlier, hoping to catch us unawares.'

At that moment, a soft tinkling sound of breaking glass echoed up from downstairs, and Kagan jumped.

Sofia nodded to Gellie. 'It seems they are even earlier than we'd thought. Go and hide in the attic. I will let you know when it's safe to come back downstairs.'

Gellie bowed. 'Yes, ma'am.' She glanced at Kagan, and then left the room in silence, closing the door behind her.

'Do you have a weapon?' said Kagan.

'Yes,' said Sofia, 'though perhaps not the type that you are expecting.' She turned to face him. 'I intend to make an example of this Dizzler. Tell me now if you have any problem with this.'

He shook his head.

'Good. Do you love me?'

'Yes. I adore you.'

'Then trust me. Go downstairs and lead the thieves to the safe in the drawing room. Hold them there until I join you.'

'But there will be others, who will be waiting by the side door. Should I...?'

'Don't question me, Kagan. Obey.'

He stared at her, almost paralysed with fear at the thought of anyone hurting her. Anger built within him, replacing the fear, and his eyes narrowed. He nodded, then left the room. The rest of her quarters were in darkness, but he knew the way well, and slipped through to the inner stairwell of the house without making a sound. He glanced down over the balustrade, and heard noises coming from the corridor leading to the side door, where the delivery had arrived that day. Kagan frowned. Sofia was right – Dizzler didn't trust him. Not only had he arrived early, but he had entered the mansion through a different door from the one that Albeck had told Kagan to unlock. The drawing room was on the floor below Sofia's quarters, and Kagan padded down the carpeted steps. He halted on the first floor landing, seeing the flickering light of a lantern from the stairs below.

'It's me; Kagan,' he whispered. 'Is Dizzler there?'

A group emerged from the gloom at the bottom of the stairs, and someone shone the lantern up into Kagan's face. There were over a dozen men in the front hall, all masked and hooded, and all carrying weapons. A figure broke away, and bounded up the stairs.

He slapped Kagan on the back, and pulled his mask to the side. 'Good to see you again.'

Kagan nodded. 'Dizzler.'

'Have you got my little map?'

'No; you're early. But it doesn't matter; I can take you straight to the safe where she keeps her gold. Her ladyship is sleeping upstairs, but her gold is kept on this floor, and I know the combination to the safe.'

Dizzler grinned. 'That's my boy. Albeck said he had some doubts about you, but I knew you'd come through for us. What about the cook? I heard he's handy with a knife.'

'He's been dealt with,' said Kagan; 'and the housekeeper won't be causing us any problems, either.'

Dizzler gestured to the group at the bottom of the stairs, and they began to climb the steps in silence. Kagan led them into the drawing room. He lit a small lamp, and walked over to a tapestry. He pulled it back, revealing a large safe embedded into the wall of the room.

Dizzler rubbed his hands together as he strode towards it.

'Alright,' he said; 'we'll clear this out first, then go upstairs for her ladyship.' He glanced at his old second in command, but Kagan kept his face neutral. 'Open it up, my boy.'

Kagan knelt down by the safe. Sofia had shown him how to open it a few days before, and he wondered if that had been part of her plan. His thoughts whirled as he went through the complicated procedure of unlocking the safe. What kind of weapon could Sofia possess that would take care of over a dozen burly men? She had told him to trust her, but what if she had over-estimated her ability to deal with the situation? Had she called for the Sander militia? Did she have other friends in the City who were coming to her aid?

The group gathered round to watch as Kagan heard the lock click. He pulled on the handle, and the door slid open. Dizzler cackled with glee. The safe was full. Sacks of gold coins were piled up on the left, while boxes of jewels and bankers' drafts sat heaped up next to them.

'And all this came from a suitcase?' said Dizzler, shaking his head.

'It was a big suitcase,' said a voice from the door.

The gang turned, and saw Sofia standing in the doorway, her red dress gleaming in the lamplight. She looked different to Kagan, though he couldn't say exactly how she had changed.

'How good of you to come downstairs, miss,' said Dizzler. 'Saves us the trouble of going up there to fetch you.'

Sofia raised an eyebrow.

'Your guard, Kagan,' Dizzler went on; 'he works for me. I'm afraid your life of luxury has come to an end, little lady.'

'Is that right?' said Sofia. 'And just what are you intending to do with me?'

'I'm installing you in my new whorehouse in the Circuit, where, hopefully, you'll earn me as much as the contents of that safe.'

'I see. I assume that you are Dizzler?'

The crew leader frowned. 'How did you know that?'

Sofia smiled. 'I shall kill you last.'

Dizzler laughed. 'Grab her, boys.'

Kagan sprang to his feet and jumped in front of Sofia, his fists raised. 'Don't touch her!'

'Oh, Kagan,' groaned Dizzler. 'Don't tell me that Albeck was right? My little sister also told me to watch out for you – she said that you'd fallen for this woman. But, you're young and foolish, so I'm going to give you one last chance, my boy. Step away, and let us get on with the job.'

'Do as he says, Kagan,' said Sofia; 'there's little point in you getting injured too.'

'Aww!' cried Dizzler, laughing. 'You hear that, boys? Her ladyship has a soft spot for our little Kagan.'

One of the men strode forwards, a crude bat in his hand, and Kagan punched him in the face before he could raise it. Another man leapt at him, and bundled Kagan to the ground. Kagan lashed out with his fists and feet, and kicked the man off him, as more approached.

Sofia shook her head, then raised her right hand. She pointed at a man who was about to kick Kagan, and the skin on his face slid off, leaving a bloody mess of open flesh. The man tried to scream, but it came out choked and garbled, and he toppled to the ground.

The other men stopped what they were doing, each staring open-mouthed at the man writhing in torment on the floor.

'Did that get your attention, boys?' said Sofia. 'Good. Now, who's next?'

She swept her hand from left to right, and six men fell, their skin rotting into pieces as their bodies disintegrated. Kagan scrambled clear as rotten body parts fell onto him. He grimaced in horror, his feet slipping on the floor as he backed into a corner.

Two men tried to run for the door. Sofia laughed, pointed, and they collapsed. Someone swung an iron bar at her, but she grasped his arm before the weapon could strike her. She squeezed, and the man seemed to wither away into a dried-up husk. Sofia closed her eyes and gasped, then let go of the arm, and the man's body crumbled into a cloud of dust.

Kagan watched from the corner of the room. Only Dizzler and one other man were left alive. The other man fell to his knees.

'Please!' he wailed. 'I'm sorry; please don't kill me.'

'Don't beg,' said Sofia; 'it's so demeaning.'

She snapped her fingers, and his eyes rolled up into his head, his face went green, and he collapsed onto the carpet.

She smiled at Dizzler. 'I told you that I would leave you to last.'

Dizzler backed away, his eyes filled with terror. 'Who are you?'

'Can't you guess?' she said, smiling. 'Though, why would you? You know nothing about this City, and you know nothing of me.'

She pointed at his stomach, and he grunted, grasped his waist, then dropped to his knees.

'Kagan...' he groaned, as he fell to the carpet; 'help me.'

'He won't help you,' said Sofia; 'and, even if he wanted to, it would do you no good. Because of what I've just done to your insides, Dizzler, in approximately five minutes, you will die in excruciating pain, and there is nothing anyone can do about it.' She stepped over the bodies on the floor, positioned a chair close to Dizzler, and sat. 'Also,' she said, 'I intend to watch.'

Dizzler writhed on the carpet, foam and spittle flecking from his mouth. He was hugging his waist as his face grew redder, then blood appeared on his lips, along with a sickly rasping noise.

'Get up, Kagan,' Sofia said from the chair. 'Stand by me. I want Dizzler to see you in his last moments.'

Kagan pulled himself to his feet, and walked over to Sofia, his eyes fixed on the sight of his old friend and mentor dying on the carpet in front of him. Sofia watched Dizzler without any emotion on her face, and Kagan longed for it to be over. Dizzler stared up at him, his blue lips trying to form words, but he lacked the strength to speak. Blood started to leak from his nose and ears, his face contorted into a mask of agony; and then he lay still, his eyes lifeless.

'So ends Dizzler,' said Sofia.

She stood, and walked over to the door. She glanced over her shoulder. 'Aren't you coming?'

Kagan pulled his gaze from the tortured face of Dizzler. 'What... I... Dizzler...'

'I think you need a drink,' she said. 'Come; we'll go upstairs and you can pour us each a large brandy.'

He followed her out of the room, his legs seeming to move of their own accord, as his mind recoiled from what he had witnessed. Saul was waiting outside by the balustrade, a bloody cleaver gripped in his left hand.

Sofia smiled. 'How did it go downstairs?'

Saul grinned. 'Both of their lookouts are dead, ma'am. I've put them on the wagon.'

'Excellent. Good work, Saul. There are another dozen bodies in the drawing room that need to be removed. Once they are all on the wagon, drive it to the Circuit and tip the bodies into a canal. Except for Dizzler. Take his corpse to the Great Racecourse, and dump it by the base of the statue of Prince Michael. Leave the wagon there, and return on foot. Then, you can have tomorrow off to get as drunk as you like.'

Saul bowed. 'Thank you, ma'am.'

'Do you need Kagan's help to move the bodies?'

Saul looked offended at the suggestion. 'No, ma'am. I can manage on my own.'

'Splendid. Good night, Saul.'

The cook grunted, then walked towards the drawing room, glaring at Kagan as he went past. Sofia climbed the stairs to her quarters, and shouted up to Gellie that it was safe to come downstairs. Kagan waited as the housekeeper was given her instructions for cleaning up the drawing room, then he and Sofia entered her rooms.

'Get me a brandy,' she said, as she reclined on a long couch. 'And one for yourself, of course. For your nerves.'

Kagan poured the drinks, then sat on the couch opposite her. His heart was still pounding, and the image of Dizzler's death agonies was imprinted onto his mind.

She took a glass from his hand and sipped. 'Lovely. Taran brandy is one of the most exquisite things in existence. Come on, drink up.'

He drained the glass in one long gulp.

She frowned. 'It's supposed to be savoured, but I'll forgive you under the circumstances. You might be wondering why you're still alive. Are you?'

He stared at her. 'I don't know what I'm thinking. My head is full, but... What happened? You killed them.'

'I think you've just answered your own question there. Yes, I killed them. And now you know my little secret, and so I should really kill you as well. Gellie and Saul know, but my subterfuge becomes more risky with every additional person who discovers the truth.' Her gaze examined him for a moment. 'You are alive for several reasons. You're loyal. I already knew that, but I was pleased when you leapt to my defence, even though you were unarmed, and had no idea of my powers. Also, you worship me, and it's nice to be worshipped; don't overdo it, though. And, lastly, I have a plan, and you are part of it.'

'A plan?' he said.

'Yes. I'm not going to tell you what that plan is; not yet, at any rate, but you will be expected to say nothing about what happened here tonight. Do I need to spell out what I would do to you if you betray my confidence?'

He shook his head.

'Good. I am taking a chance by letting you live, Kagan, and I hope you don't let me down.'

'I won't,' he said. 'I'll tell no one. You've freed me. I never need to worry about Dizzler ever again.'

'I'm glad you see it that way. Are you feeling any better?'

'Yes; I think so.' He took a breath. 'I was shocked, but now... I don't know. Somehow, I'm not surprised. I knew you were special.'

Sofia smiled, then sipped her brandy. 'You're right, Kagan, and soon the whole City will know just how special I am.'

CHAPTER 28

DARKNESS

Grey Isle, Cold Sea – 14ᵗʰ Mikalis 3421

Yendra stared at the small settlement from the roof of the Command Post. The Lostwell Brigades were out working; rebuilding houses that had been destroyed by the dragons ten days before. Others were labouring in the harbour, or clearing the ruins of the castle, and Yendra could see most of them from her vantage point.

As expected, the Crown had refused to accept her resignation, and so Yendra had decided to stay on the Grey Isle to personally supervise the recovery efforts. Her priority was to re-house and feed the hundreds of surviving Gloamers. Every day, more of them had been able to move back into a house, and every day, Yendra had gone down to speak to them in person, to offer her apologies, and to listen to their anger. The dead Gloamer militia had been sent back by ship to Dalrig, but the bodies of the locals slain in the inferno had been laid to rest in a cemetery at the rear of the settlement, and hundreds of Brigade workers had been digging the graves.

She heard a cough to her right, and turned.

'You called for me, ma'am?' said Van.

'Yes,' she said. 'Another day ends.'

Van nodded, his eyes glancing at the setting sun.

'The Queen and I have come to a decision,' she went on, 'and I wanted you to be the first to know.'

She sensed him waiting, as she cast her gaze across the small town.

'As you are aware, the Gloamers evacuated Ooste this morning, and I will soon be recalled to Pella. I intend to step back from some of my responsibilities once I have left this island. Her Majesty and I have decided to place the Brigades under the direct command of the Banner, meaning that you will be in charge of both.'

'Both, ma'am?' he said, his eyes widening. 'That's seventeen thousand men and women.'

'I know. I want you to replenish the losses the Banner has suffered – how many have died since the beginning of the Jezra campaign? Two hundred?'

'Two hundred and eleven, ma'am.'

She nodded. 'I want the Banner back at its original strength, but hire only from within the Brigades. Enlist the best the Brigades have to offer, and have them sworn into the ranks of the Banner. Also, I want you to form a new Banner reserve of a thousand soldiers, a fourth regiment, but, again, hire only from Brigade volunteers. The Banner is for Lostwell Exiles only.'

He nodded.

'That will leave you with thirteen thousand left in the Brigades. Widen their training to include more military tasks – constructing and operating ballistae, crossbows drills, and so on.'

'You want me to create an army?'

'Let's not call it that. They are a strategic reserve, without ties or loyalty to any of the nine tribes. As such, they will be available for operations that the Blades or other militia would baulk at. I don't want their deployment to be caught up in tribal wrangling – the Banner answers to myself and the Crown, and no one else.'

Van narrowed his eyes. 'Not just an army, then, but the Queen's private army?'

Yendra caught his gaze. 'That is not the sort of language we shall use in public, but yes. Currently, the King and Queen have personal control

over the Royal Guard, and, through me, the Blades. However, the repu-
tation of the Blades is so tarnished after the greenhide incursion, that it
is simply unthinkable that they would ever be deployed away from the
Great Wall for the foreseeable future. In order for the King or Queen to
activate any of the tribal militia, they need to seek permission from that
tribe, and that inevitably leads to delays and political squabbling. I
want the Banner and the Brigades to be free of all that useless bureau-
cracy; I want them highly trained, and I want them available to go
anywhere at a moment's notice. But, most of all, I want their loyalty to
lie with the Crown, and no one else.'

'I understand,' said Van. 'Should I foresee any political difficulties
with this decision?'

'No. Nothing is being done officially; in fact, this conversation never
happened. The command structure of the Banner and the Brigades is a
matter for the Crown, and the Tribal Council does not need to be
informed of these changes. This is a risky time for the King and Queen,
Van. There are rumblings of discontent coming from the tribes, and I
have doubts over the loyalty of many within the Tribal Council, and
among the remaining demigods in the City.'

'I see, ma'am. Should I start training the soldiers in counter-insur-
gency measures?'

She smiled. 'I'm glad we think alike on this. Please do so. One thing
that will become official, is your new promotion. If you are going to
command the Brigades as well as the Banner, then you will need to be
ranked higher than a major. I am going to propose the new rank of
major-general for you. I will suggest it to the Queen when I next see
her.'

'Thank you, ma'am.'

'I also have a confession. I have been reading your mind in recent
days. I wanted to be sure that you were the right man for the job. You
have led a colourful life, Van.'

'That's one way to put it.'

'The new role that the Queen and I have created for you is one that wields more power than is possessed by any of the local militia commanders. We needed to be sure of you.'

'I understand. And, having looked, are you satisfied that I am loyal?'

'I knew you were loyal, Van. I was examining your moral character, looking for signs of cruelty, greed, hypocrisy and corruptibility. You have high standards, but you haven't always been able to live up to them. I saw some of the things you did on Dragon Eyre, when you were a young lieutenant; but I have also seen the regret, shame and guilt you bear because of those events. Everyone makes mistakes, Van; I trust you have learned from yours?'

His gaze fell, and he exhaled. 'I certainly bloody hope so. Dragon Eyre changed me. I thought I was losing my mind during my last operation there.'

'I promise you this, Van – I will never order you to slaughter civilians. I am not like the gods of Implacatus, and neither are the King or Queen. We will not employ your soldiers to do the things that they ordered you to do.'

'I wouldn't be working for you if I believed otherwise.'

Yendra felt a niggle behind her temples.

Your Highness?

Yes, Salvor? I'm a little busy at the moment; can it wait?

No.

Yendra frowned, then gestured to Van. 'One moment, please. Lord Salvor is inside my mind.'

Proceed, she said to her nephew.

The King has been abducted.

Yendra blinked, and almost staggered.

His party was ambushed in Tara, Salvor went on, *and he has been taken to Maeladh Palace. The Roser militia has surrounded the building, but are awaiting the arrival of the Queen before they move in.*

The Queen has gone to Tara?

Yes, your Highness. I tried to dissuade her Majesty, but she would not take my advice. There have been no demands from the kidnappers, and no group has claimed responsibility.

Are any of the former Royal Family involved?

Lady Silva has surveyed Tara, and found no signs of any immortals present anywhere in Roser territory. She also discovered that Prince Montieth has fled Dalrig; he is nowhere to be found within the boundaries of the City. She searched Jezra, the Grey Isle, and the shipping lanes throughout the Cold Sea, but her range does not extend as far iceward as Tarstation, and our working assumption is that he has fled there.

Montieth will have to wait. I'll set out for Tara immediately. Keep me informed if anything changes.

Yes, your Highness.

She felt Salvor sever the connection, and she closed her eyes for a moment, a sickly sense of worry stirring through her stomach.

'Is everything alright, ma'am?'

She glanced at Van. 'No. I need to leave immediately.'

'Where are you going?'

'Tara. You will remain here, in command of the Grey Isle, and I shall pick up some Banner soldiers in Jezra.'

'Why would you require soldiers, ma'am?'

She turned for the stairs. 'Walk with me to the harbour; I'll explain on the way.'

It was dark by the time Yendra reached Jezra. She had taken a fast boat from the Grey Isle to Westrig, and then a wagon along the ridge that connected the two harbours. Once there, she had ordered a ship to be prepared to take her to Tara, and had organised a full company of Banner soldiers to come with her.

'Should I come?' said Jade, as Yendra walked down to the town's harbour.

'You shouldn't be required,' said Yendra. 'The men who have the King are all mortals, and after what happened with the dragons in the Grey Isle, I don't think it would be a good idea to use god powers on mortals.'

'But, they have the King. We should kill them all.'

'They will be harshly dealt with, Jade, but the priority is the safety of the King. And for that, I shall rely upon professional soldiers.'

'But, what should I do here?'

'You could go up to the walls by the cliff's edge in the morning, and kill some greenhides.'

'I'm bored of that, and without any dragons to help us, we've not been making much progress up on the cliffs. When are the flying lizards returning?'

Yendra paused by the gangway leading to her ship. 'We may have to get used to the fact that the dragons might never return. They blame me for what happened to Tarsnow.'

'Tarsnow was an idiot.'

'Please, Jade; do not say that. The dragon is dead, and no good can come from such words.'

Jade frowned. 'Will you contact me if you need me?'

'Of course. In the meantime, as Van is in the Grey Isle, I'm leaving you in command of Jezra.'

'In command?' Jade started to laugh, though it was tinged with mild hysteria. 'You're putting me in charge?'

'Yes, Jade. You have shown me what you are capable of these last few months. Don't do anything crazy.'

'Define crazy.'

'Don't joke. The life of the King is in danger, and I need you at your best. If something happens to the King and Queen tonight, the City will be in uproar. Stay ready; I'm relying on you.'

Jade's face fell. 'Please don't do that. I'm still coming to terms with the concept of obeying you; don't leave me here to make decisions on my own.'

Yendra placed a hand on her shoulder. 'It's alright; I trust you.'

Jade cringed, and glanced away.

Yendra turned, and strode up the gangway. The captain of the vessel bowed to her, and she nodded to him, then walked across the deck, passing the groups of Banner soldiers that were also going to Tara. A full company of one hundred and twenty men were gathered on the deck, all ready for battle, with their armour on and crossbows slung over their shoulders.

The ship unfurled its sails and slipped from its moorings in the ruined docks of Jezra. The wind was warm, and the vessel drew out into the open sea, its lamps burning against the purple swirls in the sky. Yendra joined the Reaper captain by the rear of the ship.

'We should reach Tara around midnight, your Highness,' he said. 'May I ask what the emergency is? I assume there is an emergency, otherwise why would so many heavily-armed men be sent to Tara at this time of the night?'

'You'll find out through the rumours, anyway,' she said; 'so you might as well hear the truth – his Majesty the King has been abducted, by forces unknown. We are on our way to rescue him.'

The captain stared at her. 'Was it the Rosers, ma'am? Have they taken King Daniel?'

'I'd rather not speculate on their identity, and I'd prefer you not to indulge in it either. What I need from you and your vessel is speed, Captain.'

'Of course, your Highness.' He turned to the helmsman. 'Make all haste to Tara.'

'Yes, sir.'

'If you'll excuse me for a moment,' said Yendra; 'I need to vision ahead.'

She sent her powers out over the swelling waters of the Warm Sea, heading for the twinkling lights of Tara in the distance. Her vision raced towards the coast and reached the high cliffs. She climbed the sheer slopes and then gazed down on Princeps Row and, to its right, Maeladh Palace. The ancient structure sprawled along much of the ridge, half-built into the cliffs and levelled terraces. The roads leading up the hillside towards the palace were packed with Roser militia, but none had entered the grounds of Maeladh. The palace appeared to be in darkness. It had been locked up, its doors chained shut, ever since the coronation of Emily and Daniel one year previously, and had been provided with a small group of caretakers from the local militia, who were supposed to keep members of the public from entering the ancient halls.

Militia were also crowded around the Aurelian mansion on Princeps Row, where the King had been staying during his visit to Tara. The bodies of the soldiers who had been escorting him were laid out in a row by the hedges surrounding the Aurelian property, and Yendra could see the blood staining their blue Royal Guard uniforms. The King's father, Lord Aurelian, was by his front gates, speaking to a group of Roser officers, while the Queen was standing twenty yards away, surrounded by members of her Royal Guard. Yendra hesitated. She wanted to speak to the Queen, but never liked to go into her head without permission.

She hoped the Queen would understand, and went in.

Your Majesty, apologies for entering your mind.

Yendra?'

Yes. I am on my way to Tara, on a ship with a full company of Banner soldiers. We shall arrive around midnight. Have there been any changes?

No. Danny's still in the palace, but we don't know what the kidnappers want. I've managed to restrain the militia from going in, but they're getting impatient, and so am I.

Please wait until we arrive, your Majesty. My soldiers are professionals; they have trained for these types of incidents.

Emily frowned. *Very well. And, thank you. Just knowing that you are on your way makes me feel better, Yendra.*

Thank you, your Majesty; I won't let you down.

Yendra broke off the link to the Queen, and took a breath.

'Soldiers!' she cried, stepping down from the quarterdeck. 'Gather round; it's time to tell you what we shall be doing.'

Roser militia were waiting for them in Tara harbour when their ship docked. The Banner soldiers disembarked, and Yendra led them through the streets of the town. A few taverns were still open, and groups of people were out on the streets, having heard rumours about what might be happening up in Maeladh Palace. Many of the Rosers stared at the well-armoured Banner soldiers as they marched through Tara, and Yendra felt a surge of pride well up in her, despite the gravity of their mission. They passed through the open plaza of Prince's Square, then began to climb the steps up the side of the cliff towards Princeps Rows, bypassing the longer route that carriages took.

At the top of the steps, they met the massed crowds of militia, who parted to let the soldiers pass as soon as they saw Yendra at their head. She brought them to a halt in front of the Aurelian mansion, and strode towards the Queen.

Emily glanced at Yendra's battle armour. 'You've come dressed for the part, I see?'

'As have you, it seems, your Majesty.'

Emily glanced down at her own armour. 'Yes. I had notions of storming the palace on my own. The Roser militia have been doing their level best to dissuade me from such a course.'

'I would also advise that you stay well clear of the palace when we enter, your Majesty.'

'I thought you might. Regardless, I am going in with you. Perhaps not in the first wave, but I'm not going to languish outside when Danny's life is in the balance.'

'Is that an order, your Majesty?'

Emily's eyes burned with defiance. 'It is.'

Yendra nodded. 'So be it.' She glanced at a Banner lieutenant. 'Appoint a squad to guard the Queen. They are not to leave her side.'

He saluted. 'Yes, ma'am.'

'Do you need to use your powers to look into the palace before we go?' said Emily.

'I did so on the ship, your Majesty. The King is being held beneath the old sunward wing, at the far side of Maeladh.'

Emily nodded, then glanced at the Banner soldiers. 'Where is Lady Jade?'

'I felt it best to leave her in Jezra, your Majesty.'

'And what if Danny is injured?'

Yendra reached beneath her armour and withdrew a small vial. 'Salve, your Majesty; the last of the supplies that were distributed to the Banner at the start of the Jezra operation. There is enough here to heal the entire company.'

Emily puffed out her cheeks. 'Good. Please tell me that we're going in now; I don't think I could take any more delay.'

Yendra signalled to the Banner company. 'Follow me.'

They set off along Princeps Row, the soldiers marching behind Yendra, as Emily's guard squad moved up to flank her. They passed the main entrance gates to the palace, and took a side road that ran below the front of Maeladh along a terrace cut into the hillside. To the right, the palace loomed amid the shadows and darkness. Of all the palaces of the City, Maeladh was the one that Yendra was least familiar with; it had been the bastion of the God-Queen when Yendra had been imprisoned on the Grey Isle, and Prince Michael had lived there for centuries before the Civil War; and Yendra had avoided going there while her brother had ruled the City. She had long considered it to be the home of her enemies, and had been glad when Emily and Daniel had selected Pella in which to live.

They passed more militia by a lower gate, and carried on, until they reached the wings on the sunward side. The gate there was also guarded, and beyond lay a series of neat, ornamental gardens. Yendra halted by the gates, and glanced down at a plan of the palace that had been drawn on a scrap of paper.

'Let me see that,' said Emily. 'I know the palace better than most people.'

Yendra handed it to her, and the Queen peered down at it in the dim light of a lamp.

'Does this little mark show where Danny is located?' she said.

'Yes, your Majesty. We intend to enter the old sunward wing in four different places, and each group will converge on the room where the King is. Every officer and sergeant has a copy of the map, marked with the route they are taking. Now, if I may, I'll carry out one last check, to make sure that there are no surprises waiting for us.'

Yendra sent her vision out and re-checked the routes into the wing, and the position of every member of the hooded gang holding the King prisoner. The Reaper captain of the ship had been right – it had been Rosers who had carried out the abduction. Yendra had been inside some of their heads, and had discovered that they were bitter opponents of the King's new laws, and also that they were waiting for someone, though who it was, not even they knew. The Rosers may have grabbed the King, but someone else was orchestrating events.

She nodded, then gestured to the Banner officers. Two groups peeled away, then swiftly scaled the iron gates, dropping into the gardens beyond, and disappearing into the shadows.

Yendra turned to the Queen. 'I again advise you to stay here, your Majesty.'

'Advise all you like,' she said. 'I can climb a gate.'

Yendra smiled. 'I have no doubt about that, your Majesty, just as I do not question your courage. But, if things go wrong, it would be wise to ensure that at least one of the City's twin monarchs emerges from this night intact.'

'You're wasting time, Commander.'

Yendra nodded, then gestured to the remaining soldiers, and they took off. Yendra ran for the gate, and scaled it, landing on the gravel on the other side. Behind her, she heard Emily land, along with the soldiers guarding her. The soldiers separated, one group running in silence to the right, while Yendra led the others directly ahead, towards the shadows of the palace wing. Narrow, sunward-facing slit windows marked the side of the stone wing of the palace, which rose to a height of three storeys. Other sections of wings abutted and led off from it in a haphazard fashion, reflecting the many different periods of construction that had gone on over the thousands of years that Maeladh had stood.

Yendra brought her squads to the wall of the palace, and they crept on, staying in the thick shadows. They came to a doorway, and two soldiers approached, standing to either side with their crossbows ready as a third eased the door open.

'It's clear,' he whispered, as he peered inside.

The soldiers lit their small oil lamps, and narrowed the shutters, angling them downwards, then they entered the building. They raced along a dark hall, then descended a flight of stairs into the basement levels. The place smelled old and unused, and even the smallest sound seemed magnified, as the soldiers crept along the stone passageways. The kidnappers had taken over a small servant's apartment deep within the bowels of the palace wing, and Yendra halted when they neared the main entrance. She knelt by the wall, and sent her vision out, locating the other three groups of soldiers that were converging on the apartment from all sides. She entered the minds of the officers, passing on her instructions, then came back to her own mind. She glanced at the lieutenant behind her.

'You know what to do. Remember, your priority is protecting the Queen. Everything else is secondary.'

'Yes, ma'am.'

Yendra rose to her feet and stole along the corridor, her battle-vision thrumming. She paused at a corner, and saw the door leading into the apartment. Using her vision, she could make out two of the kidnappers on the other side of the door, sitting with their backs against the wall. She crept to the door, and placed her fingers on the handle.

She took a breath, then ripped the door from its hinges, and rushed inside.

She pointed at the two men. *Sleep.*

Their eyes closed and they slumped to the floor. Yendra ran past them, kicking down another door and entering the main living area where the King was sitting, tied to a chair with a hood over his face. A dozen faces turned to stare at her.

Yendra swept her hand across the room. *Sleep.*

She heard noises coming from the other rooms as the kidnappers around her fell, but she ignored everything else and ran straight for the

King. She dived at him, knocking the chair over and covering the King with her armoured body.

She reached out to the lieutenants. *Now.*

The sound of windows being smashed and doors being kicked in echoed through the apartment, followed by the thrum of crossbows and the screams of those hit. Yendra pulled over a table, and pushed the unconscious body of the king behind it. She glanced up, ready to fight, but it was already over. Banner soldiers were moving through the room, checking the bodies of the kidnappers, and securing those who were sleeping rather than shot through with crossbow bolts.

A lieutenant approached and saluted. 'The apartment is secure, ma'am. No Banner casualties.'

Yendra nodded, then crouched down and removed the King's hood. His face was swollen, and there was a cut over his left eye, but he was breathing. The Queen ran over, and knelt down beside her, taking the King's hand, as Yendra cut the ropes that were holding him to the chair.

'Dear gods,' Emily sobbed.

'He's going to be fine,' said Yendra. She took out the vial of salve, opened it, and dabbed some onto the King's lips. He groaned, then his limbs juddered, and he opened his eyes. The cut over his eye healed, and the bruises on his face vanished.

'Emily?'

The Queen smiled, then leaned down and kissed him.

'I'll give you a moment, your Majesties,' Yendra said.

She stood, and saw the same lieutenant waiting to speak to her.

'We have eleven prisoners, ma'am, nine of whom are unconscious; and we killed eight of the kidnappers.'

'Good work, Lieutenant.'

'Thank you, ma'am. Shall we begin removing the prisoners from the palace?'

'Not yet, Lieutenant. The kidnappers were waiting for someone, and we need to be prepared. Have the rooms quickly searched, and send a runner outside to inform the Roser militia that the King is safe.'

'Oh, he's not entirely safe,' said a voice from the other side of the chamber, where a doorway opened. Yendra and the officer turned. An old man was standing by the door, leaning on a stick. Yendra frowned, as she peered at the old man's face. There was something about it that she recognised...

'Get down!' she cried. 'Scatter!'

The old man chuckled, and raised his hand. At once, a dozen Banner soldiers collapsed, their hands to their throats as their skin turned green. Yendra froze, keeping herself between the old man and the table where the King and Queen were crouching.

The old man pointed at Yendra. 'Don't move, sister, or you shall be next.'

'Montieth?' Yendra said. 'How is this possible?'

'Never mind that, little sister. Now, did I hear the Queen's voice earlier? Is it true? Do I have both of the pretend monarchs at my mercy?'

A squad of Banner soldier burst through a door, and peppered the old man with crossbow bolts. He flinched backwards as the bolts struck him, then he swept his left arm out, and the soldiers screamed, their flesh melting from their bodies. Montieth grunted, then ripped the bolts from where they had hit him. His face contorted in anger, then he threw down the walking stick and strode towards Yendra, his eyes lit with a savage cunning.

She pulled the Axe of Rand from over her shoulder. 'Come no closer!'

Montieth halted out of range of his sister, then smiled. 'Are you really going to stand in my way? You are powerful, Yendra, but you don't even come close to my strength. I am stronger than our mother, stronger than Michael, stronger than any other god that exists upon this world. If I will it, you will die.'

'What do you want?' she said, the axe gripped in her hands.

'It started out with salve,' he said. 'I asked politely for access to the mine here behind Maeladh Palace, and I was rebuffed. Then it occurred to me – a regime change might be in order. The mortals should never have been allowed to rule the City. It's time for your little experiment to end.'

'No,' she said, standing her ground. 'I will not permit it.'

Yendra heard the King and Queen stand by her side.

'Take the damned salve,' said Emily. 'Take it, and then go back to Dalrig.'

Montieth laughed. 'Too late for that, little mortal Queen. You and your husband are now my prisoners.'

He raised his hand towards her, and Yendra lunged at him, the axe swinging. Montieth threw himself backwards, the blade of the axe missing his head by inches. He extended his fingers, and Yendra cried out as his powers battered into her. She dropped the axe and fell to her knees, the pain blinding her. She felt her self-healing buckle under the pressure, and she slipped to the ground.

She glanced up in her agony, and saw Montieth, back on his feet, his face shining with a grim delight as he watched her suffer.

She felt herself succumb, her life force stripped away by Montieth's powers.

Barely conscious, Yendra kept her eyes open long enough to shoot out a thread of vision, using the last of her strength to send it over the swelling waters of the Straits, and into Jezra. She had to warn someone; she had to try, before it was too late.

Jade... she gasped, then the darkness took her.

CHAPTER 29

THE FRUITS OF LABOUR

Tara, Auldan, The City – 15th Mikalis 3421

Emily stared at the body of Yendra lying on the ground in front of her. Unlike the dead soldiers, Yendra's skin was undamaged, and it looked as though she were sleeping.

'Farewell, sister,' Montieth said.

'You killed her?' cried Daniel, his eyes wide.

'I had to,' said the old man. 'She was going to kill me.'

Emily fell to her knees and clutched one of Yendra's hands in hers, as tears of despair began to slide down her cheeks.

'Besides,' said Montieth; 'for three hundred years, I thought she was already dead, when, all the time, my father had hidden her on the Grey Isle. So, I won't really miss her. I'll just pretend that the last year never happened.'

'You monster,' sobbed Emily.

'Me?' said Montieth. 'She was the one swinging the axe.'

'Are you going to kill us too?'

'In time, little lady. Let's not get ahead of ourselves; there are several tons of salve I have to extract from the mine behind the palace first. But, regardless of whatever else occurs, your pretend monarchy is over. It didn't have to be this way – if you had allowed me access to this mine, then I would have permitted your regime to continue.'

'And who shall rule if we die?' said Daniel. 'You?'

Montieth laughed. 'Of course not, boy. What interest have I in ruling the City? If power was what I desired, I could have taken control at any time. No, I will leave that up to the other members of my family, once I have culled the unreliable elements.'

He turned and glanced at the side doors. The surviving Banner forces had pulled back after the carnage that Montieth had unleashed, and no sound was coming from the basement of the palace. The old man raised his hands, and the bodies scattered across the ground began to jerk and shudder. One by one, the slain Banner soldiers began to haul themselves to their feet, their eyes vacant, until all but Yendra were upright.

'Guard the two prisoners,' Montieth said to them. 'Do not kill them, but do not allow them to escape.' He glanced at Emily. 'Move away from my sister.'

Emily remained where she was, but Daniel put his hands on her shoulders and pulled her back from the body of the slain god. Montieth reached out with a hand and touched Yendra's brow. Her body began to shake, then crumbled into dust before their eyes, leaving only the polished battle armour lying on the ground. A tear fell down the old man's cheek and, for a split second, Emily saw regret in his eyes.

He stood.

'We are going to the mine,' he said to the dead soldiers. 'Bring the prisoners.'

The soldiers surrounded Emily and Daniel. Emily placed her hand on Yendra's armour, then felt arms pull her to her feet.

'Let go of me,' she said. 'I can walk unaided.'

The soldiers ignored her, and they pushed her and Daniel out of the room, avoiding the bodies of the dead, and the sleeping Roser kidnappers. Montieth took a lamp and led the way, and the group moved deeper into the bowels of the palace. They descended more stairs, then joined a wide passageway that ran directly under the side of the cliff. At the end of the corridor was a strong, iron-framed oak door. Montieth gestured to the soldiers, and four stepped forwards. They began breaking the door down, hacking at it with their swords, while Emily huddled next to Daniel, powerful hands gripping their arms.

'Salvor will have seen everything,' she whispered to Daniel.

'But what can he do? Without Yendra...' Daniel's voice almost broke, and he tailed off.

Montieth glanced at them. 'Without my sister, you are nothing. She put you on the throne, and she was the only person strong enough to keep you there. I would have had more respect for her if she had taken the power for herself, but, instead, she allowed her foolish love of mortals to corrupt her judgement, just as Michael told me she would.'

Emily stared at him. 'Which demigods have betrayed us?'

Montieth raised an eyebrow. 'None, as far as I know. Most of my nephews and nieces are cowards, and they would have been too afraid of Yendra to act against you, no matter how much they desired your deaths.'

'But Vana and Silva lied to me,' she said.

'Remind me,' said Montieth; 'which ones are they? I forget some of the demigods and their powers. Was Silva a child of my brother Isra? He had so many offspring that I lost track.'

Emily frowned. 'They told me that you weren't in Tara. If they weren't conspiring with you against us, then how could they not sense that you were here?'

'Oh, that?' Montieth said. 'I'll show you, if you like, once we are inside the mine.'

The dead soldiers smashed through the door, and large fragments of it fell to the ground. Montieth turned, and shone his lamp through the entrance. His eyes gleamed with triumph, and he set off, the soldiers shoving Emily and Daniel along after him.

They stepped through the broken doorway, and the walls of the passageway changed, from smooth blocks of stone, to a carved tunnel. Scrape marks from tools were inscribed all over the walls and ceiling. They passed side chambers as they followed the tunnel down into the depths of the ridge. Each chamber was empty, and showed nothing but bare rock.

The further they walked, the angrier Montieth seemed to get. He would peer into each side chamber, then scowl as he realised that it had already been stripped clean of any salve. Tunnels branched off from the main one, and Emily and Daniel were told to sit and wait, while Montieth conducted a search. Soldiers pushed the King and Queen against a wall, and forced them into sitting positions as the old man disappeared down a tunnel.

'I guess he was hoping that more salve would be here,' said Daniel. He looked at his wife, and took her hand. 'How are you?'

'Never mind me,' she said; 'you were the one who was kidnapped. Do you remember much of it?'

'Not really. One minute I was walking to the old house on Princeps Row, and then I heard shouts. The soldiers around me were cut down with crossbow bolts, and then someone hit me over the head. When I awoke, I was tied to a chair with a hood over my face. No one asked me any questions, or made any demands; in fact, no one spoke to me at all.'

'They were Rosers,' said Emily. 'I heard their accents.'

He nodded. 'Yes; I also heard them speak.' He shook his head. 'My own people; my own tribe. I hadn't realised how much hatred my reforms were causing, and how far some people would go to try to stop them from being implemented. Did Silva and Vana really both tell you that Montieth wasn't in Tara?'

'Yes. Well, Vana told me that he was back in Dalrig, and then Silva told me that he had disappeared completely from the City. She said that she couldn't sense him anywhere.'

'Do you think she was lying?'

'I don't know. No, that's not true. I would be dumbfounded if Silva had betrayed us; she's one of the very few demigods that I trust. Did you hear Montieth ask if she was one of Prince Isra's children?'

He nodded. 'The bastard's been alive for one and a half millennia. How could he forget who his nephews and nieces are?'

'I think that he's been sealed off from the rest of the City for so long, that he's forgotten anything that doesn't interest him. If we'd let him have this mine, then he would have slunk off back to Greylin Palace for another thousand years. That's what I should have done. This is my fault, Danny. If I'd appeased Montieth, then Yendra would still be alive.'

He squeezed her hand. 'Don't blame yourself. Whatever happens will happen, and I'm not giving up hope while we're still alive.'

Montieth emerged from the shadows of a tunnel and walked up to Emily.

'Did you know?' he said, his eyes narrow and fierce.

'Know what?'

'That this mine is almost exhausted? It's in a worse condition than the one in Ooste!' He clenched his fists and, for a second, Emily thought he was going to strike her. Instead, he turned to the soldiers. 'You six,' he snapped. 'Get into the mine and start excavating the remaining salve. The rest of you, take hold of the prisoners and follow me.'

He strode off, and the soldiers did as he had ordered. Emily and Daniel were pulled back to their feet, and were taken down a side passage to a large chamber. Montieth lit some lamps, revealing a workshop, with tables covered in tubes, bottles, and glass apparatus. There were benches by a wall, and Montieth told the soldiers to place the King and Queen there, while he inspected the equipment.

Emily and Daniel sat, and watched as Montieth examined the contents of the tables.

'This equipment is vastly inferior to what I possess in Greylin,' the old man said, shaking his head. 'It's a miracle that anyone was able to refine salve here.'

'How did you hide from us?' said Emily.

He glared at her. 'What? Oh, you're still talking about that, I see.'

'You said that you would tell us.'

Montieth smiled. 'I can do many things. I have been experimenting with salve for well over a thousand years, and am its foremost expert. There is not a soul in existence who knows more about the properties of salve than I – no one comes even close. There are things one can do, to alter the effects; things that one can add to salve, or remove, that change what it does.'

Emily saw the interest in the man's eyes. 'Such as?' she said.

He dug a hand into a coat pocket and withdrew a pouch. He opened it, and showed Emily and Daniel a collection of small vials, each containing salve of differing hues. He picked up one that was pure silver.

'This, for example,' he said, 'is concentrated salve. It is similar to a vial that Aila stole from my laboratory over a year ago. A few sniffs, I believe, were enough to restore Yendra after three hundred years in a restrainer mask. It sounds wonderful, doesn't it, but it is so concentrated, so pure, that it melts straight through human skin. It must never be drunk; its vapours are potent enough.'

'I've heard of that,' said Emily, trying to sound interested. 'Aila also used it to kill Duke Marcus.'

Montieth let out a loud laugh. 'Did she, now? My, that is most amusing. I hated that little runt, and I might even strike Aila off my list of enemies for that! Ha! It pleases me to know that it didn't go entirely to waste, despite the great effort it took to produce it.' He delved into the pouch, and withdrew a vial with a green tinge. 'Now, this one... Oh dear, this is powerful indeed. I call it *Death Salve*, and really, it's just refined salve mixed with a highly toxic substance. I had to trial many types of poisons before I found one that bound to the salve in the right way. To demonstrate its uses, I require a living mortal.' He beamed at them. 'Would either of you like to volunteer?'

'What does it do?' said Daniel.

'I'm not going to tell you; it would ruin the surprise. Actually, now that I think of it, I shouldn't use it on either of you; I may need you as leverage for a little longer.' He glanced at one of the dead soldiers. 'Go back into the palace wing, and bring me one of the sleeping Rosers.'

The soldier turned without a word, and strode away.

Montieth watched him leave, then withdrew another vial from the pouch.

He held it up. 'I added red dye to this concoction,' he said swirling it in his fingers; 'just so I wouldn't take it by accident. I call it *Anti-Salve*. It has unusual properties, and might be my proudest achievement. To mortals, it acts as a simple poison; even a tiny dose kills those with no self-healing powers. But on the gods? This is where it gets interesting. In high doses, it should be able to render a god into a mortal, permanently. Well, that's the theory; I have yet to test high doses on a god or demigod. Perhaps, once your regime is over, I can strike a bargain with the new rulers, and they will hand over one of the lesser demigods for me to experiment on. Regardless, in small doses, it suppresses their self-healing, turning gods into temporary mortals. To reverse it, one needs to wait for the effects to wear off, or one can simply take a dose of normal salve; but while it remains active, the god becomes invisible to others, and cannot be detected.' He grinned at Emily. 'Does that answer your question? To get to Tara unseen, I merely took a tiny dose of anti-salve before I departed Dalrig. Then, when I discovered that my sister was here, I dosed myself with ordinary salve, and my powers returned. Simple, and elegant, don't you think?'

'Very impressive,' she said.

'Oh, I can do more,' he said; 'watch this.'

He took a breath, and then transformed before their eyes, reshaping his features into a younger version of himself. He smiled, then did it again, losing even more years, until he looked like a teenager.

'Did you see?' he cried. 'I have gained complete mastery over my appearance, and can look any age I choose. I can enter somewhere as a feeble-looking old man, and emerge as a strapping eighteen-year-old!' He morphed again, until he looked to be in his forties. 'This is the version I prefer.'

'How is that possible?' said Daniel. 'I thought that salve only worked one way on the gods.'

'It does if you are only given a small dose every decade or so, but I have been perfecting my techniques for long centuries. Malik, my father, abused salve, until he was left a mindless shell, trapped in the body of an adolescent, but I have been much more careful, much more methodical in my approach. Do you now understand why I need more salve to continue with my research?'

'I knew that there was very little left in this mine,' said Emily, 'but the news came as a surprise to me when I was told it. Growing up, I always believed the reserves of salve in the City were as good as inexhaustible.'

Montieth's smile faded. 'Yes. I also took the supplies of salve for granted. I was aware that Naxor was taking quantities of the substance to other worlds to pay for soldiers to fight on the Great Walls, but I never dreamed that the little rat had practically cleaned out this mine. And with that idiot Malik squandering vast amounts of it in Ooste, it appears that we were both mistaken, little Queen.'

At that moment, the dead soldier reappeared, dragging an unconscious man by the heel.

Montieth's eyes lit up again. 'Bring him over here.'

The soldier hauled the body across the ground, and dropped him in front of Montieth, who crouched down by him.

'This will be a lot more entertaining if he isn't sleeping,' he said.

He placed a hand onto the Roser's face, and the man jerked awake, his eyes wide as he looked around. Montieth lifted the green-coloured vial and pulled out the stopper.

'This will get rid of that headache,' he said to the Roser. 'Sip a tiny drop.'

Emily watched as the man opened his mouth. Montieth let a small amount of the green-tinged salve touch the man's tongue, then he took a step back. For a moment, nothing happened, then the Roser started to writhe on the ground, his limbs thrashing about as he gurgled in agony. He tried to claw at his own throat, then fell still, his head lolling.

'It's just another poison,' cried Daniel. 'You killed him for nothing.'

'Patience, boy,' said Montieth; 'the best part is yet to come.'

They watched as the Roser's eyes snapped open.

'Get up,' said Montieth.

The dead Roser obeyed. He stumbled at first, then pulled himself to his feet. Montieth grinned, and walked around the Roser.

'He is dead, but completely under my control,' said Montieth. 'He will obey any order, no matter how ridiculous.' He stared at the Roser. 'Run into the wall.'

The dead man sprinted off in a rush of speed, then collided with the nearest wall. He fell backwards, sprawling onto the ground.

'Get up and do it again,' cried Montieth. 'Do it until your body ceases to function.'

Montieth cackled in glee, as the Roser got back to his feet and launched himself at the wall again, his face slamming into the smooth stone. He fell over, then rose again, blood covering his features, and ran back into the wall. There was sickening sound of bones cracking, but still the man struggled back to his feet. He swayed for a moment, then threw himself at the wall, which was dripping with blood. He smashed his face off the stones, and when he fell to the ground, he did not move again.

'Remarkable, isn't it?' said Montieth. 'Imagine putting some death-salve into the water supply of the City; within moments, I would have an army of obedient drones, ready to carry out my will. In fact, life would be much simpler if all mortals were forced to take a dose.'

Daniel stared at the bloody body of the twice-dead Roser. 'You're insane, Montieth.'

'So I have been told. True visionaries are often accused of being mad, and your attempted insult means nothing to me.'

A sound came from the passageway, and then two dead soldiers marched in, their arms laden with raw salve.

'Ah, the first instalment,' said Montieth. 'Put it down on the table, then go and dig out more for me.'

The two soldiers walked forwards, and dumped the raw salve onto the surface of the work table. Montieth rubbed his hands together.

He grinned at Emily. 'Time to start refining. The paltry amounts left in this mine should take me but a single night to refine down into a few vials of concentrated salve, and then little Queen, we shall see if you live or die.'

The hours dragged by for Emily and Daniel as they sat on the bench, watching the middle-aged Montieth work. Six dead Banner soldiers were on hand to prevent them from escaping, or even moving from the bench, while the others he had revived continued to bring in armfuls of the salve they had dug from the mine. Montieth filled glass beakers with alcohol, and a variety of other substances, and he kept a low fire burning to warm the mixtures that he was creating. Handfuls of salve were thrown in, and the solution stirred, and reduced over hours.

Montieth paid them no attention, his gaze fixed on the table, and he hummed several tunes as he admired his handiwork. Over by the wall, blood pooled under the dead Roser, then started to congeal, and Emily kept her eyes turned away from the sight of his smashed face.

'I wonder what's happening outside,' Daniel whispered. 'Do you think it's dawn yet?'

Emily shrugged, her knees up on her bench.

'With you and me in here,' Daniel went on, 'and Princess Yendra dead, who is in charge?'

'Technically, it's Salvor,' she said, keeping her voice low; 'although Van Logos might well be the most powerful person in the City right now; but I doubt that he knows it.'

'Van?'

'Yes. Earlier today; I mean, yesterday, I approved a plan to promote him. He's now in charge of the Banner and the Brigades, answerable only to us. He has seventeen thousand trained soldiers and workers under his command in the Grey Isle and on the Western Bank. He could take Pella, if he wished to. Or Dalrig.' She glanced at Daniel. 'Well, he could, if he hadn't fallen out with Kelsey Holdfast.'

Montieth poured the contents of a wide beaker into a small vial, then took a step back. So far, he had filled over a dozen vials with refined, concentrated salve, and he smiled.

'Were you watching?' he said to the King and Queen. 'To think that it used to take me days to create concentrated salve, and now I can do it in one night! I truly am a genius, perhaps the greatest genius of all time.'

A tall figure appeared at the entrance to the cavern chamber. He was wearing a Banner uniform, and had a long strip of white cloth raised in his left hand.

'I'm unarmed,' he said.

Montieth glared at him. 'Who are you? How dare you interrupt my work?'

'I am here only to talk,' the soldier said, keeping his eyes on Montieth. 'My commander wishes to know your demands, and wants assurances that the King and Queen are alive and unharmed. If you let me live, I will return to the outside of the palace, bearing whatever message you care to send.'

'Of course they're alive,' shouted Montieth, gesturing at Emily and Daniel. 'See for yourself.'

The tall soldier took a step further into the chamber, and risked a quick glance at the bench.

'Your Majesties,' he said; 'are you hurt?'

'We're alright,' said Emily. 'Is it dawn?'

'Not yet, ma'am. I am Lieutenant Cardova, of the Banner of the Lostwell Exiles. I want you to know that we are doing everything we can to ensure your rescue.'

'Did Van send you?'

'I volunteered, ma'am. Several of us did, but the commander chose me. I saw the armour of Princess Yendra when I was making my way through the basement, but there was no body. Does she live?'

Daniel pointed at Montieth. 'That bastard killed her.'

The lieutenant nodded, then glanced at the dead soldiers guarding the King and Queen. His eyes tightened, but he didn't appear shocked. He turned back to Montieth, keeping his hands raised.

'Your demands, sir? Or, do you have a message?'

Montieth raised his hand, then paused. 'Actually, you might be useful. Demands, eh? Let's see; what do I want? A ship, yes; a ship will do, for a start, then unhindered passage to Ooste, and then onto Dalrig.

I will be taking the King and Queen along with me, to ensure that my personal safety is not threatened, and then I want sworn agreements that I will be left alone, and that no foreign agents or forces will follow me into Gloamer territory. Once I am in Greylin Palace, I will hold onto the pretend royals, and allow the other members of my family to squabble over control of the City. There. What do you say to that?'

'I will pass your words onto my commander, sir.'

'Will you return?' said Montieth.

'Most likely, sir; once I have obtained a response to your demands.'

Montieth turned back to the work table. 'Then, leave.'

The soldier backed out of the entrance, then turned and hurried away.

'They won't rescue you,' Montieth said, once the soldier had gone. 'Nothing can stop me; my sister was your best chance, your only chance. It was a pity – I hated Yendra less than I hate most of those in my family.'

A group of dead soldiers arrived from the salve tunnels, but half were carrying nothing in their arms.

'The mine is exhausted already?' Montieth said, sighing. 'I'll be lucky to get one more vial out of that lot.'

———

Emily shivered from cold and tiredness. She was hugging her knees, her head resting on her hands. Images of Yendra, and of the others killed by Montieth, flashed through her mind, and she couldn't have slept, even if she had wanted to. Montieth ignored them as he went through the refinements process one last time, using up the remnants of the raw salve. The chamber was crowded with his dead soldiers, all of whom were standing motionless, their eyes empty.

'And, I think we're finished,' said Montieth, stepping back from the table and wiping his hands on a rag. He shook his head as the small number of filled vials in front of him. 'That's it; that's the last salve in the City. The only advantage of this shortage is that, before too long, every demigod will be on their knees begging me for some. He placed the vials into a bag, which he slung over his shoulder, and then turned to Emily and Daniel. 'Well, my little pretend monarchs; it's time to leave Maeladh.'

'What about the Banner lieutenant?' said Daniel.

Montieth grinned. 'We'll slip out of a side door while they are still arguing over my demands. I confess that I already have a ship sitting waiting for me – the one that I came in on.'

Daniel frowned. 'The entire palace is surrounded.'

'My foolish boy,' said Montieth. 'A Roser you may be, but I know all about how this palace was designed and built, and there are ways in and out of this mine that no one knows but the gods. Get up.'

Daniel glanced at Emily, and they stood. The Queen groaned, and stretched her aching limbs, then the dead soldiers formed up around them. Montieth led the way out of the chamber, and they followed him down a series of tunnels, all of which had long been stripped of any salve. It grew dark and claustrophobic in the narrow passage, and Emily could feel the soldiers behind her, pushing her on if she slowed. They walked for what felt like a long time, and Emily was near exhaustion when they finally came to a halt.

Montieth's lamp flashed across the end of the tunnel, then he crouched down and pushed open an old and rusted hatchway. Bright daylight broke into the tunnel, and Emily blinked, her eyes dazzled. She gazed ahead when her vision cleared, and saw the water of the great bay that sat amid Tara, Ooste and Pella. In the distance in front of them were the cliffs of Ooste, which meant that they were on the most iceward tip of the Taran peninsula. Montieth gestured to the soldiers, and they bundled Emily and Daniel forward to the open entrance. Below them were steps cut into the side of the cliff and, at sea-level, was a tiny jetty, protected by rocky outcrops that hid it from the bay.

'Did you know that this was here?' Emily whispered.

Daniel shook his head. They emerged into the sunlight, and were ushered down the worn, old steps. To their right loomed the pedestal supporting the enormous stature of Prince Michael, which was blocking the view of the main harbour of Tara. Next to the little jetty below them, a one-masted sailing vessel was tied up. Its crew had seen them, and were preparing the boat for departure.

When they reached the foot of the stairs, Montieth turned, and swept his hand over the soldiers. Over a dozen collapsed, sliding off the steps and jetty, and falling into the waters of the bay, leaving only six remaining.

Montieth laughed. 'There wasn't enough room on the boat for everyone. We'll manage with only six, I expect, at least until we reach Ooste.' He beckoned Emily and Daniel to approach. 'Quickly; get onto the boat.'

The six remaining dead soldiers shoved Emily and Daniel along the jetty, then they crossed over onto the deck of the vessel. The crew were Gloamers, Emily noticed, and they took no notice of her and Daniel, or of the dead soldiers. Montieth strode to the rear of the boat, and sat down on a bench, his contented gaze scanning the waters of the bay. The soldiers forced the two prisoners into the middle of the deck, and the crew cast off the ropes connecting the boat to the jetty. Emily and Daniel slumped down with their backs against the mast. They glanced at each other, then Daniel put his arm round her shoulder and pulled her close.

The vessel turned in the narrow gorge, and edged out towards the bay, the sail filling with the warm breeze.

'What a beautiful morning!' Montieth cried. 'I should get out more often.'

CHAPTER 30

LIABILITY

The Western Bank – 15th Mikalis 3421

The two dragons soared over the forested hills. Above them, the sky brooded in the purple half-gloaming of the hour before dawn, and Kelsey could make out rivers and mountains in the landscape. Somewhere, down there, hundreds of thousands of greenhides were sleeping, waiting for the sun's rays to revive them, and send them hurtling against the walls of Jezra.

Kelsey felt her nerves build as they approached the besieged town hugging the cliffs of the Western Bank. In the eleven days that she had been away, she doubted that much had changed, but a worry that the walls had been breached niggled away at her mind, and she almost gasped in relief when she saw the lanterns atop the defensive perimeter at the top of the ridge.

'Jezra still stands,' she said to Frostback.

'Of course it does, my rider,' said the silver dragon. 'Were you expecting otherwise?'

'No, but I have a feeling that something's not right.'

'Have you had a vision of what will be?'

'No. It's probably just nerves. What kind of reception are we going to get? What if the Banner loose their ballistae at us?'

'That will not happen.'

'But what if it does?'

'Then Halfclaw and I will spend the morning burning greenhides, to show the humans that we remain allied to their cause. Really, Kelsey, this fretting is not like you. You remind me of Aila, with your "what if" questions.'

'Sorry. This is why I need the company of other humans; to deflect my own innate negativity. When I had Aila around, it was easy to be positive, because she was always looking at things from the point of view of what could go wrong. But, on my own, my worries run riot inside my head.'

'Remember; you are a Holdfast.'

'Pyre's arse, that sounds like exactly the sort of thing my mother would say.'

'I am too young to be your mother, Kelsey.'

'You're seventy-three years old, Frostback; you're ancient, compared to me.'

'And like a newborn, compared to Aila.'

Halfclaw moved alongside. 'We are approaching the walls at the top of the cliffs. Should we slow down, and advance with caution?'

'No,' said Frostback. 'Let us soar overhead, and observe the town from above. That way, everyone will see us before we attempt to land, and we can gauge their response.'

'If even one ballista bolt is loosed at us,' he said, 'then we turn around, immediately. Agreed?'

Frostback tilted her head. 'Agreed.'

Kelsey peered into the gloom ahead of them. To their right, the sky was turning red in advance of the sun rising, and she could see the brick and stone walls of Jezra tower over the trees. There was no walkway at the top, but towers had been constructed every hundred yards, and Banner soldiers on lookout were pointing up at the dragons as they neared. Each tower had several ballistae, all aiming down into the cleared area at the forest's edge, and Kelsey held her breath as she watched the soldiers shout out warnings. Frostback picked up her speed and surged over the defensive line.

Kelsey puffed out her cheeks. No one had loosed at them. She gazed down and saw the town of Jezra at the bottom of the cliffs, and it felt like she was coming home. Even though it was still dark, hundreds of Brigade workers and Banner soldiers were out on the streets, and more were appearing with every second that passed. She wondered what they were all doing, then realised – they were rushing outside to watch the dragons.

Frostback and Halfclaw circled over the town. Apart from the crowds gathering below them, everything looked normal. The harbour was filled with ships, and the various building works had been going on apace in their absence. The new Command Post looked almost complete, and new rows of red-brick houses were being constructed close to the ruins of the ancient palace. Kelsey felt almost teary-eyed looking at it, and it came to her how much she had missed being around the people who lived and worked in Jezra.

'What are they doing down there?' said Halfclaw. 'Why are they assembling in the streets? Do they mean to attack us?'

'They would have loosed their ballistae if they wanted to attack us,' said Frostback. 'Come; let us descend.'

The two dragons circled lower, and Kelsey began to hear a low, rumbling noise. She frowned. The crowds below them were clearing a space on the flat foundations of the ancient palace, and she noticed that many had their arms raised in the air.

'Pyre's holy arsehole,' Kelsey muttered. 'They're cheering us.'

The roar of the crowd increased as they descended. Thousands of Banner and Brigade Exiles were shouting out, their voices clamouring with joy and relief. Frostback landed, then Halfclaw touched down twenty yards to her right, and the crowds surged forwards, surrounding the dragons.

Frostback raised her head, her eyes unsure.

'Welcome back!' cried a Banner officer. 'Praise the gods!'

Kelsey unbuckled the straps on the harness, and clambered down to the ground, where she was immediately surrounded by cheering men and women.

'Umm,' she said, feeling completely disorientated. 'Thanks. Thanks, I guess.'

A group of soldiers pushed through the jubilant crowd.

'Give the dragon rider some room!' their officer shouted. 'Clear the way!'

The soldiers reached Kelsey, and formed a cordon around her, pushing the others back.

The officer saluted. 'Ma'am. Might I say how pleased I am to see you here?'

Kelsey blinked. 'I don't really understand what's going on. I mean, this is great, but I didn't think you'd miss us that much.'

'Do you know the situation in the City, ma'am?'

Kelsey shook her head.

'Then, I must ask you to come with me, ma'am. Lady Jade is in the old Command Post. She will need to speak to you at once.'

'Where's Van?'

'The major-general is in Tara, ma'am.'

Kelsey frowned. 'Major-general? When did that happen? And Tara? What's going on?'

'We should proceed to the Command Post, ma'am.'

She turned to Frostback, who was still regarding the cheering crowds with some suspicion.

'I'm going to speak to Jade; I'll be back soon.'

Kelsey let the soldiers escort her through the dense mass of people, and they descended the steps to ground level.

'Why are they all cheering us?' she said, as they made their way towards the Command Post.

'They think that you have returned to save the King and Queen,' said the officer.

'Tell me what's going on, Captain,' she said, her eyes narrowing. 'Tell me, before we reach Jade.'

'Prince Montieth has the King and Queen, ma'am; he's holding them prisoner in the palace in Tara.'

'Bollocks,' Kelsey muttered. 'Where's Yendra?'

The captain lowered his gaze. 'The princess also went to Tara. I'm not certain of anything, ma'am, but there are rumours that she's been killed by her brother.'

'What? Yendra? No. It would take more than Montieth to kill her, surely?'

'That's what we're hoping, ma'am.'

They reached the old Command Post building, and entered. The captain led Kelsey to the main operations room, where Jade was sitting, alone, her head in her hands.

'Ma'am,' said the captain. 'I have brought Kelsey Holdfast.'

Jade glanced up, and wiped the tears from her cheeks.

'Two dragons have also returned, ma'am,' the captain went on; 'Frostback and Halfclaw.'

Jade stared at Kelsey, as if confused.

'Hi, Jade,' said Kelsey. 'Do you need our help?'

'My father killed Yendra,' the demigod whispered.

'We don't know that for certain, ma'am,' said the officer.

'Shut your mouth!' Jade cried. 'I know what Salvor told me. He watched it happen! And Yendra... she tried to contact me... I could feel the pain she was in; the terrible, terrible pain, and then, there was nothing.'

'Did this happen in Tara?' said Kelsey.

'Under Maeladh Palace,' Jade said, her eyes red. 'My father...'

Kelsey and the officer glanced at each other.

'Princess Yendra left Lady Jade in charge,' said the captain, 'and Major-General Logos has travelled to Tara along with an entire Banner regiment; but they cannot enter the palace for fear that Prince Montieth will kill the King and Queen.'

'I'll get back on Frostback and we'll leave right away,' said Kelsey.

Jade looked at her as if she were mad. 'Dragons are too big to enter the tunnels under Maeladh Palace. What good would they do?'

'Montieth can't stay in there forever.'

'I agree with Miss Holdfast's suggestion,' said the captain.

'Are you coming?' said Kelsey. 'Your healing powers might be useful.'

Jade glared at her.

'You can ride upon Halfclaw. His old harness is still here, presumably?'

'I cannot face my father,' Jade said. 'Don't you understand? He hates me; he would strip the flesh from my body.'

'Not if I'm there, Jade.'

'But no one will know that we're coming. I don't have the powers to contact Salvor, or anyone else, and he won't be able to contact me, because of you.'

Kelsey turned to the officer. 'Get Halfclaw's harness ready. I'm going to Tara, whether Jade comes or not.'

'Yes, ma'am.'

Kelsey strode from the room, and began hurrying out of the building, passing dozens of soldiers, who all saluted her. She stepped outside into the growing light of dawn, then stopped as she heard footsteps behind her.

'I will come,' said Jade, 'even though I am terrified of what my father might do. I owe it to Yendra.'

'Alright. Just remember the hundred yard rule.'

'I don't need to remember it; I can feel my powers switch on and off whenever you are close. Will you obey my orders?'

Kelsey chewed her lip for a moment. Jade's eyes were wild with grief and fear, and she didn't appear capable of making a calm decision, but, at the same time, Kelsey would need her.

'Sure,' she said.

'Good,' said Jade.

They set off for the ancient palace, the squad of guards resuming their duties, and escorting them through the crowds. They climbed up onto the wide foundations of the palace, and Kelsey approached the dragons.

'We're needed,' she said. 'There's a crisis in Tara. Let's get flying, and

I'll tell you all about it on the way.' She turned to Halfclaw. 'Could you please carry Jade?'

The green and blue dragon scowled.

'It's an emergency, Halfclaw,' said Kelsey; 'please.'

'Very well,' he growled.

The captain appeared, with a squad of Brigade workers carrying the spare harness. They attached it to Halfclaw's frame, while the dragon pretended to ignore their presence, then Jade clambered up. Kelsey climbed up onto Frostback's shoulders, and the soldiers on the ground pushed the crowds back. The two dragons extended their wings, and soared into the air.

'Make for Tara,' said Kelsey; 'as quickly as possible.'

'Yes, my rider.'

The silver dragon surged away at speed, racing over the town and then the harbour of Jezra. Kelsey told her what had occurred as they rushed over the sparkling, clear waters of the Straits, the dawn rays of the sun striking the waves. The sky brightened to sunward, and pinks spread across the horizon.

The journey was over in minutes. Frostback and Halfclaw soared over the cliffs edging Tara, and Kelsey laid eyes on the huge, sprawling palace complex. Banner soldiers and local militia were surrounding Maeladh, blocking every entrance and gate.

'Where shall we land?' said Frostback.

'Do you see that large courtyard on the iceward side?' Kelsey said. 'That looks big enough for you and Halfclaw, and there are officers down there as well.'

Frostback tilted her head, then descended. The soldiers in the courtyard cleared a space for them, and the two dragons landed. A figure raced through the crowd of soldiers towards them as Kelsey clambered down to the ground.

'Kelsey!' cried Van.

He reached the side of the dragon and threw his arms around the young Holdfast woman. Kelsey grimaced, feeling awkward, then saw that Van's eyes were red and tired.

He stared at her. 'Yendra.'

'Is it true?'

He nodded. 'I'm going to kill that bastard.'

'Has he still got the King and Queen?'

'Yes, but they've left Tara. I was just organising the Banner regiment to re-board the ships and sail to Ooste.'

'Ooste? Slow down, Van.'

'Salvor saw them. He said they've just got off a boat in Ooste. Montieth killed several of the militia stationed there, and he's taking the King and Queen to Dalrig. We have to stop him.'

'How in Pyre's name did he get past you?'

'There's a secret passageway that emerges from the cliffs iceward of here.'

'Right. I'm on it. Jade and I will follow them on the dragons.'

'I'm coming with you.'

Kelsey frowned. 'Aren't you a major-general now? Don't you have responsibilities?'

'Yendra's dead, Kelsey. If Montieth kills the King and Queen, then this City is screwed, and my responsibilities will mean nothing. It'll be a free for all; anarchy. Half of the Rosers I've seen would be happy if Emily and Daniel were murdered. No; I'm coming, and I'm going to kill Montieth.'

'Alright. Let's go.'

'Where now, rider?' said Frostback, as Kelsey and Van climbed up the harness.

'Ooste,' she said. 'That's where Montieth has taken the King and Queen.'

'And how will we locate them?'

'I'll be able to tell if Montieth uses his powers, but only if I'm close enough.'

Van noticed Jade on Halfclaw's shoulders.

'I thought it best if she came along,' said Kelsey.

'But she won't be able to use her powers with you here,' he said.

'I know.'

He frowned. 'Montieth has dead soldiers serving him; dead Banner soldiers. They'll kill Jade. Does she know how to use a sword or bow?'

'What about me?' Kelsey cried. 'I can't fight, either.'

'I'll watch you,' he said. He leaned over the harness and shouted down to a tall officer. 'Lieutenant Cardova; I'm assigning you as Lady Jade's escort and guard. Get up onto Halfclaw.'

The young officer saluted. 'Yes, sir.'

Cardova joined Jade on Halfclaw's shoulders, his steel armour glistening in the sunlight, then the two dragons took off. Kelsey gazed down at the glittering waters of the bay, and tried not to think about what Van had said. Dead soldiers? She recalled hearing that Thorn's soulwitch powers could raise mindless drones from the dead, but she had never seen it happen.

'If you see any dead soldiers,' she said to Frostback; 'burn them.'

The dragons cleared the bay in minutes, then soared over the harbour of Ooste. The old Gloamer ballista batteries had been taken away, and, though people stared up at them, no one tried to attack the dragons. Kelsey focussed her powers as they circled over Ooste, but sensed no powers emanating from the town.

'I can't see them,' she said to Van.

'Can you sense a god's self-healing from here?'

'No. I can only sense it if he projects his powers through the air.'

Van nodded.

'Salvor's probably trying to contact you now,' Kelsey went on; 'and I'm blocking him. Maybe I'm a liability on this trip.'

Van shook his head. 'You are the only person who can save the King and Queen now, Kelsey. Don't ever think that you're a liability.'

Kelsey glanced at him. 'What will we do?'

'Dalrig,' he said; 'that's where Montieth would go. He'd run off home to Greylin Palace.'

'Frostback?' said Kelsey.

'I heard. Greylin?'

'Aye, but be careful. They might be expecting dragons.'

The two dragons moved closer together to talk to each other, then they surged iceward, crossing the suburbs of Ooste. Fields covered the ground once the houses petered out, and the walls of Dalrig loomed in the distance. Kelsey strained her eyesight, looking for ballista batteries up on the walls, and saw them. Before she could say anything to Frostback, the two dragons ascended at a steep angle, soaring straight up into the sky until they were out of range of the machines along the battlements. A few ballista bolts were loosed at them as they sped over the line of walls, but all fell uselessly back to the ground.

'Do you see the palace?' cried Van.

'I do,' said Frostback.

'Drop us onto its roof,' Van said, 'and then get yourselves away. Once we have the King and Queen, come back and get us, but stay out of missile range until then.'

Frostback tilted her head to show agreement, then the two dragons plummeted downwards, racing towards the huge, black, fortress-like palace where Montieth and Amber lived. Kelsey clung onto the harness as the wind rushed past her. The roof of the palace was flat, and covered in what appeared to be an untidy and overgrown garden. Frostback hurtled down, but there were no ballista batteries close to the palace, and no further bolts were loosed at them. She pulled up at the last second, and hovered over a large, unkempt flowerbed, which was knee-high with weeds.

Kelsey and Van unstrapped themselves from the harness, and slipped down to the roof, while, thirty yards away, Jade and the Banner lieutenant also climbed down. As soon as all four were on the roof, the two dragons soared back up into the pink sky until they were nothing but tiny specks in the distance above Dalrig.

Van gestured for Jade and Cardova to come over to where he was crouching by Kelsey.

'Look at my garden,' said Jade, her eyes wide as she glanced around.

'They've ruined it. I spent centuries making it beautiful, and they've wrecked it in a single year.'

'We can plant a new one in Jezra,' said Kelsey.

'Can we?' said Jade. 'I'd like that. And, could I have cats for the garden, too? They can laze about in the sunshine, and I can feed them treats.'

'Could we please focus?' said Van. 'If we get through this, I'll make sure that you get a garden and as many damn cats as you want. But, first, we have to save the King and Queen from your father and sister. There's a good chance that someone saw us land on the roof, so they'll probably be expecting us. Lieutenant, your priority is to protect Jade, and I'll watch Kelsey. Neither knows the first thing about swinging a sword.'

'You say that like it's a bad thing,' said Kelsey.

'Right now, it is a bad thing,' he said. 'We have no idea how many dead soldiers and guards Montieth has roaming the palace; if and when we encounter them, leave the fighting to me and the lieutenant. If you absolutely have to fight them, then aim for their heads, or their legs. They don't feel pain, and a crossbow bolt in the guts will barely slow them down.'

'I know all this,' said Jade; 'I grew up here.'

'Will the dead respond to your commands?'

'Some of the older ones might,' she said, 'but any that have been "turned" since I left won't know who I am.'

Kelsey frowned at her. 'You're familiar with dead soldiers?'

'Yes. I've "turned" quite a few myself over the years, but Yendra made me stop.'

'I feel a bit queasy,' said Kelsey; 'this is new to me.'

'Just stay behind me,' said Van.

Kelsey's senses twitched, and she concentrated. Deep within the palace, she could feel something; powers.

'He's here,' she said. 'I can hear his powers. Somewhere far below us.'

'Does the palace have a basement, Jade?' said Van.

She nodded. 'That's where my father will have taken Emily and

Daniel. He has a sort of dungeon place down there.'

'Right; let's go.'

The two soldiers readied their crossbows, and Van set off across the roof, the others following, with the lieutenant remaining at the rear. Van skirted the overgrown hedges and shrubs, and reached the stair turret in the corner of the roof. The door was open, and he peered down into the darkness, then gestured for the others to follow. Kelsey swallowed, trying to keep her nerves from fraying as she descended the dark stairs after Van. What was she doing? She shouldn't be there; if it came to a fight, she would only hinder the others. Dark doubts clouded her mind, and she wished she had stayed on Frostback's shoulders.

They came to a door at the bottom of the stairs, and Van pressed against it, listening with his eyes closed. He levelled his bow and nodded to Cardova, who gently eased the door open. They looked through, and saw a dimly-lit corridor, with worn and faded carpets on the floor.

'There are no windows in the palace,' Jade said, not bothering to whisper. 'The main stairs used to always have a few guards posted by them, but if you go right, there is another set of stairs, for the servants.'

'Thank you, Jade,' whispered Van, 'but please keep your voice low.'

'Too late,' said Cardova. 'Two guards, approaching from the left.'

Van nodded. 'Head shots. You go left; I'll go right.'

'Yes, sir.'

The two soldiers burst out of the stairwell. They each fell to one knee, raised their crossbows, aimed and loosed. Cardova cursed, reloaded, and loosed again, then Kelsey saw a body collapse to the ground a foot in front of the lieutenant, two bolts in his face. Van gestured to Kelsey and Jade, and they left the stairwell. Three yards to the left, another dead guard was lying, a bolt through his left eye socket. Kelsey stared, then Van ushered her on, and they raced along the passageway. Cardova kicked down a locked door at the end of the corridor, and they entered the servants' stairwell. Van peered over the banister at the flight of stairs, then they set off again, running down the steps.

They passed two landings, and were descending the third flight of stairs when a door opened. A servant emerged from the gloom of a corridor into the stairwell. He paused, his eyes widening at the sight of Jade, Kelsey and the two soldiers. He opened his mouth to scream, and Cardova sent a crossbow bolt through his throat. Van ran to the opening, dragged the body into the stairwell, and shut the door. He nodded to the lieutenant, and they carried on. At the bottom of the stairs, Jade led them through a series of narrow passageways, and then down a final flight of steps, into the basement. The air felt chill beneath the mass of the bulky palace, and shadows clung to the walls. In the distance, a door was open, and light was shining out from the entranceway. Van gestured to the others, and they padded along the bare floorboards, keeping to the shadows.

He halted when raised voices echoed out from the open doorway.

'What were you thinking, father?' Amber's voice cried. 'This is madness.'

'Hush, daughter,' Montieth said in reply; 'all will be well.'

'No, it won't. You must release them, father, immediately. If you let them go, then perhaps there's a small chance that things might go back to the way they were before, but if you kill them…'

'I've grown tired of your tone, daughter. You know how I feel about a mortal monarchy; I'd rather my mother and father were back in charge, compared to mere mortals ruling over us.'

'But I swore an oath, for myself, and on your behalf, at their coronation. I have never betrayed an oath in my life, and I don't intend to start now.'

'Then, walk away, daughter. You don't have to watch what I'm about to do to the pretend King and Queen. Just walk away, and forget all about it.'

'No. This path will destroy us, father, and it will destroy Dalrig. I cannot let you do this.'

'Then, unfortunately for you, I will have to incapacitate you for a while, so that you do not interfere.'

There was a silence from the room, and Van edged forwards, until he was almost at the entranceway.

'What have you done, daughter?' came Montieth's angry voice.

'What are you talking about?'

'Have you dosed me with anti-salve? Where are my powers?'

'Mine have also gone, father. Do you recall what happened when I met the Queen before? She did something to my powers, and I could only use them again once I'd left her company.'

'Impossible,' muttered Montieth. 'Now, get out of my way.'

Van signalled to Cardova, then the two soldiers sprang up and charged into the room. Kelsey jumped to her feet and followed them.

'Don't move!' cried Van, pointing his crossbow at Montieth, as Amber's mouth opened in fright.

Kelsey and Jade entered the room after Van and Cardova. Behind Montieth and Amber, the King and Queen were sitting inside a cramped animal cage, their eyes wide with terror. Amber had positioned herself between her father and the cage, her arms outstretched as if to stop him.

Montieth turned to the soldiers, and he raised his hand, as if by reflex. Nothing happened, and his features flushed in anger.

'Take him down,' said Van.

Cardova and Van began loosing their crossbows at Montieth, peppering him with bolts. Two struck him in the chest, and he stumbled backwards, then another pair hit his torso, and he fell to the ground. Van ran at him, leaned over and smashed the butt of his crossbow into Montieth's face, even as the injuries from the bolts were starting to heal.

'On the table,' cried Emily from within the cage. 'Give him some from the red vial. Listen, Van; the red vial!'

Cardova rushed to the table as Van brought the crossbow down again, bludgeoning Montieth's head. Jade approached, staring, her eyes wide, while Amber watched, doing nothing. Cardova rummaged through the vials scattered on the tabletop, then grabbed a red-hued one.

'This?' he cried towards the cage.

'Yes,' shouted the Queen. 'It'll stop his self-healing powers.'

Cardova unstoppered the vial and ran to Montieth. Van was still over him, but the god's wounds were disappearing as soon as Van could inflict them.

'Hold his mouth open, sir,' Cardova said, as Montieth writhed and lashed out with his fists and feet.

Van pulled his jaws open, and the young lieutenant dripped some of the gloopy, red liquid into Montieth's mouth. The god screamed a roar of frustration and rage, and pushed Van away. Montieth struggled to his feet, clutching his throat, and Van drew back his fist and punched him in the face. He gripped the god by the throat with both hands and pushed him back down to the ground, choking him, as the rest of the room stilled.

Montieth gasped, his hands trying to dislodge Van's grip round his neck, but the soldier put a knee on his chest to pin him down, and tightened his grasp. Montieth's eyes were bulging, and his face turned red, as Van stared down at him, his own face just a foot above the god's.

'This is for Yendra, you piece of shit,' Van snarled, and Kelsey barely recognised his voice. Van's face was contorted with rage, and his eyes were devoid of pity, as he strangled the god.

Kelsey stepped forward, and put a hand on Van's shoulder. He glanced at her, and she shook her head.

Van released his grip on Montieth's throat, and staggered backwards, leaving the god unconscious on the bare, stone floor. Cardova smashed the lock on the cage door, and helped Emily and Daniel climb out.

'Are you hurt, your Majesties?' he said.

'That's the second time you've asked us that in the last little while,' the Queen said.

Cardova smiled. 'It's good to see you again, your Majesty.'

Amber fell to her knees. 'I am at your mercy, your Majesties. I never thought my father would go this far.'

'Stand,' said Daniel. 'You are not responsible for what your father did to us.'

Jade walked over and stared down at Montieth's unconscious form, as Cardova began binding his wrists and ankles.

'He never even noticed I was here,' she said. She looked at Van. 'I wish you had killed him. He deserves it for murdering Yendra.'

Van said nothing, then he began to weep. Kelsey pulled him close, wrapping her arms round him as great, wracking sobs left his chest. Emily and Daniel approached, and the King put his hand over Van's shoulder, while the Queen watched with a sad smile on her lips.

'What will we do without her?' said Jade.

'We carry on,' said Daniel. 'Not because we want to, but because we have to. We have to honour Yendra's legacy; we can't give up now.' He turned to Amber. 'We are taking your father into custody. You shall remain here, but we shall discuss what happened in Ooste, and your part in events, in due course.'

Amber bowed her head. 'I am at your service, your Majesty.'

'We should make our way back to the roof, your Majesties,' said Cardova, keeping an eye on the door. 'There may be other dead soldiers about.'

'The roof?' said Emily.

'Yes, your Majesty. We came here by dragon.'

'I will come with you to the roof,' said Amber. 'I will ensure no one assaults you.'

Kelsey touched Van's face, and he wiped his eyes.

'Sorry,' he said.

'You have nothing to apologise for, Major-General Logos,' said Emily. 'Princess Yendra was right to trust you, and you have proved that today. Thank you; thank you all. Kelsey, Jade, and you too, Lieutenant Cardova. I'm humbled that you think us worthy of your loyalty. Now, let's get out of this horrible basement.' She glanced at Kelsey. 'Does this mean we're going to fly?'

'Aye,' said Kelsey. She smirked. 'Your Majesty.'

'That's the first time you've ever called me that,' Emily said. 'Don't let it happen again.'

The King climbed onto Halfclaw's shoulders along with Jade and the lieutenant, while Emily sat next to Kelsey and Van atop Frostback. Amber had remained at the top of the stairs, and had disappeared back into the shadows of the palace as soon as the dragons had landed. Half-claw took a grip of the hooded and bound Prince Monteith in his fore-limbs, and then the two dragons extended their wings and took off.

'We shall fly high,' said the silver dragon, 'to avoid the ballistae batteries on the town walls.'

'That sounds like a good idea,' said Emily. 'This is my first time on a dragon.'

'Where shall we take you, Queen?'

'The Fortress of the Lifegiver first,' Emily said, 'so we can make sure the prince is settled into his new home in the dungeons; and then back to Cuidrach Palace, where each one of you will be honoured, and, of course, to tell Salvor and everyone else that we're safe and well.'

'And then?' said Kelsey.

'Then, we mourn Yendra. But, as my husband said, after that, we carry on.'

'What about Frostback and Halfclaw?' said Kelsey, as they circled higher and higher over Dalrig. 'Do you have any objections to them living in Jezra?'

'None, whatsoever.' said Emily. 'My; you get a marvellous view from up here.'

Kelsey nodded and turned to Van. He was sitting on the harness, his eyes full of sorrow.

'Are you alright?' she said.

'Thank you for stopping me,' he said. 'It's better that Monteith lives to spend his time in prison.'

'I didn't do it for him,' she said. 'I did it for you, Van.'

Their eyes met for a moment, then Frostback spread her wings, and surged away to the east in a blur of speed. Kelsey narrowed her eyes against the fierce wind, and held on tight.

EPILOGUE

Port Sanders, Medio, The City – 15th Mikalis 3421

The roof of Sofia's mansion was basking in the warm afternoon sunlight. Her ladyship was reclining on the chair next to Kagan, and he wondered if she might be sleeping; at any rate, she looked at peace, as if the events of the previous night had left no mark upon her.

Kagan closed his eyes, and tried to relax, but it was impossible. With his eyes shut, images of Dizzler's agonies flashed before him, along with the deaths of the other members of his crew. He opened his eyes again, his gaze drawn by the form of Sofia next to him.

Who was she? He had tried to ask her the previous night, but she had been more interested in drinking the brandy and getting him into bed, than discussing her past. To possess the kind of powers that she had demonstrated must mean that she was a god – had one of the Lostwell gods escaped the destruction of their world and fled to the City?

Gellie appeared at the top of the stairs and strode over, not deigning to even glance in Kagan's direction.

'Ma'am,' she said, standing before Sofia's chair.

Her ladyship opened her eyes. 'Yes?'

'News has reached Port Sanders from Tara, ma'am; news that might interest you.'

Sofia leaned up on an elbow. 'Go on.'

'It appears that, last night, Prince Montieth captured the King and Queen of the City.'

'Really? Are they dead?'

'No, ma'am. However, Princess Yendra was slain by the prince, who was then taken into custody when the King and Queen were freed.'

Sofia's face fell for a moment, and she seemed at a loss for words.

'The prince has been taken to the dungeons beneath one of the fortresses on the Great Wall.'

'Wait,' said Sofia. 'Yendra is dead? Definitely? Are you sure?'

'Yes, ma'am. An announcement was made by the palace in Pella a couple of hours ago. It's official.'

'Thank you. I will need to ponder what this means.'

Gellie bowed her head and strode away, leaving Sofia and Kagan alone on the roof.

'Is this good or bad news?' he said.

'I don't yet have an answer to that question, Kagan. It does change things considerably, and my plan might have to be brought forward.'

Her eyes fell, and she seemed troubled, but almost relieved at the same time.

'Did you know Princess Yendra?' he said.

Sofia said nothing.

'You're a god, aren't you?'

She glanced at him. 'I am, yes.'

He lowered his voice. 'Is Sofia your real name?'

'No.'

'Then, what is it?'

'Do you swear on your life that you will never repeat it to anyone?'

'I do.'

She leaned over towards him, until he could feel her breath against his cheek.

'My real name,' she whispered, 'is Amalia.'

City of Salve - The Royal Family

The Gods	Title	Powers
Malik (deceased)	God-King of the City - Ooste	Vision
Amalia	Former God-Queen - Exiled	Death

The Children of the Gods

Michael (deceased)	ex-Prince of Tara, 1600-3096	Death, Battle
Montieth	Prince of Dalrig, b. 1932	Death
Isra (deceased)	ex-Prince of Pella, 2001-3078	Battle
Khora (deceased)	ex-Princess of Pella 2014-3419	Vision
Niomi (deceased)	ex-Princess of Icehaven, 2014-3089	Healer
Yendra	Cmdr of the Bulwark, b. 2133	Vision

Children of Prince Michael

Marcus (deceased)	Duke, Bulwark, 1944-3420	Battle
Mona	Chancellor, Ooste, b. 2014	Vision
Dania (deceased)	Lady of Tara, 2099-3096	Battle
Yordi (deceased)	Lady of Tara, 2153-3096	Death

Children of Prince Montieth

Amber	Lady of Dalrig, b. 2035	Death
Jade	Adjutant of the Circuit, b. 2511	Death

Children of Prince Isra

Irno (deceased)	Eldest son of Isra, 2017-3420	Battle
Berno (deceased)	'The Mortal', 2018-2097	None
Garno (deceased)	Warrior, 2241-3078	Battle
Lerno (deceased)	Warrior, 2247-3078	Battle

Vana	Lostwell Returnee, b. 2319	Location
Marno (deceased)	Warrior, 2321-3063	Battle
Collo	Courtier in Pella, b. 2328	None
Bonna (deceased)	Warrior, 2598-3078	Shape-Shifter
Aila	Has left the City, b. 2652	Shape-Shifter
Kano (deceased)	Adj. of the Bulwark, 2788-3420	Battle
Teno (deceased)	Warrior, 2870-3078	Battle

**Children of
Princess Khora**

Salvor	Royal Advisor, b. 2201	Vision
Balian (deceased)	Warrior, 2299-3096	Battle
Lydia	Gov. of Port Sanders, b. 2304	Healer
Naxor	Lostwell Returnee, b. 2401	Vision
Ikara	Courtier in Pella, b. 2499	Battle
Doria	Royal Courtier, b. 2600	None

**Children of
Princess Niomi**

Rand (deceased)	Warrior, 2123-3089	Battle
Yvona	Governor of Icehaven, b. 2175	Healer
Samara (deceased)	Lady of Icehaven, 2239-3089	Battle
Daran (deceased)	Lord of Icehaven, 2261-3063	Battle

**Children of
Princess Yendra**

Kahlia (deceased)	Warrior, 2599-3096	Vision
Neara (deceased)	Warrior, 2601-3089	Battle
Yearna (deceased)	Lady of the Circuit, 2604-3096	Healer

THE NINE TRIBES OF THE CITY

The Nine Tribes of the City (in 3420, when *City of Salve* takes place)

There are nine distinct tribes inhabiting the City. Three were in the area from the beginning, and the other six were created in two waves of expansion.

The Original Three Tribes – Auldan (pop. 300 000) Auldan is the oldest part of the City. United by the Union Walls (completed in 1040), it combined the three original tribes and their towns, along with the shared town of **Ooste**, which houses the Royal Palace.

1. The Rosers – (their town is **Tara**, est. Yr. 1.) The first tribe to reach the peninsula where the City is located. Began farming there in the sunward regions, until attacks from the Reapers forced them into building the first walled town. **Prince Michael** ruled until his death in 3096. **Queen Amalia** ruled until her expulsion in 3420.

2. The Gloamers – (their town is **Dalrig**, est. Yr. 40.) Arrived shortly after the Rosers, farming the iceward side of the peninsula. Like them, they fought with the Reapers, and built a walled town to stop their attacks. **Prince Montieth** rules from Greylin Palace in Dalrig.

3. The Reapers – (their town is **Pella**, est. Yr. 70.) Hunter/Gatherer tribe that arrived after the more sedentary Rosers and Gloamers. Settled in the plains between the other two tribes. More numerous than either the Rosers or the Gloamers, but are looked down on as more rustic. **Prince Isra** ruled until 3078. **King Daniel and Queen Emily** rule the City from Cuidrach Palace, with **Lord Salvor** as their senior advisor.

The Next Three Tribes – Medio (pop. 220 000) Originally called 'New Town', this part of the City was its first major expansion; and was settled from the completion of the Middle Walls (finished in 1697 and originally known as the Royal Walls). This portion of the City was devastated by the Greenhide incursion in 3420. The name 'Medio' derives from the old Evader word for 'Middle'.

1. **The Icewarders** – (their town is **Icehaven**, est. 1657.) Settlers from Dalrig originally founded a new colony at Icehaven to assist in the building of the Middle Walls, as the location was too cold and dark for the greenhides. After the wall's completion, many settlers stayed, and a new tribe was founded. Separated from Icehaven by mountains, a large number of Icewarders also inhabit the central lowlands bordering the Circuit. **Princess Niomi** ruled until her death in 3089. Her daughter, **Lady Yvona**, now governs from Alkirk Palace in Icehaven.

2. **The Sanders** – (their town is **Port Sanders**, est. 1702.) When the Middle Walls were completed, a surplus population of Rosers and Reapers moved into the new area, and the tribe of the Sanders was founded, based around the port town on the Warm Sea. Related closely to the Rosers in terms of allegiance and culture. **Princess Khora** rules, but delegates to her daughter, **Lady Lydia**, who governs from the Tonetti Palace in Port Sanders.

3. **The Evaders** – (their town is the **Circuit**, est. 2133.) The only tribe ethnically unrelated to the others, the Evaders started out as refugees fleeing the greenhides, and they began arriving at the City c.1500. They were taken in, and then used to help build the Middle Walls. The other tribes of Auldan and Medio look down on them as illiterate savages. Former rulers include **Princess Yendra** and **Lady Ikara**.

The Final Three Tribes – The Bulwark (pop. 280 000) The Bulwark is the defensive buffer that protects the City from greenhide attack. Work commenced on the Great Walls after the decisive Battle of the Children of the Gods in 2247, when the greenhides were pushed back hundreds of miles. They were completed c.2300, and the new area of the City was settled. The Bulwark faced the worst destruction in the greenhide incursion of 3420.

1. **The Blades** – (est. 2300.) The military tribe of the City. The role of the Blades is to defend the Great Walls from the unceasing attacks by the Greenhides. Officials from the Blades also police and govern the other two tribes of the

Bulwark. Their headquarters is the **Fortress of the Lifegiver**, the largest bastion on the Great Walls, where **Princess Yendra** is the commander.

2. The Hammers – (est. 2300.) The industrial proletariat of the Bulwark. Prior to the establishment of the Aurelian monarchy, the Hammers were effectively slaves, forbidden to leave their tribal area, which produces much of the finished goods for the rest of the City.

3. The Scythes – (est. 2300.) The agricultural workers of the Bulwark, who produce all that the region requires. Prior to the establishment of the Aurelian monarchy, they were slaves in all but name. Eighty percent of Scythes were killed in the greenhide incursion.

NOTE ON THE CALENDAR

In this world there are two moons, a larger and a smaller (fragments of the same moon). The larger orbits in a way similar to Earth's moon, and the year is divided into seasons and months.

Due to the tidally-locked orbit around the sun, there are no solstices or equinoxes, but summer and winter exist due to the orbit being highly elliptical. There are two summers and two winters in the course of each solar revolution, so one 'year' (365 days) equates to half the time it takes for the planet to go round the sun (730 days). No Leap Days required.

New Year starts at with the arrival of the Spring (Freshmist) storms, on Thanalion Day

New Year's Day – **Thanalion Day** (approx. 1st March)
   -- **Freshmist** (snow storms, freezing fog, ice blizzards, high winds from iceward)
   - Malikon (March)
   - Amalan (April)
   -- **Summer** (hot, dry)
   - Mikalis (May)
   - Montalis (June)
   - Izran (July)
   - Koralis (August)
   -- **Sweetmist** (humid, stormy, high winds from sunward, very wet)
   - Namen (September)
   - Balian (October)
   -- **Winter** (cold, dry)
   - Marcalis (November)
   - Monan (December)

- Darian (January)
- Yordian (February)

Note – the old month of Yendran was renamed in honour of Princess Khora's slain son Lord Balian, following the execution of the traitor Princess Yendra.

AUTHOR'S NOTES

JULY 2021

Following the turbulence of Lostwell, it felt good to be writing about the City again. Going from *Gates of Ruin* to *City of Salve* also felt like a slowing of pace, and a lowering of stakes – after all, an entire world is obliterated at the end of the Lostwell Trilogy, and I knew beforehand that nothing in *City of Salve* would be quite as epic as that... The timescales also changed. The events of the Lostwell Trilogy were compressed into a mere six months of baking hot sunshine under perfect blue skies, and I wanted the City Trilogy to begin at a more steady clip; a stately progress rather than a headlong rush towards destruction.

I hope you enjoyed reading it.

RECEIVE A FREE MAGELANDS ETERNAL SIEGE BOOK

Building a relationship with my readers is very important to me.

Join my newsletter for information on new books and deals and you will also receive a Magelands Eternal Siege prequel novella that is currently EXCLUSIVE to my Reader's Group for FREE.

www.ChristopherMitchellBooks.com/join

ABOUT THE AUTHOR

Christopher Mitchell is the author of the Magelands epic fantasy series.

For more information:
www.christophermitchellbooks.com
info@christophermitchellbooks.com

Printed in Great Britain
by Amazon

57698235R00260